HAVEN FROM THE STORM

"Mr. Clive, are you perhaps playing the gentleman?"

Brandon chuckled. "Trying to, ma'am."

"And were you also perhaps thinking of spending the night outside in the cold? Curled up nice and cozy in an *open* phaeton?"

"The notion did occur to me."

"But not with a great deal of anticipation, I daresay."

Regarding him steadily in the dim glow of the lantern, Alexandra saw no reason for coyness. Whatever the tarnish to her reputation, it had already been done. And to have him outside, no doubt catching his death of cold, would improve that situation not in the least. In fact, it might make any explanations even more awkward.

She leaned forward, gazing at him with complete frankness. "So you may as well play the gentleman right here. I do trust you, you know."

Brandon wished he could say the same, but as she lay there in the straw, she looked a bewitching temptress.

On the other hand, unusual circumstances or not, the lady *was* his wife . . .

Brandon snuffed out the lantern.

REGENCIES BY JANICE BENNETT

TANGLED WEB   (2281, $3.95)

Miss Celia Marcombe's dark eyes flashed with righteous indignation. She was not a commodity to be traded or bartered to a man
as insufferably arrogant as Trevor Ryde, despite what her high-
handed grandfather decreed! If Lord Ryde thought she would let
herself be married for any reason other than true love, he was
sadly mistaken. He'd never get his hands on her fortune—let
alone her person—no matter how disturbingly handsome he
was . . .

MIDNIGHT MASQUE   (2512, $3.95)

It was nothing unusual for Lady Ashton to transport government
documents to her father from the Home Office. But on this particular afternoon a gust of wind scattered the papers, and suddenly an important page was lost. A document desperately
wanted by more than one determined gentleman—one of whom
would murder to get his way . . .

AN INTRIGUING DESIRE   (2579, $3.95)

The British secret agent, Charles Marcombe, had done his bit
against that blasted Bonaparte. Now it was time to nurse his
wounds and come to terms with the fact that that part of his life
was over. He certainly did not need the likes of Mademoiselle
Therese de Bourgerre darkening his door, warning of dire emer-
gencies and dread consequences, forcing him to remember things
best forgotten. She was a delightful minx, to be sure, but it would
take more than a pair of pleading emerald eyes and a woebegone
smile to drag him back into the fray!

THE ROGUE'S BRIDE

BY PAULA ROLAND

ZEBRA BOOKS
KENSINGTON PUBLISHING CORP.

ZEBRA BOOKS

are published by

Kensington Publishing Corp.
475 Park Avenue South
New York, NY 10016

Second printing: January, 1990

Printed in the United States of America

For Catherine,
Leslie Carmel,
and Craig

Men are April when they woo,
December when they are wed:
maids are May when they are maids,
but the sky changes when they are wives.

— Shakespeare

Chapter 1

There was a flicker of movement on the balcony.

In the room below, a rigidly laced dowager of Mayfair leaned over to whisper to the lady beside her. "My dear, have you noticed? There seems to be someone hiding up there."

Her somewhat dour-faced companion glanced upward. "Where?"

"Peeking out from behind that utterly frightful aspidistra plant."

"Um, the bride, I expect."

"And the bridegroom?"

"Never arrived."

"Ah, well. One can't have everything, I suppose. It's a lovely wedding all the same."

Turning to watch Alexandra Redcliffe descend the stairs in a cloud of white lace and tulle, the dowager heaved a sigh that threatened permanent damage to her corset. "My, how exquisite she looks! And *such* composure! I've forgotten, my dear. What is this? Her second venture down the aisle?"

"Third," came the dry comment. "She should, I daresay, be rather skilled at it by now."

Exceptionally skilled, Alexandra would have amended had she chanced to overhear. That composure never wavered as she entered on the arm of Mr. Percival Winford.

Due to the gentleman's some fifty-odd years and to a horse that had sensibly decided a fence was too high and had thus elected to let his owner go over it without him, Mr. Winford had developed a somewhat peculiar hop-and-bobble stride.

He moved at one tempo. The stately strains of the processional music moved at another. Adroitly, Alexandra managed to pace her steps somewhere between the both of them.

That composure never wavered as she slowly walked past the rows of guests, the titled and near titled of London, who had dusted off their tiaras, their silks, and their satins for what had been proclaimed as the wedding of the Season.

Give or take a few hitches, they were not disappointed.

The bridegroom, wealthy, well-placed, and exasperatingly elusive, had at last been snared. Alexandra was nearly everything a bride should be. Elegant, willowy — a bit too tall, some said, but the glowing chestnut hair and the saucy brown eyes made up for it. And for the first time in years, Lord Winford's fusty old mansion was not only shining, it was virtually in bloom.

The house, or the main gallery at least, was festooned with roses from the faux-marbled oak floors to the cherub-trimmed cornices of the ceiling. A sizable altar, hired from Lambeth Chapel, was almost smothered in white roses. Garlands of pink rosebuds ran along the backs of the gilt chairs, more than two hundred of which had also been hired to accommodate the finest derrières of Mayfair and Pall Mall.

The ample behind of the Prince Regent himself was to have been ensconced in a specially bedecked chair in front. Unfortunately, it went unoccupied. The prince neglected to show up.

His was the sole nonattendance, however, save for an elderly marchioness, who took one look at the gallery and promptly decamped, claiming she had little fondness for "hothouses" and even less for Percy Winford.

No one else seemed to mind. They endured the roses, including those that hung from every railing of the narrow balcony that rimmed the gallery, and marveled at Mr. Winford's largesse. He was usually so pinch-fisted; this wedding obviously meant a great deal to him.

"As it should for the bride," murmured Alexandra, her thoughts marching along the same lines. She glanced up at the flower-bedecked balcony, then at the old man hop-bobbling at her side. He had truly outdone himself, she conceded; it was a perfect setting.

And the last place on earth she wanted to be.

Still, there was no help for it now. Buttons polished, uniform pressed to razor sharpness, the solemn-faced young lieutenant was waiting at the altar.

The sonorous tones of the organ, also hired, rose and died. Mr. Winford, his duties completed, stepped back, gave the bridal couple a final look as if checking to see that he had gotten his money's worth, and then hop-bobbled backward to a seat in the front row.

With a tug at his collar and a nervous smile, the lieutenant took Alexandra's hand. She smiled back . . . and for the life of her couldn't remember his name.

The old vicar who stood before them was of no assistance. He mumbled. A longtime friend of the bridegroom's family, apparently he had been whisked out of retirement sans eye glasses, ear horn, or teeth.

The lack of any of these, however, did not seem to distress him. Hunching over so far his nose nearly touched the open book before him, he launched into a monotonous drone of the wedding ceremony. That is, Alexandra assumed it was the proper ceremony. To her the entire service sounded like the hum of a rather large, dyspeptic bee.

Eventually, cupping his hand behind his ear, the old vicar looked up. "Will, you, Major mumble, mumble take mumble, mumble for your lawfully mumble, mumble?"

The lieutenant looked a little confused. Finally, he shrugged and said, "I will."

"And will you mumble, mumble take mumble . . ."

Again the old man bent his ear forward, obviously waiting for the same response. Alexandra hesitated, thinking of all the papers that had been signed yesterday. The names, hers included, were already firmly affixed to the marriage certificate. The bridegroom's ring had been accepted. This union was now a legal and accomplished fact. It was her turn to offer an almost infinitesimal shrug.

"I will," she said clearly.

A second later she regretted that clarity. The vicar, apparently inspired by her example, managed to speak his last words with surprising lucidity. "I now pronounce you man and wife. Young man, you may kiss the bride."

Oh, really, thought Alexandra. Now this was pitching it a bit high. As the lieutenant turned toward her, she proffered him a firm handshake instead. "A pleasure meeting you, sir," she murmured. "Shall we lead the way to the reception?"

It was a full three days afterward before she realized she was actually married.

The note, couched in ladylike terms, was quite mild. Alexandra's screech, upon its perusal, was anything but.

One octave higher, in fact, and that shriek might have driven horses mad as far away as Leicester Square.

Without waiting for maid or carriage, Alexandra jammed a bonnet on her head, threw on a fur-trimmed pelisse, and stormed out of her house.

Oblivious to the stares of passers-by (no lady walked the streets, not even in Mayfair, without the accompaniment of a maid or footman), Alexandra marched the few blocks to Mr. Winford's house and presented herself at the door.

"Where is Miss Winford?" she demanded of the shocked butler.

"In — in her chambers," the man sputtered. He had never seen Lady Redcliffe in such a taking. "Shall I announce —"

Alexandra did not wait for him to finish. She strode through the gallery, up the same stairs she had so recently descended in lace and tulle, past the balcony with its overgrown aspidistra, and on down the hall to the next-to-last door.

A sharp knock, a soft, "Come in, please," and she was inside a very feminine bedroom, all pink and apple green and frothed with ruffles. Its occupant, just past her eighteenth birthday, had the delicate features of a Dresden doll. Indeed, she had been complimented on such likeness many times — although not within the past week, to be sure.

Nonetheless, her honey-colored hair had been freshly

brushed and her china-blue eyes were bright as she lay in bed, a ruffled counterpane pulled up to her chin.

Marching over to her, Alexandra yanked the note from her pocket and thrust it out. "Dulcie Winford! What's the meaning of this?"

The girl immediately scuddled to the far side of the bed. "Lexie, dearest, should you really come this close? You might catch it."

"Rubbish!" Alexandra plopped herself down on the edge of the counterpane. "I've had the measles. Besides, you're nearly well. The spots are almost gone. Now what *is* this? Some sort of hoax? A game?"

"Neither, I'm afraid," Dulcie whispered. Like a mouse confronted by a particularly irate pussycat, she sank under the counterpane until only the china-blue eyes were showing. "It's more . . . a slight mix-up, you might say."

"How slight?" Alexandra demanded. But the answer, if there was one, was lost under a mass of ruffles. "Dulcie, do sit up! You're mumbling as badly as that old vicar."

With great reluctance, the girl edged herself back up on the pillows. "Well, that's it, actually. He is very old, you know. He simply got a bit confused. But I'm sure you needn't fret. We can mend it—I think."

Alexandra drew a deep breath. "Dulcie, if you don't sit up and explain this note immediately, I am not going to fret. I am going to throw an absolute screaming fit! Now, I repeat, why did you send me this note? And what on earth is this drivel about *me* being married?"

"Well, you are," Dulcie said as if that settled it. "I suppose you must remember all those papers you signed?"

"Of course. As your witness."

"Perhaps—" Dulcie's voice dropped to an apologetic murmur. "Perhaps you should have read them more carefully."

Alexandra waved the note impatiently. "I was in a horrid rush. The vicar told me where to affix my sig—oh, no, you cannot mean I signed the *wrong* line?"

The china eyes were full of sympathy, although, had Alexandra not been so agitated, she might have noticed there was also more than a hint of relief in them. With a rather exaggerated amount of hemming and hawing, Dulcie at last began to make some sense. "He — you mustn't let this upset you, Lexie dear — he made just a teensy mistake. Of course, now that it's been pointed out to him, he's quite disconcerted."

"I should hope so!" Alexandra retorted. "But then, surely it's not binding?"

Dulcie looked as if she would like to creep not only under the covers but under the bed itself. "I'm afraid it is. Both legal and binding. The vicar says he's terribly sorry, but you *are* married."

Alexandra opened her mouth to utter a stream of invectives that would have made any seaman proud. Unfortunately, she had never met any seamen, and her acquaintance with invectives was almost as limited. She had to settle for, "Drat! And double drat!"

It was most unsatisfying. Unable to contain herself, she jumped up and began pacing the room. "Oh, why did I ever let you talk me into this — this *ridiculous* proxy wedding? We should have postponed it!"

From the bed came a tiny noise that sounded suspiciously like a giggle. "Now, Lexie, you know Papa wouldn't hear to that. The roses would have wilted.

"Besides," Dulcie went on, intently watching Alexandra pace a deep furrow in her pink and apple-green carpet, "the guests had been invited for months. We couldn't disappoint all those people, could we? And it was a lovely wedding, simply everyone said so. You looked absolutely beautiful!"

"In your gown," snapped Alexandra, recalling the hasty alterations and the deep flounce that had been added to accommodate her taller figure. Without breaking stride, she threw up her hands and rolled her eyes toward the ceiling. "How could I? How *could* I have let you and your father talk me into such a thing? Prancing down the aisle at *your* wedding, in *your* gown!"

Dulcie no longer even faintly resembled a frightened mouse. She calmly folded her hands over the counterpane. "Well, as Papa said, my dress cost a fortune. The guests might as well see it on someone. Naturally, I wanted to see it too."

"Naturally," Alexandra scoffed. "So there you were, peeking out through a pot of aspidistra leaves in your dressing gown. While I, a vision in white, *again,* was getting myself married to—"

The former Lady Alexandra Redcliffe ground to a thunderstruck halt.

"To *whom?* Good God, just who was it I *married?* That Lieutenant what's-his-name?"

This time there was no repressing the giggle. "Of course not, silly. You are now Mrs. Brandon Clive."

"Oh, no, it's even worse than I thought. Fetch the hartshorn, Dulcie. I am going to swoon."

"You are not. You've never swooned in your life."

"That's true," Alexandra conceded. Promptly abandoning the notion, she sank into the nearest chair and propped her chin on her fists. This was, she further conceded, just her luck. A strange lieutenant would have been bad enough. Maj. Brandon Clive was impossible!

Not that she had ever met him. Nor had Dulcie, for that matter. Papa Winford, relying on a vague arrangement made several years earlier between himself and the major's father, had shot off several letters to the Continent, insisting Major Clive come home and honor that commitment. At last, one of those missives had hit the target.

From Turkey, Maj. Brandon Clive had written back that, after careful consideration, he had resigned himself to honoring this "prior betrothal."

This letter, and the ones that followed, were coldly formal and matter-of-fact. Mr. Winford had passed them on to Dulcie, of course, and Dulcie had freely shared them with Alexandra.

It took scant reading between the lines to see that the major, with the greatest abhorrence, had finally bowed to his fate. The Clive line had to go on; he was the only one left to accomplish that deed.

It was also plain he cared little who the bride was as long as she was possessed of youth, the proper connections, and the ability to bring forth an unspecified number of little

Clives.

The last letter had made another point equally apparent. Major Clive was even less interested in the wedding itself. Explaining that he had been delayed in Constantinople, he gave the Winfords a choice: postpone the ceremony until he did arrive or stage a proxy wedding. To facilitate the latter, should it prove more convenient, the major's equerry was already en route with the pertinent documents, dutifully signed and attested and needing only the signatures of the bride and her witness. Either method, the letter suggested, was agreeable to Major Clive. Mr. Winford might suit himself.

Dulcie's father wasted no time in doing just that. Who could tell, he argued, when this indifferent bridegroom might arrive? If ever! Hobnobbing with those Turkish savages, traipsing hither and thither about the Continent, the rascal might very well find himself shipwrecked or stabbed in some Stygian alley or both!

Mr. Winford had no intention of letting the Clive fortune sink, unclaimed, into the murky waters of some Bosporian port.

"Devil take the bridegroom!" he had roared. The wedding would go on as scheduled!

And so it had. Despite the absence of both groom — and bride. The major's equerry had been chosen as a stand-in. Dulcie, who had been given no say in the matter heretofore, had been allowed to settle this dilemma. After several meetings with the solemn-faced lieutenant, she had ventured the opinion that he was quite amiable. He would, she proposed, make a most handsome substitute.

Then the measles had struck. But neither flood nor famine, let alone pestilence, was going to deter Papa Winford. This ruinously expensive wedding would march forward, he decreed, if his daughter had to be carried down the aisle on her sickbed!

"With these splotches on my face?" Dulcie had squealed. "Never!"

Thus, Percival Winford's high-handed tactics had run themselves into a stone wall. His daughter would not budge.

He would not delay the ceremony. Ultimately, he had hop-bobbled out of the room, raging, "Demme, that gown cost a packet! Someone had better be in it!"

That someone was now sitting in Dulcie's bedroom contemplating the prospect of boiling all men in oil. Beginning with Mr. Percival Winford.

"But not until he gets me out of this farrago," Alexandra muttered. She sprang from the chair. "I should like to have a few well-chosen words with your father, I believe. Where is he?"

Dulcie gauged her audience, then pulled pillows and counterpane about her as if she were battening down the hatches before an impending storm. "Papa's gone to his club. To sulk, I think. Major Clive insulted him."

"What! You can't mean he's finally arrived?"

The girl nodded. "Daniel met him at the dock last night. He wants an immediate annulment."

"Thank heavens," breathed Alexandra. She sank back into the chair. Then at once sat up straight. "Daniel? Oh, you must mean Lieutenant Who's-It."

Behind her barrier of pillows, Dulcie resettled herself quite primly. "His name, Lexie, is Lt. Daniel Symington. And you needn't look so cross. None of this is his fault, you know."

Alexandra granted the point. In fairness, she scratched the young officer's name off her oil-boiling list. "At any rate, this farrago is nearly over, thank God. I assume the annulment papers are being drawn up now."

Grimly reminding herself that she would make no mistake in her signature this time, she missed most of Dulcie's hesitant reply. Something about a message signifying Major Clive's intention to call upon Papa first thing that morning — an icy meeting in the study — Papa rampaging up to her bedroom to announce he had never been so affronted in all his days.

Alexandra interrupted with a brusque wave of her hand. "Yes, yes, Major Clive insulted your father, you told me that before. And I must say I'm not surprised. If his letters are any indication — of which I am positive they are — the man's a dreadful boor. No doubt he insults everyone he meets. But surely, lumpish behavior or no, something must have been settled. What did he say?"

"Nothing," Dulcie muttered. Her slim fingers began to fidget with a ruffle as if she were challenging it to a wrestling match. The poor ruffle never had a chance. "That is — of course he did have a few thoughts on the subject. Only *he* didn't say them."

She gave her victim a thread-ripping twist. "Major Clive didn't come here after all. He was so angry he sent Daniel — I mean — Lieutenant Symington instead. The poor dear. Lexie, you mustn't blame him. He was under orders. He couldn't help it."

"For heaven's sake, Dulcie! Help what?"

"Conveying Major Clive's — sentiments," the girl answered. The ruffle, totally vanquished, disappeared into her tiny fist. "It seems the major feels he has been duped by us all. You, me, and especially Papa, which of course is frightfully unfair. After all, Papa wanted *me* married to the Clive fortune, not you."

Plainly annoyed with the major's denseness, Dulcie let out a ragged breath. "He claims he hasn't decided whether to tar and feather Papa or simply ride him out of town on an offal wagon. Could he do that, do you suppose?"

"Nonsense," Alexandra snapped. "There *are* laws. He'd never get away with either. But what about you and me? Did he profess the same plans for us?"

"No. There was only that comment about the annulment. He said — Oh, Lexie, I simply can't tell you this part!"

With a determined look, Alexandra left the chair and walked over to her friend's bedside. "Why? I'm not precisely an uninterested bystander, you know."

"No, I suppose not," Dulcie sighed. "He — he said he'd take care of the annulment himself. At once. He said he was not about to be chained to any dried-up old dowager."

If Alexandra's mouth dropped open, it was only to be expected. Twenty-six years of age and twice widowed, she had indeed looked forward to the freedom of a dowager. But not the description!

"Why that—Where is he staying? I'll give him such a set-down—"

With sudden firmness, Dulcie reached out and pulled her down on the bed. "You will not," she said, her fingers closing around Alexandra's wrist. "Given your temper, we'll only have a bigger muddle on our hands. Oh, why did I ever tell you? I knew I shouldn't have. Still, you mustn't really take it personally, you know. Daniel—Lieutenant Symington said he tried to explain. The major wouldn't listen. The moment he heard you were Lord Redcliffe's widow—well, your last husband was rather on in years, you must admit."

"He was," Alexandra murmured, her anger abating for an instant as she remembered the kindness of the man who had died on a cold winter's day some three years past.

"And your second marriage at that," Dulcie was continuing. "I suppose it only natural for the major to leap at the conclusion you were getting on yourself."

"Oh, you suppose that, do you?" Alexandra tried to shake off the girl's hand and failed. She had never imagined her tiny friend could possess such a grip. "Dulcie, dearest, before you break my wrist, may I remind you there is *nothing* natural about this disaster. An uncivilized boor, whom I've never met, you've never met, even your father's never met, somehow winds up married to me. Well, that is going to change, I assure you. Let go of me. I intend to find Maj. Brandon Clive right now and teach him a few manners!"

But the usually convivial little Dulcie persisted in being as firm as her grip. There was no need to cause a scandal broth, now was there? Once he had gotten over his sulks, Papa would see to the annulment details quickly and quietly. In the meantime, Alexandra would do nothing and go nowhere. Except perhaps to Bath.

"*Bath?* Dulcie, whatever put that into your head?"

Confident she had won her argument, the girl released her hold on Alexandra and serenely folded her little hands atop the counterpane. "Oh, someone reminded me what a pleasant spot it was, and my Aunt Tilmatha lives there. She's the dearest thing, been widowed for years, and no children. She's always been quite fond of me. We could stay with her."

"We?"

A grin spread across the Dresden-doll face. "I'd go with you, of course. To convalesce. I'm so dreadfully worn down by this illness, I can hardly lift a finger."

Without comment, Alexandra held out her wrist. There were still a few red marks surrounding it.

"Very well then," said Dulcie, quickly changing her tune. "The truth is, I want to get away from Papa. I never really wanted to marry Major Clive. I certainly don't now, and I doubt he wants me either after this dust-up. But you know Papa. The minute he gets over his pet, he'll start thinking of all that Clive money going to waste. He'll be bound to set me dimpling and twinkling after the major, trying to win him back. And I'll not do it. Not now! Oh, Lexie, let's do go to Bath!"

"Why should we?" muttered Alexandra, still wondering why Dulcie had settled on that particular spot. She hadn't visited her Aunt Tilmatha in years, but she had another aunt in Brighton whom she utterly adored. Why not that charming seacoast town instead? Alexandra glanced at her friend's anxious face and suddenly realized why not indeed!

"Dulcie, that someone who recommended Bath? He wouldn't perchance be called 'Daniel, would he?"

"Lieutenant Symington?" The Dresden complexion flushed as red as the splotches that had adorned it a few days earlier. "Oh—he may have mentioned it in passing."

"And perhaps, also in passing of course, just happened to mention he'd be visiting there himself?"

Abruptly, Dulcie grabbed the ruffle she had throttled a short time before. She began a most industrious effort to revive it. "He may have. I—I really don't recall."

"I see," Alexandra muttered. A small inner voice told her to back away; she had had enough of Dulcie's entanglements. Unfortunately, she reflected, that timorous little voice was a bit late. It should have spoken up three days ago.

"Farrago indeed!" Alexandra scoffed at herself. "In for a penny, in for a pound. Dulcie, pack your portmanteau. I'll dash home and do the same. We're off to Aunt Tilmatha's!"

When he arrived in Bath one morning, Maj. Brandon Clive had been married exactly one week. The annulment papers had been fairly easy to obtain. The bride's signature hadn't. Lady Alexandra Redcliffe—damned if he would call her Mrs. Clive—had vanished.

Chasing across London only to be greeted by uncommunicative butlers had done little to improve the major's disposition. Mr. Winford's sulking refusal to see him had done even less. Finally, an inspired visit to Lady Redcliffe's stables and an exhausting show of interest in her horses had brought results. A garrulous ostler had at last let slip a vague reference to Bath.

Where in Bath, Major Clive had no idea. It occurred to him his young equerry was also here on leave to visit some relations or such. Rather a nice coincidence, the major thought. He decided to search out Lieutenant Symington and enlist his aid.

Just as promptly he decided otherwise. This was a matter he could handle himself.

But where to start? The City Markets? The Circulating Library? The Pump Room?

Ah, the Pump Room, of course. Sooner or later, every dowager in Bath made her way to that rather clubby spa for a glass of the hot mineral water that was highly touted to cure all ills from gout to quinsy. There they would sit, these ailing ladies, and a number of equally decrepit gentlemen, sipping and chatting in the elegant comfort of the main assembly room. No doubt his bride of advancing years would be chief among them.

Maj. Brandon Clive turned toward Abbey Square.

He was halfway down Stall Street when an elderly passer-by came to an abrupt halt beside him. "Peyton? My boy, it's been years! How are you?"

"Me, sir?" queried the major, not certain to whom the old man was speaking. Then he recognized the face. "Lord Beecham! I'm fine, sir, thank you. But I'm not—"

21

The old man hardly pumped his hand. "Good to see you, my boy, good to see you! Must run. My regards to your father!"

That, thought Brandon, as he watched the old fellow scurry away, would be fairly hard to achieve. His father had been dead for some time. Not only that, Lord Beecham had obviously confused him with his cousin, Peyton.

The latter was somewhat easy to figure out. Peyton was ten years his senior, and Brandon had scarce been in England for as many years. The callow young officer who had left for the Continent had now returned a man of thirty.

Brandon Clive chuckled. He had traveled to Bath, not in uniform but in the ordinary riding clothes of an English gentleman. No wonder Lord Beecham had confused him with his older cousin. He wondered if anyone else would.

He soon found out.

As he strode into the Pump Room, several dowagers, comfortably seated near the door so as not to miss one entrance or exit, glanced up, noted the stranger's imposing height and aristocratic good looks, and vaguely wished they were quite a few decades younger.

Mrs. Tilmatha Cawlwood, seated a little distance farther on, took one look at the newcomer's dark hair and piercing black eyes and nearly dropped her glass of restorative water. She did drop her fan and reticule. And a faggoted shawl of Norwich silk slid from her shoulders into a soft heap on the floor.

Frantically setting all these to rights, she beckoned to him in a most agitated fashion. "Good gracious me! Of all people, can you fathom it? I was just this moment thinking of you!"

Major Clive halted, searched his memory, then, successfully pulling a name out of the past, strode the few paces to her chair.

"Mrs. Cawlwood," he drawled with a polite bow. "It's been quite a while."

"Ages! I cannot imagine why you've turned up in our little town, but thank heavens you did. My boy, you simply must do something about your cousin!"

"As I recall, I seem to be blessed with several relations," he said, casually taking the empty chair beside her. "Which cousin?"

"Why, Brandon, of course. Hadn't you heard? He's returned to London and apparently he's done something terrible. Written some very rude letters or some such. And who knows what else! My niece, Dulcie—oh, she's Percy Winford's only daughter. Her mother's long gone, poor child—but such an adorable little thing. Have you met her?"

"Not yet," was the dry response.

Mrs. Cawlwood waved a fluttery hand. "Then you must. She's here, and so is her friend, Lady Redcliffe. Frankly, I'm not certain why; they've been terribly secretive. All I know is, they've somehow taken it into their heads that they absolutely despise poor Brandon. Both of them! I simply cannot feature the reason, he was always such a dear boy. But there it is, just the same. They can't abide him. In fact, they keep muttering really horrendous things like—like 'boiling him in oil'!"

"Do they?"

"Worse. It must be some mistake, surely. I can't imagine Brandon turning out like that. He was ever such a darling— oh, he had quite a temper, don't we know—but I cannot believe he'd ever be *boorish*!"

Brandon raised an eyebrow. "They muttered that as well?"

"My dear, that was the least of it. Which is precisely why I was thinking of you. You were always so much more mature and settled. And now, praise be, by some miracle you're here. You will set this straight, won't you? The girls are so upset with poor Brandon and—oh, there they are!"

She started to raise her hand. Brandon gently but quickly forestalled her. "A moment if you please. Which ones are they?"

The assembly room was somewhat crowded not only with older people but with younger family members who had been pressed into accompanying them. Under the guise of taking a sip of water, Mrs. Cawlwood pointed a discreet finger toward two young women who were surrounded by a handful of obviously admiring gentlemen. "Dulcie's the one in blue," Mrs. Cawlwood said. "The taller one in yellow is Alexandra Redcliffe. I must say that ruched bonnet does become her—and the bronzed plume is exactly the right touch. I must really remember to tell her so."

Once more lifting her hand, she managed to catch their attention. "Darlings," she called out gaily, "do come here, please. There is someone I should like you to meet."

Maj. Brandon Clive was accustomed to making instant decisions. In the few seconds it took the young women to cross the room, he made a complete reversal of tactics.

Dresden dolls had never been his cup of tea. He took one look at the tall, willowy—and eminently desirable—Lady Redcliffe, and the annulment papers almost faded from his mind.

But he did not forget Lady Redcliffe's obvious hatred of her unknown bridegroom.

As the two approached, he rose and made an elegant bow. "Your servant, ladies. Allow me to introduce myself. I am Peyton Clive."

Chapter 2

"Clive?"

The word squeaked out in unison. Good breeding not-withstanding, the name had figured too prominently of late in the thoughts of both young women to be greeted with anything but surprise. And suspicion.

Nevertheless, squeaking was hardly commendable in the general assembly salon of the Pump Room. Aware that a few heads had turned in their direction, Alexandra made a hasty attempt to recover, but the glint of laughter in Mr. Clive's eyes only make things worse. A rather sour "How'd you do?" was the best she could muster.

Dulcie made no attempt at all. Her china eyes wide with astonishment, she blurted, "Good heavens! *Another* Clive? One's more than—"

"Enough of that!" gasped Mrs. Cawlwood. "Oh, Dulcie! Please recollect your manners!"

In the process of rising, Mrs. Cawlwood managed to drop, first reticule, then fan; then the voluminous, faggoted shawl slid from her shoulders. By the time Brandon had retrieved all three, Mrs. Cawlwood had become the center of atten-tion.

"Now there, you see, a perfect gentleman," she whispered to Dulcie and Alexandra. "Whatever this taking-on about poor Brandon—which I cannot for the life of me under-stand—he was ever such a dashing little rascal. But no matter. The main thing is, we mustn't discuss that here, must we, girls?"

25

She looked at each of the young women to make sure the point was finally taken. Recalling their mysterious threats, she was half-afraid they might be tempted to dump a Clive, *any* Clive, into a pot of boiling oil. Of course, there was no such vessel available, but there was the pump in the center of the room and, concealed directly beneath it, a giant cistern of bubbling mineral water.

"The Clives, after all, my dears, are a lovely family. *Quite* lovely," she went on with great emphasis. "And quite charming too—on the whole. Of course, I do seem to recall a great-uncle of yours, dear boy. Now what *was* his name? Simpson? Yes, Simpson Clive, it was. Been dead for years, and just as well, I daresay. The man had the most disgusting habit of paring his nails at the table. It rather put guests off at dinner parties, don't you know? Why, I recollect once a paring bounced straightway into a dish of pickled—oh, *dear!*"

With the sudden realization she was in no way aiding the matter, Mrs. Cawlwood clapped a hand to her mouth. Whereupon, naturally, both reticule and fan hit the floor. Brandon, the amusement even livelier in his eyes, graciously repeated his actions of retrieval.

"Have a care with your shawl, ma'am," he murmured as he bent down, for that article, too, was in immediate danger of joining its companions. Alexandra made haste to realign the slipping garment.

Now completely flustered, Mrs. Cawlwood blurted, "So you see, girls, whatever you fancy Brandon's sins, you mustn't fault Peyton. It may have been years, but you can take my word for it, I assure you. Peyton is nothing at all like his cousin."

Beaming, she reached out to give Brandon an encouraging pat on the arm. "Of course, you aren't, are you, dear boy? Why, you've never been the least bit dashing!"

Dubious as it was, this gushing accolade served the purpose. Alexandra's anger fled. Barely choking back a whoop of laughter, she could not resist an impish, "How nice for you, sir."

Mr. Clive seemed to be having a bit of trouble keeping a straight face himself. "Thank you, Lady Redcliffe," he said.

"And now that my character has been so, ah, flatteringly established, perhaps you'd honor me with a turn around the room?"

He held out his arm, and Alexandra, to her own surprise, found herself rather eager to take it. Yet she hesitated, more leery of this sudden feeling than of the unknown man who stood before her. "Well—"

Mrs. Cawlwood, delighted with the results of her peacemaking, quickly shooed her young visitor onward with a flutter of her hands. "Yes, yes, my dear, go right ahead. It's perfectly proper, you see. That's what the Pump Room's for, to chat up one's neighbors, make new acquaintances. Heavens, you don't suppose we come here simply to drink this bilious water, do you? By all means, do toddle along. Doubtless you shall become fast friends in no time at—"

She gave Brandon an arch look. "My boy, I seem to recall an *on dit* some years past about you and one of those Clayton girls. You didn't, by any circumstance, happen to marry her, did you?"

Brandon answered truthfully, "No, ma'am, *I* did not."

Thank heavens, thought Mrs. Cawlwood. As best she remembered, those Claytons were not at all the thing. She beamed approvingly at Brandon as if he were a schoolboy who had given the correct answer to a difficult history quiz. "Then run along, my dear," she said, turning to Alexandra. "You couldn't be in more steadfast hands, I assure you. Even as a little boy, there was always one thing you could say of Peyton Clive. He's so dependable!"

With this second, equally dubious compliment, she merrily sent them on their way with the admonition not to hurry. Her dear niece would keep her company in the interim.

Dulcie, strangely enough, acquiesced without a murmur. The truth was, this newcomer had disappointed her. Having missed the humor in his eyes, Dulcie could only conclude from her aunt's comments—and from her own observations—that this latest Clive must be a very dull fellow indeed. Tolerably well featured, yes, but he had no conversation and, even worse, he was practically ancient. Why, the man must be into his third decade at the very least!

Of course, as Dulcie reflected in the wisdom of her eighteen years, Alexandra at twenty-six was getting on too, but she didn't look it. And she certainly wasn't dull!

Watching the retreating couple, Dulcie thought it had been most unfair of Aunt Tilmatha to have foisted such an onerous chore on her friend.

She sat down, gave her aunt a somewhat reproachful glance, and candidly announced, "Pity his cousin didn't arrive instead. An out-and-out router would be much more interesting."

The reticule hit the floor.

"Dulcie! Wherever did you learn such language? My dear child, you really mustn't be quite so — so frank!"

The soft-hearted Mrs. Cawlwood had never managed to give anyone a proper rake-down. She did no better this time. After some minutes of confused sputterings, she finally lapsed into a glum silence and an even glummer wish that Alexandra could be retrieved as easily as her reticule. Then they could all go home.

As luck would have it though, her new house guest seemed to have taken her earlier admonition seriously.

Alexandra was in no hurry to be retrieved. She, for one, had rather appreciated Mr. Clive's forbearance in the face of Mrs. Cawlwood's well-meaning but clearly bumbling intentions. Nor had she for a moment missed the veiled amusement in his glance.

As they meandered along the perimeter of the room, she could not deny a droll expression of sympathy. "I do feel for you, sir. It must be quite a burden."

Major Clive looked down at his companion. If he yet harbored some misgivings about Lady Alexandra Redcliffe, they did not concern her beauty or her height. While she was a full head shorter than he, at least he was not required to bend over double just to hear her. If there was anything Maj. Brandon Clive disliked, it was women who talked into his waistcoat pocket. Tucking Alexandra's hand more securely into the crook of his arm, he murmured, "A burden, m'lady? And what might that be?"

"Why, all that dependability and steadfastness. Such sterling qualities, sir. I should think a lifetime of them would prove most fatiguing."

"Not at all," came the perfectly grave response. "They're mere child's play for a man of my standards. The real accomplishment, you see, is to avoid being dashing."

Alexandra forced herself to match this gravity. "Naturally, I should have realized that at once. Never a jest. Not even an occasional lapse of drollery. How very admirable. But tell me honestly, have you never succumbed to the temptation?"

"Never. Furthermore, I pray you will not expect gallantries from me or — God forbid — any liveliness of conversation. As I said, I do have my standards to maintain."

Alexandra inclined her head in solemn accord. Opining that she had no wish to compromise such lofty ideals, she wondered aloud if Mr. Clive might not find a tour of the entire room too adventuresome for his nature.

He appeared to mull this speculation over at some length. Finally, he allowed that such a trek might be acceptable provided they advanced at a most sedate pace.

They could hardly do otherwise. If Bath was not quite the elegant resort it had been during the years of the Bonaparte wars when traveling on the Continent had been impossible and Londoners had been forced to rediscover the beauties of their own shores, the town still had its fashionable attractions. Assemblies flourished, as did its concerts and theaters. So, too, did the spas.

Foremost among them was the Pump Room. As did its fellow watering spots, including a spate of newer ones near the City Markets as well as the long-established Mineral Hospital, the Pump Room featured actual baths.

Or pools rather, to be exact.

These generously sized communal pools allowed ladies, decorously wrapped in long sheeting and attended by sternly uniformed female attendants, to soak away their infirmities, real or imagined, in small groups or large.

For the gentlemen, there were similar facilities. But for either sex, this labyrinth of steaming pools was only for the more daring. Most fashionables had scant idea where these rooms were located, nor did they have the slightest intention of seeking them out. To expose one's innards to an occasional glass of the steaming liquid was one thing. Submerging one's entire being in water that rose from seven to twenty-odd degrees above body temperature was quite another.

In fact, like Mrs. Cawlwood, there were more than a few who felt that such temperatures might indeed turn one into a human lobster — done to a turn, and ready for the funeral master's table.

Hence, male and female, young and old alike, most patrons found the general assembly room rather more appealing.

At the moment certainly, Alexandra and her escort found that to be true. The room was packed with gentry of all proportions and all states of health. Those long past the autumn of their years, their walking sticks protruding into the aisles and making treacherous snags for the unwary stroller. Dowagers who proclaimed to suffer from any number of nervous conditions and palpitations but who seemed to gather great fortitude from discussing these various ills and their treatments with any other lady who desisted in her own complaints long enough to listen.

Alexandra, at first glance, had promptly named these the "Sitters." She mentioned as much to Mr. Clive as they slowly moved past the overstuffed chairs, the straight-backed chairs (thoughtfully provided for those with back ailments), and divans that lined the walls. Hardly a seat was empty.

Moreover, a trio of musicians in the far corner seemed to be playing in accompaniment to the constant rumbling of sciatic complaints and dyspeptic sighs.

Alexandra glanced upward, and the corners of her mouth quivered. "Not quite what you are accustomed to, I expect. Have you been here before?"

"No. And more's the shame. I had no idea what a charming spot I'd missed. Soft music, the enchanting murmur of voices. Quite a rheumatic setting, wouldn't you say?"

This did win a gentle laugh from Alexandra. She straightened her face as quickly as she could. "Careful, Mr. Clive. That was very nearly a witticism."

Professing horror, Brandon declared it was no such thing.

Lady Redcliffe must have mistaken his words.

"Of course, how silly of me," said Alexandra and promptly begged his pardon. "Being a gentleman of such serious demeanor, I daresay you haven't noticed, but the Pump Room is rather a romantic spot, actually."

With a nod of her head, she indicated the dozen or so persons who strolled about the room. "As you might observe, not everyone here is a Sitter. Some of them do move about."

"They should. It's no doubt the last chance they'll have before rigor sets in."

Brandon deliberately ignored the younger people, including a lone child of not more than six or seven, who had obviously been warned to stay by his grandmother's knee and was now in the process of stealthily edging away from that elderly joint.

Instead, Brandon directed Alexandra's attention to the pump and a couple of ladies who were hobbling toward it. Both stricken in years and making heavy use of their walking sticks, they were advancing toward their goal with all the haste of a team of dying snails.

"I scarcely meant them," Alexandra said, barely glancing at the two women. Then she looked again. "Perhaps we should help them, do you think? They might appreciate it if we fetched the water for them."

"They very well might," Brandon murmured, "but it wouldn't be the least helpful. This is quite likely the only exercise they get. You'll excuse me for a moment, I trust."

"Why, yes," replied a surprised Alexandra, but her escort was already halfway across the room. In seconds, he had an aging lady on each arm. Whatever remarks he made to them went unheard by the rest of the assembly. Nevertheless, they produced a telling effect. By the time these fragile ancients had been treated to their mineral water and gently escorted back to their chairs, both of them were tittering and coyly batting their eyelashes like schoolgirls.

Alexandra batted her own in light-hearted teasing as Brandon returned to her side. "Ah, Mr. Clive, you prove my point. The Pump Room is even more romantic than I supposed."

Brandon regarded her for a second, his expression completely unfathomable. Then he smiled. "Valetudinarians always have a soft spot for us dull fellows."

Alexandra pretended to study this revelation most carefully. "Yes, that must explain it. For a moment there, I was convinced you'd betrayed your standards. You will forgive me, I trust."

This was received with a slightly disapproving frown. "I suppose I shall have to. Taking exception with a lady would be much too unsettling for my nature."

"But not for your cousin's," Alexandra muttered. She quickly caught herself. "I am sorry. Major Clive's behavior is hardly your responsibility. Shall we return to Mrs. Cawlwood and Dulcie?"

The gentleman, however, seemed in no rush to end their stroll. And neither, for that matter, was she. Mr. Clive's nearness had produced several strange feelings in her. She was not at all sure what they were or why they had come about; only that they were not entirely displeasing.

She glanced at the half-dozen or so other young couples aimlessly walking about the room and wondered if any of them were experiencing such confusing sensations. After a thorough scrutiny of the nearest faces, she rather suspected they were.

As she had previously noted, the Pump Room did have its share of visitors who were totally unburdened with afflictions of age and infirmity. Most were very young women or girls just out of the schoolroom. And most of these, to be sure, had been commanded to tag along with their elderly relations.

The surprising thing was, few of them seemed to mind. On her introduction to the spa several days ago, Alexandra had questioned this good-natured compliance. But Mrs. Cawlwood had been right. Unlikely as it seemed, the Pump Room was a perfect meeting place. Encountering the occasional young gallant (and some not quite as youthful as they would prefer to think), a young lady could stroll about, greet acquaintances of her own age, and innocently flirt to her heart's content. All this of course being perfectly respectable since she was under the eye of a family member.

Moreover, that eye — to make life even more delightful — was seldom constant. Convinced that their young daughters, granddaughters, or nieces, could not come to ruin in such proximity, the elders usually fell to discussing their ailments with so much passion, they forgot about their young relatives. As a result, this provided a well-brought-up young lady with a giddy sense of unrestraint. It was, quite possibly, the greatest freedom from chaperonage she would experience until her wedding day.

Naturally, with her record of marriages, Alexandra considered herself beyond such giddiness.

It was not until she and Mr. Clive had stopped to listen to the trio play a lackluster version of "Cherry Ripe" that she realized she had been sporting an utterly inane smile for the past several minutes.

Embarrassed, she glanced up, only to be greeted by another disapproving frown. Yet slight as it was, there was clearly no teasing behind it this time. Mr. Clive seemed truly annoyed. "Second thoughts on my cousin, Lady Redcliffe?"

"Indeed not!" gasped Alexandra. "Nothing could ever change my mind about Maj. Brandon Clive! He is without doubt the most unmitigated —"

She halted, not from loss of words — oh, no, she could think of several choice ones — but from the belated awareness that she had overstepped the bounds. Again. "Never mind. Let's just say, the less I have to do with — with your cousin, the better off we shall all be!"

"Then why are you avoiding —" the *annulment*, Brandon started to say, then recalled he was supposed to be an innocent and uninformed bystander. "I meant, that is, if you're simply avoiding the topic on my behalf, you needn't. I've not seen my cousin in a decade, and we were never particularly close, even as boys. I must admit to a certain curiosity. You wouldn't, perhaps, care to tell me just a bit of it?"

No, she wouldn't, thought Alexandra, momentarily blocked by an innate reluctance to confide in a man she had only just met. Then a second thought hove into mind. It was rather likely, wasn't it, that he would run into his cousin sometime? And did she want him to have that—that boor's version of the story? No, she most certainly did not. She wanted him to know the unvarnished truth of the matter.

Why it seemed so important for him to understand, she didn't bother to analyze. Abruptly, she answered, "Why, yes, I think I should."

With that, Maj. Brandon Clive was treated to a concise recital of his own literary shortcomings, which rather irritated him though he concealed it (had his letters really been all that boorish and indifferent?), followed by a much longer and livelier description of his wedding. This so appealed to his sense of absurdity, he burst into laughter.

"Lady Redcliffe, whatever differences may remain between you and your—ah, bridegroom, I must confess you tell an excellent story. Almost makes me wish I'd been there."

"Well, you must have been invited. Weren't you?"

Major Clive took a considerable interval to clear his throat. "Um, not exactly. Invitation cards were sent out, I would assume. But to tell the truth, no, I don't believe I ever received a *formal* invitation."

"Oh, dear, that is a shame. However, if it's any consolation, you're not the only one. Dulcie made such a slap-dash of the guest list, Mrs. Cawlwood wasn't invited either."

Major Clive peered across the room at the two women near the door. "Her own aunt?"

Following his gaze, Alexandra watched Dulcie rescue the reticule from the floor for what was very likely the dozenth time. She shrugged. "Dulcie's a dear. She's just a bit careless at times. That's why we daren't mention anything about weddings around Mrs. Cawlwood. She'd be terribly hurt that she wasn't asked to the ceremony—even if it was an innocent mistake. I may rely on your discretion, I do hope."

"You may. As for myself, I'm obliged by your candor. I can only hope you will excuse mine. My—that is, my cousin's—pockets aren't exactly to let, you know. In fact, as the cant might have it, he's full of juice. Now taking that into view, some brides mightn't be so anxious to part with his name. Yet you talk of annulment. Are you quite sure you

34

mean that?"

Their aimless strolling had brought them to a closed door at the rear of the assembly room. Now Alexandra stepped back against it in astonishment. "Good lord, yes! The man can be so full of juice he *bursts*, for all I care. I want an annulment, and without delay!"

"But there's the puzzlement, you see. There *do* seem to be delays. First, if I'm not mistaken, you seem quite content not only to let Mr. Winford handle the matter, but to let him take his own good time getting around to it. And second—well, I must confess this is the greatest puzzlement of all. The moment you learn this unwanted bridegroom, as you call him, has arrived in London, presumably the most convenient place for both of you to sign those annulment papers, you leave the city. Why? If you'll pardon my asking."

"Why, simply to avoid any wagging tongues. Mr. Clive, are you interrogating me or merely coming to the defense of your relation?"

Mentally chastising himself for his lapse, Brandon quickly slipped back into character. "Upon my word, ma'am, *neither*, I should hope. It's just that we staid fellows never seem to encounter such intriguing dilemmas. I can't help being curious, I'm afraid. And perhaps even a shade envious. Now that I've met the bride, I'm beginning to think my—my obstreperous cousin has all the luck."

A great many compliments had come Alexandra's way, the majority of them much more extravagant than this, yet none of them had flown to her head. Now she found herself blushing like some young thing pitched into her first rout party. She couldn't believe it!

Good heavens, she thought, if I open my mouth I'll undoubtedly start twittering worse than those two old ladies.

Brandon saved her from any such possibility. Excusing himself for asking—it was only that pesky curiosity of his again, he supposed—but why had she chanced on this particular spot?

"The Pump Room?" On reflection, Alexandra decided that, as a response, it was nearly addlepated. But at least she hadn't twittered.

She would have been surprised to know her companion considered her neither addlepated nor twittery. The word he might have chosen was "evasive."

"I was speaking of Bath," he smoothly continued. "Of course I don't come south often. I seldom leave" — Brandon hesitated, unable to recall for a moment where his cousin's blasted country estate was — "er . . . leave Yorkshire. But, as I seem to recall, Lord Redcliffe had a country home just outside London. Yours now, I assume — unless you've found a need to dispose of it."

There was a pause as if he expected some answer. But Alexandra, who had no idea what he was getting at, said nothing. She patiently waited for him to go on.

Brandon straightened his waistcoat. "The thought merely cropped up. Made me wonder, you see. I can understand your wish to rusticate, to add no fuel to those wagging tongues as you say. But why not have gone there instead of Bath?" Now that the question was out, Brandon shrugged as if it made no difference to him. "None of my affair, of course. Just occurred to me it might have facilitated the annulment. Bath's quite a distance, and I seriously doubt you traveled all this way for the waters. Why did you?"

"Because — because Dulcie wanted to come here."

It was nothing less than the fact, but, even to Alexandra's own ears, it sounded rather lame.

In the next breath, she caught herself up short. Logical or not, her actions were her own concern. She didn't have to justify herself to anyone. Certainly not to a near stranger!

That thought stopped her for an instant. Had she really met him not over ten minutes ago? My goodness! Then — well, it didn't matter, how dare he question her! Squaring her shoulders, she prepared to give him a sharp set-down.

The sole problem seemed to be, she couldn't think of one. Somehow, all she could think was trying to erase the look of doubt from Mr. Clive's dark eyes.

"You see, it was this way — "

She got not one word further.

From behind the nearby closed door came the sound of a cry, then a splash. Next, the door was flung open and a shrieking female attendant came bursting through. "The little boy! He's drowning! He's drowning!"

Whereupon a plump dowager, who had been most agreeably engaged in a lengthy account of her sciatica, glanced down to realize the young child who should have been leaning against her knee wasn't. With a shriek that matched the attendant's, she heaved herself out of her chair and came thudding across the room. "My grandson! Where is he? Ramsey! *Ramsey!*"

"He's in the pool!" cried the attendant. "Help him! Oh, lord, sir, please help him!" she begged, grabbing the nearest male arm, which happened to be Brandon's.

He had already started to do just that, but the two hysterical women made it impossible. First, the attendant was blocking the doorway. By the time he had moved her to one side and disengaged her clinging hands, the dowager was hard upon him.

"Hurry! Hurry!" she shrieked, grabbing at his coat and nearly pulling him off balance. Shouldering past him, she lunged into the doorway, stopped, gave a little gasp, and fainted dead away.

Brandon caught her as she fell. There was nothing to do but get this second substantial burden away from the door.

In that interim, of course, the half-dozen-or-so young gallants who had been in the assembly room promptly streamed through the passageway, as did a number of younger women. The still-shrieking attendant followed in the rear.

Brandon, now having to shoulder his way through all of them, finally arrived at the correct bathing room only to find a great deal of commotion but no practical results.

The little boy was bobbing up and down in the middle of a large pool, obviously in distress but far from dead.

Alexandra was only a few steps behind Brandon. She arrived to find one gallant unsuccessfully attempting to fish the lad out with a cane. The rest appeared to be taking a poll of their natatorial skills—or rather the lack of them.

"Can you swim?" asked one dandy.

"Lord, no," said another. "Never considered it quite the

thing, you know."

Two others were looking down at their rainment as if weighing the merits of valor against the horrid consequences of sopping attire. They couldn't swim either, they mumbled, and looked more than a little relieved when someone suggested calling a male attendant.

There was only one who seemed to realize the little boy couldn't go on bobbing forever. He couldn't swim either, he agreed, but he girded his courage and raised his arms, preparing to dive in headfirst.

Brandon, pushing through a group of excited young ladies, caught him by the collar and yanked him back. "Excellent way to crack your head," he muttered, nodding at a sign on the wall, which apparently no one else had bothered to notice.

THE HEALTH-GIVING WATER IN OUR POOLS IS MAINTAINED AT A CONSTANT LEVEL OF FOUR FEET, FOR YOUR SAFETY AND ENJOYMENT!

Without another word, Brandon quietly slipped into the pool, waded to the center, and carried the boy out. Calmly reassuring the child, who was more frightened than drowned, he directed the attendant to find a blanket, wrap the boy in it, and return him to his grandmother.

Alexandra, silently assessing the situation, decided the girl would never have the common sense to fetch two blankets. She followed her out and fetched the second one herself.

When she returned, the others had filed out of the bathing room. Brandon was standing alone, wringing the water from his dripping coat into the pool.

Alexandra draped the blanket across his shoulders. "There, sir. Not the most fitting cloak for a hero, but the best I could manage, I'm afraid."

Brandon laughed. "Fitting enough under the circumstances. What little I did scarcely qualifies as heroic."

"Oh, yes, it does!" Alexandra firmly replied. "While everyone else stood around dithering, you saved that poor child's life. I cannot think of anyone who wouldn't laud such prompt action."

"I can," muttered Brandon with a wry glance at his coat. "My tailor."

He transferred that glance to Alexandra for a moment. Then stepping back, he swung an end of the blanket over his shoulder in the fashion of a cavalier and made a deep bow. "Much as I enjoy basking in a lovely lady's approval, I must confess I'd rather do it in dry clothing. Shall we go?"

"Go?" Alexandra repeated idiotically, then blushed to the roots of her hair. It belatedly occurred to her that, instead of turning away as any lady should have, she had been admiring not only his valor but the way the wet shirt and trowsers clung to his trim figure.

"Mercy, how thoughtless of me," she babbled, making a thoroughly poor job of covering her embarrassment, "to keep you here while I chattered away. Whatever could I have been thinking of? We must fetch you a carriage."

"And find a back door," Brandon added in a practical manner. "I misdoubt the management would appreciate my dripping a path through the assembly room."

"What management?" Alexandra snapped, suddenly aware that no one save herself had come to Mr. Clive's assistance. "You'd think by now someone certainly would have—"

As if on cue, a portly little man came bustling through the door. "Ah, there you are, sir! Thank you, thank you! A thousand thanks, though small as they are to compare with the service you've rendered this establishment today!"

He rushed forward to pump Brandon's hand. "My undying gratitude is yours. Oh, my, how one trembles to think what might have happened, had you not been here. Of course we so rarely have little ones in the Pump Room. They seem to have so few chronic afflictions, you see. But naturally that's neither here nor there, is it? No excuse, no, no excuse at all for the negligence of my staff. I shall certainly reprimand them the very first chance I get."

Without pausing, he slapped a hand to his forehead. "Only, goodness knows, there's hardly been a chance to breathe, let alone bark at one's staff. What with all the commotion in the assembly room, don't you know. My other two assistants and I dashed in as soon as we heard the to-do, having no idea what had come to pass. And what should we find? Cora, that shatter-brained minion if ever there was one, clutching a dripping child in a blanket and standing there gape-jawed as a dozen ladies clustered around Mrs. Peppering—that's the lad's grandmother. Who, I might add, was fair to being smothered by all the hartshorn and vinegarette vials that had been thrust at her nose. She was awake but in such a taking as I've never seen. Went limp on us at every step. Finally, it took our entire staff just to cram—I mean—escort the dear lady and the child into a sedan chair."

Brandon, who had taken this long-winded recital in good patience, nodded his head in outrageously solemn accord. "From personal experience, I can only agree with you. The lady is definitely no lightweight. You have my sympathies, Mr.—"

"Ah, do forgive me, sir. A thousand pardons, dear lady. I am in such a state myself, I forget my manners. Please, allow me to introduce myself. Mr. Clarence Bottleswell, manager of this establishment for the past score of years. And I hope for another score at least," he said, his voice dropping to a worried mutter. "Although nothing so unsettling has ever happened here before, and, when the owners hear of it—Oh, dear, I hate to think—"

He suddenly remembered his duty and straightened up, bravely squaring his shoulders. "Ah, well, that is spilt milk under the bridge, or some such as they say. I am here solely to extend my heartfelt gratitude. I know we can never repay you, sir. But as a token of our esteem, perhaps we might offer you—and your lovely lady, of course—any guest privileges as you might find to your liking. Please, I insist! Mr.—"

"Clive," said Brandon. "And this is Lady Redcliffe."

"An honor, a great honor, I assure you. My humble establishment is yours. Please feel free to make use of our facilities at any time!"

"At the moment, I believe Mr. Clive would prefer a

discreet exit," Alexandra said flatly. "And a carriage."

That at last seemed to prod Mr. Bottleswell into the realization that one sopping gentleman and one obviously nettled young lady were not predisposed to a lengthy chat.

With a startled apology, the man bestirred himself. Beckoning the two to follow him, he abruptly turned on his heel and dashed off at such speed Alexandra and Brandon were hard put to keep pace.

By the time they had hastened down one hall, then another, Mr. Bottleswell was far ahead of them. As he came to yet another turning, he spun around, pointing to his right. "If you please," he panted. "At the end of this hall, the green door leads to the service entrance. If you will be so kind as to wait there, I'll hail a carriage from the street."

With a mighty gulp for breath and what was no doubt meant to be a reassuring smile, he disappeared in the opposite direction.

Slowing their pace, Brandon and Alexandra continued on to the turning that Mr. Bottleswell had indicated. At the juncture of the two hallways, Brandon halted. "Lady Redcliffe, you've been most considerate. Much as I hate to deprive myself of such a charming escort, it occurs to me your friends must be somewhat anxious about you by now. You'd best rejoin them, don't you think?"

"I suppose," Alexandra murmured although she gravely doubted either Mrs. Cawlwood or Dulcie had yet noticed her absence. By now the assembly room must be a-buzz with the hashing and rehashing of the recent events. And of course those events were bound to grow with each retelling.

With a hint of amusement, Alexandra wondered how long it would take before the story stretched to enormous proportions. By afternoon, no doubt, the courageous Mr. Clive would be credited with saving a dozen or more unfortunates. Plus slaying a sea serpent in the process as well.

Yes, she thought, she really should return, and not simply for curiosity's sake. No matter what the circumstances, rushing pell-mell down vacant halls with a disheveled gentleman would scarcely enhance any lady's reputation.

Lost in her thoughts, she had traveled a few steps farther.

Now she looked back to find Mr. Clive hadn't moved. He grinned. "You needn't tarry on my account. Or are you afraid that, like Mrs. Peppering, I might swoon and you'd have to bodily lift me into the carriage?"

The thought of such a ludicrous possibility surprised a laugh from the lady. "Oh, very well. Since I'm no longer of any assistance, I'll leave."

She started to retrace her steps, but, as she did, from somewhere came a blast of chilly air. Brandon automatically pulled the blanket tighter about his shoulders.

"Then again," Alexandra said firmly, "another few moments will hardly matter, will they? Mr. Bottleswell may be some time — *will* be some time," she amended. "Carriages for hire are not that plentiful in Bath."

Provided he had even managed to flag one as of yet, she further considered, they could be sure he would have any number of words for the driver before he brought him along to the rear. Mr. Clive, she said abruptly, could not possibly wait outside all that while. He would undoubtedly catch his death.

Major Brandon Clive, who had survived many a rain-soaked mission without so much as a sneeze, seemed to accept this reasoning in perfect solemnity. "How true," he sighed. "And with my delicate constitution — well, one shouldn't take needless chances, should one? What do you propose?"

"To wait for it myself, of course. I suggest you find a draft-free corner and remain there. I'll come back for you as soon as the carriage arrives."

"Then what?" mustered an amused Brandon. "Hand me into it like some dottering old guffer?"

Alexandra did not hear this. She was already walking down the hall and wondering how the Pump Room had managed to acquire such an idiotic staff. The one attendant she had seen was, to be sure, a mindless gape-jaw. As for the others, where were they? There was only the manager's word that they even existed.

His word? Alexandra allowed herself a very unladylike snort. Mr. Bottleswell had words to let, but none of them had suited the purpose. Scrabble-skulled little gabster, had he offered Mr. Clive so much as a brandy? Or the comfort of his office while a proper conveyance was fetched?

"Dreadful little man," she muttered aloud, unaware that Brandon had quietly followed behind her. "Now which door did he say? Ah, there it is, the green — oh, dear, there are *two* green doors. I do wonder which."

Approaching them, she glanced from one to the other, then with a shrug, picked the nearer one.

Without breaking stride, she opened the door and marched in. "My word, why ever is it so dark in . . ."

Well, at least it's only four feet deep.

That was her first thought as she surfaced in a wallow of flailing and sputtering.

Her second was much more dire. I've lost my bonnet!

Hard upon that came the mortifying discovery that the heroic Mr. Clive was standing in the doorway. Simply standing there, doing absolutely nothing!

Alexandra drew herself up to her full height, an action that served to bring her bosom just above water level. The clinging fabric of her dress emphasized every curve.

She quickly folded her arms and achieved a rather admirable air of nonchalance. "Oh, is that you, Mr. Clive? If you are looking for the exit, I do believe I've found it. It's the *other* green door."

"So I gathered."

Having had the prudence to remain in the doorway until his sight adjusted to the dimness and having just as readily ascertained that the lady had come to no actual harm, Brandon was in no great hurry. He ambled leisurely to the poolside.

"Very kind of you, I must say, to have demonstrated the point so graphically, but really, Lady Redcliffe, as I may have mentioned before, there was no need to go to such lengths on my account."

"I didn't," Alexandra replied with the utmost gravity. "As you might recall, Mr. Bottleswell offered us the use of his pools. I simply couldn't resist availing myself of his hospitality."

"I see. Merely a brief respite on such a hectic day? Quite understandable. However — well, you've been so helpful and I do hate to complain — but I am rather anxious about that carriage. Shall you be long?"

"No, I believe I am quite finished, thank you."

"Then, perhaps you'd like an assist?" Brandon said, reaching his hand out to her. In lieu of taking it, however, Alexandra glanced around at a sodden mass floating near the center of the pool and determinedly waded out to it.

"Lady Redcliffe, I do hope you'll forgive my asking, but what the blazes are you doing now?"

"Retrieving my hat," Alexandra replied. "You don't expect a lady to rise from her bath improperly attired, do you?"

Calmly wringing out the pathetic item, she donned it and tied the dripping strings beneath her chin. The sagging amber plume threatened one eye. Alexandra neatly tucked it behind her ear and waded back to the edge of the pool. "There," she said, taking his hand, "I do think I am ready to go now."

Brandon started to lift her out. Unfortunately, Mr. Bottleswell picked this exact moment to come bounding to the door and announce he had at last found a carriage.

"Good heavens!" he cried upon spying this latest disaster and immediately rushed forward.

As he neared the edge of the pool, his foot slipped in a puddle of water. Naturally, he righted himself by grabbing hold of the nearest person, which happened to be Brandon. Caught off balance, Brandon not only knocked Alexandra back into the water, he pitched in with her.

When the two of them resurfaced, Mr. Bottleswell had not moved. Aghast, he moved his lips but nothing seemed to come from them. At last, in desperation, he resorted to the one statement that had kept him in good stead through a great many years. "May I be of some assistance?"

Brandon dashed the water from his face. "Well, if it's no great bother, you might oblige us with two dry blankets."

"And that carriage," chimed in Alexandra, again batting

the plume from her eye. "We'd prefer a rather fast driver too, if you please."

"But not *this* fast!" she protested as they racketed up High Street toward Mrs. Cawlwood's house. The coachman had taken one look at his prospective passengers and his expression had sent them both into peals of laughter. Now convinced he had taken up two wrong-uns who were not only sopping but daft as well, he was sparing no horses to be rid of them.

Inside, every jolt over a cobblestone seemed to fling water from the lady's hat directly into her face. But why the devil she, and the gent as well, should find that so comical was beyond the driver. "Loonies, the both of them," he grumbled to himself. "And dripping all over me seats to boot!" He made short work of getting them to upper High Street.

"Definitely loonies!" he concluded when, with a flourish, the gent handed the lady down from the carriage "like they was goin' to some fancy-dress ball." He was even unhappier when the gent bade him wait.

"Not on your tuppence, gov'ner," the driver growled. Paid or unpaid, he turned his horse with every intention of making a rapid disappearance and then pulled up short, thunderstruck.

"Gor, it's a bloomin' parade!"

It was nearly. Commissioned to give Mrs. Cawlwood a brief and discreet explanation of Alexandra's disappearance, Mr. Bottleswell had followed orders all too diligently. He had been so brief and so discreet, Mrs. Cawlwood had found it impossible to fathom whether Alexandra had been half-drowned by Mr. Clive or abducted. Or both.

But they had set off for upper High Street, that much Mrs. Cawlwood had ascertained. Of course, this only served to put the lady into an added dither. Abducted to her own home? Impossible!

Or was it? Horrors! Surely modern laxity hadn't gone that

45

far!

Mrs. Cawlwood did not wait to ponder such thoughts twice. The girl was her guest, her responsibility so to speak.

Reticule and fan had gone flying as Mrs. Cawlwood burst from her chair. Thundering out of the Pump Room and into the street, she had commandeered the first passing carriage. No matter that its owner had another destination in mind. When Mrs. Cawlwood plopped herself in beside him and ordered the driver to "Put 'em to it!" she got no argument from the slender, silver-haired gentleman inside. With remarkable presence, he merely nodded to his coachman. "Phelps, as the lady says, 'put 'em to it.'"

A mystified Dulcie, finding herself abruptly deserted by her aunt, had proved no less resourceful. Pausing only to snatch up the fallen reticule and fan, she had sallied forth to hail a sedan chair, wheedled its present occupant out of it, and now had its two bearers hotfooting it up the hill in pursuit of her aunt.

Not far behind her was Lieutenant Symington. He had sauntered toward the Pump Room, hoping for a pleasant morning's encounter with the charming Miss Winford, but he had arrived to witness no more than a blur as that young lady hopped into a chair and beseeched its two young bearers to "follow that carriage!" Then, "Oh, do hurry, lads! A guinea each if you catch it!"

Lieutenant Symington's first impulse had been to stop and laugh. Two boys on foot after a team of horses? Ridiculous!

But the boys, it seemed, were unaware of that fact. With Dulcie clinging to the solitary chair between them and urging them onward, the pair had promptly balanced the poles on their shoulders and set off with every intent of winning that reward.

Daniel Symington had not stopped to laugh again. With the sudden thought that only dire straits would have pitched a sheltered young lady into such action, he had dashed after them.

Now third in line, he pounded up the hill, hardly noticing the two wolfhounds who raced about his legs and playfully nipped at his heels. Unable to resist the commotion, they had broken their leashes and joined in the pursuit.

46

And so, finally, had the starched-back butler who had been walking them. Feeling such duty was much beneath him and with no great love for Lady Poddingly's hounds, he had been tempted to let them go. Wiser thoughts had prevailed, including the certainty that her ladyship would have his head if he lost them.

When a stern, "Here, Jocko! Here, Stedley!" had failed to suffice, he had allowed himself a dignified trot after them, but the dogs had defeated decorum. Sweat pouring from his face, the butler was now at a most undignified gallop.

Not so much as a flicker disturbed Mrs. Cawlwood's own redoubtable butler's features as he opened the door to the very disheveled persons of Alexandra and Brandon.

"Thank you, Chives," said Alexandra, removing and handing him her ruined bonnet. "You may as well dispose of this, I expect." Eyes sparkling, she turned to her companion, who seemed equally amused. "And this is Mr. Peyton Clive. I do think, under the circumstances, he might welcome a small brandy before he leaves for his own lodgings."

"I would indeed," Brandon replied. "A rather substantial one, if you please."

"Very good, sir. May I take your"—the butler glanced up, noticed the gentleman was bare-headed, and adjusted to the situation without a qualm —"blanket, sir?"

If this roused another burst of humor from his audience, it did not seem to distress Chives. Nor did the flustered arrival of Mrs. Cawlwood with an amiably confused escort whom she identified as Lord Chambers. "It was his carriage, you see," as if that explained everything.

Mr. Clive had hardly been shown to the library and presented with his brandy when Dulcie rushed through the door. And hard upon her entrance came a breathless Lieutenant Symington.

None of this brought so much as a raised eyebrow from Chives; not even the two dogs who bounded into the hall behind the lieutenant.

It was the intruding butler who finally made him see red. Gentry rushing pell-mell into the hall was one thing, but a member of his own trade behaving so abominably? Chives' eyebrows shot up to his hairline. Firmly collaring the dogs as well as this latest arrival, he marched them all outside and proceeded to give the human third of this trio a good raking-down.

That settled, he straightened his coat and went back inside. The hallway was filled with people, all talking at once and no one, as far as Chives could see, making an ounce of sense. He waited until there was a brief lull in the din, then gravely approached Mrs. Cawlwood. "Begging your pardon, madam. There appear to be two deceased chair boys on the front steps."

Dulcie, who had been bombarding Alexandra with so many questions she had yet to receive one answer, suddenly whirled around. "Oh, they're not dead, they're just out of breath. I promised them two guineas if they'd hurry, you see. Although come to think of it, they didn't actually catch up to the carriage. Still, they did come quite close. I suppose they deserve their reward anyway. Would you mind, Chives?"

Bowing, the butler took two coins from a small cloisonné box on the hall table and went out the door.

"Now, Lexie!" Turning to her friend, Dulcie proceeded to give her a hard scrutiny from head to toe. "You look positively disgraceful. What on earth have you been about?"

"A great deal of water, obviously," murmured Alexandra, who had been trying to slip away up the stairs. With very little success, she noted wryly. She had barely made the third step before the girl halted her once more.

"Later please, Dulcie. I can't have—"

Have what? Anyone seeing her in this bedraggled condition? Half the town, it seemed, already had. Not to mention the rather kindly looking stranger Mrs. Cawlwood had acquired in her haste and, of course, Lieutenant Symington, who was staring up at her in unabashed amazement.

"Oh, all right," Alexandra sighed, realizing she would get nowhere until she had settled their curiosity. As quickly as possible, she recounted the morning's occurrences, including Mr. Peyton Clive's heroics and her own twice-dunking.

The telling was slowed by Mrs. Cawlwood's repeated "dear

me's" and "oh my's." Finally, this good lady collapsed in a chair and would have no doubt required her hartshorn had not the newly acquainted Lord Chambers sat down beside her and begun patting her hand. At this action, as Alexandra noted, Mrs. Cawlwood seemed to perk up considerably.

"Mr. Clive is in the library," Alexandra finished. "Warming himself with a brandy."

"At this time of day?" gasped Mrs. Cawlwood. "Surely, a sherry would been more appropriate, or perhaps even a claret —"

But Lord Chambers ventured to find the strong libation not only fitting but richly deserved. "Quite a resourceful chap, I'd say. I should very much like to meet him."

"And I," promptly echoed Lieutenant Symington. "I have never had the opportunity of meeting the major's cousin."

"Well, yes, of course," muttered Alexandra, not particularly pleased with this reminder. For a short while, she had forgotten Mr. Clive was in any way related to the odious major. "If you'll excuse me, I'll just run along up stairs and wring myself out. Doubtless, should you gentlemen care to repair to the library, Mr. Clive will be happy to meet — never mind! Here he is. Mr. Clive, may I present Lord Chambers."

Rising, the older gentleman put out his hand. "A pleasure, sir."

"How do you do," said Brandon, taking the proffered grasp.

"And this," began Alexandra, "is Lieutenant —"

"*Symington!*" blurted Brandon, who had just turned to come face-to-face with the young man in uniform. "That is, I presume that's your name," he added, quickly covering his outburst.

"*Sir?*"

That was all the suddenly crimson-cheeked young officer managed to say. Taking his equerry's hand and pumping it vigorously, Brandon gave him no chance to say anything further. Still pumping away, he began edging the lieutenant toward the door. "Ah, no doubt you've noticed the resemblance between me and my cousin. Quite remarkable, some say. Never noticed it myself. Now I suppose, like everyone else, you're agog over this fiddle-faddle at the Pump Room. Yes, well, no problem there, we can soon fix that. Doubtless you'd like to pop along to my lodgings with me. I'll tell you all about it while I change."

A confused lieutenant, feeling himself inexorably propelled away, looked at his superior in complete consternation. "Sir, I really don't understand. I only just arrived, you see, and—"

"The ladies appreciate it, I'm sure," Brandon finished, never once easing his grip or his progress toward the door. "We'll leave them to their peace, shall we? Meantime, you and I can have a nice long talk."

Without slowing his pace, Brandon glanced back over his shoulder. "You ladies will excuse us, I trust. If we may, the lieutenant and I will call again when we're more—appropriately attired."

Lieutenant Symington looked down at his uniform and could find nothing amiss. But by the time he had reassured himself of his impeccability, it was too late. Somehow he was already out on the front steps, and the door had been firmly closed behind him.

Lord Chambers, having had a great many more years than Daniel Symington, needed no such urging to take his leave. The ladies did indeed need their peace, he agreed, and, with a gracious adieu, he left them to it.

"Such a kind face, don't you think?" murmured Mrs. Cawlwood. "Been a widower for years, so he tells me." And as this added observation seemed to put her more in a dither than ever, she promptly took to her bed.

It was some while later when Dulcie suddenly came out with a similar thought. "Do you think *he* has a kind face?"

She was sitting on Alexandra's bed, watching idly as her maid, whom she had brought with her from London, dried and arranged her friend's hair. Alexandra, now attired in a becoming and much less clinging cambric day dress, was not really listening. She was thinking of her own personal maid and, more particularly, of her recently acquired lady's companion. The *de rigueur* older woman, whose presence was supposed to lend countenance to a young lady otherwise unguarded by husband or family.

Thank heavens, Alexandra thought, she had brought neither of those women to Bath. Between the two of them she would have faced hours of scolding for her so-called scandalous behavior of the morning.

She came out of her woolgathering as Dulcie peremptorily repeated her question. "Well, has he, do you think?"

Alexandra thanked the maid and dismissed her. "Who?" she said, as the woman left the room. "Lord Chambers?"

"No, no, I was speaking of Mr. Clive. I rather like him, I think, but I don't suppose I'd call his face especially kind. I'd say it was more devilish, wouldn't you?"

Alexandra laughed in surprise. "Yes, I would," she agreed, recalling the banter they had shared during that hectic carriage ride. "But I wouldn't admit as much in his presence if I were you. I have Mr. Clive's assurances that ordinarily he's quite dull."

"Nonsense. I may have thought so at first, but I don't any longer. And neither do you, Alexandra Redcliffe! Don't think to gull me. I saw the way you looked at him. In fact, I do believe you're falling in love with Mr. Peyton Clive."

"Me! Impossible," Alexandra said in a flat voice. She had never been in love, and she had no intention of starting such foolishness now. Love meant marriage, and she had had more than enough of that, thank you. "No, Dulcie. No entanglements for me. I intend to devote the rest of my life to spinsterhood."

This provoked a giggle from Dulcie's pink lips. "You can't be that, silly. You've already been married."

"And married—and married!" snapped Alexandra, remembering to add her latest fiasco. "I do believe I've had my full share of men, don't you?"

But Dulcie, displaying a sudden wisdom far beyond her years, caught more in this statement than Alexandra had meant to divulge. "You haven't loved any of them, have you?"

"Why, Dulcie, of course I did. Lord Redcliffe—"

"Was my mama's second cousin," her little friend swiftly

interrupted, "and he was terribly kind. I know because he did the kindest thing anyone's ever done for me. He brought you into the family, and that brought you and me together. You cared for him, I could see you did. But, Lexie, he was so old. You were never really 'in love' with him, were you?"

"No," Alexandra replied truthfully. "But I've always wished I could have been."

She shook her head sadly, recalling the man who had been the father her own had not. It wasn't the role he had sought. He had simply accepted it when it became clear that no other was possible. "He wasn't really that old, you know. It was just that he was terribly ill, and he kept it from everyone, even me, until very near the end."

"I remember. Let's don't talk about that," murmured Dulcie, who disliked sadness but doted on tales of derring-do and danger. "Anyway, your first marriage must have been much more romantic. I mean, giving your hand to some heroic, young suitor. Then rushing to his side as he lay dying."

Alexandra's lips curved into a bitter smile. "Oh, yes, that was very romantic."

Dulcie refused to be deterred. "And now there's Mr. Clive, isn't there? He's not dying, of course. But he is a hero of sorts and very likely the only one in Bath at the moment. Are you quite sure you wouldn't care to marry again?"

"Quite sure."

"Well . . ." hesitated Dulcie, pondering the situation. "Then there's only one thing for it. You'll have to indulge in a mild flirtation."

Alexandra broke into a fit of laughter. "Very well, Dulcie, if you insist."

Besides, as she realized later, the idea appealed to her rather strongly.

Dulcie, of course, was delighted with her own suggestion. The thought of a discreet, but deliciously wicked, flirtation between a beautiful widow and the current hero of Bath was too much to keep to herself.

52

But whom to confide in? That was the problem. Aunt Tilmatha wouldn't do; *everything* cast her into a fluster.

After searching her mind, Dulcie decided Lieutenant Symington would make a trustworthy confidante. She could hardly wait to maneuver him into a solitary audience.

It wasn't, as it turned out, at all difficult. By tea time, three young gentlemen were ensconced in Aunt Tilmatha's drawing room. The impeccably dressed lieutenant — he had changed uniforms twice to make certain of that fact — plus two flamboyantly clad dandies who had been sketchily introduced to Mrs. Cawlwood's charming new guests and were anxious to further that acquaintance.

They were not disappointed. Their three hostesses looked particularly charming that afternoon. Dulcie in sprigged muslin and Alexandra in green-striped cambric were all any swain could ask. Even Mrs. Cawlwood's once-pretty face seemed to have regained some of its youthful glow. For reasons of her own, she had eschewed her usual afternoon grays in favor of her very best mauve sarcenet and a new lace cap she had been saving for some extremely special occasion.

Dulcie was the soul of patience through one cup of tea and several compliments on her fetching appearance. When the conversation inevitably switched to the events of the morning, she smiled in a rather secretive manner and left Alexandra and her aunt to fend for themselves.

Most decorously, she asked Lieutenant Symington if he would care for a stroll through the garden.

The young officer immediately rose to attention. "I'd consider it an honor, Miss Winford. That is, should your aunt approve. May we, ma'am?" he added, bowing respectfully to Mrs. Cawlwood.

That lady, busy with thoughts of her own, consented without a quibble. Her garden, to her regret, was too small for a bench, let alone any improprieties. Cautioning Dulcie to take a shawl, she waved the couple off.

Dulcie ignored this parting advice. It was barely autumn and the tiny garden, hemmed in by brick walls, was a sunny spot of dead calm.

Unfortunately, stroll as slowly as one might, a tour of

Mrs. Cawlwood's garden took all of three minutes. By the time Dulcie had regretted the passing of the roses, and Lieutenant Symington had remarked on the budding of the asters, they had traversed every foot of the area.

Dulcie suggested they might sit on the edge of the small fountain in the center.

"He does splash a bit," she admitted, with a rueful look at the squat Neptune whose lips squirted water not only on the heads of the two dolphins beneath him but, on occasion, far beyond. "Of course he only misbehaves when the wind is blowing, and it's not. Shall we?"

"After you, Miss Winford," said the lieutenant with hardly a glance at the razor-sharp crease in his third uniform of the day. He waited until Dulcie had seated herself on the narrow, moss-speckled rim of the fountain, then followed suit. "Most pleasant, I must say," he commented, cheerfully ignoring the way the narrow stone ledge jarred into his buttocks. It was the only time he had ever envied a lady her buffering petticoats. "I — ahem, well, this is the first we've ever been alone, isn't it? I've been wanting to speak with you."

"Oh, yes, and I, you. Only now that we *are*. Alone, I mean, I do wish you'd stop calling me 'Miss Winford.' I've decided to confide in you, you see. Which I can hardly do unless we're great friends, and we certainly can't be that if we keep Miss-and-Mistering each other all our lives. I shall be Dulcie and you shall be Daniel, don't you agree?"

"It could hardly be the other way round — Dulcie," he answered, trying out the name and finding it quite to his liking. He gave her a teasing, if slightly embarrassed, grin. "And now that we're such great chums, may I also confide in you?"

"Naturally, but not at the moment. It's my turn. I wanted most especially to ask your opinion of Mr. Clive. Is there anything amiss with him, do you suppose?"

"Miss Winford, I hardly think — the major is my superior . . ." He halted, gulped, then attempted a hasty amendment. "I mean —"

This, in turn, was cut short by the airy wave of a small hand. "Daniel, do stop sputtering. The name is 'Dulcie,' as

54

you might be kind enough to remember, and I know exactly what you meant. The major is your superior officer, and, as such, you feel it would be most improper to discuss his character. Particularly, I imagine, since you couldn't think of anything nice to *say* about him. But I shouldn't ask you that, at any rate. I have not the slightest interest in your major. He's obviously an ill-mannered hither-and-therian and the least mentioned, the better."

With an impatient glance at her companion, Dulcie primly resettled herself on the ledge. "I was speaking of Mr. *Peyton* Clive. He's not your commanding officer. So there is no reason not to be perfectly frank with me, is there? And don't tell me you've only just met him. I'm quite aware of that. Even so, you did walk back down the hill with him — at least I assume you did — so you must have formed some opinion by now."

"Well, haven't you?" she prompted when no response was forthcoming.

"Several, I expect," muttered Daniel, tugging uncomfortably at his collar. He had been saved from one gaffe by Dulcie's innocent misinterpretation. That had been a relief, certainly, but it still hadn't made him happy. Nor had his long chat in Mr. "Peyton" Clive's lodgings that morning. The lieutenant felt as if he were fast sinking in a sea of deception.

Yet, even though he had his orders, he could not resist at least a small defense of his superior. "He is not ill-mannered."

This brought a laugh from the dainty figure beside him. "Oh, Mr. Clive has quite adequate manners, I've already noticed that. In fact, Lexie seems to find him highly charming, although she claims he prefers to be dull."

Dulcie primly smoothed out her skirts. "I don't believe that any longer of course. And my aunt seems to feel he's a fine fellow but a bit wanting in dash. I don't believe that either. Especially after this morning. It's almost — well, you'll think me silly to say so, I imagine — but it's almost as if he were two persons in one. Good heavens! You don't suppose *he's* a hither-and-therian, do you?"

"I never thought so," mumbled Daniel. Then remembering his orders, he spoke up clearly. "That is, I'd certainly never suppose so. The Clives are a distinguished family, and blood tells, so they say. The major's always been an honorable man. I've never had any reason to doubt his word."

Until now, he added to himself on a dubious note.

Dulcie looked even more dubious. "Well, I'm glad you've found *one* good quality about him. Now, you needn't look so puckerish. I know you must feel obligated to stick up for him. And I suppose I shouldn't have been quite that outspoken, no matter how dreadful he is. Forgive me?"

She smiled so winningly, Lieutenant Symington decided he could forgive the lady most anything. "Of course. Sometimes, I will admit, he can be a tad harsh. But he is still—"

"Honorable?" Dulcie sweetly interrupted. "Fine, I shall accept that. Though I pray God that's the *only* way he resembles his cousin. The fact is, you see"—she looked up at the lieutenant with a grin that held more than a hint of mischief and just as much of resolve —"I've decided Lexie will marry Mr. Clive."

Lieutenant Symington had to grab hold with both hands to keep from pitching backward into the fountain. "Dulcie, she *is* married!"

Had he known his new confidante better, he would have realized such a minor snag would never halt Dulcie Winford. She swept his objection away with an idle flick of her fingers. "A mere bagatelle. Papa's snits never last more than a few days. I imagine he already has the annulment papers well in hand. They should be here any day."

The lieutenant, who knew very well where the annulment papers were, was growing more uncomfortable by the minute. "I'm not quite sure I understand. You're expecting your father to bring them from London himself?"

"Goodness, no. Papa hates to travel. That's why I insisted on coming to Bath, you see." If he didn't, Dulcie saw no reason to explain. "Papa will send them by post of course. And the moment they arrive—why, all Lexie has to do is sign them. Then we can get on with it."

"We?"

"You and I, naturally." A somewhat exasperated Dulcie was beginning to wonder if she had picked the wrong confidant. She had never suspected Daniel Symington of being such a slow-top. Nevertheless, quite taken with him despite this irritating drawback, she decided to be generous. Besides, as she reminded herself, she might very well need his assistance. If Mr. Clive should be as slow to catch the drift as dear Daniel seemed to be, she was going to need all the help she could get.

She smiled at the confused young officer as if to assure him he was doing just fine. Which he wasn't, in Dulcie's view, but it never paid to let a man know he wasn't precisely needle-witted.

"You see," she went on patiently, "Lexie's had such terrible luck with marriage—marriages, I should say. Several of them now, to be exact. So naturally she has no intention of trying it again. She fancies herself determined to become a dowager and wear puce and lace caps and all sorts of dreadful things just like a very old lady. Of course, she is a *little* old, but not very, do you think?"

"Hardly," murmured Lieutenant Symington, trying to envision the vivacious Lady Redcliffe quietly taking her place among the rheumatic dowagers in the Pump Room.

"And she is my very best friend in the whole world despite our differences in ages," Dulcie went on. "Do you think that odd?"

The lieutenant, who was less than two years Alexandra's junior, opined that he saw nothing in the least odd about it.

"Neither do I," Dulcie continued blithely. "I'm quite grown up, you know. And even if she weren't my dearest friend, which of course she is, I should have really felt obligated nonetheless. I mean, if it weren't for me—and Papa—she would never have gotten involved with that horrid major of yours. We really must set things right!"

There was that "we" again, observed the lieutenant. The feeling came to him that Mrs. Cawlwood's tidy garden was fast becoming as treacherous as any battleground. During their short acquaintance, he had become rather fond of Lady Redcliffe. He was more than fond of Miss Dulcie Winford. Moreover, until the past few hours, he would have blindly followed Maj. Brandon Clive through hell and beyond.

57

Summoning forth all his strategical training, Lt. Daniel Symington came to a snap judgment. He was, he concluded, in a perfect quandary.

"Just what exactly did you have in mind?" he ventured hesitantly. "After all, if Lady Redcliffe doesn't wish to remarry—"

He was cut short by an exasperated sigh. "Oh, you men! That's only what she says, not what she means. It's because she's never been in love, you see.

"At least,"—an impish grin tugged at the corners of Dulcie's lips—"not until today, that is. I don't believe Lexie knows it herself yet, but you may take my word for it. She is in love with Peyton Clive."

Good Lord, thought Daniel. This was becoming even more complicated than he had imagined. "Are you sure? How could she have fallen in love that fast? She's only known him for a few hours."

And I'd only known you for a few minutes, Dulcie thought. But naturally she did not put voice to such sentiments.

"Sometimes a few hours can be long enough," she said instead and waited for Daniel to mull over this sagacity.

He decided to adhere to the facts, if only as a delaying tactic. "Look, Dulcie. No doubt you mean well, but if she were to wed again, it would be her—what, third marriage?"

"Fourth."

"That many? Good Lord, what an awful lot of weddings. I shouldn't wonder she's bored with them. In fact, despite what you think, I'd be inclined to believe Lady Redcliffe means precisely what she says. Besides, she does have a husband now. Perhaps if she got to know him, really know him, she might be tempted to—"

"Put a saber through his black heart," Dulcie said flatly. "Not that she actually would, of course. Lexie's much too kind-hearted for that, and I doubt he has a heart anyway. Believe me, Lexie wants no more to do with that man than I!"

She paused, like a governess trying to impart a lesson to a backward child. "Daniel, do try to understand. Lexie is my dear, dear friend. I do not wish to see her in lace caps, and I do not wish her tied to someone she detests. I want her to be happy. I want her to have a husband she loves!"

A good soldier knew how to accept defeat gracefully. Lt. Daniel Symington mimicked the act of handing his sword to his tiny Dresden-featured conqueror. "I am yours to command, General Winford. What are your orders?"

"Oh, nothing very dramatic," a laughing Dulcie informed him. "We simply throw them together at every chance. And if Mr. Clive should prove difficult—although I rather think he won't—we both saw the way he looked at Lexie, didn't we? But on the unlikely chance he should move a bit slowly, you'll simply point out to him how wonderful Lexie is, and how a man of his advanced years needs a wife to ensure he doesn't go careening about the countryside getting the ague, or gout, or whatever it is old men get. Oh, yes, and there's Mr. Druberry!"

"Druberry," Daniel automatically repeated. He was still having trouble imagining the major as a gout-ridden old codger.

"Mr. Altheus Druberry," said Dulcie in a tone that plainly evinced her disregard for that gentleman. "Thank heavens, he wasn't here today though I cannot imagine why. Attending his mother, I expect. At any rate, he is so awfully prosy, it makes one's teeth ache. By some great misfortune, we had to meet him our first day in Bath. And even more unfortunately, he has developed a *tendre* for Lexie. You will keep him out of the way, won't you?"

"Certainly," murmured Daniel, who had managed to escape this gentleman's acquaintanceship during his several visits to the Cawlwood home. "But how? Dulcie, you simply can't dash about plucking beaux for someone else like"—he glanced about him—"like a garden bouquet! This bloom looks quite nice, we'll pluck it for Lady Redcliffe. This bloom's wilted, let's toss it away!"

Lieutenant Symington thought this a rather handsome analogy. He was more than a little provoked when it was greeted by an outright giggle.

"Don't be such a gudgeon," chortled Dulcie. "I said Mr.

Druberry was prosy, not a *posy*."

"I intended that," answered Daniel, stiffening on his two inches of ledge, "as a mere figure of speech. The point is, one cannot go about selecting one's friend's friends, no matter how great a friend that friend might be."

If Daniel realized he had rather over-befriended that statement, he didn't let it stop him. Now that he had set his back up, he had no intention of being distracted. Neither by his own rhetoric nor by that appealing Dresden face so close to his own. To avoid the latter pitfall, he sternly delivered the remainder of his objections to a nearby aster bud.

"I cannot fathom throwing Maj—Mr. Clive at anyone. He's not a man to be pushed! I mean, that is, I *assume* he's not. No man likes to be pushed. And for that matter, just how in the devil am I supposed to dissuade this fellow Druberry? If Lady Redcliffe welcomes him and Mrs. Cawlwood welcomes him, which apparently they do if he's here most every day, then how to you propose I stop him? Set myself by the doorway, maybe, and give him a bash with my sword handle every time he appears? Well, I can tell you, I won't. It's very bad ton!"

Dulcie seemed to think precious little of this argument. As a slight breeze picked up, she simply nodded her head in a noncommittal fashion.

Then her laughter rang out. "Can't you simply picture it? Good day, Mr. Druberry, *thump*! Good-bye, Mr. Druberry, *thump*! I must say the notion does appeal to me."

"Dulcie!"

This admonition had no more effect than his previous words. The breeze ruffled a ribbon at the waist of Dulcie's dress. She casually realigned it. "All right, although I must say you are a terrible spoilsport. We'll simply have to think of something a bit more diplomatic, I suppose."

She bent forward, catching his gaze with a definite hint of teasing in her own. "You can be diplomatic, can't you, Daniel?"

"I should like to think so," he retorted, belatedly aware he was being ribbed and all the more put out because he had been slow in recognizing the fact. "I fancy I have conducted myself quite tolerably in a good many delicate affairs of state — both here and abroad," he added, with the air of a seasoned man of the world putting the naive little provincial in her place. "After all, I am an officer —"

"And therefore a gentleman!" said Dulcie triumphantly, completely unabashed by this set-down. "Oh, I knew I could count on you, Daniel! I simply knew it! A gentleman would never desert a lady in distress. Particularly now that you have two of us!"

"I do?"

Daniel Symington was not given to fanciful thoughts, but it did occur to him that arguing with Miss Dulcie Winford was tantamount to jousting with the wind. It simply moved around one and continued on its way, completely unperturbed.

"To be certain!" Dulcie said. "You are going to help me help Lexie. And that shall rescue us both, don't you see. Lexie won't have to wear puce and lace caps and I shan't have to feel sorry for her. And Mr. Druberry will be banished — quite tactfully, of course. Although I daresay Lexie wouldn't protest if you did thump him, as long as it wasn't frightfully hard. She doesn't care for him either, you see. She's just too polite to say it. And neither does Aunt Tilmatha, at least I don't think so. But I suppose it wouldn't do at any rate. Thumping anyone on her doorstep would send her into absolute dithers."

"I thought," Daniel said ominously, "I made my position on that matter quite clear."

"Yes, yes, you did. Still, I do wonder. Perhaps just the tiniest whack? As a warning?"

"No!"

Laughter danced in the china-blue eyes. "Well, it seems like such a little thing to ask. But if you insist, I suppose we shall have to devise another means. I promise, I'll ask of you no conduct unbecoming to an officer and a gentleman."

She paused, thought a moment, and said most seriously, "Which, thank heavens, you are because, judging from a certain major, one is not always necessarily the other, is one?"

And that, in Lieutenant Symington's opinion, was quite enough from Miss Dulcie Winford.

Already appalled at the crack in his loyalties, Daniel could not abide a further dent in his superior's armor. Still, even in his anger, he could not meet such a winsome enemy head on. Staring directly in front of him, he gave not just the one hapless aster bud, but the entire plant, the benefit of his outraged opinion.

His major, he declared, was a gentleman of the first stare. If his letters had been a little brusque—which they hadn't been, not at the beginning—it was only natural. Admittedly, from what Dulcie had quoted, they might have been a bit formal and lacking in emotion, but that was understandable, too. Major Clive was hardly the type to write love letters to a girl he had never met. He wasn't of a mind to marry anyway, but he had honored the obligation because he *was* a gentleman.

Of course, the major *had* once mentioned something about a promise of his own making. A promise to his father upon entering the service, that by the age of thirty he would resign that commission and start a legitimate nursery to carry on the Clive name. Or at least that branch of it, the major being an only son.

If that was killing two birds with one stone, it didn't make his actions any less honorable, did it?

Then to resign that commission, with the greatest reluctance, only to find himself married to an aging widow—No, no quickly forestalled the lieutenant as Dulcie began to protest, Lady Redcliffe was not like that. Nothing at all! But the major hadn't had any way of knowing that beforehand. He thought he had been hoodwinked by a—a—

The lieutenant groped for the appropriate description. He could hardly use the word "barren" in front of a young unmarried girl even if she were exasperating. He finally seized an alternative: "dried-on-the-vine."

Yes, dried-on-the-vine, and very possibly a scheming adventuress at that. It was little wonder, wasn't it, that the major had cut up rough? And if those last letters had been too pound-dealing for Dulcie's liking, well, the lieutenant would have her know the major wasn't always like that. No, sir, not by a long shot. During the past three years, Major Clive had served as personal envoy for not only one, but two ambassadors. His tact had saved many a ticklish situation from the court of the Hapsburgs to Constantinople.

In short, as the lieutenant concluded, the major was not only an officer and a gentleman, but a diplomat as well!

Pleased with this defense, he looked at Dulcie only to be greeted by a peal of disbelieving laughter.

And that, in a certain young officer's opinion, was more than enough!

Lt. Daniel Symington was unaccustomed to baring his innermost feelings. He was quite definitely unaccustomed to being laughed at by a hoydenish girl!

His face scarlet with indignation, Daniel stiffly bowed himself out of the garden and the Cawlwood residence. He marched down the hill, firmly convinced Miss Dulcie Winford was the most infuriating female west of the Byzantine!

Chapter 3

Major Clive, who had been of a mind to drop in briefly for tea and then coax Alexandra away for a carriage ride, had hit somewhat of a snag himself.

Unlike in Bath, in London it was not only fashionable but virtually obligatory to ride out each evening at the stylish hour of five o'clock. In the city, a gentleman without his own stables plus a choice of several conveyances was considered a very strange bird indeed.

Ladies also vied with each other in the rich appointments of their carriages, complete with liveried footmen and powdered coachmen with French kid gloves. Some favored the smaller, sportier curricle or perhaps a ladylike vis-à-vis cozily designed to hold only two persons.

The meeting ground, without exception, was Hyde Park. There, riding slowly down the tree-shaded lanes, ladies and gentlemen of the ton greeted one another with many a pause for chatting and gossip.

It was also a ripe setting for both fleeting and serious flirtations.

And not always with ladies of rank, as Brandon remembered with a wry grin. Hyde Park, at five, was also the hunting ground for certain "straw-damsels." Those professional courtesans, known more often as the Fashionable Fallens or Cyprians and sporting, from one time to another, such whimsical sobriquets as the Brazen Bellona, the Venus

Mendicant, the White Doe, or the Mocking Bird, were no bedraggled creatures of the gutter. No, not by a far cry. These were damsels who had "guineas in the funds" and accepted only the titled or near titled as their lovers.

For a moment, Brandon regretted his long absence from London.

Then he managed to recollect his thoughts. Bath, as he had discovered, was far different from London indeed. The steep and narrow cobblestone streets made equestrian traffic difficult. Residents and visitors alike walked or took a chair. Even a hired hack, as Brandon had learned only that morning, was somewhat of a problem to come by.

There were few private stables, and such public ones as there were were on the outskirts of town. After several futile attempts at hiring a presentable carriage, Major Clive had given up.

Tomorrow, he decided, he would fetch his own phaeton. Upon his arrival in Bath, he had sought out the best livery stable, having no desire to leave his spanking new team with just anyone. And the cleanest, best-equipped stable he had found belonged to a certain Mr. Cryll. There was only one drawback. Mr. Cryll's establishment was at the farthermost reaches of town.

Now descending the steps of the Seven Seas Inn, Brandon halted as a second drawback occurred to him. His phaeton was a high-perched racing style, considered rather too daring for ladies. Some timid souls considered it a downright dangerous contraption. Would Lady Redcliffe? No, concluded Brandon, remembering her pluck. He rather thought she wouldn't.

He continued on his way, heading up the steep hill toward Mrs. Cawlwood's home. It was only a few blocks away from his lodgings, but he had scarcely covered any of that distance before a very red-faced young officer came barreling around a corner and nearly knocked him into the street.

Since, as he soon discovered, Lieutenant Symington's destination was just a short walk past the Seven Seas,

Brandon thought it only polite to offer escort to his obviously distressed equerry. Besides, it seemed to be the sole means of satisfying his curiosity. Lieutenant Symington, plainly in no disposition to chat, was already forging down the hill.

Reversing himself and lengthening his stride, Brandon soon caught up with him, but it was not until Daniel was inside the house — his grandmother's, he muttered — that he at last remembered his manners. Grimly commenting that he intended to change his uniform for one that was not begrimed and moss-stained from sitting on the ledge of that damned fountain, he bade the major make himself at home.

Brandon, even more curious now, did just that. Following Daniel upstairs, he waited patiently while his young equerry changed.

As might be expected, he found his equerry's solemn explanation, and Miss Winford's less-than-solemn reaction, perversely amusing. Lieutenant Symington did not. Feeling mightily abused from all sides, Daniel shrugged into the tunic he had been wearing that morning when the major had so abruptly shuttled him from Mrs. Cawlwood's house. He still saw nothing amiss with the tunic, but he was beginning to feel there was a great deal amiss with his beloved major.

Stiffening himself to his full five feet ten inches, he scowled into the mirror, searching for any epaulet gone awry, any button improperly done up. Satisfied, he then turned and permitted himself a rare privilege. He directed an even fiercer scowl at his superior.

"I must say I've never before had reason to doubt your—" Honor, he started to say, but even in his anger, he realized that was coming a bit too strong. He settled for "judgment!"

"Never?" said Brandon, making a herculean attempt to stifle his amusement. "Well, I find that a little hard to believe. We've been together, what, three years? Surely I must have made a misstep or two somewhere along the way."

"Very few," Daniel said loyally before recollecting he was very put out with this major of his. "But nothing like this! It may be impertinent, but, in view of this morning's developments, I feel I have a right to ask. Sir, what are your intentions toward Lady Redcliffe?"

Brandon Clive was made of stern stuff. The last vestige of a smile disappeared from his lips, and, if he found his equerry's self-righteousness more amusing than impertinent, he did not betray the feeling. "Why, Daniel," he drawled. "I believe that's a question usually asked by the girl's father. Don't tell me you've adopted Lady Redcliffe?"

"Certainly not!" Dismay spread across Daniel's face. He was in deep waters, and he knew it, but, once started, he was determined to wade through them.

He took a deep breath. "It's just that I'm rather fond of Lady Redcliffe. And then there's Dulcie wanting me to help — ah, never mind, that's another matter. The thing is, sir, this morning while you were changing clothes, you ordered me to keep silent. About your real identity, I mean. But why? When you arrived in London, you were so hipped you wouldn't even let me tell you about her. All you wanted was a speedy annulment — the speedier the better, you said. *And* it was the only reason you came to Bath, so you claim. Yet now that you've met Lady Redcliffe, you appear to like her and she seems to like you. Why don't you tell her the truth instead of" — the lieutenant painfully cleared his throat — "instead of *wooing* her! At least that's the way it looks to some of us. Which doesn't make sense, because you're already married to her. Or are you only funning with her? If you are, I'd say that was most unfair. I think — oh, blast it all, I don't know what to think. Frankly, sir, I'm not sure about this whole business!"

"Neither am I," Brandon replied. He looked up to see Daniel's expression and smiled, but there was little humor in it. "No, it happens to be the truth. I'm at a bit of a loss myself. My first impulse was simply to play the lady along — to take her measure, so to speak — then foist the annulment papers on her and demand an immediate signing. But now?"

He reached out, idly fingering the nearest bedpost as if lost in thought.

"Yes?" prompted Daniel. He quickly dragged up a chair and seated himself in front of his superior.

Brandon shrugged. "Now, frankly, I seem to be finding myself somewhere between Scylla and Charybdis. The lady exceeded my expectations."

Far exceeded them, he amended to himself.

"In fact, I could even go so far as to call her captivating if I had a mind to. But that may very well be the problem."

"Sir?"

"Yes," Brandon said thoughtfully. "Captivating, enchanting . . . entrapping. Very little difference in those words when you get down to the meat of them. And no matter how honeyed the bait, Daniel, I dislike being trapped!"

The lieutenant's chair shot back a good two inches. "But surely you can't mean that. Good lord, sir, I thought you understood. She didn't plan the wedding that way. No one did. It was simply a hare-brained mistake. On the vicar's part!"

"Was it?" Brandon retorted. "Or did someone, perhaps, simply take advantage of a doddering old man? Of course, it's merely a thought, but it does make one wonder, doesn't it? From his letters I'd judge Mr. Winford to be excitable perhaps and certainly as stubborn as a jenny in a post-road mire, but no bumbleskull. And neither is Alexandra Redcliffe. I'd say when the lady really wants something, she can be quite determined."

"Well, she doesn't want *you!*" Daniel blurted. Upon realization of what he had said, his face reddened to the color of his tunic. "Beg pardon, sir, but—well, that just won't fadge. If you're thinking she married you for your money, why should she? Lord Redcliffe left her full of juice!"

"Are you certain?"

"Er, no. Not personally of course. One can hardly ask a lady for an accounting of her finances. But there's a country estate, so I hear. And the town house in London and the stables, and servants and—"

And why hadn't she brought any of them with her? Daniel

68

suddenly thought.

He remembered something Dulcie had said in passing. What was it? That they had been accompanied to Bath by only one maid—and Dulcie's at that—because there hadn't been room in the coach? The lieutenant was hardly familiar with the traveling habits of ladies, but his own mother, whose circumstances were comfortable if not exactly lavish, never seemed to travel without at least two attendants. And his grandmother never went anywhere without her own personal maid—not even to the Pump Room, which was where she was now.

He turned back to the puzzlement at hand. Did modern women travel so scantily attended by choice? Or was Lady Redcliffe, in fact, badly dipped?

Since an answer to these self-imposed questions was plainly beyond him, he veered off on a different tack. "Well, even if she is dipped—which she probably ain't—what difference would it make in the long run? She don't mean to stay married to you."

"So she says," Brandon agreed matter-of-factly. "But then why hare off to Bath?"

He waved a hand, cutting off the inevitable interruption. "Yes, I know, to avoid any scandal. She told me this morning. She also told me she knew I—that is, Major Clive—had arrived in London that very day. Yet she hared off all the same. Seems to me any woman as anxious for that annulment as she claims to be would never have gone anywhere without first getting her hands on those papers."

There was another long silence, this time on Daniel's part, as he tried to assimilate this newest development. Before, he had thought the major had taken quite a liking to Lady Redcliffe. Dulcie certainly believed so.

For now it seemed the major didn't like Lady Redcliffe at all. Daniel screwed his face up in concentration. "Sir! I must protest—I think. It seems to me you're as good as calling Lady Redcliffe an adventuress!"

"No, I wouldn't say that."

"No, sir, being a gentleman I'm sure you wouldn't. And neither would Mr. Winford," Daniel added, much struck by a new idea. "No adventuress could have gotten around him—at least not for long! I guess it won't be long anyway," he continued, his face falling woefully. "Mr. Winford's set on marrying Dulcie to you and nobody else."

"Unless," Brandon interjected, "he thinks perhaps he's found a bigger fish."

If this didn't exactly bring the lieutenant out of his doldrums, it did manage to catch his attention. He sat up straight. "Bigger than you, sir? I'm afraid not. Why, Mr. Winford sought you out himself. He wrote letters all over Europe—"

His superior officer held up a hand for quiet. "Yes, but did it ever occur to you that, between those letters and the wedding, he might have chanced upon someone more favorable and nearer to hand?"

Not only had the idea never occurred to Lieutenant Symington, he didn't think much of it now either. "Nonsense! Not with all your blunt!"

Brandon shrugged. "I have sufficient of that, I suppose. But there are a few other men, equally plump in the pockets, who have something I don't. Something that Mr. Winford might consider a very high drawing card indeed. I wonder, has Miss Winford had any titled suitors lately?"

"Good Lord, I hope not," groaned Daniel, so cast into the dismals by this implication that he hardly noticed Major Clive arise from his chair. Nor did the suggestion that, if they hurried, they might still join the ladies for tea elicit any comment from him. Numbly, Daniel reached for his hat and followed Major Clive out the door.

It was only when they were halfway up the hill that he began to wonder.

"Begging pardon, sir, but just why are you going there for tea? I mean, I assume it's hardly Mrs. Cawlwood that's attracting you. I know it's not the tea! It must be Lady Redcliffe. But after all you've just said, why in the blazes should you want to see her again?"

"I enjoy her company," Brandon said matter-of-factly. He

had scarcely failed to notice the lieutenant's confusion nor the distraught look at each mention of Miss Winford's name. Hiding a smile, he put a sympathetic hand on his equerry's shoulder. "Women are a perplexing lot, aren't they?"

"Amen to that!" came the heartfelt reply. If Lady Redcliffe had confounded the major, it was nothing compared to Daniel's feelings about Miss Dulcie Winford. Having come to the conclusion that young lady would be a handful for any man, Daniel was of a mind to be as far away from her as possible. Also, as close as possible. He simply couldn't decide which.

"Life," he sighed, "was a lot simpler in Turkey."

Brandon solemnly agreed with him. "No matter. You shan't be in my service much longer. My decommission should come through soon, and you'll be reassigned. I could put in a word for you if you like. You could be back on the Bosporus within a month. Would that be soon enough?" He cast a wry glance at his young equerry as they continued up the hill. "Or has, perhaps, the damage already been done?"

"I'm afraid it has," was the woeful answer. With that, the remaining distance was trod in silence. Two officers of His Majesty's army, their minds niggled by doubts, soon presented themselves at Mrs. Cawlwood's house.

As Brandon noticed, their hats were not the only ones Chives had carefully placed on the hall table. Three other gentlemen's toppers were there, lined up in a neat row.

Daniel, making the same head count, took on an expression that suspiciously resembled that of an exceedingly jealous suitor. "There were just two when I left here. Wonder whom the third one belongs to?"

He was not elated when he found out. Escorted into Mrs. Cawlwood's drawing room, he nodded to the Messrs. Cavendish and Sharlett, who had not only been there earlier but who now seemed entrenched for the afternoon. While Alexandra was presenting Mr. Clive to these, Daniel turned a sharp glance on the newest arrival. Compared to the rainbow fineries of young Cavendish and Sharlett, this worthy in a subdued gray coat and highly starched collar points seemed a very drab bird indeed.

And not just any bird, thought Daniel, noting the way the man's chest puffed out as he rose to be introduced. He looked like a damned pouter pigeon!

"Oh, yes," said Alexandra as if in complete accord, which in fact she was, had he only known. "And may I present Mr. Druberry."

Daniel's gulp was almost audible. "Mr. *Altheus* Druberry?"

The chest puffed out a bit more. "The very same, sir, I am flattered, I must say, that you have heard of me. Is it possible"—the gentleman turned to cast a fawning smile on Alexandra—"that one of these lovely ladies has been extolling my virtues?"

Daniel looked from Alexandra to Mrs. Cawlwood and counted his blessings that Dulcie had not yet reappeared in the drawing room. "I believe there was some mention of your name," he finally mumbled.

Alexandra, having a good idea of what that mention might have entailed, swiftly came to his rescue. "Goodness! Why are we all standing about? Please, gentlemen, seat yourselves. I'll just ring for a fresh pot of tea, shall I?"

She turned to Mrs. Cawlwood, who had been absent-mindedly munching on a currant bun. "What, my dear? Tea? Of course, we'd all like some more, I'm sure. And perhaps a few more cakes as well. The currant buns are nice, don't you think? But no more poppy seed cakes, if you please! I can't abide them."

"Shall I go ask what else there might be?" Alexandra politely inquired.

"Yes, would you, dear?" Mrs. Cawlwood beamed a thankful smile at her. "Tell Cook some of her penny-pound cake would do. Or even plain bread and butter. I rather think gentlemen are always fond of that, don't you, Peyton, dear? Reminds them of their childhood."

"Of course," Brandon soberly agreed.

Alexandra had a sudden vision of Brandon as a small boy

72

eating his bread and butter and was rather disgusted to realize she found it touching.

She quickly glanced away as Mrs. Cawlwood recalled another discrepancy in her tea party. "Dulcie! Wherever is that girl? If you would, dear, you might remind her that we do have guests. Surely it couldn't take an hour to change her frock. At least not a simple afternoon frock. I cannot think what's keeping her!"

Alexandra could. Not once in the past several days had the Messrs. Cavendish and Sharlett failed to present themselves for tea. Mrs. Cawlwood seemed quite unperturbed by this constancy, but Dulcie found it a dead bore. Though she was a good two years younger, she had promptly dismissed them as mere boys who hadn't a whit of conversation.

This had been confided in private, and Alexandra had found it impossible to disagree. The two young dandies dressed to the nines, smiled a great deal and never spilled tea on their trousers. And that, thought Alexandra as she left the room, seemed to be the sum total of their accomplishments.

But then, there was always Mr. Druberry, who had sufficient opinions for twelve men and never failed to voice them.

Little wonder Dulcie had been delighted to find a few moss stains on her skirts. This had given her an excellent opportunity to leave the company. Even smaller wonder she seemed in no hurry to rejoin it.

When the tea replenishments were taken care of and Cook was mollified (she was quite proud of her poppy seed cakes), Alexandra dutifully went to her friend's bedroom.

The young girl, now freshly attired in pink muslin, was by the window. Looking down into the garden, at the fountain to be exact, she wore what could only be described as a smile of pure mischief.

Alexandra paused in the open doorway. "Dearest, your aunt's rather expecting you downstairs."

Dulcie whirled around. "Oh, Lexie, I'm afraid I simply can't. I have a most dreadful headache!"

Accepting this indisposition with all the solemnity it deserved, Alexandra made the proper comments. "Naturally, you mustn't exert yourself. You stay right here and rest. I'll make your excuses to the gentlemen, including, let's see, Mr. Druberry—"

"Ooooooh!" moaned Dulcie, clasping her temples in a frightful show of pain.

"And Lieutenant Symington, of course."

Dulcie's drooping posture righted itself at once. "He's returned? Aha, I knew he would. That is, I mean—well, with so many guests, I really can't leave you and Aunt Tilmatha to entertain them all. It wouldn't be right. No, not right at all." She flew to the mirror. "Wait half a second, dearest Lexie, I'll go with you."

Mincing this way and that before the mirror, she adjusted an errant blond curl, then spun around. "There! How do I look?"

"Lovely," Alexandra pronounced without so much as a hint of a smile. "But your headache?"

"Oh, that!" replied Dulcie, gaily taking her arm and urging her along. "That was ages ago. I'm quite well now, thank you. Shall we rejoin your many suitors?"

"Mine?" Halting their progress, Alexandra firmly removed Dulcie's arm from her own. "You're being much too generous, aren't you?"

"Not in the least. Why, they're practically all yours anyhow. Except, perhaps, for the 'little boys.' And you really can't count them either way. They're just as happy with one of us as with the other."

"So it would seem," murmured Alexandra, who found the moonish glances of young Cavendish and Sharlett more than a bit embarrassing. Whether the object of their affection was she or Dulcie, it appeared to make no difference. The pair immediately switched their tongue-tied admiration to whomever was nearest.

"Perhaps they're just short-sighted," she said.

"Hah!" scoffed Dulcie. "The only thing they're short of is

74

between the ears. You may have them both with my blessing."

"Thank you," Alexandra muttered dryly as they continued down the hall. "The same, I take it, holds true for Mr. Druberry."

"You can be certain of it!"

"And Lieutenant Symington as well, I suppose?"

Dulcie flashed her an impish grin. "Well, since you've so many, perhaps I could take just one. If I choose to," she continued airily. "I really haven't decided. Have you?"

"Have I what?" said Alexandra, minding the hem of her skirts as she started down the stairs.

"Decided on Mr. Clive? He's yours too, you know."

"I seriously doubt that," Alexandra snapped. Feeling inexplicably irritated, she swept on down the stairs and into the drawing room without another word.

She was not the only one to feel riled. In her absence, apparently, Mr. Druberry had seen fit to enlighten his audience who appeared to be ruffled, on several subjects, one of which was directed exclusively at Mr. Clive. However, Alexandra noticed, the recipient of this tirade was calmly regarding its donor in amused silence.

Mrs. Cawlwood had fluttered valiantly to his defense. "But really, Mr. Druberry, I daresay it couldn't be helped. The dear boy had no idea. I mean, how was anyone to know she might fall in a pool?"

"That, madam, is beside the point," Mr. Druberry intoned.

Spying Alexandra, he immediately stretched to his full height, which was not considerable, and rushed to her side.

Escorting her to a chair, he managed to inform her that she had made much too light of the morning's misadventures, only a chance remark had led him to the truth of it, and that he was truly shocked a lady had been led into such danger.

All this was delivered without a pause for breath. Alexandra thought it rather remarkable. After a speaking glance at

Mr. Clive, she politely thanked Mr. Druberry for his concern, adding that since she had come to no real harm, she thought it best to forget the entire escapade.

Oh, but he couldn't, Mr. Druberry insisted. There was, he added with a grave lowering of his voice, a matter of some, ah, delicacy he wished to discuss with her. Perhaps Lady Redcliffe might enjoy a brief stroll in the garden? Unless, of course, she was overly fatigued by this morning's disaster?

Dulcie, overhearing, glanced out the window and noticed that a breeze seemed to be picking up rather satisfactorily. She was all too quick to encourage the gentleman. "Nonsense, Lexie's never tired. She'd love to show you the garden. And do be sure to take a close look at the Neptune, Mr. Druberry. The view can be quite refreshing—at times."

Both Alexandra and Mrs. Cawlwood tried to protest at the same instant. Dulcie shushed them with a cheerful, "Heavens, do run along, you two. Aunt Tilmatha and I will keep these other charming gentlemen well entertained, I assure you."

"How nice," muttered Alexandra, making a mental note to stand well upwind of the unpredictable sea god. She had had enough dousings for one day. And pompous as Mr. Druberry might be, it seemed rather unkind to ruin those meticulously starched collar points.

Alexandra led him as far from the fountain as Mrs. Cawlwood's miniscule bower would allow.

"There," she said brightly. "You've seen the garden, and the, uh, breeze seems to be stirring again. Let's go back inside, shall we?"

But Mr. Druberry, having set his mind to his mission, was not easily dissuaded. He tried to take Alexandra's hand. Failing that, he suggested they take a seat and was quite discomfited to realize there were no chairs. Finally, he elected to take a wide-legged stance beside a prickly but flowerless rosebush.

Puffing out his chest, he conveyed his trust that Mr. Clive

would not tarry long in Bath.

"I have no idea," retorted Alexandra, somewhat shocked by this blatant inquisitiveness. "Mr. Clive's estate is in the north. In Yorkshire, I believe. I assume he's merely stopping in Bath on his way home from—"

Mr. Druberry pounced on the obvious hesitation. "Ah, yes, from where indeed?"

"I really couldn't say. I would suggest, since you seem to be so interested in Mr. Clive's affairs, you ask him yourself."

Far from being put off by this coldness, Mr. Druberry rewarded her with a triumphant smile. "I did! And I must say the chap was rather evasive about it. He mentioned some anonymous friends in Folkestone. Whereupon Mrs. Cawlwood immediately seized the reins, saying no doubt he'd been to visit his childhood bosum bows—the Peltinghams or Sheltinghams, or some such—and wasn't it fortunate that 'dear Peyton' had just happened to pass through our little town on his way home? Mr. Clive," the gentleman finished ominously, "did not disagree."

"With what?" came Alexandra's arch reply. "That he's returning from Folkestone to Yorkshire? Then one might presume, mightn't one, that those are precisely his intentions."

"One might," concurred Mr. Druberry with the air of a man who had just caught the cat with the canary feathers still in its teeth. "Unless one stopped to think that our little town is hardly the most direct path north. It is, in fact, a most strangely circuitous route."

"Is it? Geography was never my strong suit. Furthermore, I fail to see how any of this is my concern. Or yours, either."

She might as well have saved her breath. Mr. Druberry took no more notice of the rebuff than of the rosebush he was so perilously close to backing into.

Adjusting his stance until he was nearly on tiptoe, he launched into a convoluted recital of the purity of his intentions, his wish that, despite such brief acquaintance-ship, Lady Redcliffe had realized the esteem in which he held her, and his most ardent hope that, in her innocence, she might see fit to rely on a friend whose knowledge of the vagarities of men far surpassed her own.

Innocence? Vagarities? The man rattled on, so enmeshed in his own eloquence, Alexandra doubted he could make heads or tails of it himself. She certainly couldn't.

"Mr. Druberry," she interrupted. "Perhaps you didn't know. But I happen to be a widow. Twice over."

"Of course you are, dear lady," he said, again reaching for her hand and attempting to pat it. Alexandra promptly clasped her hands behind her back.

Mr. Druberry had to content himself with an awkward pat on her elbow. "Ah, yes, well—that's just my drift, you see. One cannot help but be aware of your plight. No husband to guide and protect you. Your father gone—"

"Only to Scotland," Alexandra briskly interposed. "He's quite alive."

"He is?" In his astonishment, Mr. Druberry stepped backward, only to make contact with a particularly vicious rose thorn. With a most ungentlemanly expletive, he popped forward again. "A thousand pardons, dear Lady Redcliffe," he gasped, trying to rub his leg and regain his dignity at the same instant. "But I thought—that is, I assumed, since you'd mentioned having your own home in London—that rather naturally you were alone in the world."

"I am, in a way," Alexandra said coldly. "And I may assure you, sir, that is exactly how I prefer it. However, since as you have evinced such kindly interest in my welfare, I shall be more than happy to satisfy your curiosity. My mother died when I was a child. And my father has been remarried for some years now to a Glaswegian woman who had wealth but no title. My father had a title and no wealth, thanks to a penchant for gaming and a charming, but absolutely useless, head for managing his business affairs. They make an ideal couple. Moreover, my dear step-mama and I are in perfect accord. She never darkens my doorstep. And I never darken hers."

"Ah!" exclaimed Mr. Druberry, who seemed to find this revelation immensely satisfying. "I suspected as much. Two hearts which—if I may be so bold as to suggest—might someday beat as one cannot conceal the truth from each other. You *are* alone!"

"Not quite," muttered Alexandra, again reminded of a zealous maid, an even more zealous companion, and a staff of servants who seemed to feel it their duty in life to protect her from any vicissitude, whether she wished to be protected or not.

Mr. Druberry knew nothing of this and most certainly wouldn't have listened had she tried to tell him. Having decided she needed the protection of a stalwart male (and who was more stalwart than he?), he was not to be deterred.

"I do understand," he said with a glance that was obviously meant to be sympathetic. Unfortunately, it only made him look all the more like a disappointed pigeon. "You're very brave, but there's no need to pretend with me. In truth, dear lady, this morning's incredible misadventure simply stresses the fact. You are unaware—as of course you should be—of the scoundrels of this world. Rogues who would lure fragile, helpless innocents such as yourself into a morass of dangers. And worse! I pray you, my dear Lady Redcliffe, do let me advise you. It would be my most privileged honor if you would consider me your mentor and your protector against any scoundrel who might besiege you. I am not given to rowdiness, of course, but you may trust me, my dear brave little lamb. I would be a towering bulwark in defense of your honor."

His brave little lamb had been hard put to choke back her annoyance. Now she did not have to. She was just plain choking. Even on tiptoe, this towering bulwark barely reached her chin.

Frantically searching her skirt pocket for a handkerchief and finding none, Alexandra resorted to hiding her face in her hands until she was somewhat better composed. "Forgive me," she gasped. "I—I seem to have swallowed something the wrong way."

"Amazing you could have swallowed it at all," murmured a dry voice.

Startled, both Alexandra and Mr. Druberry whipped around to find Mr. Clive right behind them.

Casually removing a large, snowy white handkerchief from an inner coat pocket, he handed it to Alexandra with a nod to her companion. "Hope I'm not intruding," he drawled. "It looked so pleasant out here I thought I'd take the air myself."

"And eavesdrop as well?" snipped Mr. Druberry.

Brandon raised an eyebrow in exaggerated surprise. "Why, sir," he protested in a much aggrieved tone, "such a thought never entered my mind. What do you take me for? A scoundrel?"

The little man's chest ballooned in indignation. "I may tell you, Clive, I find nosy-poking most offensive!"

"Couldn't agree more," returned Brandon. "Terribly uncivil, isn't it, to poke into another's life, be it a man's—or a lady's?"

"Now see here!" It was only with difficult restraint, and with the memory of that rosebush so close to his legs, that Mr. Druberry kept from hopping up and down in extreme dudgeon. "I resent your inference. If you think I was prying into Lady Redcliffe's affairs, you are very much mistaken! I shall have you know, my intentions were of the noblest! I was merely offering this dear, innocent lady the benefit of my advice and my protection, which, God knows, she needs! What with some—some scoundrels about, who care not a fig for her safety. Or her honor!"

"And might I be considered one of them?" Brandon quietly asked.

"Well, if the boot fits—" Mr. Druberry started to bluster. Then it occurred to him he was trapped between a prickly bush and a foe who not only rose head and shoulders above him but looked as if he might be exceedingly handy with his fives.

Mr. Druberry shot a glance down at the one and up at the other and decided the better part of valor was to sidle away. Quickly maneuvering himself so that Alexandra was between him and both his enemies, he gave her an abrupt nod. "My lady, I will take my leave of you now. You will understand, I trust, that a man of dignity"—he paused to favor Brandon with a most disapproving frown—"does not stoop to squabble with virtual strangers. Therefore, I bid you farewell in the hopes we may soon speak again in more fitting circumstances. And in privacy!"

With the briefest of bows to her and none to Mr. Clive, he compressed his lips into a forbidding line and stalked off.

"My, my," drawled Brandon. "I do believe that fellow is a bit huffed with me."

"I can't imagine why," said Alexandra with a laugh. "Were you actually eavesdropping?"

"Really, madam! Now I am most truly aggrieved. I strode out here at Miss Winford's suggestion for nothing more than a lungful of air. It's hardly my fault if Druberry was so busy orating. And you were too busy choking back a few choice words, to notice my approach. My intentions were also of the noblest."

"Oh?" queried Alexandra. "And just what were they?"

"Why to rescue you from a great gust of wind, which"—Brandon glanced toward the door through which Mr. Druberry had disappeared—"thankfully has subsided."

"For the time being," Alexandra acknowledged. "But I doubt it's permanent."

Brandon nodded. "We can be certain of that. Still, much as I hate to say it the noble Mr. Druberry was right in one respect. I owe you an apology."

"For what perchance? Offending my guest?" Alexandra returned the handkerchief to him. "I must allow you did rather twit the gentleman, you know."

"No such thing," replied Brandon. "I was most easy on the man. Much more so than he deserved in fact. If I had been a less dignified sort of fellow, I might have very well planted him a facer."

Alexandra's lips quivered. "I suspect he more than half thought you would. Well, I do thank you, sir, for not creating a scandal broth in my hostess's garden. And if you are apologizing for even entertaining such an idea, then—"

"I'm not," Brandon said bluntly. "My only regret is not acting more wisely this morning. It was careless of me to entangle you in that little escapade. You might very well have been harmed."

"The devil you say!"

The words were out before Alexandra could stop them. In truth she was sorely disappointed. Was Mr. Clive turning out like every other man she had known? Convinced that a lady should be eternally wrapped in bunting?

Good lord, she thought, things will never change. Men do as they like, but the slightest mishap and they're positive a woman's constitution—not to mention her honor—is irreparably damaged.

It was a most fretting state of affairs. The only thing a lady could honorably die of was boredom!

"Mr. Clive," she said crisply. "I do not accept your apology. To put the truth with no bark on it, I must say I am slightly annoyed that you even felt the need for one. As you might remember, you did not entangle me. I rather entangled myself. And I assure you my constitution is not so fragile as to be completely undone by a mere dunking. Nor, I think, is my honor. It may come as a surprise to you, Mr. Clive, but—once the child was safely rescued of course—I found the entire episode rather entertaining."

She gave the gentleman a sharp look and added dryly, "Now I suppose you're shocked no end."

"Why, no," murmured Brandon somewhat taken aback. "But I hardly thought any lady would—"

"I suppose you think," Alexandra interrupted, "that a lady should be content with an occasional rout party or a ball at Almack's Assembly Rooms. Or, in Bath, perhaps a decorous visit to the Pump Room. I assure you, sir, a lady can find such a life quite restricting!"

Brandon, by now having recovered himself, seemed to consider this unexpected anger quite interesting and amusing. He was remembering the way Alexandra had looked with that soaking bonnet on her head. "Good Lord," he said, chuckling. "Does this mean every time your life goes a bit flat, I'll have to find another pool for you?"

"No, thank you!" Alexandra retorted. Ordinarily she would have been surprised at her own vehemence. It was hardly polite to upbraid a gentleman no matter how sincere her feelings, but the gentleman *had* disappointed her. Somehow, she had expected more of him.

"Laugh all you like. Yet I doubt any man would settle for such limitations. Do you go to London, sir?" she asked abruptly.

"I've been there on occasion, yes."

"Do you know Bond Street? Or St. James?"

These were perfectly reputable streets that contained, among other establishments, the likes of White's, Boodle's and Brooks's. The latter were clubs for men, and gaming was the principal entertainment. Brandon hoped Lady Redcliffe wasn't thinking of invading this strictly male domain.

"I do happen to frequent White's from time to time," he answered, affecting a teasing drawl. "Were you thinking I might sponsor you as a member?"

"Of course not," snapped Alexandra. "I wouldn't dream of entering any of those rooms. Besides, standing hour after hour over a green baize table and, more often than not, losing one's entire fortune in the process, strikes me as absolutely childish. I merely used those streets as an example. Have you ever walked along them? Alone?"

Brandon, having no inkling of her real meaning, merely shrugged his shoulders. "Naturally. There's no danger. I've strolled that area many a time in my younger days."

"In the mornings? Or in the afternoons?"

"Both, I suppose, I fail to see what difference that makes."

"Naturally you wouldn't, you're a man. Now a lady intent

on shopping might pass through those same streets in the mornings, assuming, of course, she's accompanied by a maid or footman. But in the afternoons? Horrors! A lady, no matter how innocent her mission, would never dare set foot or even drive by there in the afternoons. Her reputation would be in shreds. That's just another of a lady's restrictions, you see, among a great many more. I daresay you wouldn't care for any of them."

"No, I'm fairly sure I wouldn't," replied Brandon, recognizing what was, for him, an entirely new point of view. Having led a most freewheeling life, he could hardly visualize the unseen fetters a well-bred young woman might face.

But to give him credit, he did try. London was Lady Redcliffe's home and Brandon's too, despite his long absences on the Continent. He tried to picture it through her eyes and admittedly fell short.

The London he knew was a man's world. The clubs, the shops, the hotels were all dedicated to gratifying the wants of the wealthy gentleman. Horse racing, gaming, hunting at one's country estate — these were all tailored for the aristocratic male. Any woman who entered into such activities did so only in the most decorous fashion.

"Good God!" he expostulated. "You must feel utterly stifled!"

This was emitted with such fervor that Alexandra, in her astonishment, forgot her own anger. A most infectious peal of laughter broke from her lips. "Oh, not quite *that* stifled, sir. You must forgive me, I do tend to be a bit outspoken. It's only that I get somewhat irked now and then. A lady mustn't do this. A lady mustn't do that. A lady never goes anywhere alone! Not in London, at any rate. I've no desire to be considered hoydenish, of course, but I do confess I get tired of being so awfully well chaperoned all the time.

"After all," she said, adding an amendment to her previous complaint. "I do behave myself quite properly for the most part. And as for this morning's events, I daresay none — save for Mr. Druberry perhaps — think the worst of it. Now if I were some naive school miss, of course, that would be much different. But I'm not. I'm twice widowed and I cut my wisdoms years ago. A woman of my age can certainly take care of herself!"

"By all means," Brandon agreed in a most somber voice. "You are a virtual *grande dame*, which, unfortunately, leads me to a slight dilemma. I was about to propose a drive in my phaeton tomorrow, my only hesitancy being that you might find it too daring a conveyance for a lady. I see now that a woman of your mettle would find that no obstacle. However, I'm afraid I must hesitate for a second reason. I fear the perch may be too precarious for a lady of such advanced years."

"Well," returned Alexandra, mimicking the accents of a very feeble old dowager, "it depends. Is this contraption of yours well sprung or not? I cannot abide being jounced about, you know."

"It's very well sprung, madam."

"Then, by Jupiter, you almost persuade me. Assuming, of course, you bring along three or four footmen to hoist me onto the perch."

Brandon looked at her slender figure and decided it would hardly take the effort of one arm to lift her into the highest seat. "I shall bring what's needed, my lady. Shall I also procure a vinegarette of smelling salts and perhaps some hartshorn for your nerves?"

"Don't be impertinent, young fellow. I shall bring my own."

Chuckling, Brandon suggested they tour the rest of the garden if it would not be too exhausting for her ladyship.

Alexandra allowed she might have the strength on the condition they took exceeding small steps.

"I believe that would be quite sensible," Brandon agreed. Judging the distance of the small garden, he estimated that four normal strides would easily bring him to a brick wall.

Thus, slowly and with a pace that was almost mincing, they proceeded around the area several times, being of course careful to evade the ever-treacherous Neptune.

Their conversation fell idly from one thing to another. "Did Mr. Clive plan to remain in Bath very long?" Alexandra asked, rather grimacing at the notion she was becoming as big a nosy poke as Mr. Druberry.

Yet Mr. Clive didn't seem to mind her curiosity. He hedged naturally, but the truth was, he didn't know the answer himself. Alexandra was just as undetermined when the same question was put to her. She shrugged, saying their sojourn depended somewhat on Dulcie and a great deal more on Mr. Winford. If he didn't send those annulment papers soon, Alexandra supposed she would simply have to return to London and force the issue herself.

Of course, as she quickly added, it was early days yet. The post coach did take time. It would be foolish to rush back to London only to find the papers had arrived in Bath.

Mr. Clive concurred such haste would be most foolish indeed. "A few days, I daresay, shouldn't make all that much difference. Are you anxious to be home?"

"Not at all!" exclaimed Alexandra and immediately rued her outspokenness. She had no wish to explain why she had found this sedate watering hole more pleasant than she had expected. Instead, she tried to cover her lapse by extolling the virtues of London.

"Do you frequent the city, Mr. Clive?"

"Not often," said Brandon truthfully before recollecting he was supposed to be a country gentleman. But that was all right, he decided upon further reflection. Some country gentlemen rarely traveled to London either. "There's the estate, you see. So much to do," he murmured evasively.

"Oh, yes, and so far to the north, isn't it? You must never get to town. How awful for you."

And for me, too, came Alexandra's unbidden afterthought. I do wonder just how far Yorkshire is from Mayfair.

Promising herself to search out an atlas at the Circulating Library the very next chance she got, she went on to tell Mr.

Clive of the delights of the London theaters. Just last season, for example, Mr. Kemble had not only presented Mozart's *Don Giovanni*—in English, mind you—but *Hamlet* on the same program at Covent Garden. It had been a most uplifting evening.

Then of course she was certain Mr. Clive would have enjoyed *The Beggar's Opera*. Its star, the famous Eliza Vestris, had not only been enchanting but—oh, dear, it was almost too shocking to relate—she had actually displayed her limbs in the role of Macheath. Quite a few ladies, Alexandra revealed, had left the theater at that outrage, herself included. But not of her own volition, as she recalled. It was simply because her companion, one aghast Mrs. Opal Hatchcombe, had threatened to march up on stage and hit Miss Vestris over the head with her reticule if they did not leave.

And then there was Drury Lane, where Edmund Kean had once again—

Noticing Mr. Clive's amused glance, Alexandra suddenly stopped short. Good heavens! How embarrassing. It must sound as if she were deliberately trying to lure the man to London.

She immediately switched to some inane remark about the prospect of tomorrow's weather, that at least got them onto the subject of tomorrow's outing and the question of where they would go.

It was only when Alexandra happened to recall Dulcie's chatterings about a long-ago visit with Aunt Tilmatha, that either of them chanced upon a suggestion.

"Landsbrown? Landstown?" Alexandra mused aloud, trying to remember. "Ah, *Landsdown*, now I recall. I haven't the foggiest notion where that might be, I'm afraid. But undoubtedly it's near by. There are the remains of a Saxon fort there, I believe, which King Arthur is supposed to have besieged, or something to that effect. At any rate, Dulcie mentioned she'd once been taken there on a picnic in honor of her birthday. She found it terribly exciting."

"Which birthday?" Brandon asked.

Alexandra laughed. "Her sixth, I believe."

"Then I doubt we shall find it anywhere nearly as interesting," Brandon said dryly. "Or do Saxon ruins hold a particular fascination for you?"

"Not really," Alexandra admitted, and by mutual accord they dismissed that possibility.

"Although I do rather like picnics," she ventured as an afterthought and looked up, only to be met by the stoic expression of an officer who had endured more than his share of cold field rations in a diversity of open terrains. And most of them, he recalled, had been damnably inhospitable.

On occasion, however, Maj. Brandon Clive found it polite to be gracious under fire. "Fine," he conceded. "A picnic it shall be. If only you'll name the spot."

This, naturally, took a great deal more thought and several turns around the tiny garden. But at last it was Mr. Druberry who came to the rescue. In absentia, to be sure. Alexandra was quite careful not to say who, in one of his many discourses, had mentioned this as-yet uninvestigated wonder.

"A maze?" drawled Brandon. If this suggestion appealed to him no more than a clutch of tumbled-down Saxon ruins, he did not let it show. "Somewhere off Trowbridge Road, did you say?"

"So I understand," said Alexandra, wondering if the notion was too childish. Apparently it wasn't. Mr. Clive seemed rather amused. "It's quite new," Alexandra added, "so I've been told. Er, someone mentioned it at tea the other day, I think."

It had been Mr. Druberry's intent to escort her to this latest attraction himself, but Mrs. Cawlwood and Lady Redcliffe had also been present at the time. Mr. Druberry's request had gotten lost in the general shuffle of conversation. Fortunately.

"Mrs. Cawlwood claims it's been the talk of Bath all summer," Alexandra blithely continued. "Although she

88

seems to have serious doubts it will last another. According to her, its owner—a Mr. Paley, I believe—doesn't know a yew from an alderberry. Knowing the man, she says, his hedges will be nothing but bare sticks by next year."

"A maze one can see through? Hardly sounds worth the effort," Brandon surmised.

This objection was promptly brushed aside. He was assured that Mr. Paley's maze was, in fact, only a little less grand than the massive labyrinth of London's Hampton Court. Even Mrs. Cawlwood, who hadn't seen it personally, of course, but had listened to every account of its progress, had to admit it hadn't gone to seed, yet.

Mr. Clive was also assured that Lady Redcliffe thought she might find Mr. Paley's creation most amusing.

"Unless of course you shouldn't care for it at all," she added, allowing herself a wistful glance in Mr. Clive's direction. "I wouldn't like to insist."

"The thought never entered my mind," lied Brandon. "I'd be most willing to oblige."

Alexandra had a simple reason for her insistence. The thought had just come to her if she had already seen the maze with Mr. Clive, she would have a perfectly valid excuse for not seeing it again with Mr. Druberry.

Thanking Mr. Clive prettily for his acquiescence, Alexandra declared that, as long as he was providing their means of transportation, it would most certainly be her duty to provide the picnic luncheon. Mrs. Cawlwood's cook was a gem, she added. She was certain the woman would be only too happy to provide a substantial basket of delicacies.

Brandon smiled, remembering many a dubious Turkish meal he had devoured without knowing the contents, or wanting to know them, and reckoned that no matter what Lady Redcliffe and this gem of a cook devised, his digestive system would be equal to the task.

"Meanwhile, I shall ascertain the exact directions to this fascinating labyrinth. Mrs. Cawlwood might know, I should think. I'll ask her. Later," he added, after a glance toward the house. If Mr. Druberry had gone off in a huff, he hadn't let it take him very far. His stocky form was plainly evident just inside one of the drawing room windows. He seemed to be dividing his time between a dialogue with his hostess and casting thunderous looks at the two outside.

Brandon hastily suggested they take another turn around the garden.

"If you like," Alexandra agreed, thankful she wasn't given to dizzy spells.

"I suppose we really should get back to our guests," she couldn't resist teasing, for she too had spied the figure at the window. "But it is so pleasant out here. Makes it difficult for one to want to return inside, doesn't it?"

"Very difficult," muttered Brandon with another glance at the house.

"And of course being from Yorkshire, you must simply hate being cooped up indoors. A town must seem terribly confining, I expect, after all that open space and such a lovely climate. At least, I imagine it must be. I know so little about Yorkshire, I'm afraid, and I must confess I had no idea it was such a sunny spot."

"Sunny?" Brandon questioned.

"Well, it must be. Your face is quite bronzed." Alexandra glanced up at him and laughed. "You needn't look so taken aback. It's very becoming. One seldom meets sun-bronzed gentlemen in London, you see. I rather think I'd like to know more about Yorkshire."

So would I, thought Brandon. He made a mental note to read up on the subject.

With a few desultory remarks that might have fitted any shire in the country, he put what he hoped was an end to this particular discussion by saying that his own holdings in Yorkshire were really too small to be worth the mention.

Small to the point of nonexistence, he added to himself.

Alexandra was positive she was being ragged.

"Aren't you being a bit modest, sir?" she said with an arch appraisal of his attire. "I have had two husbands, and I know

90

a coat from Weston's when I see it. I also recognize Mr. Hoby's touch with a pair of boots. You may not go to London often, Mr. Clive, but you obviously order your clothing from some of the best establishments on St. James Street. Furthermore, you're staying at the Seven Seas Inn, are you not?"

"I am," Brandon said.

"Well, according to my ever-knowledgeable hostess, that happens to be the finest lodging in Bath. One would almost suspect, sir, that you are a man of substance."

"And if I were?" Brandon murmured. "Would that be of any import?"

The strangely arrested expression on his face puzzled Alexandra for a second. Then, assuming this was simply more of his ragging, she answered him tit for tat. "It depends," she replied saucily.

"Perhaps, Lady Redcliffe, I am merely a reckless plunger, making a great show on a few pence, with my pockets to let tomorrow. Would that disappoint you?"

"Oh, most assuredly," Alexandra retorted.

It was a purely teasing remark, but there was a sharpness in her tone that she had not intended. Mr. Clive's words had cut too close to the quick. Her own father had been a plunger. A light-hearted, devil-may-care punter who had been neither able to control his impulses nor withstand the consequences. The results had soured him into a man Alexandra hardly knew. Their financial losses hadn't mattered to her, but the change in her father had produced a wound that would never quite heal.

She looked up to find Brandon watching her closely and forced a pert smile to her lips. "Best stop twitting me, Mr. Clive, or you might just ruin your reputation. You couldn't possibly be reckless. You are steadfast and stoic, remember?"

"Ah, so I am," Brandon said easily. "Must have slipped my mind. I'll try not to let it happen again."

A stray leaf brought his attention to the fact that the wind was rising. With a glance at the drawing room window, which was now empty, Brandon turned back to Alexandra with an exaggerated bow. "It appears one of your suitors has retired from the field. Shall we return inside?"

Chapter 4

They walked in to discover the Messrs. Cavendish and Sharlett on the point of departure. Mr. Druberry apparently had already departed. At least he was nowhere in sight. Daniel and Dulcie were sharing a téte-à-tête chair in a far corner. Dulcie, her Dresden face looking most impish, was whispering furiously. Daniel looked as if he couldn't decide whether he would like to take her in his arms or bolt for the Antipodes.

He could easily have done either for all the notice their hostess was taking of them. Mrs. Cawlwood, having moved from her place by the window to a slightly more commodious settee, was looking not only flustered but pleased.

The reason for this state was fairly simple to understand. Lord Chambers was sitting beside her.

With a bow to Alexandra and Brandon, his lordship casually reseated himself beside the lady as if they had been boon companions for years. Mrs. Cawlwood seemed to find the arrangement most satisfactory.

Such proximity must have appealed to Mr. Clive too, Alexandra realized. Somehow, she found herself sitting beside him on an identical settee directly across from the older couple.

If such closeness rattled her, she tried hard not to let it show. The truth was, she was nearly as flustered and pleased as Mrs. Cawlwood. Acutely aware that his thigh was pressing against hers, she sat as straight as possible and hoped no one would notice her cheeks were becoming uncommonly hot.

She seized upon the first subject that sprang to mind. "Perhaps," she said, not daring to look at Mr. Clive, "Lord Chambers might know the direction of the maze."

"The maze? My very own idea!"

A stocky figure emerged from the hall, only to be greeted by a choking gasp from Mrs. Cawlwood. "Mr. Druberry! Pray forgive me, I'd forgotten you were still here!"

Altheus Druberry came forward with a darkly murmured, "So apparently had everyone else. But no matter," he added in a tone that said it clearly did matter. "Since all you ladies seemed to be otherwise engaged, I was indulging myself in a moment of solitude just outside the doorway. Most refreshing, as a fact. A man of my pressing schedule has so little time to pause quietly and reflect." He turned to Alexandra. "How interesting of you to mention the maze, my dear lady. As you may recall, I only recently proposed a jaunt to that very spot. Pray let me offer my services. I flatter myself that I have an exceedingly fine sense of direction and I would be most pleased to accompany you through Mr. Paley's magnificent wonderland. Indeed," he added, with a scowling glance at Brandon, "I am persuaded you should prefer a guide who can not only lead you through it but knows how to get there!"

"Too slow by half, Druberry," Brandon drawled. "The lady has already offered to show me the maze."

"Lady Redcliffe, you cannot be serious. Our country roads can be a baffling lot to those who aren't acquainted with them. The roads in that area are a confounded maze themselves. You simply can't go tearing about the countryside with a stranger. In fact, I shouldn't put it past this gentleman to drive you out in some utterly preposterous contraption like a—"Druberry searched his mind for the most unladylike conveyance he could imagine—" like a high-perched phaeton!"

"I believe that's precisely what it is," Alexandra replied. "Of course he has offered to bring along some smelling salts in case I grow faint from terror."

It was a gibe she immediately regretted. The situation, as she reminded herself, had been distasteful from the beginning. Now it was completely out of hand. Mr. Druberry's chest was swelling at an alarming rate. Mr. Clive was saying nothing, but there was an ominous look in his eyes. Mrs. Cawlwood looked as if she dearly wished she had a reticule to drop.

With an expression of total bafflement, she began to chatter about Trowbridge signposts and empty teapots and impertinent cooks, who were too scarce to discharge.

Dulcie and Lieutenant Symington were doing nothing to improve matters either. Judging from the sounds emanating from that corner, they were suffering from acute strangulation or else doing their best not to laugh their heads off.

If Lord Chambers seemed no less amused, he was a great deal quieter about it. "Perhaps I can be of help," he ventured. He began to give Mr. Clive directions to the Paley maze.

The maid entered with a fresh pot of tea and Alexandra poured for everyone. Whether they wished it or not.

In the general confusion of "Cream? One lump or two?" it was Dulcie who finally solved the impasse. Her eyes still damp with laughter but looking more than a bit annoyed as well, she rose from the corner seat and walked over to stand by Alexandra. "There is only one thing for it now," she said firmly. "We'll all go!"

And with that, the problem was settled. If some members of the group did not especially relish the idea, at least no objections were raised. With a decisiveness that would have impressed General Wellington, Dulcie mapped out the plans. Since there were so few vehicles of any sort at their disposal, Mr. Clive could bring his phaeton. Lord Chambers, as Dulcie had already witnessed during her mad dash up the hill that morning, had a carriage that would seat five, assuming its occupants were congenial. Would his lordship be so kind?

At his nod, Dulcie smiled in triumph and glanced around. Was there anything else?

"Well," hesitated Alexandra. "I did promise a picnic nuncheon, but I doubt, under the circumstances, we need bother."

"Definitely not, under the circumstances," muttered Brandon.

Dulcie blithely ignored this last comment. "A picnic? Splendid idea!" she cried and promptly enmeshed the absent Chives in her battle plans. He and the provisions could tag along, in a borrowed hack perhaps, at the end of their little caravan.

"There," she said, dusting off her dainty hands as if she had accomplished some physical chore. "It's all worked out perfectly, hasn't it?"

Hardly, thought Alexandra. Judging from the uncomfortable silence that followed, the jaunt had all the makings of a minor disaster.

The only one who seemed content with Dulcie's plans was Dulcie.

As soon as the last guest had left and Mrs. Cawlwood had dithered off with grave misgivings to consult her butler and cook, Dulcie whirled on her friend with a most disgusted gleam in her eye.

"Lexie, I do believe Mr. Clive has turned you into a complete ninny!"

"I wouldn't be surprised," Alexandra murmured without thinking. Then she blinked and, with a wry smile, admitted, "I do seem to be in a constant muddle these days. A maze sounds most appropriate, somehow. You don't mind too awfully much, do you?"

Relenting a little, Dulcie said she supposed not. She expected she might even enjoy the outing tremendously. Or would have, had not Mr. Druberry been included.

"Lexie, your brains have truly gone to mush! Why in heaven's name did you have to mention it in front of him?"

"I didn't," came the dour correction. "As you may recall, he was in the hallway at the time. Oh, Dulcie, I am sorry. I

96

know how much you dislike Mr. Druberry, but I had no idea how to dissuade him. I had — well, to be honest, I had other things on my mind."

Alexandra sat down on the settee she had recently shared with Mr. Clive. For an instant, she imagined she could still feel the warmth of his thigh against hers. Immediately, she jumped up and switched to the other settee, motioning for Dulcie to take the one she had vacated.

She waited until the girl had neatly arranged her muslin skirts on the damask cushions. "The fact is, you see, I have a feeling that I made a complete cake of myself."

"You certainly did!" Dulcie agreed.

"Oh, very well, then. I've done it twice today. Or thrice," Alexandra said, remembering her ungainly pitch into Mr. Bottleswell's spa. "At any rate, this seems to be my day for firmly placing my foot in my mouth. I did it again in the garden with Mr. Clive. At least I fear I did. Whatever started me ranting on so, I'll never know. But I went on and on about being stifled by propriety and hating to be overchaperoned and — well, then somehow I got around to practically demanding he take me to the maze. It suddenly occurred to me that, to go jaunting off alone with him — on top of all I'd said — he might just have gotten the wrong impression. I was afraid he might mistake me for —"

"Some hurly-burly female," Dulcie flatly interrupted. "No, that would never do. That's not at all what I had in mind."

Alexandra nodded, not really understanding but not terribly interested either. She was, in fact, rather disgusted with herself.

All her talk of independence, and yet at the merest suspicion of danger she had retreated like a frightened rabbit.

But not from Peyton Clive. She was honest enough to admit that, if only to herself. What she mistrusted were her own jumbled feelings. The gentleman's nearness had a way of provoking the most unladylike thoughts. For a moment, recalling the pressure of his thigh against hers, Alexandra wondered if she would really mind being treated like a hurly-burly female.

"Well, of all things!" she gasped. Scandalized by her own imagination, she hurried on to thank Dulcie for her timely intervention.

"Think nothing of it," the girl replied, her face screwed into a deep frown of concentration. "If you wished safety in numbers, you certainly have them now. And by one too many, to be sure!"

At Dulcie's scowling face, Alexandra broke into helpless laughter. "Oh, dear, I have made a cake of it, haven't I? Well, it's only for a few hours, and Mr. Druberry shan't bore you to tears. I promise. I shall keep him occupied — somehow."

"And ruin everything?" Dulcie muttered. "No, indeed. I shall tend to Mr. Druberry myself. With a little help," she added slowly. Then a grin spread across her face. "Of course. Don't you fret, Lexie. We'll take care of everything!"

Having delivered that cryptic reassurance, she tripped off, leaving Alexandra to worry why she felt a minor disaster had just loomed into major proportions.

Late the next morning, dressed in a fawn-colored velvet suit à la militaire, complete with chocolate-toned frog fastenings down the front of the jacket, Alexandra pinned on a tiny cocked hat of matching velvet and adjusted the curve of its deep-brown plumage so that it would not tickle her ear.

"Very nice," pronounced Dulcie, appearing in the doorway. "Much better than that dripping feather you wore yesterday."

She whirled into the room to show off her own outfit, a dress of pale blue with matching pelisse and a bonnet with a ruching of deeper blue that demurely peeked from beneath the brim. "Too light-colored, do you think?"

"Not a bit," decreed Alexandra. "We're only going on a civilized outing, you know, not a mad traipse through the woods. You look adorable."

"Thank you, I rather thought so," said Dulcie, watching as her friend turned back to the mirror. She watched for a few seconds longer, then emitted an exasperated sigh. "Whatever are you doing?"

"Forcing smiles," Alexandra replied. "I have a feeling that's about all I shall be doing today."

"Nonsense. I told you, we'll take care of everything. What time is it?"

Alexandra flipped open the cover of the delicate timepiece pinned to her shoulder and glanced down sideways of it. "The time is precisely eleven o'clock. And if all's well, I shall cheerfully eat my hat."

Dulcie ignored this last. "No wonder I hear voices downstairs. This was the hour we decided to meet, wasn't it?"

"You decided." As Alexandra recollected, no one else had had much to say about Dulcie's plans. The girl had taken it upon herself to decree who would ride with whom. Alexandra could hardly wait for the outcome of that decision. No doubt, since Chives had managed to borrow a gig for himself and the provisions, Dulcie would insist on putting Mr. Druberry in the rear with the chicken salad.

Silly, Alexandra mentally chided herself. Even Dulcie wouldn't go that far . . .

As she and Dulcie descended the stairs, the hall seemed to be full of men and roses.

On closer inspection, however, Alexandra quickly amended that notion. There were men, all right—four of them, to be exact—but the roses turned out to be none other than Mrs. Cawlwood herself.

Darting here and there, hastily greeting the nearest gentlemen, "Peyton, dear boy, and Lieutenant Symington, how prompt you are," welcoming Lord Chambers, "How very nice to see you," and directing a patient Chives about the food, "Are you quite sure you've not forgotten something?" She was a flurry in rose pink.

Actually, the dress was quite becoming to her little dumpling of a figure. And so was the large, fringed paisley shawl, which persisted in slipping from her shoulders.

It was the hat that stopped Alexandra. A full-brimmed concoction, it boasted more roses than the lady's garden could ever hope to emulate.

Unable to resist a smile, Alexandra glanced around to find exactly the same expression on Dulcie's face. "Oh, dear," the girl sighed. "Aunt Tilmantha will take up enough space for two people."

The notion did not seem to faze her however. She tripped on down the stairs, calling out gaily, "How lovely, we're all here. Is everyone ready to go?"

The mass of roses tilted upward. "Why, no, my dear. Mr. Druberry hasn't arrived yet, and I must say I'm a bit surprised. He's usually so dreadfully punctual. Isn't he, Lord Chambers?"

"He is that," his lordship replied flatly. He cleared his throat. "However, if you are worried, dear lady, I suppose I could go and fetch him."

Mrs. Cawlwood, snatching at her slipping shawl, mumbled that his lordship was much too kind but she doubted such was necessary.

"Indeed not," Dulcie promptly agreed. "Mr. Druberry assured me he wouldn't miss our little outing for the world. I'm sure he'll be along presently."

Threading her way through the hall, she bestowed a mischievous smile upon Mr. Clive and asked if she might see his phaeton.

"My pleasure," responded Brandon. He grinned as Dulcie, with a few deft maneuvers, ushered them all out the door.

Lord Chambers' coachman, who had been keeping an eye on both teams of horses, gave the phaeton's reins to Brandon and went back to take his place on the driver's seat of his lordship's carriage.

Brandon wrapped the reins around the brake pull of the phaeton and stepped backward, only to find Dulcie right beside him. "I hope you approve, Miss Winford."

"Oh, I do!" she exclaimed as she admired the superbly appointed vehicle with its team of four, matched blood chestnuts. The glistening wheels reached as high as her head; the high-perched seat was nearly twice her height. "It's—why, it's fair bang up to the marker, sir!"

"Dulcie," wailed Mrs. Cawlwood. "Such language! Wherever did you learn that horrible cant?"

"I don't remember," Dulcie replied in all innocence, but she flashed a wicked smile at Lieutenant Symington, who incriminated himself very nicely by flushing to the roots of his sandy hair.

Brandon smoothly stepped into the breach by offering Miss Winford a drive at some future date. Today, as he took care to emphasize, he had rather promised to take up Lady Redcliffe.

Dulcie seemed to find that a splendid idea. As did Alexandra. She silently agreed the phaeton was not only bang up but top of the trees, to add her own sparse acquaintance with cant to the matter.

The silk roses quivered in agitation as Mrs. Cawlwood craned her neck upward, gazing in horror at this contraption, which was, in fact, more suitable for racing than for mild outings in the countryside. Not wanting to hurt "dear Peyton's" feelings but unable to find the right words, she finally ventured the opinion that such a magnificent vehicle was no doubt ideal for gentlemen but rather too sporting for ladies, didn't one agree? Perhaps the lieutenant, being an officer of course and doubtless accustomed to all sorts of rigorous action, might accompany Mr. Clive. The ladies would be more comfortable in Lord Chambers' carriage.

"There," she said, hitching up her shawl. "I'm sure this arrangement will suit all us much better, don't you think?"

She was to learn her error when she glanced around. From their expressions, it seemed, a good four members of the assemblage did not find this arrangement in the least suitable.

With a sigh, Dulcie took charge.

Directing their attention to his lordship's equally elegant, although more sedate carriage, she uttered a cry of delight. How clever of his lordship, she announced. Instead of the closed carriage she had seen yesterday, Lord Chambers had brought along an open chaise. "Isn't this wonderful, Auntie!" she exclaimed, presenting her hand to his lordship and climbing into the seat. "There'll be room for your hat!"

And before the lady knew it, Mrs. Cawlwood was ensconced in the seat opposite with Lord Chambers at her side and Dulcie was urging the lieutenant to leap in beside herself. "Oh, do hop in, Daniel. You must know how gentlemen hate to keep their cattle standing. Isn't that so, Mr. Clive?" she added with a dimpled grin.

"Indubitably," said Brandon, much amused, and almost as impressed, by the girl's maneuverings. The chit would make a great battle tactician, he decided, and proceeded to match her promptness of action.

Since he, Alexandra, and Chives were the only ones left standing, Brandon lost no time in making a choice. He immediately lifted Alexandra onto the high seat of his phaeton and climbed up after her. Grabbing the reins, he turned to look back at the carriage only a few feet behind. "Shall we be off?"

"No!" quailed Mrs. Cawlwood. "We cannot leave without Mr. Druberry!"

Dulcie turned a most solemn face to her aunt. "I'm afraid it can't be helped. The horses, you know. Too terribly cruel to keep them fretting."

She leaned out of the carriage. "Chives, you'll bring the gentleman along, won't you?"

"If you like, Miss," replied the butler. He turned to go into the house. Not by a trace of expression did he reveal what he thought of this outing or of the gentleman in question.

Dulcie, still leaning out, glanced over her shoulder at the driver of his lordship's carriage, then hailed the phaeton with a wave of her gloved hand. "I do believe we are at last ready, Mr. Clive. Shall we?"

"Yes, ma'am!" returned Brandon with a formal military salute.

And they were off.

The only one to see them off was a solitary figure briskly

approaching Mrs. Cawlwood's house from the opposite direction. That he was displeased was a mild understatement compared to a few minutes later, when Chives neatly tucked him into the gig between the chicken à la Russe and the caramelized apple tart.

Deftly weaving his team through the narrow streets of the town, Brandon had soon put quite a space between himself and Lord Chamber's cautious driver.

Alexandra, having noted Mr. Clive's dexterity with the reins, had relaxed her tight grip on the edge of the narrow seat and was finding the fast clip rather exhilarating. Almost as exhilarating, she admitted to herself with a wry grin, as were the envious stares of a good many feminine pedestrians.

Furthermore, as she also duly noted, that envy encompassed not only the phaeton but its owner as well.

Stealing a sideways glance at her escort, she could hardly deny that he deserved the attention. For practicality's sake, he had stowed his tall-crowned hat under the seat and his black hair was slightly ruffled by the breeze. But the buff coat, the intricately tied cravat, even the top boots were the height of impeccability.

At first, nevertheless, Alexandra had been slightly disappointed. She had expected any man dressed by Weston's to appear in a many-caped driving coat, but the day was too warm for that. While Mr. Clive might be an adherent of fashion, he was obviously no slave to it. Alexandra silently forgave him this one omission.

Watching him judge corners and traffic and shoot past them to a nicety, she paid scant heed to their route. It was only when they reached the outskirts of town that she happened to look back. Lord Chamber's carriage was nowhere to be seen.

A bit dismayed for more reasons than one, she called Mr. Clive's attention to the fact. "We should pull up and wait, don't you think? Isn't Lord Chambers the only one who knows the way?"

"No," said Brandon, neatly skirting a dray wagon with inches to spare and setting his team at even a faster clip now that they had reached the high road. "Symington tells me he was on leave here last year when Mr. Paley blocked out his creation. Studied it rather carefully, he says. On several occasions. So I'd hazard he not only knows the maze but how to get there too."

Well, thought Alexandra, a heap of good that does us. Lieutenant Symington was nowhere in sight either.

"So do I," Brandon continued conversationally. "Ascertained the direction from my landlord. Quite a useful fellow, if a bit chatty for my taste."

Alexandra took the hint. The blood chestnuts were fresh and as unaccustomed to these strange roads as their owner. Mr. Clive obviously wanted to give his entire attention to driving. Alexandra closed her mouth and contented herself with the passing scenery.

She soon saw the reason for his concentration. Only a league or so beyond Bath, they left the main road, and their route became a series of sharp turns into one country lane after another.

"Good heavens," she murmured. Mr. Druberry had been right; the roads to Mr. Paley's estate were a maze unto themselves. Mr. Clive, she noticed, seemed to know what he was doing.

Relaxing as they slowed to a sensible pace, she smoothed the wind-blown plumage of her hat and idly observed Mr. Clive ply the reins with the practiced ease of a Four Horse Clubsman. The sun dappled through the overhanging trees. The feathers gently ticked her cheek. It was not an unpleasant sensation.

"Ah, Paley's Folly," said Brandon, spying a large white gate. As he drew the team to a halt before it, a young boy came running from one of the two sentry boxes alongside. With a respectful tug at his cap, he removed the padlock that held the two sections of the gate together. Then, with a whoop and a leap, he jumped on one section and rode it as it swung backward and then the other. Judging from his delighted expression, this free-swinging ride was the thrill of his day.

Beaming, he scrambled over to the phaeton and tilted a well-scrubbed face up to Brandon. "Ain't supposed to do that. Mr. Paley says it plumb sags the gate. Ye won't tell, will ye, yer honor?"

Brandon, thinking the gate must be fragile indeed if this lad's slight weight threatened its destruction, vowed that his lips were sealed. A fee box lay just to the left of the gate. Brandon tossed a coin into it, then lobbed a second to the youngster. "Straight ahead to the maze, son?"

"Yes, sir!" The boy glanced at the coin in his small fist, then at the phaeton. Plainly his admiration for both was boundless. "Only we ain't open yet," he continued happily. "Don't rightly know if we will be. Old Custy's laid up with the quinsy. Howsomever, they's lots of flowers 'n' things. And good, wide paths. 'Spect them chestnuts of yers might favor a tool through the gardens. They sure are prime 'uns, ain't they?" he said, gazing at the team in admiration.

Then apparently feeling he had been less than diplomatic, he darted a look up at Alexandra and quickly added, "And the pretty lady, too. 'Spect she'd favor a squint at the flower beds and such."

Alexandra barely swallowed a laugh. It was clear which the boy thought prettier. "I 'spect I would," she said gravely. "But it can be only a brief squint, I'm afraid. We're expecting another carriage to join us shortly."

Satisfied that he had set matters to rights, the lad happily waved them forward with the promise that he would keep a sharp eye for the other carriage.

They drove on Mr. Paley's paths that meandered back and forth across the estate past a number of fading flower beds. After a few minutes Alexandra decided Mrs. Cawlwood's prediction had indeed the ring of truth. Of course, it was coming on autumn, as she reminded herself, and one could hardly expect too much. Even so, Mr. Paley's gardens left a great deal to be desired.

Therefore, she was more than a little surprised when they finally came upon the maze. The hedges, although a bit erratically groomed, were lush and verdant and incredibly dense.

"And so tall!" she gasped in amazement as the phaeton drew up by the entrance. The yew hedges were more than twice her height. "These were planted only last year? My word, they must have sprung up like magic!"

"More like overnight," responded Brandon, once again relying on his innkeeper's loquacity. "Which explains, I imagine, why the locals have dubbed it Paley's Folly. Seems the man's initial efforts died almost as soon as he put them in the ground. So this summer, at ruinous expense, so I'm told, he imported a second crop of yews. Full grown. In the considered opinion of my host, they won't last the winter."

"Most interesting, sir. Were you planning to remain here until that demise?"

The unexpected voice startled the horses, and their equally unexpected lurch nearly unseated Alexandra. With a muttered curse and even faster thinking, Brandon managed to bring all of them back into their original positions.

Only then did he glance down to his left. "Good morning, Druberry. Creeping up on people can be a dangerous habit."

"You should know!" snapped this much-affronted gentleman, forgetting the fact that creeping had been precisely his intent. Rather pleased to note how clearly voices carried in the quiet country air, he had tiptoed up to the phaeton. It had been most upsetting to realize the occupants were discussing nothing more scandalous than yew hedges.

The horses had been even more upsetting. Never mind that he had spooked them himself, their sudden lurch had sent him scuddling backward at a most undignified rate.

Feeling much maligned, he straightened his hat and cautiously circled the phaeton to present himself at the other side. "My compliments, Lady Redcliffe. May I set you down?"

"It would appear you've already tried that," Alexandra replied, and, if her tone was a bit acidic, she thought it only served the man right. No thanks to him, she had nearly alighted head first. "You made good time, I see. Did you have a pleasant ride out?"

His chest swelling visibly, Mr. Druberry informed her that being bounced about in the back of a gig was hardly his idea of jollification. However, the prospect of Lady Redcliffe's companionship had spurred him onward, no matter how trying the journey.

The others, he went on to explain, were just around the corner of the maze and the picnic nuncheon was spread. If Lady Redcliffe was now ready to step down, he would be only too happy to escort her.

When she showed no signs of moving, he sought to further entice her by commending the appearance of the nuncheon. The chicken salad, he added, looked most particularly appetizing.

He was so pathetic in his entreaties, Alexandra finally took pity on him. "If you like, you may help me down now, sir. Is there a place for Mr. Clive to leave his horses?"

"There is," said Mr. Druberry, making a contemptuous gesture toward a stand of trees opposite the maze. "His lordship has kindly directed me to say that his driver will tend the various equipages during our stay. The gentleman may leave his conveyance with the others.

"Unless of course," he added, with a disparaging glance at the four matched chestnuts, "one perhaps feels one's team is too unruly to manage between the trees. I understand they're rather close together."

Oh, the devil with you, thought Alexandra, seeing all hopes for a pleasant outing fading before her eyes. One might as well insult a gentleman's manhood as to insult his horses or his driving ability.

"I expect Mr. Clive can manage very nicely," she said, rushing into the gap. "He's accustomed to spirited horses, I believe. Now please assist me, sir. I feel it is most impolite to sit here nattering while the rest are waiting."

With that, she practically plummeted herself into Mr. Druberry's arms and dragged him away. A look backward as they rounded the corner of the maze told her she had barely forestalled the gathering storm. With a thunderous expression on his face, Mr. Clive was smartly turning his team and heading for the trees.

Thanks to Chives' resourcefulness, a table and chairs had been wrested from one of Mr. Paley's minions. Graciously set with linen, gleaming cutlery, and a tempting array of delicacies, the nuncheon was ample evidence of Chives' competence.

Upon Alexandra's arrival, the rest of the party had already disposed themselves around the table. Mrs. Cawlwood was at the head, Dulcie at the foot. The lieutenant and Lord Chambers had taken two chairs on one side. On the opposing side, they had, not so thoughtfully as Alexandra observed, left three adjacent chairs for herself and her two so-called suitors.

She promptly took the middle one, wishing for the first time in her life that she had been plumper than any of the various dowagers she had seen in the Pump Room. How convenient an ample girth and one of those vast plateaus of corseted bosoms must be in a situation like this. A natural no man's land, so to speak, effectively separating two hostile forces. Neither of her dining partners would have been able to see the other.

Alexandra looked down at her own slight figure and decided, in her case, nature was going to be of no help at all. She would simply have to contrive a less fulsome barrier.

One glance around, and she found the answer right in front of her.

Mr. Druberry was seated to her left when Brandon slipped into the remaining chair. While he was generally acknowledging the rest of the company and thanking Lord Chambers for providing care for their vehicles, Alexandra was fast filling a plate with every savory within her reach.

His lordship, thinking the lady must have a ravenous appetite, merely grinned and redirected his attention to

Brandon. Raising his glass, he commended Mr. Clive on the excellence of his blood chestnuts and said the grove had seemed the best place to rest such fine animals. He prayed Mr. Clive had not found the spot too cramped for their needs.

"Not at all," Brandon replied. "I managed to tuck them in rather comfortably in my ham-fisted fashion," he added with a dark glance at Mr. Druberry. "Only uprooted two trees in the process."

"Two?" exploded that worthy. "Sake's alive, man, can't you control that team better than—"

Alexandra chose that moment to deposit a whole meat pasty in his open mouth.

Smiling innocently at the poor man's distress, she assured him that Mr. Clive was again only teasing. Then placing the heaping plate in front of this worthy gentleman, she urged him to eat his fill.

As fast as she could, she loaded another plate and set it before Brandon.

"Much obliged," he said dryly, then peered around her. "Now look here, Druberry—"

Alexandra was kinder to him. This time she broke a pasty in two. Only half of it went into his mouth.

Later, when the nuncheon party had broken up and Alexandra and Dulcie were returning from availing themselves of Mr. Paley's rather Spartan facilities for females, Dulcie broke into a bout of giggles that could not be restrained.

"Oh, Lexie, I'm sorry, but I couldn't keep a straight face a moment longer. What a picnic! It was absolutely delicious!"

"Was it?" Alexandra muttered. "I don't seem to recall tasting much of it."

"I shouldn't wonder. But I wasn't speaking of the food although, come to think of it, it was rather exceptional. I must remember to compliment Aunt Tilmatha's cook. She'll be most pleased to learn that the gentlemen, in particular, enjoyed it. Especially the Misters Clive and Druberry, don't you think? I mean, they seemed to be so taken up with chewing, they hardly uttered a word. Very unlike them, I must say. And most unlike Mr. Druberry. I just don't understand it."

"The devil you don't," snapped Alexandra as Dulcie succumbed to another fit of giggling.

As both of them well knew, neither man had stopped eating because Alexandra hadn't given them the chance. Throughout the meal, they had glowered across her at each other, but, at the first hint either had been about to open his jaws for other than chewing, Alexandra had declared they simply must try this tidbit or that—and had promptly popped it into their mouths.

Lord Chambers, the lieutenant, and Dulcie had steeled themselves to keep the conversation going without so much as a smile. Mrs. Cawlwood found the entire nuncheon astonishing.

Alexandra found it absolutely exhausting.

The thought of an afternoon in the maze had seemed quite nice at its inception. Now, seeing the three gentlemen don their hats and head for the entrance of the maze, Alexandra thought the idea seemed intolerable. She hoped the place would never open.

At the moment she seemed to be in luck. One of Mr. Paley's minions was staunchly declining to unbar the entrance. Mr. Paley, it seemed, had absented himself to Tunbridge Wells for the sennight. And the custodian, Custy, whose perch overlooked the perplexity of yew hedges and whose duties involved directing bewildered visitors out of it, was abed with the quinsy. Only those two had the authority to open the maze.

Deferent but firm, Mr. Paley's subordinate pulled at his forelock and refused to budge. The prospect of losing a party of elegants in the shrubbery did not appeal to him. Nor, as he informed them, was such his responsibility. With all due respect, they would be most welcome to wander to their hearts' content next week or any afternoon thereafter. But not today!

Upon that, he gave a final yank to his forelock and scurried off before a word of rebuttal could be offered.

"Well, of all the impudence!" cried Mr. Druberry. He whirled around to Lord Chambers. "You see, sir, that's what comes when gentlemen try to deal squarely with lackeys! It simply cannot be done! I've a good mind to hail that fellow back and teach him a few manners with a stick!"

"If you could find him," his lordship murmured. The man had melted into the trees. By now, no doubt, so had every other chap in Mr. Paley's employment. "My friend, I do believe you'll discover that we have been left to our own devices. Being as there seem to be no other visitors, I daresay we'll not see another human face until we return to the main road."

"Oh, dear!" interjected a quavery Mrs. Cawlwood. She craned her head up at the towering hedges and evinced a shudder that made the roses on her hat flutter like a chorus of opera dancers. "I really shouldn't like being lost in there. And without a soul to assist us. Oh, no, indeed not! I, for one, am delighted the man would not open. Lost or no, I misdoubt I should care to go wandering through the thing anyway. It looks quite creepish."

"Why, Aunt Tilmatha, it doesn't seem in the least creepish to me." This from Dulcie, of course, who was more than a little disappointed. Gazing at the three bars that were firmly locked across the entrance, she uttered a wistful sigh. "Such a perfect day, I'm certain it would have been great fun, but I suppose we have no choice."

"Nonsense," said Mr. Druberry.

Doffing his hat, he strode over to the entrance and, with an action that threatened to burst his coat, he sank to his haunches and waddled under the lowest bar.

This brought a laugh from Alexandra. She had seen ducks waddle before but never an oversized pigeon.

Mr. Druberry, however, took her gaiety as a sign of approbation. He straightened up on the far side, obviously quite pleased with his own agility. "Now, since the young ladies are so anxious to see the maze—and no reason they shouldn't, I might add. We paid good money for the privilege of the entire park when we entered. Furthermore, it is, as you now see, quite easily at our disposal."

Replacing his hat at a jaunty angle, he motioned them forward. "The gentle sex, first, of course. Ladies, if you will kindly follow my example."

"Oh, no!" wailed Mrs. Cawlwood.

"Oh, yes!" enthused Dulcie.

Oh, God, thought Alexandra, envisioning not only herself but Mrs. Cawlwood's plump little figure scrabbling under the bar.

Mr. Druberry, swelling with importance, was quick to assure them they would have not the least difficulty. He was already on the other side to assist them. And as for the maze itself? Well, in all modesty, Mr. Druberry had to admit he had been blessed with an unerring sense of direction. He would have them in and out as swiftly as a cat could find cream.

"Come, come, my dear ladies. You shan't be lost, I promise. You can trust me with your lives."

Mrs. Cawlwood wouldn't even trust him with her shawl. When he reached through the bars, suggesting that he might hold that charming bit of rainment while she scuddled under, Mrs. Cawlwood clutched it to her and retreated in the opposite direction.

In a flitter, she declared the rest might go if they dared. She herself would be quite content to wait for them under Chives' protective eye. Well, no, of course that wouldn't answer, would it? Chives and the gig had already left for town.

No matter, she supposed she would wait just where she was. Outside the entrance. She would be perfectly safe there alone and there was no use arguing. The others might explore to their utmost desire, but she was not going into that place.

Furthermore, she had no intention of scuddling under anything.

"Can't say I fancy the thought myself," Lord Chambers immediately concurred. "Dear lady, what say we leave the youngsters to indulge themselves while we take a short stroll around the grounds? I imagine, with a little thought, we can contrive to amuse ourselves during their absence."

The silk roses bobbed coyly. "Why, I expect we can. If you're certain the girls—"

"Will be perfectly safe," interrupted Mr. Druberry. At the mention of the word "youngsters," his chest had puffed up with pride. Pity, he thought. These old people simply couldn't match his agility. Offering the two a smile so sychophantic, it bordered on disgusting, he urged them to toddle along.

"And never you fret," he called after them. "With Altheus Druberry in the lead, we shall be back here before you are!"

For the past several minutes, Brandon had been standing to one side, apparently in idle conversation with Lieutenant Symington. Now, as he stepped forward, he dryly muttered, "I admire your confidence, Druberry. Seems to me Hannibal said about the same thing when he set out for the Alps."

"Mr. Clive!" Glaring at him across the barrier, Mr. Druberry rose to his full stature. His chin barely cleared the top bar. "May I say I find your attempts at jocularity completely assinine!"

"Of course," Brandon replied. "I'm a great believer in pound-dealing myself. Feel free to say whatever you like. I naturally, shall be only too glad to claim the same privilege. Shall we perhaps square off for insults at ten paces?"

"Good heavens," exclaimed Dulcie. "How exciting! Shall you be long at it, do you think?"

"I," declared Mr. Druberry, "shall take no time at all for such childishness. Now, ladies, if you please. Simply bend down and give me your hands. I shall assist you into the maze as a gentleman should. The others"—squatting down on his haunches and poking a chubby hand under the bar, he directed a scowl at Brandon—"the others can follow along or not, presuming they can manage to get themselves under."

"We most certainly can!" blurted Lieutenant Symington.

He had held his tongue until he could stand it no longer. This pompous little pigeon was outside of enough, and Daniel was more than ready to tell him so.

Only the slight pressure of Brandon's hand on his shoulder kept him back.

With a wink to his equerry, Brandon allowed as how they just might be able to creak through. "But I really find no need for it, do you, Lieutenant? Let's see if we can't all manage something a bit easier than crawling in the dirt."

Whereupon Alexandra found herself in his arms, being effortlessly lifted not only over the top bar but over the head of Mr. Druberry as well. Brandon set her gently on her feet and then, in one easy motion, put a hand on the same bar and vaulted over it.

Daniel promptly followed suit with Dulcie. Then he vaulted over, knocking off Mr. Druberry's hat in the process.

This worthy's reactions played across his face somewhat like the muggings of a very bad pantomimist at a country fair. Not only had four people just sailed over his head but his fine new hat was now lying in the dust with a heel mark firmly indenting its crown. It was beyond outrage!

He scrambled for his cherished topper and plopped it on his head, dust, dent, and all. "You—you show-off!" he sputtered at Brandon. Then at Daniel, "And you, you young scalawag! Just see what you've done!"

With the innocence of a cherub, the lieutenant begged pardon for the "accident." Alexandra, miserably failing to hold back her laughter, only made things worse.

"Pray, do let me brush that off for you," she gasped, reaching for the hat. But at the same time its owner jerked his head, and all she achieved was to send it rolling into the dirt once more.

Brandon retrieved it. Without a word of thanks, Mr. Druberry snatched it away, yanked out his handkerchief, and began brushing like mad.

With great ponderance, he informed Lady Redcliffe that he felt it only his duty to apologize for certain "rowdies in their party." Indeed, the very idea of pitching ladies over a fence trespassed all bounds of gentility. He could only hope that their delicate nerves were not shaken to the point of permanent decline.

This patronizing little speech did for Alexandra what she could not seem to do for herself. It completely wiped the smile from her lips.

Rather archly, she thanked the gentleman for his concern and allowed that her "delicate nerves" had withstood the crossing just fine. "Furthermore," she could not resist adding. "It was, you must admit, most effective."

"Was it not?" giggled Dulcie. "Gracious, Mr. Druberry, had we done it your way, our dresses would have been as grimy as your hat!"

Score two for her feisty friend, thought Alexandra. In a stroke, Dulcie had punctured Mr. Druberry's pretensions to both fashion and gallantry.

His mouth drooped like a bullied child's. "I regret, Miss Winford, that you find my efforts so laughable. I was merely trying to prove helpful in my small way. Had I realized you preferred being pitched over a fence, I would have been only too happy to oblige. Thought of it myself, naturally. But to actually lay my hands on your person? Really, I considered that most unseemly. Of course, that was before I knew you approved of rowdiness."

Confident he had put the girl in her place, Mr. Druberry turned to Alexandra, assuring her that she need not worry. He knew *she* would never have countenanced such behavior, had she had the choice.

"Do follow me, Lady Redcliffe. I shall endeavor to make the remainder of this excursion more suitable."

He tossed an icy stare back at Brandon and Daniel. "I'll direct the way for the ladies, if you don't mind."

"By all means," Brandon drawled. "As you say, you're the unerring pathfinder. We poor show-offs and scalawags will just tag along in the rear."

With a further stare that said plainly, See that you do, Mr. Druberry turned into the nearest path, studied the flanking yews with great concentration, then wet a pudgy forefinger to test the wind, and cried, "Aha! This way, ladies! Stay with me!"

As he forged down the path, Alexandra looked at Brandon. "What was the wind to do with it?"

Brandon shrugged. "Haven't the foggiest. You don't really want to stay with him, do you?"

"Well," she hesitated, glancing up at the confusing hedges and then at their leader's dwindling figure. Apparently unaware that the ladies were not right behind him, he was moving ahead at a brisk pace. "Hardly," she agreed, "but I don't wish to be lost either. Perhaps we should catch up."

"In a moment," Brandon answered.

Bending over to adjust the cuff of his boot, he waited until he spied Mr. Druberry disappearing around the first corner. "Sorry," he said, straightening up. "I'm afraid we can't. Our illustrious leader seems to have vanished."

He looked around, imitating Mr. Druberry's fierce concentration, then licked a finger, and held it up. "Aha! This way, Lady Redcliffe. Stay with me."

Alexandra turned to observe that Lieutenant Symington and Dulcie had lagged even farther behind. It was obvious from their expressions they weren't in the least worried about getting lost.

Alexandra heaved a sigh of exasperation as Brandon took her arm and smoothly steered her through a concealed opening in the hedges. "Mr. Clive, this is an entirely different path. What are you doing?"

"Merely taking a shortcut, Lady Redcliffe."

"Really? And just how certain can you be of that?"

"Very," replied Brandon. Taking a fold of paper from his pocket, he dangled it in front of her, then promptly repocketed it. "I told you my landlord was a rather enterprising fellow. He not only knew the key to the maze but, for a modest sum, offered to draw me a copy of it. I thought it a wise investment."

Alexandra glanced backward once more. Their younger companions were nowhere in sight. "And Lieutenant Symington has a copy as well, I take it."

116

"Didn't need one," said Brandon, deftly steering her around another tricky corner. "As I mentioned, he was here when our elusive Mr. Paley constructed his pride and joy."

"Yes, but that was over a year ago, wasn't it? And the hedges have been replanted. How could he possibly remember?"

Brandon grinned. "The plan's the same, and Symington has—that is—appears to have an excellent eye for detail. He evidently memorized the whole layout."

"Amazing."

Furnished with this information, Alexandra relaxed and began to enjoy the walk. The sun was warm, the grass beneath their feet was as soft as a carpet. Utterly lost herself, she was content to follow her escort's lead.

One pathway looked the same as another to her, and it was only when they had made a number of bewildering turns that she realized Mr. Clive must have a considerable memory as well. He hadn't once referred to the map.

She was about to repeat her verdict of "amazing" when a plaintive yell came echoing across the hedges.

"Halloo? Lady Redcliffe? Miss Winford? Where are you?"

"Mr. Druberry!" Alexandra gasped. "I'd forgotten about him. He must be looking for us frantically!"

"No doubt. Wait here, I'll set him at ease."

Stepping a few paces away, Brandon cupped his hands to his mouth and shouted, "Druberry, one of us seems to be lost! It couldn't be our noble 'pathfinder,' could it?"

"Me? Absolutely not!" came back the indignant bellow. "It must be you!"

"Could be! But lost or not, Lady Redcliffe and I have arrived at the center!"

"Already? Impossible! Lady Redcliffe, don't despair! I'll find you! I'm almost there!"

Brandon chuckled as he rejoined Alexandra. "I have a suspicion our friend is merely whistling in the dark."

Alexandra turned on her heel, noting the yew hedges that seemed to surround them from every side. She threw a dubious look at her guide. "So are we, I think. Mr. Clive, my sense of direction may be far from unerring, but this is definitely not the center."

"It isn't?" Brandon's eyebrows shot up in exaggerated surprise. "Dear me, could I have made a misturn? Perhaps the map was wrong? Well, I suppose there's nothing to do but yell for assistance from the 'great pathfinder.' Wait here, or better yet . . ."

Taking Alexandra's hand, he led her around the nearest corner. "Perhaps you'd rather wait here. This spot appears to be a bit more comfortable."

And, of course, there it was. A square, dead center of the maze, with benches upon which the weary but triumphant seekers could take their rest. The sheltered area was interspersed with beds of freshly planted asters and, in the middle, was a gurgling stone fixture.

"Oh, no!" Alexandra laughed. "Not another fountain!"

"We'll stay well clear of it," said Brandon, escorting her to a bench in the farthest corner. He took a seat beside her, then immediately rose again. "How remiss of me, I've neglected to yell for Druberry. Shall I?"

"If you like, sir," Alexandra said primly. "No doubt you would be delighted with his company. Especially since you seemed to relish it so dearly at nuncheon."

"Among other things," murmured Brandon, reseating himself. "Never ate so many meat pasties in my life. Thanks to a certain lady who kept jabbing them into my mouth."

"I did not jab!" Alexandra retorted. "And even if I had, it was your own fault. You persisted in trying to goad that poor —"

She suddenly laughed. "Oh, how unfair, sir! You were doing it on purpose, weren't you? It wasn't Mr. Druberry you were twitting. Not primarily at any rate. It was me! You enjoyed every minute of it, didn't you?"

"Let's just say it was a novel experience. I haven't been hand-fed since I was in the nursery."

"No? I wonder," Alexandra quipped and immediately wished she hadn't. Mr. Clive's answer had reminded her of a most indelicate *on dit*, but of course ladies were never supposed to know of such things.

Not bloody likely, they don't, she thought.

This particular bit of gossip had made the rounds of every tea table in London as soon as all the gentlemen had disappeared. Rumor had it that Harriette Wilson, the most glittering straw-damsel of all, had entranced many a beau by offering dainty morsels from her fingertips. Not only that, she had dangled petite bunches of grapes from between her bare toes and invited her current lover to munch accordingly.

The gentleman—according to rumor of course—had thought this most exciting. Alexandra had merely thought it a bit messy. And no doubt ticklish as well.

"I only hope they weren't purple grapes," she muttered. "The poor girl must have the most stained feet in London."

"Pardon? Did you say something about grapes?"

With a gasp, Alexandra looked up to find Mr. Clive regarding her with quizzical amusement.

"No!" she blurted. "I mean, I guess I was just thinking out loud. I thought—I thought it would have been nice to have had some for our nuncheon!"

"Ah, yes, too bad we didn't. They'd have been easier to pop into my mouth than meat pasties, I daresay." Grinning, he casually leaned back and rested his elbows on the top railing of the bench. "Shall I bring some around this evening?"

Alexandra had told herself many times she was too old to blush. She told herself the same thing now, but somehow that didn't seem to keep the heat from rising in her cheeks. She tried to ignore it.

"That won't be necessary, sir. If you wish any more 'popping' done, you'll have to find someone else. No doubt there are a great many women who would be only too willing to oblige."

"Wouldn't know," Brandon said easily. "I'm only interested in one."

There was no denying the blush this time. It threatened to go clear to the roots of the glossy chestnut hair and very

119

likely would have, had it not been for Dulcie's aptly timed intervention.

Her blond head appeared around the corner of a hedge and with a trilling, "I've won, at last!" she came skipping up to Alexandra and Brandon. A disappointed-looking Lieutenant Symington trailed behind her.

"Won what?" questioned Alexandra, relieved and at the same moment annoyed that she was no longer alone with Mr. Clive. "No, don't tell me. Let me guess. The lieutenant knows the maze, so I understand, yet you've been a while getting here. I can only imagine you refused to let him lead. You insisted on finding the way yourself."

"Yes, and I did! Isn't it splendid!"

Brandon smiled, then allowed it was his turn at the guessing game. "I'd say, from the look on Symington's face, there was also a slight wager involved. Dare I ask what it was?"

Dulcie had the grace to lower her eyes. "Well. Actually, it was a kiss but he lost so he doesn't get it. Oh, this has been great fun, hasn't it?" she went on, whirling about to look at the square. "And what a darling little fountain! Look, Daniel!"

Before he could answer, a more dubious thought struck her. "Where," she asked, "is Mr. Druberry?"

"Almost here, or so he claims," said Brandon. He stood up. "I think, assuming Lady Redcliffe agrees, we'll begin to wind our way out. Would you two care to accompany us? Then again," he added, with an understanding smile at the lieutenant, "perhaps you'd care to stay longer and admire the, er, asters or some such."

Daniel gave the impression he would very much prefer to tarry, but Dulcie beat him to the choice. "Oh, no, let's all go! I'll lead, shall I?"

"It's a different path," warned Daniel.

"No matter," declared Dulcie with a flippant wave of her hand. "I found the right way once. I'll wager I can do it again. Please, Daniel, let me lead."

The lieutenant bowed in surrender. "Be my guest. But

only if I'm allowed the same stakes."

Already studying her exit strategy, Dulcie barely gave him a thought. "Why not? You're bound to lose anyway. Now, let's see. Ah, there's the other opening. Lexie, Mr. Clive, would you please follow me? And Daniel, don't you dare try to get in front!"

Alexandra finally got a word in edgewise. "Dulcie, hold up a moment, please. I'm afraid we've forgotten Mr. Druberry again. He hasn't called out to us any more. You don't suppose he might have fainted—or anything?"

"No such luck," muttered Daniel and then he suddenly reddened at his want of tact. "Beg pardon, Lady Redcliffe, but Mr. Druberry's in prime health. I heard him pounding up one of the wrong paths as we came in. If you ask me, he's just too stubborn to call for help."

Alexandra could hardly deny the logic of that estimate of the gentleman's character. Still, she hesitated. "We can't simply go off and leave him, can we?"

Highly anxious to exhibit her newfound talents of exploration, Dulcie gave her friend a sharp tug on the sleeve. "For heaven's sake, Lexie, he's only lost in a maze, not quicksand! Nothing could possibly harm him. Besides, he's probably already found his way out by mistake. Now do stop dawdling. Let's go!"

Blithely she led them through the opening and just as blithely up one pathway and down another until they were so far from the exit even Daniel and Brandon had trouble finding the way out.

When they finally emerged, only Mrs. Cawlwood and Lord Chambers were waiting for them. Mr. Altheus Druberry was nowhere in view.

To Alexandra and Dulcie—each for her own particular reasons—time had seemed to pass so quickly in the maze, they could have sworn the adventure had taken only a few minutes.

Neither had noticed the sun was beginning to cast long shadows through the trees and would not have noticed now, had not Lord Chambers pointed out the fact.

Much as he disliked breaking up such a charming party, he said with a fond gaze at Mrs. Cawlwood, the roads in these parts could be rather tricky at night.

And pitch black to boot, he added. Mr. Paley's acreage spread for miles, and there were no houses until one reached the main road. Even there, there were few lights to guide the way after dark. It might be better for all concerned, including their teams, he continued on a serious note, if they left in good time.

Although his matched grays were on the gentle side, it was plain his lordship valued his cattle as highly as did any Four Horse man.

Which of course brought up the problem of their "illustrious pathfinder." He was still in the maze.

A rather reluctant "Hallo!" from Lord Chambers brought an echoing reply that this worthy was certain he was almost at the center and hadn't the slightest desire for assistance.

"Blast if that isn't just like the fellow," muttered Daniel. "Almost wish I'd taken my boot to his skull piece instead of his hat. It might have drummed some sense into him."

He raised his voice. "Mister Druberry! I will give you precisely ten minutes, then I am coming in after you! Sir!"

When no answer was forthcoming, Mrs. Cawlwood uttered a highly exasperated "Tut! I had no idea the man was so taken with yew hedges. One seems fairly like another to me. What on earth could provoke him to dodder so long when he knows we're all waiting?"

"Vanity, thy name is not always woman," said Lord Chambers with a droll glance at his fellow male companions. "I think you will find, my dear lady, that all of us gentlemen possess it in good measure. Although fortunately," he added in a tone of derision, "not always in the same vein."

Looking up at the sky, he judged the slanting rays of the sun, then shrugged. Despite his inclination, Lord Chambers was not the sort of man to leave a companion to the terrors of the night, though, to be honest, he was sorely tempted.

He put that thought aside and motioned to Brandon. Perhaps, he politely suggested, since Mr. Clive was not familiar with Bath roads, he might care to leave at once. The others might wait for their missing cohort if, of course, that should meet with approval from the remainder of the party.

"Lord, yes!" exclaimed a vexed Daniel. Druberry's stubbornness didn't bother him half so much. It was the man's damned incompetence. "These roads are definitely a muddle after dark. I know; I've been coming here to visit Grandmama since I was in leading strings. Got lost on a hired pony once, thought they'd never find me."

He chuckled. "Turned out I wasn't any happier when they did. I got my hide blistered seven ways from Sunday."

Finally realizing he was rambling, he flushed and shot an embarrassed look at Brandon. "Sorry, that's another story. I'll go in and fetch the little pouter pigeon—that is—the gentleman. You go right ahead, sir."

"And take Lexie with you," Dulcie sweetly interjected. "There'll barely be room in his lordship's carriage for the five of us as it is."

Of the entire party, only Dulcie found Mr. Druberry's bullheadedness not the least irritating. Determined to give Lexie and Mr. Clive their solitude, she had planned several ruses to keep Mr. Druberry from their side. Stepping hard on his toe, so that he couldn't keep up, had been one plan. Sending him back after her pelisse, which she had carefully left in the carriage, had been another. If all else had failed, she had been more than ready to faint dead away in his arms.

She had been a bit disappointed at first, of course, to realize her acting talents were not going to be needed. Dulcie was certain she had a flair for the dramatic.

But she had eventually forgiven Mr. Druberry for his thoughtfulness. In fact, to give credit where credit was due, she had to concede he had solved the problem rather well by getting waylaid all by himself.

And apparently was determined to remain so. With some grim satisfaction, Mrs. Cawlwood muttered that she had known such a creepish place would bring them all to no good. Certainly Mr. Druberry was proving her point. She only wished, she added with an impatient tug at her shawl, that he weren't taking such an uncommonly long time in doing it.

"Lieutenant Symington," she said with uncharacteristic firmness, "would you please fetch Mr. Druberry *now*? And as for you, Peyton dear. I'm quite sure Lord Chambers has the proper idea. You really should go on.

"Perhaps—" With Mrs. Cawlwood the voice of authority could only go so far. At the thought of the perilous phaeton, her tone quavered upward a full octave, but she plunged on bravely. "Perhaps, dear boy, you'd rather take me up with you. I do know the roads a bit."

It was hard to tell whose relief was greater—Dulcie's, Alexandra's, or Mrs. Cawlwood's herself—when Brandon graciously declined the offer. "Never fret, ma'am. As you see, the phaeton and I managed to get Lady Redcliffe here without so much as damaging a feather on her hat. You have my word we'll get her—and that charming bit of chapeau— back to Bath in the same condition."

That he didn't keep one half of his promise was not Maj. Brandon Clive's fault. Some blame belonged to Alexandra; the rest to a hay wagon.

With a tip of his hat and a parting "see you in town," Brandon swung the team toward the front gate and then turned right, correctly taking the sole lane back to the main road.

Alexandra, again noting his prowess on the narrow turns, was paying no attention to the road ahead. She was wondering if she had the nerve to ask if she might handle the reins for just a few minutes. But as they rounded a curve, Mr. Clive suddenly pulled his team to a halt. At the same time, he threw out an arm to keep Alexandra from pitching forward out of the seat.

"What is it?" she cried, then realized that, if she had been looking straight ahead as one normally should have, she would never have asked such a silly question.

The reason for their delay was obvious. A clumsy Kentish wagon had turned over, dumping its load of straw and effectively blocking the entire lane. The driver and his helper seemed not only to be taking the mishap in stride but were clearly in no panic to rectify it. They would, they reckoned amid much head-scratching and straw-chewing, have to appeal to Mr. Paley's boys for help. They also reckoned that might take quite a spell.

"Quite," agreed Alexandra, observing neither seemed particularly anxious to go in search of that help. She looked at the dense thickets and trees flanking each side of the lane. "We can't possibly go around, can we?"

"Impossible," said Brandon. He thought a moment, then beckoned to the wagon driver. "I noticed a side path back there as we rounded the last curve. Does it lead to the Bath road?"

That brought on further discussion between the man and his helper. In fact, so much so, that they each required a new straw to chew on during their musings.

Finally, they came to a consensus. "Reckon it might. Reckon it might not."

Brandon let out a heavy breath. "I say we chance it. If we wait for those fellows to make a move, we'll be here until Michaelmas."

"Or at least until Mr. Druberry and party catch up with us," teased Alexandra.

"Madam," Brandon said grimly. "You have just settled the matter. We chance it!"

With an expertise that the lady could only call remarkable, he backed the spirited chestnuts to the turning and double-switched them into a lane even narrower than the first.

Brandon put his team down it cautiously. Then after a few minutes, the frown on his face cleared and he urged the chestnuts to a gentle clip. "Looks tolerable enough," he explained. "Well traveled, you can tell from the wheel marks ahead. I vow we'll make the high road with plenty of daylight to spare."

Alexandra only hoped he was right. She had never imagined there were so many thickets near Bath. The narrow lane meandered and meandered, switching first one way, then that. And the heavy wheel tracks that had inspired Brandon's confidence began to peter out into one dubious side trail after another. Eventually, they disappeared altogether.

As did the sunlight.

In the dusky gloom, Brandon was forced to slow his chestnuts to a snail's pace, a precaution of which they obviously did not approve. At last, keeping a firm rein on their exuberance, he pulled them to a dead halt.

"Lady Redcliffe, the barest hint of a suspicion has been niggling at my mind. I wonder if the same thought could have occurred to you."

"We're lost?"

"That would seem to be about the gist of it."

"I rather imagined it might be," said Alexandra, trying to match his calm tone. Nonetheless, the truth had to be recognized. Complete darkness was fast approaching, and, with it, a most definite chill was seeping through the insubstantial velvet of her riding suit. Holding herself erect, Alexandra tried to ignore the latter, but the former was impossible to deny.

Thickets and trees bounded them in all directions. Any minute now, she thought, it would be too black to see the horses in front of them, let alone the road.

"Well, we do have some lanterns, don't we?" she asked. Simultaneously, she felt the springs give a bounce and glanced sideways to see she was talking to an empty space.

Brandon had already had the same idea. Having tied the reins firmly to the brake stick, he had leaped to the ground and was striking a tinder to light the traveling lamp attached to his side of the phaeton. Moving around to the other side, carefully shielding the light with his hand, he lit the other.

"For what it's worth," he muttered, dousing the taper and restoring the tinderbox to his pocket. The highly ornate lamps were primarily designed for just that. Ornamentation.

126

They might signal one's approach toward an oncoming vehicle, but, as for illumination, about all they did was light up the front wheels of the driver's own carriage.

And a damned sight of help that is, thought Brandon, peering at the darkening road beyond. What someone should devise was a pair of head lamps for the horses!

Removing one from its holder, he gave Alexandra a reassuring wave, which fooled neither of them, and walked a bit down the road.

As he returned, Alexandra leaned perilously over the side of the phaeton. "Any more tracks?"

"Yes, one set. Obviously a farm wagon," Brandon acknowledged. Coming to stand by her, he looked up and, in the dim light of the lantern, saw not the slightest trace of anxiety on the lady's face. That rather impressed him.

"They cross this road," he went on, "and lead off to the left."

He pointed to what was apparently another side road just ahead. Alexandra took his word for it. All she could see was a wood filled with shadows.

More to keep her nerve up than anything else, she politely commended Mr. Clive for his discovery. "These markings? Were they fresh, do you think?"

"Exceedingly," Brandon replied, not mentioning the equally fresh horse droppings he had nearly stepped into. "Which means there must be a farmhouse, or some such, nearby. No farmer is going to go larking his precious team about the countryside in the dark."

"Of course not," agreed Alexandra, surmising that Mr. Clive was just as concerned for his own team. If there was a farm in the vicinity, they had no choice but to find it. And not only for the horses' sake, she thought with a wry grimace. Larking about in the darkness was no great boon for a lady's reputation either.

No doubt Mr. Clive had already arrived at the same conclusion. And since he was clearly doing his best, Alexandra was determined not to add to his worries.

"Now then," she said brightly, "it would seem shelter is just around the next turn. I am quite ready to forge ahead if you are."

She expected a resounding affirmation. What she heard sounded more like a muffled curse. "Pardon?"

"I said, er, among other things, I could use Symington right now."

Alexandra peered down at him in surprise. "The lieutenant? Why? Oh, I see. You're thinking he'd know the road."

"Not *this* road," Brandon muttered. "I wouldn't presume anyone's knowledge of this godforsaken pig trot. Except maybe for our unknown farmer, if he actually exists. Even if he does, the problem now is getting to him."

Brandon replaced the lantern, then leaned an elbow against the side of the phaeton. "Without some light to guide us, we can't even make it another few feet. Now if Symington were here, I'd have someone to walk ahead with the lanterns while I drove the team."

Alexandra made a move to get down. "I may not be an officer of the guard, but I can certainly carry a couple of lanterns!"

Reaching up, Brandon set her firmly back into the seat. "No doubt you could," he concurred in less than amiable tones. "But that great a scoundrel I am not, Lady Redcliffe. No woman is going to go stumbling off in the night while I tamely follow along at my ease. Besides, you're not exactly shod for it. Those dainty little slippers may be fit for the gentle grass of a maze, but they're no match for the rocks and potholes of this road. I daresay you might get twenty paces before you sprained an ankle. Just how much help would that be?"

"None," sighed Alexandra, admitting the logic, if not in his first argument, at least in the latter. But she was not to be deterred. "Very well then. You walk, and I'll drive."

"What?" Listen, my girl, these are no docile nags for a lady's gig. They may be standing quietly now — they've been trained to. But one touch of the reins, and you'd find them the devil to handle. You cannot drive this team!"

"I'll wager I can," piped Alexandra, borrowing a phrase

from Dulcie. Actually, although she considered herself a rather good driver, she was afraid he might be right. She had never handled a team of four such spirited horses, but she took care not to let Mr. Clive know this fact.

Firmly drawing up her kid gloves, which in truth were so sheer as to be little more protection than silk, she informed the gentleman he was proving to be as bullheaded as a certain Mr. Druberry.

Hearing the explosive snort that resulted, she knew she had scored a telling point. Without pause, she pressed it further. "I pray, sir," she said archly, "that you do not intend to leave me here freezing while you quibble the night away. Either I walk or I drive. Make your choice."

Brandon made it although to say he was displeased with the selection was an understatement. He grabbed first one lantern, then the second, and stalked to a position in front of the horses. With the utmost trepidation, he turned his back to them and started down the road.

"All right!" he barked. "Let 'em out easy. And for God's sake, don't run me over!"

"I'll try not to," Alexandra replied sweetly. Biting her lip, she untied the reins, only wishing she could cross all ten fingers at the same time.

She squinted at the dim silhouettes of her new charges. In the daylight they had been normal-sized horses. Now, they seemed enormous. "Please," she whispered to them. "I'll be kind to you if you'll be kind to me."

The chestnuts must have heard her. There could be no other explanation.

Brandon, feeling much like a misplaced crab, was sidling along in front, trying to keep one eye on the road and the other on his team, ready to jump for their heads at the first sign of bolting.

The fact that they didn't astounded him.

But no more so than Alexandra. Now as nervous as she was cold, her teeth began to chatter with the intensity of rocks inside a hollow barrel. "Good boys. Lovely boys . . . steady as we go," she said under her breath.

Realizing she would soon have them as edgy as she was, she gave it up as a bad job. She clamped her teeth shut but found that, while it stopped the chattering, it did nothing to soothe the horses. Not daring to let up on the encouragement, Alexandra decided there was only one alternative.

She would have to hum.

So, accompanied by a hastily improvised buzz of "Cherry Ripe," the little caravan slowly veered to the left, following a single set of tracks into the night.

Desperately humming away, Alexandra went through "Cherry Ripe" twice, then on to "Greensleeves" and was well into what snatches of *Così Fan Tutte* she could remember when Mr. Clive called a halt.

"Thank God," Alexandra sighed. Apparently the chestnuts had liked her selections, for they had behaved admirably. Even so, they had disliked the dark as much as she had, and they had flinched at every rustle of a leaf or chunk of a dislodged stone.

Forced to keep an unrelenting grip on the reins, Alexandra felt as if her arms were being wrenched from their sockets as she tied down the lines.

Looking skyward, she hugged herself against the chill while offering a silent prayer of thanks and an equally heartfelt addendum. Pray God this farmer had not only an understanding wife but a warm stove as well.

And perhaps, if it weren't asking too much, a few candles would be nice.

This postscript came only when she had blinked and strained to see past Mr. Clive's bobbing lanterns. The outline of a building loomed before him. It was all too patently the only one around, but not a trace of light shone from it.

"Is anyone at home, do you suppose?" she called out.

The rasp of a door opening sounded encouraging. The harsh echo of Mr. Clive's laugh did not. "There is," he called back, "but I seriously doubt they'll bestir themselves to greet us. Lady Redcliffe, I'm afraid we're going to have to provide our own hospitality."

"Well! How dreadfully unfriendly!" snapped Alexandra, nearly falling off her perch in an effort to see the door. Unhappily, not only the dark but a large blob of tree made this impossible.

The best she could do was right herself and, in the haughtiest voice she could achieve, call out, "Nevertheless, sir, we cannot simply barge in!"

The two lanterns bobbed back to the phaeton. In their dim glow, Alexandra came to the conclusion she had never seen a man's face register as much disgust and as much amusement at the same instance.

Returning the lanterns to their sockets, he climbed into the seat and took the reins. "I assure you, they won't say a word."

He chucked the reins and the phaeton moved forward. At last Alexandra's view was unobstructed.

She took one look and the haughtiness dissolved in a gulp. "It's a *barn*!"

"Ah, you noticed," Brandon said. Jumping down, he helped her alight, then once again freed the lanterns, and handed them to her. "Pray enter, milady. You'll find the residents of this noble establishment just inside.

"I regret that you must join them," he added as he started to unhitch the chestnuts. Alexandra was practical enough to realize this commiseration was meant not for her but for his horses.

Still, dismayed as she was, she had to admit to a certain curiosity about these unseen hosts. Whoever, or whatever, they might be.

Lifting both lanterns high, she led the way into the barn.

And promptly halted, a startled laugh escaping from her lips.

"They" were two of the shaggiest draft horses she had ever seen. Furthermore, Mr. Clive had been right. They didn't seem to mind the intrusion in the least. Standing placidly in their stalls, they scarcely gave the newcomers a glance. The fresh straw in their feed boxes was clearly of much more interest to them.

And to Mr. Clive as well, it seemed. He led his team in. Then nodding toward a large mound of the same hay at the rear, he politely inquired if she were not too fatigued to hold the lanterns a few minutes longer.

"Of course," murmured Alexandra and proceeded to trail around as directed. He found a watering trough, recently filled, thank heavens, and deemed suitable for the chestnuts. He wiped all of them down with handfuls of straw. He inspected the empty stalls, also recently mucked out, thank heavens. He tucked each animal into place and gave it a reassuring pat along with a suitable amount of fodder.

Finally he looked up and said, "I am sorry." And this time, Alexandra knew he was not talking to the horses.

Tired and chilled, she set the lanterns down with a thump. "No apologies needed, sir. This is no more your blame than mine. Less even," she added with a weary laugh. "If I hadn't twitted you about Mr. Druberry, perhaps we'd have never taken this route. No matter, it's done. In fact, it's quite an adventure. The best thing now, it seems to me, is simply to find a place to rest."

But where? Even a recently mucked-out stable did not present the most aromatic choices.

It appeared Mr. Clive's fastidiousness matched her own. Wrinkling his nose in distaste, he grabbed a lantern and began to poke into the shadowy recesses of their new abode.

"Ah, a ladder," he said. His head tilted upward. "And a loft, I would imagine. Let me see."

He was up and back down in a matter of seconds. Returning to Alexandra, he executed a grandiose bow. "Your hayloft awaits, milady. And no finer could one ask for, I might say. Fresh straw, great quantities of it, and a natural perfume as enticing as the sweet scents of Picardy."

Alexandra rather doubted the last, but at this point anything seemed preferable to standing on her feet all night. Modestly gathering her skirts about her legs, she made for the ladder.

Brandon, never immune to a pair of shapely ankles, could hardly resist an admiring glance or two as he helped her up.

In fact, had Alexandra chanced to look back, she might have said he resisted not at all.

"I left the lantern on the ledge," he cautioned. "Have a care not to knock it over."

When she was safely up, he set the other lantern at the bottom of the ladder, then blew it out and clambered up after her.

Alexandra, finding there was enough headroom to stand erect, promptly did so, the better to look around. The loft was small, but it was mounded with straw, and the aroma, if not quite Picardy, was nonetheless fresh and sweet.

With an exhausted sigh, she lowered herself onto a particularly inviting mound. Then immediately sat up straight.

"Bit prickly, is it?" said Brandon, his head emerging through the opening.

"Not half so much as these feathers on my hat. They tickle."

Alexandra unpinned the velvet concoction as Brandon swung himself over the ledge. He watched her place it out of the way, then sink back into the straw. "No doubt a blanket would be appropriate at the moment," he said. "Unfortunately, I don't happen to have one."

Alexandra, her eyes already heavy with drowsiness, simply buried herself in deeper. "The straw will do nicely, thank you. It's warm."

It was also early yet, thought Brandon. Moreover, the wind was on the rise. Their loft was bound to get quite a bit chillier before the night was out.

Their loft? It came to him that, even under the direst circumstances, a man did have his obligations. He swung a leg back onto the ladder. "I think perhaps I'd best stay below — to keep an eye on the team — or such."

Oh, no, not his precious horses again.

That was Alexandra's first thought. Her second thought brought her fully awake. "Mr. Clive, are you perhaps playing the gentleman?"

Brandon chuckled. "Trying to, ma'am."

"And were you also perhaps thinking of spending the night outside in the cold? Curled up nice and cozy in an *open* phaeton?"

"The notion did occur to me."

"But not with a great deal of anticipation, I daresay."

Regarding him steadily in the dim glow of the lantern, Alexandra saw no reason for coyness. Their situation, as she reminded him, was scarcely the height of propriety. Whatever the tarnish to her reputation, it had already been done. And to have him outside, no doubt catching his death of cold, would improve that situation not in the least. In fact, it might make any explanations even more awkward.

She leaned forward, gazing at him with complete frankness. "So you may as well play the gentleman right here. I do trust you, you know."

Damn! thought Brandon. He had every intention of being honorable. And now to turn those big, trusting eyes on him!

Good Lord. At this rate, he would require more than a cold wind to get him through the night. He would need a bloody snowstorm.

"Besides," continued Alexandra, having no idea of the mental anguish she had inspired, "it would be nice to have someone to talk to. I'm no longer sleepy. Are you?"

"Not at the moment," Brandon muttered, but he sorely wished he were.

Looking around, he chose a heap of straw several feet from her, plumped it up, and sank into it. Maybe, he decided, if he could get comfortable enough — and keep his eyes off the lady — he would doze off despite himself. Asleep, any man was a perfect gentleman.

"There, I'm fairly cozy," he said, making good his first intention. "Now we can talk. Know any boring stories?"

Alexandra's soft laugh sent the second intention right out of his mind. He looked.

At the slim figure lying so gracefully against the fragrant straw. At the burnished tousle of chestnut hair. At the enticing curve of her lips and the thickly fringed eyes that seemed to glow more green than hazel in the flickering light.

Suddenly he jumped up to snuff out the lantern.

"Er—danger of fire, you see. Thought it might be wiser to douse it—if you've no objection."

"None," Alexandra concurred, a little surprised at his haste but otherwise thinking it a very sensible precaution. "Anyway, it's rather fun talking in the dark."

Vowing to get hold of himself, he encouraged the lady to reminisce about her childhood, her likes, her dislikes, anything so long as it diverted his attention.

But this too proved his undoing. As it turned out, they seemed to have a great many preferences in common. Somehow, without either noticing, it seemed only natural, as they laughed over approval at one thing and commiserated over their disapproval at another, that they moved closer together.

And somehow, when Alexandra began to shiver from the wind whistling through the chinks in the loft, it seemed just as natural for Brandon's arms to go about her shoulders.

When his lips met hers, Alexandra could not have said. Nothing was sudden. Bit by bit, the world receded and the strong yet comforting arms around her seemed only right, only—natural.

For Alexandra, it seemed not as if she had been waiting a lifetime for this moment, but that this moment had been waiting for her.

Then so, nearly, did it seem for Brandon. Telling himself he was being less than a gentleman—and even more than a fool—did no good. One touch of Alexandra's soft lips, the feel of her slender, pliant body in his arms, and Maj. Brandon Clive's intentions drifted away like the sands of the Anatolian deserts.

Besides, dammit, he had every right. Unusual circumstances or not, the lady was his wife . . .

He pulled her closer, parting her lips with his, and the passion built between them, deep and utterly intoxicating.

"Circe of the maze, you bewitch me."

The husky murmur was almost a groan as his mouth gently traced the outline of her throat and his hands enmeshed themselves in the tousled riot of her silky hair.

Alexandra felt his hands move over her body, gently but impatiently loosening the fawn velvet. And with his hot mouth on hers, it seemed as if her slim fingers caressed him of their own accord, helping him shrug off the coat, the ruffled shirt, the tight-fitting trowsers.

She responded completely to the urgency of his love-making, returning pleasure for pleasure, stroking him with her fingertips until he could contain himself no longer. Murmuring love words that had no meaning—yet meant everything to Alexandra—he took her with a swift, yet considerate passion that she had never known. Nor even realized could exist.

Without thought of modesty or hesitation, she lay entwined with his lean, hard body and exulted in this most wondrous adventure of all.

It was only when the faint rays of sunlight began filtering through the ill-fitting walls of the loft and they were searching for their assorted articles of clothing that Alexandra felt the first heat of embarrassment flush her cheeks.

But that was not to last. By the time both were dressed, they had been forced to pluck so much straw from each other's clothes and hair, they were fairly doubled over with laughter.

"Allow me, milady," said Brandon. With an elegant bow, he plucked another straw from Alexandra's tumbled hair.

Watching her as she repinned it in some semblance of order, then retrieved the jaunty little hat, and placed it atop her curls, Brandon smiled. Lady Redcliffe might not be returning in the pristine condition he had promised.

But her hat was in perfect shape.

Chapter 5

Even better, the post mail arrived at Mrs. Cawlwood's house before they did.

Upon walking in, they found the lady's attention had been completely distracted by a vexing missive from London and most likely would have remained so, had her niece left well enough alone.

But of course Dulcie was not the type to leave even the slightest intrigue unplumbed. Especially when the missive concerned not only her but several directives not at all to her liking.

Delighted to see the two of them returned safe and sound and even more delighted to escape the woeful remonstrances of her aunt, Dulcie fairly pounced on them as they entered the drawing room.

Wherever had they been? She and Aunt Tilmatha had been up all night, as evidenced by the fact that both ladies were still clad in very frilly dressing gowns, and naturally, as Dulcie explained, they hadn't had time to change because they had been up waiting and worrying. Then the post had come, which had upset Auntie even more . . .

Dulcie stole a look at her aunt, decided not to pursue that subject, and, without losing a beat, asked Mr. Clive what time it was.

When he pulled out his pocket watch to show her that it was nigh onto seven, she declared that capital! It seemed

Daniel and Lord Chambers, after waiting and worrying with the ladies until well past midnight, had finally gone off to their respective lodgings. If the missing pair had not returned by full light, his lordship had declared, they would put out a search party.

Clearly they had not yet done so, as Dulcie went on to observe, because they had promised to stop by before they set off. Perhaps if Chives—Dulcie turned away to call the butler who was still in the process of closing the front door—perhaps if Chives would be so good as to hurry, he might find them before they left home. It was rather useless, didn't they all agree, to go searching about the countryside for someone who wasn't missing?

Chives, at any rate, accepted her logic in perfect seriousness. He hastened out the door.

In this brief respite, Alexandra motioned to Mr. Clive that he might as well do the same.

But Dulcie gave them no time for even the briefest adieu. Whirling back to them, she took each by the arm and insisted they be seated. Now that Chives was gone, they simply must tell her, and Aunt Tilmatha of course, all about it. Were they really and truly all right? What had happened? Had the phaeton overturned? Had they been waylaid by footpads? Or even a highwayman?

"Gentlemen of the shade, minions of the moon," Dulcie blithely quoted. And carried away by her own rhetoric, she soon had Lexie and Mr. Clive fleeing through the night pursued by a deadly, but dashing of course, band of highwaymen who at last surrounded them, black capes atwirl, swords and pistols gleaming in the moonlight, and demanded their money or their lives!

"Swords?" gasped Mrs. Cawlwood. Until that moment, she had been glancing from her prodigal guests to the letter and back again, plainly undecided over which to fret most. Now the letter dropped from her fingers, totally forgotten. "Pistols? Oh-h-h-h, my!"

She collapsed in her chair.

"Dulcie, really!" muttered Alexandra. But, little though she realized it, the girl's ridiculous fantasy had been a godsend. Whatever nervousness and abashment she had felt on the ride back evaporated as she rushed to Mrs. Cawlwood's side.

She assured her hostess that nothing of the sort had transpired; they had simply gotten lost. Not daring to look back at Mr. Clive, she further assured the lady that a "placid farm couple" had not only taken them in but had shared their own provender with her and Mr. Clive.

Of course, that provender had happened to be straw. Furthermore, they hadn't precisely put it to the same use as their "hosts." Alexandra thought it prudent not to go into details.

She also thought it prudent to ignore the choking sound that Mr. Clive couldn't quite seem to restrain.

The farmer had pointed them homeward, she hurried on to say.

This, too, was a statement of fact — as far as it went. In the revealing light of dawn they had chanced upon a farmhouse some distance from the barn. Its owner, with many a dubious look but nary a comment, had steered them back to the main road.

Alexandra, pleased to think she had glossed over these explanations rather smoothly, cast a questioning glance at Mr. Clive. "Done, sir?"

"Admirably," agreed Brandon. He offered his apologies to Miss Winford and her aunt for any distress his remissive sense of direction had caused them.

Mrs. Cawlwood, utterly relieved to learn that they had been menaced by neither footpads nor highwaymen, was only too ready to forgive and forget. "Poor dears, you must have had a dreadful night!"

"To the contrary," Brandon murmured, "but I'm sure *all* of you ladies must be quite fatigued. So, if you will excuse me, I'll take myself off to my own quarters. Mrs. Cawlwood, Miss Winford," he said, bowing.

139

He bent politely over Alexandra's hand. "Lady Redcliffe. Or might I possibly call you by your Christian name?"

The lady flushed, he noted, but there was also a twinkle in her eyes that pleased him greatly. Her answer was little more than a whisper. "Under the circumstances, I think it — it might be appropriate. Shall I walk you to the door?"

"That would be advisable," Brandon muttered.

With the utmost formality, he took her arm and escorted her into the hallway. At the front door, he stopped and looked over his shoulder, making sure they were well out of the others' sight.

Then, grinning, he reached behind Alexandra and plucked a small piece of straw from the nape of her hairline.

"I do hope that's the only one we missed," he murmured.

Breaking it in two, he handed her half and tucked the other into his pocket.

Before she knew it, he had kissed her lightly on the lips and was gone with a soft, "Au revoir — Alexandra."

Amidst a flurry of emotions, the lady discovered another sensation. She was starving.

Now there, she thought, was one feeling she could deal with. Not having eaten since nuncheon the day before and wishing only to change her attire and delve into an enormous breakfast, she tried to slip past the drawing room and up the stairs.

No such chance.

Now that all distractions had departed with "dear Peyton," Mrs. Cawlwood had retrieved the fallen letter. With a fresh set of "oh, my's!" and "modern laxities!" she had once more collapsed in her chair.

She looked up, scarcely noticing a figure in rumpled fawn velvet trying to sneak past.

Dulcie's eyes were much sharper. Obviously feeling the need for reinforcements, she plunged into the hallway, caught her friend by the elbow, and virtually dragged her into the drawing room.

"Dulcie," Alexandra hedged. "This letter — whatever it is — if it's something between you and your aunt, perhaps she'd rather I didn't intrude."

She certainly hoped so. Her stomach was beginning to ache.

But Mrs. Cawlwood seemed perfectly willing to have a third party share her woes. She mutely handed the missive to Alexandra, then proceeded to demonstrate that Dulcie was not the only member of the family to harbor a flair for the dramatics.

Throwing a hand across her forehead, she uttered a heartrending moan. "Whatever shall I do?"

"Nothing," Dulcie said flatly. Then remembering her manners and how much she had come to like her sweet, dithery aunt, she quickly knelt by the old lady's chair. "Please, Aunt Tilmatha, you mustn't fret. You've done nothing wrong. And neither, for that matter, have I!" she added defiantly. Rising, she fetched a stool from across the room, placed it beside Mrs. Cawlwood's chair, and sat down to assuage her aunt as best she could.

Taking the fragile, veined hands into both her own, she began to murmur a series of reassurances that made no sense, even to her, but that Mrs. Cawlwood seemed to find quite soothing.

Dulcie looked across to Alexandra, who had taken a seat on the nearest settee. Resigned to her fate and the ache of her empty stomach, Lady Redcliffe was conscientiously poring over the letter. Or trying to. She hadn't gotten far past the first line when Dulcie spoke up.

"It's Papa, you see."

"No, not really," Alexandra admitted. Trust Mr. Winford to save a few pence on franking charges, she thought. The single sheet of paper was crossed and recrossed with so many lines it resembled an epistolary cat's cradle.

She gave up. "Perhaps it might be quicker if you simply told me what he said."

This idea seemed to meet with general approval. Both ladies were all too willing to reveal the contents. Unfortunately, both of them chose to do it at the same time.

At last, seeing that Alexandra was understanding them no better than Mr. Winford's penmanship, Dulcie arrived at the gist of the matter with more than a slightly exasperated clarity.

Papa, along with a great many other directives, was demanding dear Aunt Tilmatha keep a tight rein on his daughter. It had occurred to him — belatedly it would seem — that Bath might be filled with as many adventurers as London. He wanted none of them around his only daughter. Until he had made a suitable match for her, he wanted no shilly-shalliers hanging about. Moreover, Aunt Tilmatha had been directed to keep an eye out for a certain Lieutenant Symington, whom Papa had just heard was also in Bath. And while he had nothing personal against the lad, the Symingtons were no nabobs and furthermore Papa hadn't liked the way the boy had been making sheep's eyes at her in London. He didn't want any of the same going on in Bath!

"And furthermore and furthermore!" Dulcie went on hotly. "Papa actually called dear Aunt Tilmatha a skitter-wit! He says, knowing her, she's likely allowed me to run pell-mell and — oh, Lexie, he's practically demanding she lock me in my room or he's coming to fetch me! Well, I'll not have it! And I'll not have him hurting Aunt Tilmatha's feelings so!"

She jumped up. "I'm going to write Papa right now. I haven't the slightest wish to go home yet and there's no use him fancying himself into another snit. Which he'll do at any rate. Papa does love to take umbrage, you know. I'm sure he'll be satisfied if I complain that we've hardly met anyone in Bath and that I'm dreadfully bored and I wish I were back in London because I miss Reginald Snavely!" Dulcie giggled. "Papa hates the Snavelys. He'll let us remain here forever, if we choose. You don't mind, do you, Aunt Tilmatha?" she quickly added.

"Forever?" muttered Mrs. Cawlwood. "Well, I suppose

not—"

"Thank you. You are a dear, Auntie, and Papa won't descend on us, I promise. I shall tell him that you're a perfectly rigid chaperone and that I have been the soul of propriety. Which, come to think of it, I have been. Haven't I, Auntie?"

Dulcie, expecting approbation, was a little taken aback at a fresh moan from Mrs. Cawlwood. "Oh, dearest, but you haven't!" wailed that lady. "Ah, me, what to do? What to *do*? I have a responsibility to your father, although I must say I don't relish being called skitter-witted! But rigid? Oh, dear, no, you mustn't say that. I've been much too lax, I fear. Why, Lieutenant Symington has been here every single day, at least I think he has, hasn't he? Well, if not, near enough anyhow. I must profess I like the boy, but now your father doesn't approve and—good heavens, my dear! At the door last night when he left. Doubtless you thought no one could see, but I did, Dulcie! You let him *kiss* you!"

"Oh, that." Dulcie dismissed this mortifying accusation with a wave of her hand. "One has to pay off one's wagers, you know. Of course I didn't really expect I'd have to. I was quite certain, if I'd found the way in, I could find the way back. And no doubt I would have if everyone hadn't been rushing me about. So you see, I truly had no choice. Papa says one must always honor one's debts."

Mrs. Cawlwood, who had not been privy to the wager in the maze and who no more understood this explanation than the Copernican theory of the equinoxes, seized on the only word that did make sense to her. "Debts?" she gasped. "Never tell me you've borrowed *money* from Lieutenant Symington!"

Her niece, clearly astounded, was quick to reply she had done nothing of the sort. Whatever must Aunt Tilmatha be thinking of? A lady did not borrow funds from an unrelated gentleman. Not once. Not ever. Not in a thousand years.

With a sigh of relief, Mrs. Cawlwood settled back into her chair. Then immediately popped forward again. "The lieutenant! Dear me, I've never done this before. I'm not even

143

sure how one goes about it. Where is Chives?"

When it came to muddled explanations, Dulcie now found herself receiving as good as she had given. She turned a puzzled face to Alexandra, then back to her aunt. "He's not returned yet, I expect. Why do you ask?"

"Because," said Mrs. Cawlwood, obviously girding her courage, "I must tell him Lieutenant Symington is no longer welcome in my house."

"Aunt Tilmatha, *no*! You can't mean that!

"I'm afraid I must, dear. A shame too. He did seem like a rather nice boy. I am acquainted with his grandmother, you know. A charming lady, most respectable. My stars! I do hope your father doesn't expect me to bar *her* from my door!"

"He cannot force you to bar anyone!" Dulcie cried.

"Well, I suppose not. Well, of course he cannot!" For a moment, righteous indignation threatened to overcome Mrs. Cawlwood's resolve. But mettlesome or not, Percival Winford was her late sister's husband and Dulcie's father. To a woman of Tilmatha Cawlwood's upbringing, parental authority was not to be flaunted.

She girded her courage again. "Your father only wishes to protect you. And though I daresay he might have worded it better" — much better, she thought, skitter-wit indeed! — "he is completely within his rights. That kiss was very, very naughty, my dear. I must confess I don't quite understand. He did seem such a polite boy and of course his grandmother is above reproach. I wonder, what with this mystifying wager — if it were truly all his fault."

"Not all," Dulcie admitted with a guilty look at the carpet. "I suppose, if I'd truly objected, he'd never have had the nerve to collect his winnings."

"I thought not," Mrs. Cawlwood said sharply. "But that's neither here nor there at the moment. The real fault is mine, I'm afraid. I have been much too permissive for your own good. I shan't allow that to happen again. Your father has plainly bade me to ban all shilly-shalliers from this house and, unkindly worded or not, I must agree it's a most

144

sensible demand. I intend to comply with his directives."

"Oh, Aunt Tilmatha, please, you wouldn't! You mustn't!" cried Dulcie. "Daniel's no adventurer! Tell her, Lexie, tell her he isn't!"

Alexandra, naturally averse to entering this family uproar, had picked up the letter again more as an excuse to keep herself out of the argument than anything else. In consequence, she had managed to pick out a few lines including the part that seemed to be under discussion now.

At Dulcie's urgent plea she had no choice but to look up. "No, truthfully, I cannot say I would ever apply that term to the lieutenant. And for that matter, to actually be precise"— she hesitated as she glanced down at the letter—"neither does Mr. Winford. He only demands—er, requests that Mrs. Cawlwood keep an eye out for Lieutenant Symington."

"And it's not because he made sheep's eyes at me either," blurted Dulcie. "It's only because the Symingtons are not disgustingly rich. That's all Papa cares about. Well, not all of course. He can be a perfect dear at times, but he is dreadfully snobbish about money, I'm afraid. You aren't, are you, Aunt Tilmatha?"

"I should certainly hope not!" the lady retorted. "I have never considered wealth the standard for judging a gentleman's quality!"

That established, she suddenly fell into a deep study, punctuated by doubtful glances first at Dulcie, then Alexandra, which at last ended in an even more doubtful sigh. "I suppose a small rout party might do. Nothing elaborate, you understand. I hardly think I could survive a major crush. I don't imagine Chives could either. But a small jollification? Yes, I think that might do quite nicely. And I do apologize, my dears. You're quite right, you've been here for days, and I should have planned some entertainment. Only, I must confess, it simply never occurred to me."

She reached out a hand to Dulcie. "You must forgive an old lady, my child. Young girls do like to meet other young people. I should have realized that. No wonder you've been bored."

"But I haven't!" protested Dulcie. Flying to her aunt's side, she made haste to assure her that any declarations of boredom and loneliness were only to mollify her father. "We have been having a most interesting time! Have we not, Lexie?"

She didn't wait for an answer. "However, we do love parties! And we haven't a thing to wear to a ball, but a rout party? Oh, yes, I think Lexie and I can manage quite nicely there."

She gave Mrs. Cawlwood an exuberant kiss on the cheek. "Thank you, Auntie! What a rollicking idea!"

"Good heavens, I pray not!" gasped her aunt. "I'll have no rollicking in this house!"

"Why naturally not, Auntie. I cannot imagine what made me use that word. I meant convivial, of course. Yes, a nice, quiet, convivial evening with only the most unexceptional people — and perhaps just one shilly-shallier — for spice, you know."

"Dulcie!" quailed her aunt.

The girl laughed. "Oh, Auntie, I was only teasing. I don't suppose you'd know any out-and-outers at any rate."

"Not one!" exclaimed Mrs. Cawlwood, who was already composing a mental guest list. Mr. Druberry, of course. The girls might not be overly fond of him, and neither was she for that matter, but he *was* unexceptional.

Furthermore, Mrs. Cawlwood felt she owed him some recompense for the trip back from the maze. His stubbornness and pomposity had nettled everyone, herself included. She had offered not one objection when Lord Chambers, to everyone's relief, had rather brusquely dumped Mr. Druberry at his house before bringing the ladies to theirs.

Which was fortunate in one part, she reflected. The man had no way of knowing that Alexandra and dear Peyton had been stranded overnight. Thank goodness! He could be a terrible gossip at times. Still, the rest of the group had treated him rather shabbily, she thought. She would have to put him on the list.

Rising, she informed her house guests that she was going into the library to make the invitation list while it was still fresh on her mind. The girls might go on into the morning salon for a bite of breakfast if they liked.

Alexandra liked the idea immensely. Deciding a bath and change of clothing could wait, she followed Dulcie to the breakfast table.

She was content to let Dulcie chatter on about party dresses and ribbons until she had eaten her fill. But finally, replete with kidneys, eggs, and three particularly delicious scones, she concluded she had been patient long enough. "Well?" she said, breaking into the girl's prattle. "Where are they?"

Dulcie looked up from a bowl of figs and cream. "The ribbons?" she asked between bites. "Actually, I haven't decided on pink or green. There must be some decent shops near Abbey Square. We could go—"

"Later," Alexandra interrupted. "The annulment papers. I assume they came with your father's letter. Do you have them? Or does Mrs. Cawlwood?"

"Neither of us," came the vague reply. Obviously Dulcie's mind was still on party trimmings. "Papa didn't send them. He said he couldn't find Major Clive. Oh, dear, this does present a problem, doesn't it? If I wear the pink muslin, I shall need pink ribbons, of course. But then the yellow— which is ever so much more sophisticated—practically cries out for green ribbons. A very pale shade of green naturally. Or perhaps, a wide sash instead? I simply cannot decide. Which should it be, do you think?"

But Alexandra had already left the room.

She put off any thoughts until she had bathed and dressed herself in a satin dressing gown with a becoming lace fichu that framed her throat. Then settling herself on a chaise, she accepted a blanket from Dulcie's maid and dismissed the girl.

"I'll have a nice nap," she muttered. "And I'll think things

147

through afterward when my mind is clearer."

A few minutes later, she heard Dulcie pass her door. And sometime after that, Mrs. Cawlwood.

Neither stopped in although Alexandra was more than half hoping they would. They, too, had spent a sleepless night and both were plainly intent on remedying that loss with a peaceful morning's nap.

"So shall I," Alexandra told herself confidently.

She made herself comfortable — and her eyes would not close.

There was no denying the fact. Like Dulcie, she was in a quandary, but, unlike her dear, chattering little friend, the purchase of a few ribbons would not solve the dilemma.

Lady Alexandra Redcliffe was suffering from a lack of guilt.

She had been trying, ever since she had walked in the door, to suffer pangs of remorse and shame, and she had failed abysmally. After much soul-searching and striving, the best she had managed was a pang of hunger.

Now even that had disappeared.

Despairing of sleep, she threw back the blanket and went over to her dressing table. Sitting down, she picked up the hairbrush and decided to punish herself with not merely the required one hundred strokes but two hundred.

The brush flew, and the chestnut hair crackled with static as each strand bounced and flared about her head. Alexandra regarded the wild, disheveled appearance staring back at her from the mirror. "You may as well face it," she mumbled, taking another scalp-digging stroke. "You are a fallen woman. What's more, you shameless hussy, you not only enjoyed, you relished every moment of that fall!"

There was no use denying that either. The present question was, what next? Have a raging affair with Peyton Clive? Hie herself to Coventry?

Or Landsdown, perhaps?

Alexandra smiled wryly, remembering the mention of a nearby Saxon fort that King Arthur might, or might not, have besieged. Hadn't his queen taken vows after her ill-fated romp with Sir Lancelot? Of course. Alexandra recalled reading the story as a girl. Guinevere had gone to France with her knight. Then she had returned to England, not to rejoin her husband, but to retire from a world too much with her. The story had seemed most romantic at the time. The Lady Guinevere, robed in purest white and carrying an ever-present candle, as she renounced her passions for the tranquility of the convent.

But where? The practical matters of joining the cloistered life had never entered Alexandra's head. Now it occurred to her that, to enter a cloister, the first step presumably would be to find one. That in itself would present a problem, she admitted and tried in vain to recall where Guinevere had ended up. In Coventry? Somewhere in France? Surely nowhere so close as Landsdown. Was there a convent in Landsdown?

Alexandra peered into the mirror, trying to imagine herself as a nun, and dismissed the entire notion with a very ungenteel snort. She was, she concluded, neither flagrant enough for a raging affair nor pious enough for a nunnery. She was certainly not going to France, and, with her sketchiness in geography, she had no idea where Landsdown was—let alone Coventry.

"But I do know the way to London," she told the glass.

It was the only solution. She would, she decided, return to the city. There she would force the annulment papers on the elusive major herself. And she would stay there! Far, far removed from the temptations of a certain gentleman's charm.

Convinced she had just given herself the most sensible advice possible, she went back to the chaise and pulled the blanket snugly around her.

"With or without Dulcie, I am going home," she muttered. "There are simply too many Clives in my life." Whereupon she forced herself to think of other things until she finally dozed off.

But her dreams could not be controlled that easily . . .

One of the faces seemed disturbingly familiar. *"Guinevere, chère Guinevere,"* he murmured. *"J'y suis, j'y reste — avec tu, mon petit chou. On va faire l'amour."*

"Oh, Lancelot, darling, why can't you ever speak English? You know my French is as poor as my geography."

"Quite so. Afraid it slipped my mind again." He removed the plumed helmet and his armor creaked as he stretched out beside her. "Cozy spot this, I must say. Come closer, *ma belle dame* of the hayloft, and we shall stay here forever."

"Well, it does sound tempting. But, no, I hardly think we should tarry here much longer. The straw is getting into your armor. And there is that little matter with Arthur, you know. It seems he has disappeared. I am afraid, my dashing knight, I shall have to leave France. I must go back to England and find him myself."

"Then I shall go with you."

"No! That would never do! Oh, Lancelot, do you not see? Much as you tempt me, I must escape both of you. If not, I shall have to purchase a white robe. Do they come with pink ribbons or green, I wonder? Oh, neither likely. I shall be forced to wear stark white, with a candle of course, while I wander aimlessly through the countryside in search of a nunnery. You wouldn't perchance happen to know of one, would you?"

"Not offhand."

"Pity. Neither do I. And I've no sense of direction whatever. Doubtless by the time I stumble upon one, my robes will be filthy, and I shall have candle wax all over my fingers. It sounds most depressing."

Nodding in solemn agreement, the knight extracted a kerchief from his elbowplate and wiped his perspiring forehead. "Rather uncomfortable, too, I daresay, but at least you would not clank with every step. *Alors,* were it not for my vow, I would forsake this shell of metal in a trice. It tends to

150

grow cumbersome, especially on a warm day."

And even more cumbersome, the lady had noticed, on warm nights.

Suddenly she remembered it was those very same nights that had put her in such an intenable position. "I must go!"

"To England, *mon amour*?"

"No, to wash my feet again. Ever since you insisted on munching those purple grapes from my toes, I can't seem to get the stain off."

"Ah, but such a lovely way to dye," the knight exclaimed. "Forgive me, my dear. I simply couldn't resist that," he added as he crushed her to his breastplate. "But you cannot leave me! What should I do, where would I go without *mon petit chou*?"

She pushed him away because the points of his pallettes were gouging into her chest. "You do keep calling me that. What does it mean?"

"Ah, it is a most romantic term of endearment in my language. But in yours, alas, I fear it does not translate well. It means 'my little cabbage.' "

"I agree. It certainly does sound better in French. No, no!" she cried as he attempted to clasp her to him once more. "I mustn't be near you. There's no future for us. I must hie myself to London and you — well, you still fancy that quest of yours, I suppose."

"What? Oh, yes, the grail. Nice of you to remind me. I'd rather forgotten all about it. Last I heard it was in Yorkshire, but I daresay if it's been there for centuries, it can wait a bit longer. I'll get there eventually. In the meanwhile . . ."

He clanked both arms around her. "Just one more time? or two? For remembrance's sake?"

Greatly distressed, she slipped from his metallic embrace. "You are my own true love, but I cannot. Please!" she cried as he began to tug at his breastplate. "Do not try to tempt me again. You shouldn't! You mustn't!"

"I can't," muttered the perspiring knight. "My armor must have rusted shut. It won't come off."

It was early afternoon when Alexandra awoke. Wondering why she felt little more rested than she had when she had lain down, she hurriedly pulled the bell. Within a few minutes, thanks to the ministrations of Dulcie's clever maid, she was dressed in gold French muslin with a chocolate-striped spencer, her chestnut curls pulled back into a simple cascade.

The dream forgotten, she decided her fatigue could only be blamed on the fact that she was hungry again. Although how she could be was a marvel, she thought, considering the immense breakfast she had stored away.

However, food seemed the most practical idea at the moment. She was going to need all her strength when she faced Dulcie with her decision to leave.

Going downstairs, she crossed her fingers that neither her willful little friend nor her hostess was in the dining room.

The trick worked. Only Chives was present, deftly removing two nuncheon plates from the table. The other ladies had finished some while ago, he explained. Madam, having decreed the party would be this coming Friday evening, had now gone calling on friends to spread the word of her intentions. Miss Dulcie was in the library, penning invitations. If Lady Redcliffe would care to take a seat, her own nuncheon would be served posthaste.

Thanking him, Alexandra was soon treated to a bountiful plate of Melksham ham, garden peas, and parslied potatoes in cream sauce. She left the table, more than a bit embarrassed to realize she had finished every bit of it.

"I really must get back to London," she murmured to herself. "If I stay here, Chives will have me plumper than any Pump Room dowager."

Thus, further steeled with resolve, she went into the library. "Good afternoon, Dulcie."

The girl sat at a dainty escritoire. Notepaper spread about her, she added a swirling flourish to an invitation, then held it at arm's length to admire her handiwork.

152

"Isn't it? A perfectly gorgeous afternoon, that is. Yet here I am, trapped in a fusty old library, trying to remember my schoolroom penmanship. Not that I really mind, of course. It seemed the least I could do, now that Aunt Tilmatha is going to all this trouble to toss a bash just for us.

"Besides," she added with a definite twinkle in her eye, "the guest list is almost perfect. It seems Auntie has discovered any number of young gentlemen to invite."

Alexandra was not taken in for a second. "I gather she's decided not to bar Lieutenant Symington after all."

The twinkle grew more pronounced. "Not after I told her the story about the time Papa banned strawberries from the house because he thought they weren't good for me. That only made me want them all the more naturally. I sneaked off to a playmate's house and ate three whole baskets full."

"Dulcie Winford, you are an absolute minx." Coming forward to take a look at the very substantial guest list, Alexandra shook her head in mock disgust. "Mrs. Cawlwood took the hint, I see."

Dulcie giggled. "Aunt Tilmatha may be dithery, but she's rather bright for all of that. As soon as I mentioned the fact that I was biliously ill for a week after and that I've never much cared for strawberries since, she promptly sat down and added Daniel's name to the list. Moreover, she's out now, polling her every acquaintance for the names of any more suitable young gallants that might be in town. Not that she would ever admit it, of course, but I know exactly what she is up to. She thinks, with a party full of handsome young men, my head will be so turned I'll forget Daniel."

"And will it, do you suppose?" asked Alexandra.

Dulcie laughed. "Naught but time will tell, will it? However, you needn't fret. There is only one bid that interests you, I should imagine. I have already written it out. In fact, I took very special pains, and I must say it looks rather nice. Here, take a peek."

Smiling at the girl's own opinion of her workmanship, Alexandra took the proffered invitation. "Mr. Druberry's no

153

doubt," she murmured, expecting this to be only more of Dulcie's teasing.

Her face sobered as she glanced at the meticulous little swirls and flourishes. For a moment she wavered. Then taking a deep breath, she laid the paper on the escritoire. "Dulcie, I'm quite sure Mr. Clive will be pleased to attend, but you will have to entertain him yourself, I'm afraid."

Her friend, having been reminded that the almost perfect guest list contained at least one glaring flaw, had decided to get the worst over with. Now laboriously and reluctantly beginning another invitation, she did not look up. "Don't be a goose, Lexie. If you're imagining you must sacrifice yourself to Mis-ter Al-the-us Dru-ber-ry" — she penned the name as she spoke — "all evening, you can simply put that notion right out of your head."

Finishing the note, she applied sand from an ornate shaker to set the ink, then blew it off with a definite look of annoyance. "There! One bid for that pompous little pigeon puff! I do hope Aunt Tilmatha's happy now. She knows he and Mr. Clive are nearly at loggerheads, but she insisted on inviting the man all the same. She says they're both gentlemen, they'll be too polite to indulge in any real dust-up. A shame," she murmured, reaching for an envelope. "It would be much livelier if they did."

"Dulcie!"

But the girl blithely went on scrolling and flourishing. There was, she continued, not the slightest cause for Lexie to work herself into a pet. If need be, she and Daniel would take turns distracting Mr. Druberry. Lexie, she added with an impish grin, could distract Mr. Clive in any way she liked.

And I fear that's all I am to him, thought Alexandra. Nothing more than a distraction.

Leaning over the writing table, she firmly took the quill from the girl's hand and returned it to the inkwell. "Dearest, please listen to me. I am sorry — and I must apologize to your aunt as well. She's been so kind, but, after all, the party

154

is really for you. I'm sure she'll understand. I shan't be here Friday evening."

"Of course not," said Dulcie, refusing to take her seriously. She retrieved the quill and set it to a fresh piece of paper. "A promising to-do with all sorts of interesting guests. Including a certain Mr. Clive. No doubt you'd rather be upstairs knitting the whole time."

"No, I'd rather . . ." Alexandra began and faltered. Heaven only knew what she really wanted. She dared not even think about it. She squared her shoulders. "No, I shall be in London."

It finally began to dawn on Dulcie that her friend might be serious. With exaggerated care, she returned the plumed implement to its holder and looked up. "Why?"

That was exactly the question Alexandra had not wanted. To say she was fleeing from Peyton Clive would only set the girl probing into areas she had no wish to divulge. She settled for the least painful answer.

"For the annulment papers of course. Apparently your father is stymied, and I am tired of waiting. If I'm to have them, it would seem my only recourse is to go back and demand them myself."

She braced herself for the protest bound to come. As soon as this change of plans sank in, Dulcie would leap up from her chair, crying that her friend could not possibly leave without her!

But Dulcie neither leaped nor cried. To Alexandra's surprise, she merely leaned back in her chair, a smile of triumph spreading across the Dresden features. "Splendid! I knew it! This is exactly the way I planned it. You're going to marry him, aren't you?"

Surprise turned to outright amazement. "Who?" was the best Alexandra could manage.

"Why, Mr. Clive of course. No wonder you are so anxious to be free. Has he proposed yet? Officially, I mean?"

"Certainly not!"

"Oh, well, I expect he'll get around to it. Perhaps tomorrow or the next—"

She suddenly clapped her hands. "Friday! Of course! Lexie, darling, we must find you an absolutely smashing gown. When Mr. Clive sees you Friday evening, you'll look so lovely he can't possibly resist. Oh, this is splendid! Just wait until I tell Auntie her little rout is turning into an engagement party!"

"Dulcie Winford, you'll say no such thing! Listen, you simply don't understand any of—where are you going?"

"To forage through Auntie's writing box. These silly little invitation slips are too small. I need some real letter paper."

She was gone before Alexandra could turn around. And back almost as quickly.

Waving several sheets of lavender paper, she darted past Alexandra and reseated herself at the escritoire. "Now, let's see," she said, picking up the pen.

Alexandra's protests, she merely ignored. "Darling, do sit down and stop sputtering. I can't think." She stared at the ceiling for a moment, then with a triumphant "Aha!" began to write.

Finding that no matter how much she sputtered, she was getting not the least response, Alexandra finally forced herself to draw up a chair and sit still until the girl had finished.

At last Dulcie put down the pen. Alexandra fixed her with a firm eye. "Now would you mind listening to me?"

"As long as you like, Lexie, dearest. But there's no use to put yourself into such a swivet. The problem is solved. Care to see the letter?"

"No! Yes!" blurted Alexandra, snatching the paper as rapidly as she had changed her mind. Knowing her impetuous friend, she wouldn't have put it past Dulcie to have written Mr. Clive a congratulatory letter.

But the salutation read, "Dear Papa."

With a heavy sigh, Alexandra began to read the text.

By the time she had finished she had run completely out of sighs, heavy or otherwise. "Dulcie, this is utterly preposterous!"

She read it again.

Amid the hasty swirls and flourishes, Dulcie had managed to convey the impression of extreme duress. Had dear Papa no regard for her feelings? Here she was, she declared, unwed, unwanted, and with her prospects dwindling at an alarming rate. She was, she further avowed, tantamount to being on the shelf. An old maid, Papa! Why, just that morning she had spied a wrinkle, and already the rumors were starting. In fact, someone in Bath had referred to her as an ape leader! Oh, Papa, she had actually heard the person say it. How humiliating!

Alexandra looked up. "Dulcie Winford, you are scarcely past your eighteenth birthday. Who called you an ape leader?"

"Me. When I was upstairs just now. I said it in front of the mirror—out loud."

"And the wrinkle?"

A giggle escaped the smooth pink lips. "It was Aunt Tilmatha's actually."

"Oh, Dulcie."

"Well, it's the truth. I didn't say it was mine. I simply said I saw one."

Alexandra went back to the letter.

The upshot of which proclaimed that, being the dutiful daughter Dulcie was, of course, she would have been content with her father's choice of bridegroom. But since he was obviously in no rush to secure the annulment papers, his loving daughter could only infer that dear Papa no longer found Major Clive suitable.

In which case, Dulcie had added with a mighty flourish, she might as well accept Reginald Snavely. He had asked her first anyway. As long as Papa seemed to have no other plans for her now, she thought it only honorable to return to London—within the next two days or so—and accept poor Reginald's offer.

"Good lord," moaned Alexandra. "Did he propose mar-

157

riage to you?"

"Yes. In a park swing at Hampton Court when we were both about seven years old. I pushed him off. Dreadful little snip, I didn't like him any better then than I do now. Did you read the postscript?"

"I did," said Alexandra and laughed despite herself. She read it once more aloud.

"P.S. Dear Papa, I know how much you dislike the Snavelys, but I'm sure your generous nature will shine forth once they become family. And pay no attention to any rumor your might hear. I don't believe for a minute that the Snavelys have lost all their money."

Alexandra put down the letter. "Dulcie Letitia Winford, you are incorrigible. Either tear this up at once, or I shall do it for you."

"Whatever for?" said Dulcie, snatching her composition out of harm's way. "Didn't you say you were tired of waiting for that annulment?"

"Yes, only—"

"Then there's nothing else to be said. Once I've put this teensy little burr under Papa's saddle, he'll hound that bothersome major out quick as a wink. The papers will arrive in no time, you can be certain of that," she added, gaily waving the letter. "And you shan't even have to think of leaving—which I must say is terribly inconsiderate of you, at any rate. How can Mr. Clive possibly propose to you Friday evening if you aren't here?"

Alexandra counted to ten. Then as calmly as she could, she tried to dissuade Dulcie of her illusions. There was no reason—not one single reason in this entire befuddled world, she iterated—to believe Mr. Clive would propose to anyone on Friday.

She might as well have saved her breath. Dulcie, once she got her perfect little teeth into something, did not let go easily. "Nonsense, no one can ever be that sure of a man's intentions unless—that's it! You've been fibbing to me, haven't you? Of course, he won't propose Friday because he

158

shan't need to. He's already done it! Oh, Lexie, you sly puss. How awful to lead me on so. I shall never forgive you! Now, tell me every detail. When was it? Last night while you were lost? Or this morning, when he brought you home?"

"Neither!" retorted Alexandra. "And I do wish you'd stop playing the fool. I have no desire to be married to Mr. Clive—or any man. I am going home tomorrow."

Never had she spoken so sharply to her friend. Dulcie's blue eyes flew wide open. "Lexie, you cannot mean that. You're in love with him."

It was Alexandra's turn for complete astonishment. "Ridiculous! A man I've scarcely known three days?"

And one very unexpected night in the straw, she thought, the heat rising in her cheeks. "He—has a certain charm, I'll admit. But even if he is seriously considering—which of course he is not! And neither am I! I have been married quite enough, thank you."

"But never to the right man," Dulcie promptly announced. For a moment, she had been worried, but that fleeting blush had not escaped her. She sat back, grinning, reassured that she had been on the right track all along, whether dear Lexie knew it or not.

Obviously Alexandra didn't. Rather crossly, she informed her friend that husbands were no laughing matter. "You are such an innocent, Dulcie. Do you imagine marriage is all sweet mist and roses? Well, I may tell you for a fact, it is not. Husbands—even the kindest of them—are no knights in shining armor. They take sick, they snore, they—"

Knights? Straw?

Oh, no! thought Alexandra as her dream came flooding back to her. Peyton as Sir Lancelot du Clive? Good lord, had she actually called him her own true love?

This time the redness that overcame her was a great deal more than fleeting.

Dulcie laughed in delight. "Mr. Clive looks quite healthy to me. I seriously doubt he'll snore for years yet. And even if he should, it's of no importance. You're still in love with

159

him. Admit it."

"Never!" Alexandra snapped.

"Very well then, tell me otherwise. Look me straight in the eye and tell me you do *not* love Mr. Peyton Clive."

Alexandra looked her in the eye. That part was easy.

"I do not—" she began and fell silent. She cleared her throat and tried again. The words simply would not come. "Oh, all right, perhaps I do not *not* love him," she cried angrily. "But I am going home all the same!"

And with that, she flounced out.

She would have been a little surprised and a great deal more suspicious, had she happened to glance back. Dulcie was no longer smiling. In fact, several solemn emotions played across the Dresden face, but defeat was not one of them.

The girl sat for a few minutes gazing out the window. Then calmly sealing the letter to her father and setting it aside, she selected a fresh sheet of paper. With a tiny smile and even less regard for her penmanship, she scrawled a hasty note.

Chives, upon being summoned to the library, was sent off with two missives posthaste.

Chapter 6

Both found their mark with a speed that not even Dulcie could have anticipated. A chance encounter with an outbound postrider sent one letter off to London before Chives had gotten a block from the house.

The second encounter was not quite so chancey. As the addressee was already climbing the hill toward Mrs. Cawlwood's home, Chives had only to stop and wait. With a bow, he delivered the second missive into the correct hands.

"Shall there be any answer, sir?" he asked, having stood aside until the note had been torn open and conned.

"Answer?" came the explosive reply. "My God, how could anyone answer this?"

Mrs. Cawlwood's butler displayed not the slightest trace of curiosity. "I see, sir," he said. "No doubt you'd prefer to relay your sentiments in person. May I escort you to the house?"

The harsh laugh was equally explosive. "Thank you, no. If I had any sense, I'd escort myself straightway back to Turkey!"

Hard upon which, Chives was left to wonder why a gentleman who had plainly been intent on seeking Mrs. Cawlwood's abode should suddenly turn on his heel and stalk off in the opposite direction.

Major Clive chuckled as he handed the note back to his

equerry. "I don't think Miss Winford intended for me to see this."

"No, sir, I am quite certain she didn't," replied an unsettled Lieutenant Symington. "And there's the devil of it, sir! How can I be subtle when I don't even understand what the blazes is going on!"

"That does make your mission a bit more difficult, I expect."

Brandon turned to the mirror, looking for circles under his eyes and wishing he had gotten an hour or two more sleep before his subordinate had barged in.

"Have a seat, Daniel," he said, tightening the sash of the long robe he had hastily thrown on, "and let's see if I have the gist of Miss Winford's urgent message."

Returning to his bed, he punched up the pillows and sprawled back against them, his weight supported on one elbow. "The way I read it, your Miss Dulcie wants you to influence Mr. Peyton Clive — subtly of course — to keep Lady Redcliffe here in Bath. The question is, now how does she suppose he might accomplish that feat? Kidnapping? A convenient cosh on the skull?"

"Sir!" Appalled by the burden Chives had placed in his hand, Lieutenant Symington was in no mood for frivolity. In his considered opinion, his superior was taking the predicament much too lightly. He was quite certain, he replied in disapproving tones, that Miss Winford would never condone any such brutality. She merely thought it more — Daniel groped for the appropriate word — more *politic* for Lady Redcliffe to remain in Bath, instead of chasing through London in search of an errant bridegroom.

Frowning at the note, he laid it on the small table beside his chair. "As you see, sir, since Mr. Winford cannot find you, Dulcie seems to think he's tarrying, but then she doesn't know the truth. You're here! I must say, sir, I think it would be most unfair to send Lady Redcliffe on the same, mad goose chase!"

"Agreed," said Brandon in an amiable fashion although he was not so certain Alexandra's quest would prove as fruitless as Mr. Winford's. Beneath that beautiful exterior, the lady had needle-sharp wits. Possibly, just possibly, she might ask enough questions to learn his true identity.

Brandon smiled to himself. He was not quite ready for any such revelations yet. Without disturbing his position, he reached out an arm and slipped the note from the table.

"Must have changed her mind," he muttered half to himself, recalling the reasons Alexandra had given for entrusting the procurement of the annulment papers to Mr. Winford.

He looked up at Daniel. "She's planning to leave tomorrow? The lady appears to be in somewhat of a rush, doesn't she?"

"Naturally!" blurted Daniel. "She's—"

"Yes?"

This encouragement was mild, almost idle, or so Daniel thought. His face ablaze, he gave an angry tug at his collar and decided, subtlety be damned! Compared to this, verbal fencing with Turkish satraps was child's play. He was tired of mincing words.

"Dulcie says she's in love with you, sir."

"Miss Winford? My, my, I had no idea."

"Not Dulcie! Lady Redcliffe!" thundered Daniel. Good Lord, he thought, was the man entirely void of feeling? He had known his major to find humor in some very odd circumstances, but this—this mildly interested nonchalance was pitching it far too high. Lt. Daniel Symington was a romantic at heart. In his book, one did not trifle with a lady's affections, not even in jest.

His patience now as constricted as his collar, he spaced each word clearly so that there could be not the slightest misunderstanding. "Dulcie is convinced that Lady Redcliffe is in love with you." God help her, he thought. "And you with her!" he declared.

This shot seemed to come no nearer the mark than the first. To Daniel's chagrin, the major rose from the bed, threw back his head, and laughed outright. "Miss Winford does stick her fingers in a great many pies, doesn't she? My

163

sympathies, Daniel, you may never know a day's smooth sailing again although I dare say it might be worth the voyage."

The lieutenant leaped to his feet. "Just a minute, sir! If you mean to infer Dulcie is—"

"A very captivating young lady," Brandon interrupted. "Also a determined little minx as doubtless you've already discovered. One finds it hard to disoblige her. And now if you'll excuse me, Lieutenant, I'd like to dress and find myself some nuncheon. Care to join me?"

Daniel's "No, thank you, sir, I've eaten," was more than a frostily polite refusal. It was a fact and a most uncomfortable one at that. He had just come from a heavy meal, foisted upon him by a grandmother who thought him far too skinny, when he had encountered Chives with the note. Now, not only was his mind upset, but his stomach appeared determined to follow suit.

He was only too happy when the major dismissed him. For the first time in his life, Lt. Daniel Symington, on leave from His Majesty's Light Horse Guards, felt compelled to disobey an order.

Brandon, having eaten a hearty nuncheon with not the vaguest sign of any gastric aftereffects, returned to his room. The inn's valet respectfully dogged his footsteps, then bowed as Brandon pointed to the buff coat lying crumpled in the corner.

"Sponged and pressed, sir?" the man asked as he picked up the garment.

"Whatever," murmured Brandon. His attention was on a packet of papers lying on the dresser.

"Indeed, sir."

Shaking his head at the cavalier treatment of such fine apparel, the valet began to search the pockets. Gentlemen did leave such odd things in their clothing, he thought. He always made it a point to leave any valuables on the guest's dresser before leaving the room.

164

He did so now although there seemed to be only one thing in this gentleman's pockets — and hardly valuable in the valet's opinion. Nevertheless, his training stood him in good stead. He laid the piece of straw on the dresser as carefully as if it were a gold sovereign.

"What's this?" Brandon said. He picked it up. Then, with recognition, a smile played across his lips that was anything but devoid of feeling. Tucking it into the pocket of the gray cord coat he now wore, he reached for the packet. He tapped it a couple of times with his forefinger, then asked the valet if there happened to be a safe on the premises.

"Yes, sir. In the proprietor's office."

Brandon handed him the packet. "Then put this in it if you please, but first, I'll need a pen and some letter paper."

"Very good, sir."

When the valet had brought the necessaries and backed himself respectfully out the door, Brandon sat down to write.

His efforts were more to the point than Daniel's. That young man had gone trudging up the hill to admit his failure. It was not a mission he relished, but, if nothing else, Daniel Symington believed himself to be a man of courage.

Now, standing hard by an aster bush in Mrs. Cawlwood's garden, he was not so certain. A wrathful band of Turkish bandits had not undone his bravery. A wrathful Dulcie was something else again.

Storming up and down the path in high dudgeon, she refused even to look at him. "What do you mean Mr. Clive won't help us? Good grief, Daniel, I daresay you weren't the slightest bit subtle!"

"I was! That is — well, no, I suppose I wasn't, but it wouldn't have mattered anyway. That's what I've been trying to tell you if you'd only stand still for a minute. He didn't care. He hardly even seemed interested."

Dulcie had reached the end of the tiny garden. Reversing her steps, she paced by him without a glance. "Mr. Peyton Clive flatly refused to help? How *could* he?"

To Daniel, it seemed his collar had been shrinking steadily by the second. It had started with the major. Now, his head swiveling back and forth as he tried to keep Dulcie in his range of vision, he felt as if he were being garroted during a cricket match. Tugging again at the tight collar, he made a mental note to see his tailor as soon as possible. Any fool who had stuck his neck out this far, he reasoned, needed a uniform at least two sizes larger.

Giving up all hope of catching Dulcie's eye as she sailed past, he drew himself to attention and addressed his answer to the nearby aster bush. "I hardly believe it my place to conjecture how, or why, a man behaves as he does. And for the sake of accuracy, I must say he did not flatly refuse. At least, not in so many words. The—Mr. Clive, that is, was fairly amiable about it, but there was no mistaking his meaning."

"No?" Dulcie suddenly whirled to a stop in front of him. "Daniel, what exactly did he say? Can you remember?"

"Naturally!" The lieutenant's intuition may not not have been infallible, but his ability to recall factual information was a point of pride. "If you must know, he called you a determined little minx."

"Oh." Dulcie's pout made it clear she was not overly fond of that description.

"He also called you a very captivating young lady."

"That's better."

"And he said he found it hard to disoblige you."

To Daniel's amazement, his young lady greeted this regretful news with a broad smile.

"That's much better!" Dulcie cried. "It means he will most likely change his mind and help us after all."

Considering his opinion of the major's attitude, Daniel thought this most unlikely, but he was careful to keep that thought to himself. Well enough that Dulcie was once more her usually cheerful self. The last thing he wanted to do was set her off again.

What he did want was her advice. For Lt. Daniel Symington was a very troubled young man. He liked Lady

Redcliffe. Should he reveal the truth to her or not? Loyalty had stretched him one way, his sense of honesty another. And where, he thought, heaving a mighty sigh, had that put him? At a bloody standstill, that's where!

"Dulcie?"

His would-be adviser, obviously busy with thoughts of her own, looked up at him with a slow, sweet smile. "Yes, Daniel?"

"I—I need to talk to you, I think."

Blast! he thought, what a lame beginning. Dulcie might be feisty, even a bit meddlesome—although the major hadn't been impolite enough to actually say so—but she was also clever. If he didn't watch his words, he would no doubt soon have her madder than ever. And that, he decided, would be more than he could cope with. Wrestling with one's conscience was sufficiently arduous. Soul-wrestling in the company of a pacing bundle of fury was impossible.

Taking a deep breath, he was about to begin when he found he had lost her attention completely.

She was watching Chives struggle through the garden door with two rather unwieldy burdens.

"A bench!" she exclaimed. "How nice, but do you think there's room?"

"No, Miss Dulcie, there is not," the butler replied in a most disapproving manner. Setting the bench down near the adjacent wall, he pulled the second burden, a long-handled spade, from beneath his arm and started to dig.

"However, madam feels that, since the garden has been put to such great use lately," he paused to bestow a cryptic glance on the lieutenant. "We must accommodate our guests. I have been instructed to remove this rose bush. It is an Irish Gold tea rose," he added, the disapproval in his tone now equaled by regret.

"Then you mustn't!" Dulcie protested. "If it's one of Auntie's favorites—"

"It isn't," Chives gravely informed her. "Madam is not particularly fond of the Irish."

The digging took some while, but there was no complaint

from the lieutenant. He considered the incident a good omen. As soon as the doleful Chives had removed the rosebush, Daniel pulled Dulcie down on the bench.

"Miss Winford. Do you — do you believe in honesty?"

With a sigh of exasperation, Dulcie moved as far away as their seating would allow, which wasn't very far. It was a small bench. "Of course," she said. "I also believe I gave you permission to address me by my given name."

Having gotten his courage up, Daniel was not to be distracted. "But honesty at any cost? Even if that honesty betrays an order — a trust, I mean. Even if it means causing unhappiness now — instead of later?"

Dulcie gave him a sharp look. "Are you quite sure? About the later part, that is?"

"Yes, I'm almost positive."

"Almost? But you don't really know for a fact, is that it?"

It was Daniel's turn to be exasperated. "Blast it all, Dulcie, how can anyone know the future for a fact?"

"Exactly. You see, Daniel, I've found that things have a way of working out in the end. So why upset anyone needlessly? Honesty's rather nice, you know, but not when it's unkind. Sometimes it's just another name for meddling, and I wouldn't advise that at all!"

My God, thought Daniel, look who's talking.

The expression on his face brought a giggle from Dulcie. "Oh, Daniel, what is this? Some sort of military problem?"

"Military?"

Even as he said it, Daniel knew he was going to take the easy way out. Coward, he thought. And did it anyhow. "Yes, that's it, a military problem."

Well, it was, in a way.

"But what if it weren't?" he added cautiously. "What if it were, say, a matter of honesty between a man and a woman? Don't you think each should be completely truthful to the other?"

The giggle turned into laughter. "I should certainly hope not! My goodness, Daniel, do you want to take all the romance out of life? Without secrets, I can't imagine how

168

dreadfully dull things would be."

She fluttered her eyelashes in mock coyness. "In fact, I have a few secrets myself. Don't you?"

That settled it for Daniel. Pot calling the kettle black or not, Dulcie had advised him not to meddle. Dulcie had advised him that people were entitled to their secrets. Furthermore, as any good military man should know, discretion was the better part of valor.

Thus having convinced himself, he went a step beyond. From now on, he silently vowed, he was going to be discreet as Hell. Dulcie could poke into other people's lives all she liked, but not Daniel Symington. He had already stuck his neck out, and it had proved most uncomfortable. His nose, he was going to keep to himself.

Reassured, his strategy firmly resolved, the lieutenant took his leave of Miss Dulcie Winford. As he walked down the street, he was also pleased to note that his collar seemed to have loosened considerably in the past few minutes.

Unfortunately, he had forgotten another maxim that every good military man should know. Namely, that to the strongest belongs the victory. A mere officer of His Majesty's Light Horse Guards was no match for a tiny, but determined, Dresden doll.

Dulcie had been employing her own strategy when he arrived. As soon as he left, she went back to it.

Having used umpteen excuses to keep her maid busy and therefore unavailable to aid in Lady Redcliffe's packing, Dulcie marched into a bedroom turned topsy-turvy with traveling accouterments.

Eyeing the two already overflowing portmanteaus and the welter that remained strewn across the bed, she was delighted to note her friend was making an absolute hash of the task.

Alexandra would have been hard put to disagree with her. How on earth, she wondered, could her own maid have packed so much into such little space? The dresses Alexandra crammed in seemed to pop out of their own accord the instant she turned her back. Still, she refused to give up. With a dubious glance at Dulcie, she tackled another frock, but the flounce on the skirt simply would not cooperate. No matter which way she crammed and poked, the ruffly fabric persisted in escaping the case.

Vexed to the verge of tears, she finally balled up her fist and planted the flounce a resounding facer. This achieved her nothing, of course, except the realization of how stupid she must look doing battle with a piece of muslin. Shaking her head, she glanced up with a woeful smile. "I'm afraid I'm not very good at this."

"You certainly aren't. Here, let me help."

Before Alexandra could stop her, Dulcie dumped the contents of both portmanteaus on the bed. "The only thing to do," she said brightly, "is start all over."

"And very, very slowly, I see," Alexandra snapped as she watched the girl begin to fold a dress, refold it, then, declaring she must have done something wrong, shake it out, and start afresh. "You vexatious little imp, I know exactly what you are doing, but it won't work, I assure you. Tomorrow, packed or not, I am leaving. And don't think to dissuade Chives from booking my seat on the morning's mail coach either. I have already asked him to procure a ticket. If he fails, I shall do it myself!"

"Fiddlesticks! You haven't the slightest idea where the coach station is."

"I'll find it."

"No doubt, after getting yourself lost several times." Laying aside any pretense of folding clothes, Dulcie plopped herself down on the bed and watched as Alexandra resumed her attempts at packing. "Need I remind you that this trip is entirely unnecessary?"

"I think not," Alexandra muttered heavily. "You have been reminding me for the past three hours. Don't you suppose you might give it a rest?"

"Only if you'll stop that silly packing. I declare, you're making such a shambles, it is getting on my nerves."

"Fair enough," gritted Alexandra, viciously poking a fringed Norwich shawl into the nearest portmanteau, "because you, my dear girl, are beginning to get on mine."

They might well have been close to dagger's point, had not Dulcie's ever-present giggle chosen that moment to erupt. "I am not. The only one who's making you nervy is you."

It was a perceptive thrust. Long after the two had hugged and made up and Dulcie had been persuaded to leave her friend "time to think for a few minutes," her words rang through Alexandra's mind.

True, she thought, pushing aside a tangle of clothes and sitting down on the spot Dulcie had so recently vacated. It was herself she didn't trust. And why should she?

Wedded thrice, and not one of them a marriage — not in the real sense of the word. Any sensible woman would have learned her lesson by now, but, oh, no, *she had* had to fall cup-over-teakettle for a man she had known less than three days. Worse, she had no idea whether he truly cared for her or not.

She glanced across the room, saw her own miserable reflection in the glass, and promptly stood up. "Alexandra Redcliffe, you are a fool. Go home!"

The portmanteaus were almost packed, their contents a sorry sight indeed. A flounce draggled out here, a fringe there, but at least they were in. Alexandra was just tackling the large hatbox when Chives announced himself at her door.

"Come in," sighed Alexandra, by now convinced that all lady's maids were magicians on the sly. Five assorted hats had arrived in that box, nested in silk wrappings, with nary a feather or ribbon in less than perfect shape. She couldn't seem to fit in *two* without crumpling them beyond recognition.

She turned around. "Chives, are all the maids still busy?"

"I believe so, milady. Miss Dulcie has them polishing silver for the rout party. May I be of some assistance?"

"Only if you can conjure four hats into the size of peas. "No, I am merely jesting," she quickly added, seeing the affronted look on the man's face. Apparently butlers did not consider conjuring as part of their duties.

She gestured toward the tray he was carrying. "Is that letter perhaps for me?"

"Milady." He presented it to her. "I also have some rather unfortunate news, I am afraid. The inside seats for tomorrow's coach seem to be booked full. Would you care for one on the outside?"

Outside? Clinging for dear life to one of those narrow wooden seats atop the coach? Battered by the wind and begrimed by every cloud of dust from the road? "No, I would not," Alexandra declared, "but I shall do it anyway. If you will, procure me an outside seat."

The butler was appalled. So, for that matter, was Alexandra. Yet she was determined. It was, she vowed as she ripped open the letter, going to take more than a hail of wind and dust to stop her.

All it took was a total of three heavily scrawled lines and signature:

> Having ascertained your hiding place, I shall arrive in
> Bath this week. I trust, madam, you will employ no
> more ruses to thwart me.
>
> Maj. Brandon D. Clive

Dulcie was elated. Having just sent Chives off with the last of the invitations, she was only too content to sit back and murmur the most insincere sympathies as Alexandra stormed about the library.

Careful to keep a smile off her face, Dulcie agreed with her friend's every condemnation. Yes, Major Clive simply had to be the vilest man alive. A complete out-and-outer. A positive rake-shame.

No, of course, no gentleman would pen such a letter. How could anyone accuse dear Lexie of trickery? And thwarting?

Incredible! Even more incredible, how could anyone manage to be so insulting in just three lines?

No, no, she was not making light of the situation. No, indeed. Dear Lexie had every right to be outraged. There was no doubt about it. The man was an absolute rapscallion.

And a most convenient one at that, Dulcie added to herself.

Fingering the note her furious companion had thrust upon her just a few minutes earlier, Dulcie was quite willing to give the devil his due. The major was an awful person, of that there was no question, but he did have an excellent sense of timing. Unwittingly, she thought, he had accomplished with a few words what she had been unable to achieve with hours of pestering.

Dear Lexie would be staying in Bath. She and Daniel wouldn't need Peyton Clive's intervention after all.

In fact, according to Dulcie's lights, it would simply be too perfect. The major would arrive — being of course even more despicable in person. Dear Lexie would take one glimpse at him and fly into Mr. Peyton Clive's arms. The annulment papers would be signed, Lexie would accept Mr. Clive's proposal, and they would live happily ever after.

Dulcie Winford did love happy endings — especially when she had engineered them herself.

Alexandra, still whirling about the room in extreme dudgeon, happened to glance at the girl's face. She ground to a halt. "Dulcie Letitia Winford, don't you dare grin at me!"

"I'm not," Dulcie promptly fibbed. "It must have been a stomach ache! From nuncheon, no doubt. The peas were atrociously undercooked, didn't you notice?"

"No!" snapped Alexandra. "At the moment, I've more on my mind than an indigestible dish — the rotter!" — Dulcie took this to mean Major Clive and not the peas — "And so should you! After all, if it had not been for you and your father, I'd have never encountered this — this . . ."

She snatched up the letter and shook it at the girl, "this lout!"

173

Thus chastised, Dulcie put on a suitably mournful face. Unfortunately, it kept slipping. The only solution, she decided, was to think terrible thoughts.

But the most horrible thought that came to mind was the possibility of her own marriage to Maj. Brandon Clive. And Dulcie considered that no possibility at all. The major felt he had been equally hoaxed by herself and Papa; he had said as much in one of his previous letters. Once those annulment papers were filed, Dulcie had no doubt of the outcome. Major Clive would hie himself off faster than a dry leaf in a windstorm.

Poor Papa, she thought. He could fuss and fume all he liked, but her once-prospective bridegroom was a lost cause. He would want no part of the Winfords now.

Declaring to herself that things had a lovely way of turning out in the end, she serenely ventured that same opinion to Alexandra.

"For the *best*? Oh, don't they just?" gritted Alexandra. Running out of epithets and energy, she sank into a chair beside the escritoire. As she did, a square of paper fell from her pocket. It was the envelope that had housed Major Clive's note. Alexandra had not meant to show it to Dulcie.

But now, after the girl's smug platitude, she could no longer resist. She picked up the envelope. "Kismet, my dear. I wonder if you shall love the way this turns out."

She flipped it over and laid it on the writing desk. On the back, obviously as an afterthought, were two more heavily scrawled lines:

I trust Miss Winford has kept the ring I sent. We may be needing it after all.

With somewhat grim satisfaction, Alexandra sat back and watched as her friend stormed about the library in absolute panic.

Vowing that nothing, neither fire nor flood nor unnatural

acts of God, would ever make her wed Maj. Brandon Clive, Dulcie ran upstairs and flung herself on her bed.

Alexandra, feeling dreadfully repentant, ran after her and only made things worse by repeating the girl's own platitude. But attempting to reason with her brought not the slightest response.

Finally Alexandra's practical nature asserted itself. "The first thing we must do," she said, "is start acting sensibly. Both of us. It is not the end of the world, you know. When Major Clive comes, no matter what he wants, I'll stand by you. And if he—well, if he really does have marriage in mind, he can't very well toss you over his shoulder and carry you away. It simply isn't done!"

She reached for Dulcie's arm. "Come along now. We'll think of something, I'm sure. Or more likely you will," she added with a smile. "You're ever full of clever little plans."

"I am, aren't I?" Dulcie said as if just realizing a marvelous fact. "Why, of course I am. And it's perfectly simple. I don't know why I didn't think of this before."

She seemed to go from panic to giggle with no effort. "I shall practice being utterly horrid. By the time Major Clive arrives, I shall be so good at it, he shan't *want* to marry me. Of course! Once he sees what a shrewish wife I should make, he'll wash his hands of me for ever and ever. Papa will never suspect a thing. He already knows from the letters that Major Clive is not particularly fond of us. He'll never know that dreadful man almost changed his mind!"

As far as Alexandra was concerned, the odious Major Clive deserved every trick imaginable, but what about Dulcie's father? Was he, in fact, as easily manipulated as his daughter seemed to think? Alexandra was beginning to feel a bit sorry for him until she remembered he had very nearly pushed Dulcie into an unwanted marriage.

She decided to let Mr. Winford fend for himself. As long as men stomped through, disregarding all others' feelings in their path, women had the right to side-step. It was the way of the times.

Alexandra offered no objections as Dulcie set herself to

exploring any number of "*horrid*" possibilities.

They were still plotting when a mighty thud-thud-thud of the front door knocker resounded through the house.

Dulcie gulped in mid-sentence, and the china-blue eyes opened to enormous proportions. "It's him! Oh, Lexie, not this soon! I'm not ready! I haven't practiced!"

Alexandra wasn't ready either. If it were only for herself, she would have marched straight down, snatched the annulment papers from his hand, signed them, then slammed the door in his face!

But there was Dulcie to consider. The idea of slamming the door still appealed to Alexandra, but she recognized it as a temporary solution at best. Maj. Brandon Clive would have to be dissuaded permanently.

Squaring her shoulders, she waited for the much gentler knock on the bedroom door.

Dulcie snatched it open, and Chives stepped into the room, announcing a visitor for her.

"We know!" cried Dulcie. "That knock sounded like the devil himself! He must be terribly angry, isn't he?"

The butler delicately cleared his throat. "The gentleman does seem considerably agitated, I believe."

In complete dismay, Dulcie appealed to Alexandra. "What shall I do?"

"See him," Alexandra said firmly. "He cannot force you into marriage."

"Indeed not!" Dulcie replied, gathering her courage. "Only Papa can do that, and he'll never know."

She turned to Chives. "Tell Major Clive I shall receive him in the library."

Without altering his expression, Chives announced that he had already ensconced the gentleman in that very room. Then, once more clearing his throat, he begged pardon but thought he should perhaps clarify Miss Dulcie's misconception.

"I have no knowledge of a Major Clive," he said gravely. "The gentleman in the library is your father."

Dulcie went rigid for a good sixty seconds.

Then she politely dismissed Chives and flung herself on the bed again.

No amount of cajolery would work this time. Dulcie refused to leave the safety of her room. She declared she was not coming out until Papa left, and that was final! Major Clive, she felt quite sure she could handle. She knew she could manage Papa. But not together! They had no right being in Bath at the same time. It was monstrously unfair.

The suggestion that Major Clive had not yet appeared made no difference to her. He *would*, she cried, and she knew exactly what would happen. He and Papa would join ranks to force her into a hideous marriage from which she most certainly would pine away in despair. As long as she was doomed to pine anyhow, she would just as lief do it in her own room rather than with that awful Major Clive, and Alexandra could tell Papa just that. She was not coming out ever!

Rising, Alexandra went to the window for a deep breath of fresh air. Thence to the mirror to straighten her mussed hair. Then back to the window for several more deep breaths.

Thus somewhat fortified, she turned around and sternly addressed the bed. "Very well, I am leaving. Someone must meet your father, and, if you won't, then I suppose I shall have to. But it's *you* he's expecting, you know. Must I go alone?"

"Yes."

Alexandra threw up her hands in disgust and marched out of the room.

Common sense, however, made her slow down before she reached the stairs. Between Dulcie's panic and Mr. Winford's considerable agitation, someone had better keep a cool head.

She paused to calm herself, then proceeded down the stairs, wondering what had so excited Dulcie's father that he had put aside his hatred of traveling to come all the way to Bath.

Not the annulment papers, she thought. He hadn't been able to find Major Clive for the signing. Perhaps some letter concerning Dulcie's behavior had put him in the hips.

But what letter?

Alexandra halted on the lower step.

Mrs. Cawlwood had threatened to write one, but, as far as Alexandra knew, she had never gotten around to it. Neither had Dulcie until today. And Chives had posted that mere hours ago. Mr. Winford couldn't possibly have received it yet, unless, of course, by some weird chance he had managed to intercept it.

Oh, my, Alexandra thought as she continued on into the lower hall. If Papa Winford had intercepted that letter, no wonder he was in the hips.

With vague notions of the unknown Reginald Snavely running through her mind, she threw open the library door and walked in.

She took another deep breath.

"Why, Mr. Winford, what a pleasant surprise! Have you come to taste the famous waters of Bath?"

Percy Winford came up from his chair with an impatient nod of greeting. "I have not. We've water in London, if I wanted it, which I don't. Hardly ever touch it myself. Where's Dulcie?"

"In her room," Alexandra answered matter-of-factly. "She refuses to come out."

She took a chair and awaited the normal reaction.

It was not forthcoming. Apparently Dulcie had pulled such shenanigans before.

With no more than a passing "Harrumph," Mr. Winford resumed his seat. "Daresay she'll trundle out fast enough when she gets hungry. Always does. What's she puckered up about this time?"

"Er—I'm not quite certain."

Which was true, Alexandra told herself. With Dulcie's darting little brain, one could never be certain of anything.

"But do tell me," she quickly added and put on a bright smile, "what brings you so far from London? Dulcie tells me how much you dislike traveling. It must have been an exhausting trip. No doubt you're simply perishing for some refreshment. I'll ring for some now, shall I?"

She started to rise, but Mr. Winford waved her back to her seat. "Later. First I've a mind to know what's going on here. And you'll do as well as Dulcie. Better, I expect. She has a way of gabbling on so, it takes a man all day just to catch the drift."

No doubt, thought Alexandra. His so very innocent looking, little Dresden doll had often proved herself a past master of misdirection. Under Mr. Winford's steady eye, Alexandra only regretted she were not half so good at it herself.

All her attempts failed. Tea? Sandwiches? A sip of sherry? Mr. Winford would have none of them. Not even the glass of port she suggested at this ungodly hour. He wanted to know if his daughter was behaving herself.

"Why, naturally." A bit taken aback by the abruptness of the question, Alexandra was nonetheless just as swift in defense of her friend. "Whatever should make you think otherwise?"

"Experience," Mr. Winford said flatly. "That gal of mine is a handful, always has been. Occurred to me I'd best hie myself down here before she gets herself into some new scrape or another. If she ain't already."

He gave Alexandra a suspicious glance. "Which, if she ain't—as you say—I find mighty surprising. Dulcie's forever fancying some young scamp or the next. Nothing serious, you understand. She always forgets about him the next week. Still, she needs a firm rein for all of that. Why I let her cozen me into traipsing off here, I'll never know. Told myself that scrabble-skulled sister-in-law of mine could never keep her in tow. Appears I was right too, wasn't I? She's not even here!"

Alexandra leaped to the second defense. "I believe, sir, that you'll find Mrs. Cawlwood has been a most proper chaperone. She's merely stepped out—for a brief time—to call on friends."

Dulcie's father emitted a scoffing laugh. "Brief? Knowing Tilmatha, she'll likely be gabble-goosing for hours. Small wonder that daughter of mine tends to run on so. Comes by it naturally—from my wife's side of the family, of course."

"Of course," muttered Alexandra. "So you're here to relieve Mrs. Cawlwood of her duties, is that it? You've come to fetch Dulcie home?"

Mr. Winford regarded her with a glance that said his suspicions had just been confirmed: Women were the silliest creatures going.

His patience apparently strained to the limit, he went about putting her straight. If fetching had been his intention, he retorted, why in blazes would he have bothered to come himself? He would have sent his carriage and a couple of servants to do the job. And he himself would still be in London, safe in the comfort of his own study instead of this fussy little room Tilmatha had the nerve to call a library.

Library! he harrumphed, casting a disparaging look round at the ruffled cushions and the lace doilies on every chair arm. Hardly a book, he sneered, let alone a humidor. Blast, the woman hadn't even managed to provide a decent footstool!

Alexandra didn't really suppose, did she, that he would have endured that confounded coach for God-knew-how-many leagues, not to mention having his bad leg jounced and bounced with every jolt, simply for the dunder-headed reason of fetching?

Remembering that self-same—and most well sprung—coach had brought her to Bath, Alexandra doubted he had suffered as unduly as he imagined.

She refrained from saying so. How thoughtless of her, she murmured. Of course Mr. Winford would only endure such hardships for a most sensible reason. Would he mind terribly if she asked what it might happen to be?

With a look that told her she was still being ridiculously silly, Mr. Winford opined he thought the answer should be obvious. He had come to see Major Clive.

"He's here?" gasped Alexandra. "You've seen him?"

Dulcie's father pinched his nose in a dubious attitude. "Not me, but I reckoned you had. Bath's a small town, much as I recall. I was thinking for certain you'd run across him by now."

Alexandra assured him she hadn't. "He did send a note, however. I received it today."

The thought of its contents made her angry all over again. It took some effort to control her voice, but she managed. "He informed me he would be here soon, but he failed to mention a specific date. Perhaps he has not arrived yet."

"Hmmmm," reflected Mr. Winford. "Can't see why not. But he'll hove in directly, I expect. The bank draft was sent two days ago."

Alexandra was confused and said so. Mr. Winford was scarcely surprised. Women never had the slightest head for business.

He favored her with a condescending nod. "Something ladies never understand, I reckon. You just expect your bills to be paid, and fiddle-de-dee where the money comes from. But a man needs a packet of blunt on hand, no matter where he is. And that, of course, is how I tipped to his whereabouts."

"I see," murmured Alexandra. "You traced Major Clive through his bank. Most commendable."

Mr. Winford would have considered it much more commendable if the lady had remained in a state of confusion. He was rather irked by her quick grasp of the situation.

"Er—yes," he mumbled, scratching his chin. "At any rate, I'd had tinker's luck finding the fellow. Blasted disobliging of him, I must say. You'd think he'd have the grace to keep himself available, wouldn't you?"

In Alexandra's opinion, Maj. Brandon Clive was possessed of no grace at all, but, according to reports, he had made himself available at the outset. He had gone to the Winford house and had been refused admittance. Alexandra could not resist asking if such had indeed been the case.

"May have," Mr. Winford blustered. He obviously was not pleased with the reminder. "Doesn't matter; he should have

181

known it was too early by half. A man cannot do business when he's riled. I've always said that. If you want to come to terms with a man, you bide your time until he's simmered down. Well, I've bided. And by now, I figure the major's simmered down. Soon as I find him, we'll sail along as cozy as two boats on a pond."

"How nice," murmured Alexandra, placing her hands in her lap and studying them. To her, it sounded as if they all were headed for the reefs. She looked up to find herself under extremely doubtful scrutiny.

"Why the long face, my girl? Don't you see, I've finally got the major pinpointed. Those annulment papers are as good as signed. I thought that's what you wanted."

"I did—I do."

Alexandra forced a smile and a somewhat disjointed murmur of thanks. Yet she was far from satisfied. One could hardly enjoy one's own freedom at the expense of another's, and she was beginning to feel that was precisely what Dulcie's father had in mind.

She approached the subject cautiously. "I'm sure you are right. No doubt the major will be happy to sign those papers straight away. I imagine I'm no less eager to be rid of this inane marriage than he is. In fact, I imagine he'd be delighted never to cross paths with any Redcliffe—or Winford—again. And we'll be most willing to oblige him, won't we?"

"Here now—just a moment," hedged Mr. Winford. Apparently the chair had grown uncomfortable for him. He proceeded to reposition himself two or three times before he continued.

"No need to cut a chap off short, I always say."

"Oh, but surely he deserves no better, sir. I mean, after that insulting message he sent you. Why, he accused all three of us of trickery and dishonor and—well, all sorts of deceitful things. Bad enough for Dulcie and me, I must say. But also to impugn your honor, sir, a gentleman of the first order? Disgraceful! You can't possibly intend to be sociable with such a man!"

A nice thrust, thought Alexandra. She was stricken to find it hadn't made the slightest dent.

Without so much as a squirm, Mr. Winford opined that she was being a mite too harsh on the major. "Forgive and forget, that's what I always say. We musn't fault a man for a few words spoken in anger. Used to be a bit hot-blooded myself, I'll admit. But it's of no matter, men can take these things in their stride."

Smugly, he reached over to pat her hand. "Don't fret your pretty head over it. This is strictly between gentlemen. You ladies wouldn't understand."

This lady understood perfectly. Quietly moving her hand out of reach, she said, "You're assuming, of course, Major Clive is a gentleman. What if he isn't?"

Balderdash! exploded Mr. Winford. "Come to grips with yourself, gal. You're getting as skitter-witted as Tilmatha. Course he's a proper 'un. Owns a house in Mayfair, don't he? Member of White's, ain't he?"

And he's rich, thought Alexandra. All the credentials for a perfect gent!

"Even so," she replied calmly, "I do wonder if the 'gentleman' will be quite as open-minded as you seem to anticipate. Very likely, he still thinks we've tricked him, you know."

"Ah!" Dulcie's father settled back in his chair, the picture of confidence. "All we need is a bit of clarification. Once I explain the whole of it, the major will see it was merely an innocent mistake — on the part of that dunderheaded vicar! We'll have matters cleared up in a tick. And then, thank God, we can get back to where we started. I'll have Dulcie and Clive hitched before the month is past!"

There, thought Alexandra, it was finally out. She glanced up, willing her thoughts to her friend somewhere above. Don't worry, Dulcie, the best laid schemes can gang awfully a-gley within a month.

Furthermore, she added to herself, Maj. Brandon Clive might prove more recalcitrant than Papa Winford imagined. However, she wasn't banking on it. Judging from his letters, the major could be counted on in only one respect. He would do the most odious thing possible!

Still, Dulcie's father hadn't found him yet. In the meantime, maybe, just maybe, she could persuade Mr. Winford to forget the entire venture.

Not that she had much hope of that. Nevertheless, she felt it imperative to try.

"Sir, I'm sure every father wishes his daughter a suitable match, in time. But Dulcie's quite young yet, you know, and a hasty marriage is not always a happy one, as believe me, I can personally attest. You want your daughter to be happy, don't you?"

Percy Winford looked at her as if she were half-cocked. "What's happiness to do with this? I am speaking about marriage!"

Alexandra refused to be daunted. "So am I, sir. The plain truth is, Dulcie does not wish to wed Maj. Brandon Clive."

"Why in thunderation not? She hasn't even met the man!"

"Exactly," said Alexandra, taking a hardy breath. "Perhaps, since she would be committing herself to a lifetime, she might eventually prefer marrying someone she knows, perhaps even loves."

This was outside of too much for Mr. Winford. Not only was such fiddle-faddle ridiculous, he scolded her, but it was shockingly improper! He would have her know that he and the late Mrs. Winford—God rest her soul—had shared a marriage for a good decade. And not once, in that many years, had either sunk to such depravity as to even mention the word "love."

"Absolute nonsense!" he went on, by now having gathered up a good head of steam. "I must say I'm amazed at you, gal. You're old enough to know better. Next you'll be telling me you picked that first husband of yours—what was his name?"

"Charles Farthington."

"Of course, one of the Bruton Street Farthingtons—rum bunch, the lot of them. I shouldn't doubt, what with all that romantic claptrap cluttering up your mind, you *did* pick him yourself."

Alexandra stiffened. "Then you'd be amiss, sir. He was my

184

father's selection. But I suppose I should thank you for mentioning it."

She did not bother to explain why. Yet as painful as that first marriage had been, she considered this an excellent reminder. She had promised to stand by Dulcie, and stand by her, she would. Her feisty, innocent little friend would not be ramrodded into the same fate!

With a bitter smile, Alexandra glanced up, wondering if the girl were still lying prostrate on her bed. No matter, she thought. Panic would not keep Dulcie down for long. Doubtless, she would soon be at the mirror, practicing resolute faces and planning all sorts of evasions.

She would need every one of them, Alexandra calculated. For Mr. Winford had wasted no time puzzling over that oblique thank you. He had simply ignored it.

Instead, he proceeded on the assumption that Alexandra had brought about her own downfall. She would have never gotten in the aforementioned pickle, he asserted with little sympathy and even less tact, if she had had anything but a fool for a parent.

As Alexandra had had little choice in that selection either, she let him maunder on without bothering to interrupt. The more he went on about filial obedience and a sensible father's duty to decide his offspring's future, the more Alexandra was convinced. No amount of reasoning was going to sway Papa Winford. Even if Major Clive should escape him, he would always be determined to marry his daughter to a husband of his own choosing, not hers.

If Alexandra had harbored any qualms about Dulcie's machinations, they were gone now. The girl was correct. One did not batter one's head against a stone wall when it was much simpler to step around that wall.

Well, so be it, thought Alexandra. Papa Winford, I have a feeling you are in for some very fancy side-stepping.

It occurred to her, her life might have been much different had she arrived at that conclusion some ten years earlier. But she hadn't. She had confronted her own father head on.

"And all that netted me was Charles Farthington."

She hadn't realized she had spoken aloud until Mr. Winford suddenly broke off whatever he was saying and jabbed a stubby forefinger in her direction. "Knew I could depend on you, my girl. You'll tell her, will you?"

"Er—tell who? What?" mumbled Alexandra, who had heeded not a word of what Mr. Winford had considered a very pertinent discourse.

"Tell Dulcie, of course," he said in disgust. "Keep your wits about you, Alexandra. I was just saying you've never told Dulcie the facts about that Farthington business, now have you?"

"No," Alexandra answered truthfully. "I haven't. She's somehow gotten the idea it was all very—sentimental and tragic. I never bothered to say otherwise."

"Then it's high time you did! Show her what happens when you hurdle spade-over-shovel into marriage with a downy-faced boy—and one with his pockets to let at that!"

Mr. Winford shook his head in amazement. "Always knew your father was a loose string. But I'll be blasted if I understand why he ever let you talk him into hitching up with that family. The Farthingtons haven't had two guineas to rub together in twenty years."

"Well, my father didn't know that, and he is not a loose string," Alexandra said coldly, wishing she felt more strongly about coming to his defense. Unhappily, Mr. Winford's opinion had a ring a truth to it that she was hard put to deny.

"He is a—a man of convenience, one might say. He and Charles' father were two great friends at the gaming table."

And two great fools as well, she added to herself. Both had blithely left their fortunes at White's and Brookes's.

"Papa was so used to putting up a bold front, he didn't realize Mr. Farthington was doing the same. When Charles applied to him for my hand, it suited Papa's sense of—convenience. Without a dowry, my prospects were rather dim, and the Farthingtons were a suitable family. Suitable in all ways, so Papa assumed. He thought the whole arrangement quite a capital idea."

Alexandra's lips curved into a grim smile. "Until the day

after the wedding. When he applied to Mr. Farthington for a small loan and found Mr. Farthington was just about to do the same. Papa had no use for any of them after that."

Mr. Winford uttered a gruff snort. "Should have known better in the first place. And so should have you, my girl."

"I suppose," Alexandra murmured. Her mistake, however, had not been in wanting to marry Charles Farthington. She hadn't. Her mistake had been in confronting her father, but she had been only sixteen, and she hadn't realized he was a man dedicated to the path of least resistance. The more she had railed and pleaded and balked, the more he had thought of the peace and quiet he would have when she left the house. He had set the wedding date as soon as possible.

Alexandra mentioned none of this to Mr. Winford, who in any event would have missed the point, had he bothered to listen. Which he probably wouldn't have anyway. He was too busy congratulating himself on his own acumen.

No fool-headed stripling for his own daughter, he thought. Being the excellent, sage father he was, he had picked a man of thirty years. A good age. Solid, sensible, a time of life when a man had left his wild oats behind, but was still in peak condition to handle a rambunctious gal of eighteen.

And in peak financial condition, too, but of course that went without saying. Once he had remembered that long-ago "betrothal," Percy Winford had ascertained the Clive assets before he had even bothered to find out if Maj. Brandon Clive was still breathing.

"My God, I've got to find the man!" he blurted, suddenly remembering his mission. He sprang up from his chair although not so fast as to be unmindful of his bad leg. "You talk to Dulcie, Alexandra. I'll be on my way."

"But—but surely," stammered Alexandra. His abrupt movement had taken her completely by surprise. "Surely, you can't be leaving. You—you haven't seen Dulcie!"

"Later," said Mr. Winford, gingerly testing his knee. Sometimes, when he had been sitting a while, it had the trick of freezing up on him. He had no time for such foibles now. "She's still in her room, you say? Well, she'll come out soon enough, once you set her straight on this romantic bosh. Ha! Stuff and nonsense! You just tell her what it's like to marry some addlepated boy who's got no more sense than to go break his fool neck and leave you a widow after—how long was it?"

"Two weeks."

Mr. Winford snorted. "Some romance. Useless waste of time, I call it. All that expense of a wedding and for what? A fortnight with a goose cap who gets himself killed on some idiotic, drunken dare and leaves you without a farthing to boot. Har!" he barked, slapping his thigh, on the untwingy leg, naturally. "Rare joke that, eh what? A Farthington without a farthing to his name? You just tell my little minx that, and we'll have no more conniptions. Rather, she'll be thanking her old father for using his bean. And don't you think to pretty up the story either, you hear?"

"I shan't," Alexandra said. If she did tell Dulcie—and it occurred to her, she very well might—there was no point in lying. Dulcie might have been too young to take notice, but, as Dulcie's father had so bluntly reminded her, others hadn't forgotten that brief marriage.

Neither had she. Ten years had softened the blow but not the truth. Charles Farthington had been a spoiled, selfish boy who had clumsily pawed his bride for a total of two nights and then had returned to the all-important pleasures of his nineteen-year-old life. The ever-present bottle and evenings of witless pranks with his macaroni friends.

Alexandra followed Dulcie's father into the hall where he gathered up his hat and cane from the marble-topped table near the door. "Your gloves, sir," she said, retrieving the overlooked items and handing them to him. "I imagine Mrs. Cawlwood will be sorry to have missed you."

"No doubt," grumped Mr. Winford. He looked as if he were not in the least sorry to have missed her. "Tell her to prepare a room for me—that scatter-wigged Tilmatha will likely never think of it herself—and make sure she has a decent sherry fetched up. Woman's always had the weirdest notions about tea time. She persists in serving tea!"

"Oh, you'll be back by then, do you think?"

"Can't see why not. Little town like this. How far away can a man get? If the major's here — and I full reckon he is, despite the fact you ain't spotted him — I'll wink him out in a flash."

Mr. Winford started for the door, and, as Chives seemed to be nowhere about, Alexandra hastened to open it herself. "Where, if you don't mind my asking, sir, do you plan to start winking?"

Doffing his hat, Mr. Winford gave it a confident pat. "The Seven Seas, a' course. That's where the bank draft was sent."

With a reminder to "talk some sense into that fiesty gal of mine," he hop-bobbled off down High Street.

Alexandra still stood in the doorway watching long after his stumpy figure had limped past the crest of the hill. Then, at last having made up her mind, she slowly closed the door and went upstairs to Dulcie's bedroom.

Alexandra sat down on the bed and leaned back on the palms of her hands.

After a moment, she said, "He's gone."

There was a silence, then a tremulous "Where?" emanated from the crumpled form beside her.

"To the Seven Seas Inn," Alexandra said. "He seems to think he'll find Major Clive there."

The next series of sounds would have seemed an impossible jumble to the ordinary person, but Alexandra correctly inferred them to mean that Dulcie was as firmly convinced of her father's powers of detection as he was. Especially since, as no doubt luck would have it, all the fates would join in to help.

"Oh, Lexie, what now?" Dulcie wailed plaintively. "He'll find him, I know he will! And he'll bring him back here. Oh, but maybe not. Maybe he won't come. Maybe he'll flatly refuse to marry me now. Maybe he'll — oh, dear lord, what am I saying? Of course he'll come. It's no use, fate's against me. They will come back, arm in arm, all cozy as you please. And they'll gobble me up quick as — quick as a currant bun!"

"Possibly," muttered Alexandra, refusing to be drawn into an argument. She had enough doubts of her own going through her head. Major Clive at the Seven Seas Inn? So was his cousin. Had they met yet? Would Peyton Clive be delighted to know she would soon be free? Or indifferent? Would he propose Friday night as Dulcie had predicted? If he did, would she accept?

Accept?

Good grief, what a ridiculous notion!

She certainly would not accept. Besides, as she sternly reminded herself, this was no time to be mooning over Peyton Clive. She had Dulcie to consider.

Taking a handkerchief from her own pocket, Alexandra handed it to Dulcie. "Your father proposes to be back by teatime. And I daresay, with or without the major he will. Men, I've found, have a way of being quite prompt when there's food or drink in the offing. Now blow your nose. You'll feel better."

The order was obeyed with the desired result. Dulcie even managed a woeful smile. "No doubt you're right. Papa does like his sherry. Was he—did he run terribly roughshod over you?"

"A little," Alexandra conceded. "He insisted I tell you a story. And I've decided I shall, but not for the reasons your father supposes. I want to explain about Charles."

"Oh, but I already know!" the girl exclaimed. Distress momentarily gave way to excitement. "It was all so wonderfully tragic. Your handsome bridegroom, daring to ride neck-or-nothing over the Hyde Park hedges—"

"And broke that neck on the third hedge," Alexandra said flatly. "It was tragic," she added, her voice slowing dying away as the memories intruded. She quickly shook her head to clear the mists of a decade. "But it was neither wonderful nor romantic."

She proceeded to relate the harsh truth of her first marriage with one exception. A few days earlier she would have been hard put to intimate that the physical aspects of that union—any union—were less abhorrent than its daytime realities. Now she knew differently. Charles' insensitive fumblings were relegated to the past where they belonged. Peyton Clive had taught her what the act of love could be. Had been.

With a smile, she remembered the hayloft and the first thought that had come to her after their intimacy. So this is what it is all about, she had marveled.

Dulcie promptly jerked her back to the present. "If your first marriage was all that dreadful, why are you smiling?"

"It was. And I'm not," Alexandra snapped, sharply bringing herself to attention. "I told you about Charles Farthington for only one reason. You must not make the same error I did. You must not let your father push you into a marriage with a man you don't know and don't love!"

Dulcie, taken aback at this sudden vehemence, could only stare at Alexandra wide-eyed.

"Well, of course I don't want to do that," she agreed. "But how are we to stop it?"

Alexandra was honest. "I'm not sure. I haven't gotten that far."

She leaned back on her palms, apparently in a deep study, but that was only for Dulcie's benefit. The fact was, she hadn't a clue. The obvious thought was to escape. But to where? Brighton perhaps? Dulcie had another aunt there.

No, she thought, rejecting the notion as fast as it came to her. The idea of dashing about England with Papa Winford and Major Clive baying at their heels seemed rather unsatisfactory. Moreoever, they would soon run out of aunts.

Not surprisingly, Dulcie's thoughts had been traveling along the same lines. Alexandra heard her mutter "Brighton" and, turning, saw a flash of hope whisk across the girl's face, but it was gone as soon as it had come. Sinking her chin into her fists, Dulcie adopted an expression as glum as Alexandra herself felt at the moment.

"No ideas?"

"None," mumbled Dulcie. "Have you?"

"Not a glimmer," Alexandra admitted. She sighed. "I daresay we'll feel quite silly if we're only building mountains from the proverbial molehills. We could be, you know. We've no certainty the major will cooperate with your father."

She had meant this as a spark of cheer, but Dulcie seemed to have no sparks left. She didn't even bother to raise her head. "He will. Why else would he have mentioned the ring?"

Yes, there was that, Alexandra conceded. The wedding band, sent from Turkey, and that hastily scrawled addenda to the major's last note. "I trust Miss Winford has kept the ring I sent. We may be needing it after all."

Cheeky brute, she thought. She had never seen the item, but she had no doubt it was some garish piece of barbarity ablaze with all sorts of outlandish and uncomfortable stones.

"I only hope you had the foresight to pitch it out with the trash!"

Coming slowly out of her own thoughts, Dulcie cast a vague look at the dresser and a dainty traveling case which lay thereon. "I don't believe so. I rather recall tossing it amongst the pearls Papa gave me on my last birthday — he can be a dear. Sometimes. I know I brought the pearls with me to Bath. Maybe the ring's still with them. Shall I look?"

Alexandra shrugged and, without much interest, Dulcie scooted herself off the bed and walked over to the dresser. With a glance at the mirror and a slightly annoyed, "Why didn't you tell me my hair was mussed?" she opened the jewelry case. Drawing out a small velvet bag, she tipped it over and a pearl necklace slithered out. She tipped it again, and a flash of gold came to rest beside the necklace.

Dulcie turned, holding up the ring to let the sunlight glint against it. "Pity it's not from — from someone else."

Reseating herself on the bed, she placed the ring in her palm and held it out for inspection. "Actually, it's rather pretty, don't you think?"

More than that, Alexandra realized as she bent forward for a closer look. Major Clive's "barbaric" offering was a great disappointment. Not a stone, chunky or otherwise, glittered from the slim circle of gold. Its only ornamentation was a filigree so delicately wrought she had to peer even

192

closer to distinguish the pattern.

How disgusting, she thought, it's exquisite, but she had no intention of saying so.

"Passable," she sniffed. She pushed Dulcie's hand away.

As she did, the ring toppled and fell on the bed between them. Dulcie let it lie. "I suppose," she said, eyeing it with no more interest than before, "that, legally, it's more yours than mine. Do you want it?"

"Absolutely not!" Glancing down at her bare fingers, Alexandra uttered a scoffing laugh. "I already have two wedding bands in my own jewelry case. I certainly don't need another!"

"No?" murmured Dulcie, completely unmoved by this outburst. She, too, looked down at her friend's ringless fingers and thought it little wonder Lexie had put the first ring away. Apparently young Mr. Farthington had been a very sad romp indeed. But why was she not still wearing the second?

Dulcie shrugged. She had asked that question once and had found the reply so vague it had not been worth the listening. She didn't bother to ask again.

If she had, Alexandra wouldn't have answered. Couldn't have—not to the young girl's satisfaction.

The horror of her first marriage was easy to explain. But a marriage of benevolence? How could one possibly explain that?

Oh, the facts were simply enough. Widowed at sixteen, Alexandra had had no choice but to return to her father's house. He hadn't objected. However, as his financial assets were as nonexistent as her own, they had been quite up against the wall and most likely would have fallen through it, had not her father met his Scottish lady.

She had had a modest fortune and had known how to hold onto it. He had had a house mortgaged to the rafters and had never managed to save a pence. Alexandra had thought it a very practical arrangement.

She had been the only snag. Her new Scottish stepmother had made it clear she wanted to take her bridgegroom home to Glasgow. She had also made it clear those plans did not include a nearly grown, and already widowed, stepdaughter.

Then a fairy godfather had appeared. Or so it had seemed to Alexandra at the time. Lord Redcliffe had emerged from out of nowhere — actually, it was from only a few doors down the street in Mayfair — and had offered her his name and his protection.

So, at seventeen, Alexandra had put away her first wedding ring and accepted a second.

She had known Lord Redcliffe was fond of her, no, even loved her in his way, but he had been so much older and already ill. He had offered mainly out of kindness, she had known that too and had accepted gratefully.

For six years, she had remained a faithful companion to this gentle man.

But never a wife.

After the funeral, she had wrapped the ring carefully and tucked it into her jewelry case as one might stow away a keepsake from a cherished relative.

Scooping up the filigreed ring, Alexandra firmly pressed it into Dulcie's hand. "Put that somewhere — anywhere — out of sight. The only way that ring is going on your finger is over my dead body!

"Although," she added with a crooked smile, "I do hope we can came up with a rather less painful alternative."

What they come up with — or, to be more factual, what came up to them — was Papa Winford.

Deep in discussion over a number of half-baked ideas, each of which seemed no more fruitful than the last, both of them started at the sudden rap on the door.

Dulcie's "come in" was automatic, and her father was in the room before she was aware of it.

As Mr. Winford hop-bobbled toward them, both sat on the edge of the bed as silently as two schoolgirls waiting to be disciplined.

Pulling up a nearby chair, he eased himself into it, then

eaned back to regard them with a piercing stare. "I've news for you, my girls. Alexandra first."

"Sir?" Alexandra, feeling all the more like a naughty student, half-expected him to draw a ruler from his pocket and rap her on the knuckles.

Instead, he withdrew a thick envelope and flicked it into her lap. "A present, my dear. Find yourself a pen and sign em."

Alexandra looked down at the bulky envelope. The front was blank, save for the word "Clive" neatly inscribed in one corner, but there was little doubt as to what it contained. "The annulment papers," she said dully.

"Nothing less! Knew you'd be pleased as punch," said Mr. Winford, trying to instill some enthusiasm. What was amiss with the silly chit anyway?

Scratching his head, he decided it could only be one of two things. Either the gal had been staying with Tilmatha so long she had misplaced her own senses, or she had reckoned on keeping Major Clive for herself.

Well, he concluded, they would just see about that. If the gal didn't soon straighten her thinking cap, he would do it for her!

"Come along, girl. There's no need to dally. You'll find the major's signature already there, nice and plain as a body could ask. All we need is yours. Open her up now, and let's get on about it!"

With a glance at Dulcie, who neither returned the glance nor uttered a sound, Alexandra did as commanded. There was no mistaking Maj. Brandon Clive's imprint on the documents. It was the same heavy scrawl with which he had penned his letters.

Even worse, the documents looked as legal as could be.

Blasted luck, thought Alexandra. Not for her own sake, of course, but for Dulcie's. They needed every delay they could find, but there was none to be found at the moment—not even the lack of a pen. A large plumed quill lay beside an inkwell on a lamp table by the window.

Reluctantly Alexandra took the documents over and appended her signature to them. Some justice in London, she noticed, had witnessed the major's signing. Before she could put down the pen, Mr. Winford was there to witness her own signature.

An instant later he had the papers restuffed into the envelope and safely tucked in his pocket. "There," he said, giving the pocket a final, satisfied little pat. "Nothing to it, eh what? Quick and painless as slipping a rabbit from a snare."

Alexandra looked at Dulcie and doubted the rabbit would have shared that analogy. "Quick, at any rate," she murmured. "I'm rather surprised you found the major so fast."

She was even more surprised when Mr. Winford suddenly jerked back a step.

"Said I would, didn't I?" he grumped and promptly hobbled back across the room to his daughter.

Informing her he had no time to waste chitchatting, he ordered her to stay put—and out of mischief. He would be back in a few days at the most with a special license, and Dulcie could spend the interval finding something to wear for her wedding. Something simple, mind her. He had already pegged a fortune on a splashy wedding—even if it had netted the wrong bride—and he was not about to repeat any such nonsense.

Turning to leave, he commanded his daughter to keep her nose tidy and do absolutely nothing until he returned.

"I want your word on that, gal! You hear me?"

Dulcie heard. Her eyes had grown wider and wider at each word. It was obvious she was incapable of uttering such a promise, much less keeping it.

Throwing an arm around her, Alexandra held her close and, in the confusion, almost failed to notice their visitor was fast heading for the door.

"Mr. Winford! You've only just come to Bath. Surely you're not starting back to London now?"

Dulcie's father came to a reluctant halt. "Why not?" he barked, throwing the words over his shoulder. "You want those papers filed, don't you? Or do you?" he added, suddenly turning around.

"Of course. But it's growing so late—it's nearly teatime. Why, you've not yet had your sherry. And Mrs. Cawlwood? She hasn't returned, I don't believe. Surely you'd like a word with her."

"Not likely!" retorted Mr. Winford. "I'll take a nip of sherry on my way out. And Tilmatha can wait, my horses can't. Got a fresh team waiting outside. No point in frittering away the blunt it took to hire 'em. And no point in frittering away my time either, girl. I've got to be on my way!"

"Very well," said Alexandra, thinking that, even with a sniff of all that Clive money, Mr. Winford was still in a most inexplicable rush. "But please, answer me this before you go. Since you and Major Clive seem to have come to some— some sort of agreement, shall we be expecting him to call?"

"Don't know," mumbled Mr. Winford. He reached for the doorknob.

"Well, where is he now? At the inn?"

"No. Went riding."

And with that cryptic response, Dulcie's father hied himself off to London. He didn't even pause for a sherry.

"Pesky females," he muttered to himself as his coach rumbled through the afternoon on the high road to London. "Forever asking too many damned questions. But not the right ones, thank God!"

Reflecting on this gave Percy Winford a good deal of satisfaction. Before long and with no more than a dozen shouts to his driver to mind the potholes, he settled back, rather pleased with himself. He had outfoxed them all, by Jove!

For the fact was, Mr. Winford had come to no agreement of any sort with Maj. Brandon Clive.

But he would, he assured himself. In the meanwhile, what was the harm in a little evasion? The main thing was to have those papers filed and get himself back to Bath. With the annulment safely tucked in the past and a special license safely tucked in his pocket, Mr. Winford reckoned there would be no holes in the net when he ultimately threw it over the major.

"Fellow's eely, damned if he ain't," Mr. Winford grumbled, protecting his bad knee as the coach hit a particularly rough spot on the road. "But he's not getting away this time!"

That settled, Mr. Winford thumped on the roof of the coach and bellowed at his driver to "spring 'em along!" Twingy knee or not, he was in a race with time. Not to mention a small item like the truth. For he still hadn't met Brandon Clive.

Percy Winford had arrived at the Seven Seas Inn to find no one about, save for an angry proprietor and a no-less-unhappy egg merchant, who had claimed it was hardly his fault the inn's floor had been so heavily waxed he had fallen and smashed more than six-dozen, perfectly good, fresh eggs. No more had it been his fault that he had had to use the front entrance instead of the service door because no one had been there to admit him.

Whereupon the proprietor was only too quick to inform the merchant that he would have been admitted correctly had he arrived in the morning as a proper tradesman would, instead of having blamed his tardiness on slow-laying chickens, and just look at the mess he had made!

Between upbraiding the bespattered egg man and ordering about a scullery maid, who had been on hands and knees with a cloth but who had only seemed to be making things worse, the innkeeper had been understandably in no mood for conversation.

Furthermore, having launched into a profuse apology only to discover that this Mr. Winford, by name, had not been seeking quarters but merely gratis information, the innkeeper had lost interest in him rapidly.

Yes, he had replied, throwing up his hands as the huge puddle of goo seemed to grow ever wider, there was a gentleman by the name of Clive in residence. Been there for some time. No, the gentleman was not in at present. Yes, he

vas quite certain. Hadn't he himself procured a horse from
he rental stables for this particular guest? The gentleman
aad gone riding. No, he did not know which path the
gentleman had taken nor how long the gentleman would be
gone.

Making it quite clear he had answered enough questions
n the face of adversity, the innkeeper had redirected his
attention to the hapless scullery maid, telling her in no
uncertain terms to stop behaving as if she were stirring
omelets and clean up the bloody floor!

His directions to the egg merchant had been even more
succinct. The man, having complained of a bruised elbow
due to sudden impact with the Seven Seas overwaxed floors,
had been told he would soon find his elbow in a most
inconvenient orifice if he did not exit immediately.

The egg man had at once taken the cue and had made
himself scarce. Unfortunately, the inn's valet had seemed to
have no such sense of timing. He had picked that exact
moment to wander in, saying a gentleman guest by the name
of Clive had directed a packet to be put in the safe. (What he
hadn't said was that the mission had slipped his mind; he had
been carrying it around in his own pocket for some while.)
With a broad flourish and a look of pitying smugness at the
scullery maid, he had proffered the envelope to the proprie-
or to be put in safekeeping.

With an equally broad flourish, his employer had told him
o lay it on the desk for the time being and to pick up a cloth.

Mr. Winford, of course, had missed none of this exchange. While the others had been watching the shocked
valet forfeit dignity in pursuit of an elusive egg yolk, Dulcie's
father had sidled over to the desk for a peek.

A moment later, having not only ascertained that this
copy of the annulment papers were as legal and tidy as the
one he carried but also contained a vital element his copy
lacked—namely, the major's signature—Mr. Winford had
come to a rapid decision.

What need was there for the major to go rushing about,
seeking Alexandra's signature, and hailing that long way

back to London for the filing? Mr. Winford would do it for him. After all, the man was near family. Dulcie's father had considered it only his duty to pay his future son-in-law a favor.

Having quickly diverted all eyes to a far corner in which three eggs lay cracked, but untrammeled, in oozing repose, he had pocketed the papers. Then having bid the Seven Seas Inn a genial good-bye, he had hop-hobbled out the door.

Now, as he jounced along toward London, Mr. Winford congratulated himself once more. What a stroke of luck! Moreover, if the major soon discovered the papers were missing, which Mr. Winford had no doubt he would, he would be forced to send a post to London for a new set, and that would take time.

Time enough for a wily old man to return and spring the trap!

Alone inside his coach, Mr. Winford slapped his good knee in triumph. With a gruff chuckle, he threw out an imaginary net and began to haul it in.

Chapter 7

Had Alexandra the slightest suspicion of such a hoax, she would have doubtless been tempted to crack a few dozen eggs herself—over Mr. Winford's head.

As it was, the "facts" seemed dreadfully clear. Major Clive had met with Dulcie's father and not only was still willing to marry the girl but had apparently approved the acquisition of a special license to hasten that marriage.

Upon Mr. Winford's exit, Alexandra had automatically risen to close the door he had left ajar. As she turned around, her only thought was, Dear lord, where do we go from here?

If she had no idea, someone else had a very definite notion. No sooner had the sound of the departing coach reached their ears, than Dulcie had sprung off the bed in an absolute flurry.

Ringing for her maid and calling for Chives to bring her luggage, Dulcie began pulling out drawers and dumping their contents on the bed. Alexandra's surprised protests slowed her not a bit. Scuddling to the armoire, she proceeded to toss out one dress after another with the announcement that she was not waiting around to be trapped like some helpless animal. She was leaving, and, if Lexie wished to go with her, she had better get her own things packed immediately.

Alexandra ducked as a frothy sprigged muslin sailed through the air and landed on the bed. "Dulcie, stop behaving like a maniac! Where do you think you're going? Home to London? How could that possibly help?"

"It won't!" Dulcie cried, tossing a spangled sarcenet gown after the muslin. "I am running away to—to Brighton!"

The maid arrived with Chives right behind. "Bring my portmanteaus! Bring my trunk! Bring everything! Lady Redcliffe's too!"

She suddenly twirled around. "Oh, Lexie, you will come with me, won't you? We've got to go!"

"How?"

That stopped the girl, but only for a second. "I'll—I'll have Chives hire a coach, that's it! Even in this town, there must be one for hire somewhere. Chives!"

The butler had already hustled off in search of the luggage. Dulcie started to run after him, then abruptly changed her mind, and darted back into the room to fetch her reticule.

She dumped the contents on the chest, woefully lamenting what she had just suspected. "Drat, I have spent most of my pin money, and I forgot to ask Papa for more. Perhaps Aunt Tilmatha could—or you!" she added, suddenly brightening. "You have scads of money. Surely you've enough with you to hire a coach, haven't you?"

"I have," Alexandra muttered. Now that the surprise was over, she was beginning to think a bit more clearly. Pulling up a chair, she seated herself and regarded Dulcie with a quelling stare. "However, I am not leaving Bath. Neither are you."

Ignoring the girl's startled wail, she told Dulcie to cease blathering, as well as tossing clothes about, and start listening to reason. Dashing about England would only delay the problem, not solve it. If there was no changing Mr. Winford's mind, which unhappily seemed to be the case, they would simply have to attack from the opposite angle.

"Major Clive?" said Dulcie. Although still plainly dubious, she had at least stopped dumping frocks on the bed. Now, carelessly pushing aside a mound of silks and muslins, she plopped herself down on the edge of the coverlet. "We change *his* mind, I suppose?"

"We do. He is here in Bath, and your father isn't. A rather

nice arrangement when you pause to think of it. All we have to do is convince him that you're such a horrid little minx, you'll never make a fit wife for anyone."

Dulcie glanced away, and a wounded expression lengthened the Dresden doll face. "Not for *anyone*? Ever?"

She looked so pathetic, Alexandra could not resist a smile. "Oh, darling, of course you'll be an adorable wife to some man — all in good time. We simply want the major to think otherwise. Don't you remember? It was your idea in the first place."

"Yes," Dulcie muttered, looking even more forlorn as she sank her chin into her fists. "Only that was before I actually thought I'd have to face him. I still think I'd rather go to Brighton."

"Well, we're not!" said Alexandra with a great deal more confidence than she was feeling. What if the man were so monstrous, he would never even notice Dulcie herself was being disagreeable?

The thought was so ruinous, she promptly shoved it from her mind. "Dulcie, he is only a man. If the two of us cannot run circles around him, we are not worthy of the name 'woman.' We shall stand our ground right here in Bath. In fact — right here in this house. I doubt Mrs. Cawlwood will object to one more guest tomorrow night."

"Invite him to the party? Oh, Lexie, you couldn't!"

"I can, and I will. Major Clive is going to receive a personally conveyed invitation within a very few minutes. From me."

This double shock had its effect. Dulcie immediately jumped to her feet in protest. "You're not going to that inn? You can't! A lady, alone, walking —"

"The public streets?" Alexandra calmly interrupted. "Outrageous in London perhaps, but perfectly acceptable in Bath, I should think. If anyone should ask, you may tell them I've gone to — oh, to the Circulating Library, if you think that would sound more genteel."

She rose. "Mrs. Cawlwood left word saying she'd be back before teatime, and so should I, I would imagine. But if not,

I daresay you can contrive to entertain any visitors until we return. I expect there will be a few, don't you think? Perhaps Lieutenant Symington amongst them?"

Having deliberately introduced this last name and gratified with the result it inspired, Alexandra went to her own room to change into a walking ensemble.

Having just as deliberately dressed her best, to inspire her own confidence, Alexandra arrived at the Seven Seas Inn in a merino wool suit of deepest cherry red with a jet-trimmed chapeau cocked fetchingly over one ear. A fringe of matching jet on her cherry-hued parasol danced merrily with each step she took.

But, alas, upon closing that parasol and walking into the reception hall of the inn, Alexandra discovered neither her attire nor her hard-won air of confidence was to be admired by anyone. The reception area was empty.

Taking a deep breath, she strode forward and nearly fell as she skidded on the freshly waxed floor.

A good deal more cautiously, she edged herself toward the innkeeper's desk. A bell sat atop it. Just as she reached out to give it a firm clap, an amused voice spoke out behind her.

The egg man and his injured elbow would have had a sympathetic ally in Alexandra. Startled, she spun around and her heel made contact with a particularly treacherous blob of wax.

The red parasol went skittering in one direction, Alexandra in another. The next thing she knew she was sitting flat on the floor gazing at a pair of cuffed riding boots.

She looked up. "Peyton! I mean, Mr. Clive. How—how nice to see you."

Brandon grinned as he bent down. "I must say it's flattering to have a beautiful woman at my feet, but this is hardly the place, don't you think?"

He suddenly sobered as he lifted her to a standing position. "Alexandra," he murmured, not taking his hands from her waist. "You are beautiful."

He bent forward, his lips seeking hers, and Alexandra found herself more than a little disappointed when he abruptly pulled back. "Good lord, woman, you intrigue me so I can't even think straight. Are you hurt?"

"What?" Alexandra said dreamily. Collecting herself, she thrust herself out of his grasp and stepped back hard.

Too hard.

Strong hands caught her before she fell but not before the slender heel of her slipper skidded sideways. A flash of pain shot through her ankle.

Brandon, seeing that pain reflected in her face, did not bother to ask a second time. He scooped her up in his arms.

"Damned landlord," he muttered angrily. "Fool seems to think this floor needs polishing every time a footprint falls on it. Is it your ankle?" he asked.

Alexandra nodded, instinctively tightening her arms around his neck although the pain seemed to be lessening already. She wondered why she hesitated to declare that fact, then realized it was because she liked it just fine where she was.

The truth made her cheeks burn. "It's nothing," she babbled hastily. "Only a slight twist, I'm sure. You—you may put me down now."

Brandon, who was by no means abhorrent of the situation himself, ignored this last request. "May be worse than you think. However, I've some liniment in my satchel upstairs that never fails. Cures men and"—horses, he had started to say. He thought better of it—"and ladies too, in a trice," he amended. "I'll have to fetch it of course. In the meanwhile, I could set you down here, I suppose."

He glanced at a nearby chair, then pursed his lips as if in deep concentration. "No," he added, shaking his head. "It won't do. I don't imagine you'd care to remove your stockings in public."

"My *stockings*?

Brandon laughed. "Just one, but you will have to remove it. For the liniment, you see."

"Now, really!" Alexandra protested, looking wildly

205

around. What if someone came in? "I—I don't wish any liniment. Please, put me down!"

"Can't. Worse thing for a sprain is to put weight on it. Now, let's see." He glanced toward the stairs. "My room's just at the top there, first door on the right. Quite handy as you can see. You could be up and back in less than a trice, and it does provide a certain amount of privacy. I wonder—under the circumstances of course—if we shouldn't find that more appropriate?"

Alexandra could only stare at him. Appropriate? Allowing herself to be carried into a man's bedroom? In a public inn? The suggestion was scandalous. Alexandra could hardly believe her ears.

An instant later, she believed them not at all. "Very well—under the circumstances," she heard herself saying.

It was the last thing she said for some while. Never had a man's nearness affected her like this. Somewhere between fantasy and reality, the thought drifted through her mind that she might well be content to dwell in Peyton Clive's arms forever.

In fact, she found it rather disappointing that the trip up the stairs was so short. Almost before she knew it, they were in the room and she felt herself being gently lowered into a deep, comfortable armchair in the corner.

Brandon stepped back with reluctance, his eyes lingering on Alexandra's face. Then abruptly he strode over to the armoire against the far wall.

Damn, he thought, almost forgot the liniment!

Opening the armoire, he pulled out a satchel and delved into it. "Your stocking if you please," he said without turning around.

Alexandra, watching the play of muscles across his broad shoulders, made not the slightest demurral. Obediently, she removed her right shoe and, reaching beneath her skirts, peeled off the gauzy silk stocking.

No more did she object when he returned, holding a large brown bottle in his hand. Pouring a small amount into the cup of his palm, he went down on one knee before her.

206

"Milady?"

Alexandra held out her right foot.

She shivered as the cold liquid touched her skin. Then as his hands began gently massaging her ankle, there was only warmth. A warmth that seemed to pervade her entire body.

"Better?" Brandon murmured huskily.

Alexandra nodded. Instinctively she bent forward, and, when their lips touched, she could not have said. She only knew that now she shivered, and it was not from cold, as he kissed her deeply, his hands reaching up to clasp her face to his as if he wished never to let her go.

She scarcely felt the movement when, once more, he picked her up in his arms and carried her to the bed.

Laying her softly on it, Brandon stepped back to remove his coat. For a moment, he hesitated. Should he be the gentleman and send her away?

Hell, no, he groaned to himself. The lady was not only willing, she was his wife. And he wanted her. Wanted her as no other woman he had ever known. At that moment he could not have sent Alexandra away, had even the hounds of Satan been after him.

She felt his strong hands move along her body, tossing away the frivolous hat, undoing the buttons with impatient fingers until they lay together, the smoothness of her creamy skin molded against the firmness of his own.

Brandon's lips captured hers in a hard, demanding kiss, bruising her mouth. Yet she clung to him all the tighter. Her hair, fanned out in a riotous array, made a pillow for his head as he whispered murmurs of desire into her ear.

It's not love, she thought. He never mentions love. But she didn't care. She wanted this, wanted it from the moment she had seen him, and had known it would happen when she agreed to be carried up those stairs. Alexandra did not lie to herself. She did not struggle against her own emotions.

She gave herself to him totally, matching kiss for kiss, stroking his body until he moaned with the agony of passion. He took her again and again, first urgently, then tenderly, drawing her passion to heights no less than his own.

At last, they lay quietly, breathing deeply. With Alexandra's head against his chest, Brandon lightly fingered a chestnut curl and smiled. "I set out to remedy you, madam, but I do believe 'tis you who've remedied me. And most delightfully, I must say."

Alexandra snuggled closer to him. "Happy to be of service, sir, but I fear the doctor must leave you now. It must be growing late."

Stifling a yawn, she wrapped a blanket about her and swung her feet over the side of the bed.

She let out a gasp of pain as her heel hit the floor.

"Your ankle?" asked a surprised Brandon. Pulling her back onto the bed, he gingerly tested her right ankle. "I don't understand it. My liniment never fails."

Alexandra looked down a little sheepishly. "That leg feels fine. I—I'm afraid it must have been the left ankle I twisted."

Brandon threw back his head and laughed. "An understandable mix-up. Come along, I'll have it matching the other one in—"

"In a trice?"

"Exactly."

Still laughing at Alexandra's embarrassment, Brandon applied a second treatment. And as even the lady had to admit, his confidence in the liniment was justified. By the time they were both dressed, Alexandra found she could walk without a trace of pain.

She started toward the door, then stopped, suddenly realizing it would be hardly discreet to traipse down the stairs in full view of any Seven Seas lodgers. "Would—would you mind taking a look?"

"Of course," said Brandon, immediately comprehending. "As a matter of fact, there's a back stairs. Perhaps you'd rather go that way."

"I believe I would."

Nodding, Brandon opened the door and peered both ways. "Hall's clear. I'll escort you home. For a fee," he added with a grin.

As he bent toward her, his lips seeking hers, Alexandra

suddenly uttered a gasp. "Major Clive!"

Brandon's head jerked backward. "How did you—now listen, I can explain—"

But Alexandra had no time for his sputterings, didn't even hear them. She grabbed his arm. "Oh, for goodness' sake, how could I have forgotten! That's why I came—to find him. He's here, at the inn! Have you seen him?"

"Who?" muttered a very wary Brandon. A glimmer of understanding was just beginning to dawn on him.

"Major Clive, of course!" Out of the corner of her eye, Alexandra noticed the rumpled bed and her cheeks flushed almost as red as her suit. How mortifying, she thought. Dulcie was depending on her, but the minute a man's arms had folded about her, she had let that mission fly right out of her head.

"Your cousin!" she blurted, lowering her head to cover the shame of her own folly. "That—that—oh, never mind, I shan't go into that. He is your relation. Nevertheless, I do have something to say to him, and I fully intend to see him today!"

At this, she looked up to find a rather strange expression on her lover's face. "Why, Peyton, didn't you know he'd arrived?"

Brandon took care in his answer. "The only Clive I know of at this inn is myself. If I may ask, what leads you to suspect otherwise?"

"Dulcie's father," Alexandra replied. "He met with the major here. Today."

"Oh, did he?" said Brandon, thoughtfully rubbing his chin.

"Indeed! Not only that, it seems they've agreed the major is still to marry Dulcie. Within the month, so her father says. He's gone back to London to purchase a special license."

That he had also gone back to file the annulment, Alexandra did not mention. She was a little afraid that, if Peyton realized she would be free within a few days, he might propose. And even more afraid he might not.

209

Oh, really! thought Alexandra, her imaginings were getting more impossible each day.

Hearing Brandon mutter something about the validity of that license, she quickly snapped back to attention. "Valid? Oh, Dulcie's father will see to that, you can depend on it. But it shan't work, no matter how determined he is. Dulcie doesn't want to marry the major, she never did. One shouldn't have to marry a man one doesn't love. And Dulcie shan't!" Alexandra hurriedly went on. "Maj. Brandon Clive will soon find he cannot ride roughshod over her, or me either! That's why I've come, to give him a personal invitation to the party. We mean to give him a taste of his own medicine!"

With a stubborn thrust of her chin, she declared her intention of leaving, only to have Brandon catch her by the arm. "Party?" he said. "You don't perchance mean Mrs. Cawlwood's little get-together tomorrow night, do you? Seems I received a bid to that effect myself."

Suddenly there was a throb in Alexandra's voice. "You—you'll be there?"

The assurance that he would be was promptly followed by a blunt query. Why, since she and Miss Winford seemed to have so little regard for the major, should they bother to issue him a bid?

At the explanation, he laughed out loud. "The little imp. What do you suppose she'll do?"

"I'm not certain," said Alexandra, moved to return that amusement with a smile of her own. "But she means to treat him in an outrageously shabby fashion, you can be sure. With any luck he'll be so put off, he'll skitter back to the Continent as if the very devil were after him. Which, come to think of it, is quite likely the case already," she added, then abruptly clapped a hand over her mouth. "Oh, dear, I do keep forgetting that man is related to you. You won't tell him, will you?"

"Not a word to anyone," Brandon soberly vowed.

"Thank you." Relieved that she hadn't destroyed Dulcie's strategy before it began, she felt silent for a moment, plotting her own. Suddenly she looked up. "Peyton, what time is it?"

He drew out a pocket watch and snapped it open. "Just on half past four. I suppose you're expected back at Mrs. Cawlwood's for tea fairly soon, are you not?"

"I suppose," Alexandra vaguely echoed. "But this is more important. I shall simply have to be late, that's all. Yes, of course," she said, abruptly making up her mind. "You may show me the rear stairs, if you will. And I'll come right in again by the front. The major's been out riding, so I understand. No doubt that is why you've missed him so far. Perhaps he's returned by now, and, if he hasn't, he will soon. No Englishman, not even a barbaric Englishman, likes to miss his tea. I shall merely wait for him downstairs until he appears. It's my duty to see that he accepts an invitation to that party. Our plans depend on it, and I shan't leave here until he does."

As she reached for the door handle, Brandon stepped into her path. "I wonder," he said, clearing his throat. "Do you think that wise? That is, a lady waiting alone in a public area of an inn? And what if my, er, 'barbaric' cousin should cut up rough? It might very well prove embarrassing for you. Better, I should think, that I escort you back to Mrs. Cawlwood's, then let me handle this in your stead. If my cousin is in Bath, as you say, I can pin him down later tonight in his chambers. That might be easier for all concerned, wouldn't you agree?"

Alexandra studied his face. "You won't reveal our plans?"

Brandon solemnly put a hand over his heart. "Not a word."

"Well . . ." murmured Alexandra hesitantly. "I suppose you're right. That might be more suitable." She pondered a moment longer, then suddenly brightened. "Of course. And you could see to it that he actually came. You could bring him yourself."

"I shall do my utmost."

This was spoken in such earnestness, or at least so it seemed to Alexandra, that she had no doubt he would succeed. Thus reassured, she waited until her escort had properly hatted himself, then allowed him to lead her quietly down the rear stairs.

Once having made the street, they looked back and then at each other with slightly conspiratorial smiles, confident they had been seen by no one.

The inn's valet, however, having finally been relieved from egg mopping and rewaxing, had been in the servants' quarters on the third floor, changing his garments and reestablishing his tattered dignity with a nip of brandy. He was just descending those same stairs from the top floor when a gentleman, whom he recognized, and a lady, whom he did not, exited from the second floor. All he caught of her was a glimpse of cherry-red suit and the back of a hat a-dance with jet fringe.

Upon entering the lower reception area a short time later and discovering a parasol that very much matched that outfit, he had little doubt to whom it belonged. Reaching beneath the chair under which it had skidded during Alexandra's slide across the room, the valet whisked it out.

After speculating a moment, he decided discretion left only one option. He neatly tucked the cherry-red parasol with the fringe of jet into the armoire in Mr. Clive's room.

Alexandra and Brandon arrived at the Cawlwood house only to find Dulcie and Lieutenant Symington approaching from the opposite direction.

"Daniel and I have been for a stroll," Dulcie murmured. And this, outside of the barest polite greeting to Mr. Clive, was all she did have to say.

She went on into the house, leaving Alexandra to marvel not merely at her friend's uncharacteristic want of conversation but at how any girl could look so elated and so downcast at the same instant.

She found no answer in the lieutenant. With even less to say, he seemed to be staring at Mr. Clive in a most inexplicable fashion.

A hundred questions darted through Alexandra's head.

212

Divining the answer to none of them in either man's face, she eventually shrugged and followed Dulcie's example and went into the house.

With a strained, "After you, sir," the lieutenant ushered Mr. Clive in behind her.

Chives, standing patiently by the door as they filed in one by one, took the gentlemen's hats and placed them in meticulous alignment on the hall table. "Madam and her guests are in the drawing room," he announced. "Miss Dulcie, I believe, has just joined them. This way, if you please."

Since all three of them were by now quite familiar with the whereabouts of Mrs. Cawlwood's drawing room, his offer to lead the way was hardly necessary. Nevertheless, the lieutenant and Brandon obediently trailed along in his wake, leaving Alexandra a moment to scrutinize her appearance in the ormolu mirror that hung above the table.

Noticing that the cherry-red suit bore no telltale wrinkles from her recent adventure, Alexandra blushed a little, then firmly told herself that, if she could keep her face as composed as her outfit, she would have no problem.

Taking a substantial breath, she removed her hat and placed it beside Mr. Clive's very correct black topper. Only then did she recall that, while dressing herself and borrowing his comb to assemble her tangled locks, he had donned an entirely different outfit. She knew exactly what he was wearing now, a proper afternoon suit of fine black wool with gleaming shirt points and a deftly folded high starcher. But for the life of her she could not remember what he had been wearing when he had walked into the inn.

And why should that possibly matter, she scoffed at herself. What will I be trying to remember next? His undergarments? Nonsense. My back was turned. I didn't peek. I'm quite convinced I didn't.

Adamantly tucking an errant curl into place, Alexandra proceeded into the drawing room.

Her entrance was scarcely noticed. The occupants of that room seemed to have paired themselves off according to

213

mood.

The Messrs. Sharlett and Cavendish, clearly having no one else upon which to bestow their smiles for the nonce, were smiling at each other between constant sips of tea. Dulcie and the lieutenant, once more ensconced on the solitary tête-à-tête, were exchanging speaking glances. On the settee, Lord Chambers was doing his best to console an obviously agitated Mrs. Cawlwood.

By the window, Mr. Altheus Druberry was expounding his opinions to the sole remaining occupant of the room. As that happened to be Mr. Clive, Mr. Druberry's observations were hardly being given the attention that worthy considered his due. His chest seemed to puff a bit more with each passing moment.

Brandon, too disinterested even to be goaded by these thinly veiled remonstrances, idly glanced toward the door. His expression of boredom suddenly transformed itself into a wry smile.

"Ah, there you are," he said as Alexandra moved toward him. "Mr. Druberry fears I've overstimulated you . . . by our stroll in the afternoon air," he added after a wicked pause. With not the slightest trace of expression, he walked over to the tea table, poured a cup, and brought it to Alexandra.

"Thank you," she said, taking the cup and saucer with none-too-steady hands. She was delighted she hadn't been holding them a second before. They would have crashed to Mrs. Cawlwood's carpet without fail. Alexandra glanced at Mr. Clive, uncertain whether to wither him with a stare for being such a horrid tease or to silently bless him for giving her this brief interval in which to recover.

Instead, once she had recovered, she decided two could play the game. She gave him a glittering smile, then turned her full attention to Mr. Druberry.

"So kind of you, sir, to be concerned," she sighed, raising a limp wrist to her forehead. "I declare I am almost faint from exertion. Such a long walk and such a hectic pace. You, sir, I'm sure, would never subject a lady to such an undignified romp."

214

"Indeed not!" pronounced Mr. Druberry, immediately drawing up a chair and delivering her into it as if she were fragile china. He had already made several blustering noises, attempting to draw Lady Redcliffe's attention to himself. None of which had seemed to meet with the least success.

But now? Altheus Druberry could hardly believe his luck. The lady was not only hanging on his every word but was looking up at him with appealing eyes as if begging him to become her champion. His chest puffed out to amazing proportions.

And Brandon, watching Alexandra sit back with a triumphant smile on her face, had little trouble interpreting her thoughts— There, Mr. Clive! You deserve a bit of pomposity for giving me such a start.

Touché, he thought, but he did not concede the battle. Instead, he added a riposte of his own. He assumed the look of such absolute contrition, Alexandra nearly choked on her tea. "You were saying, sir?" he inquired politely.

"I was saying—" thundered Mr. Druberry, then caught himself upon seeing he had attracted stares from the others in the room. He lowered his voice to an irate rumble. "I was saying, Mr. Clive, that women are very dainty creatures. No gentleman of Bath would think of marching a lady up and down these hilly streets. Especially in the afternoon air!"

He paused to let this dire revelation sink in. "Obviously you are unaware, sir, but I may tell you I have it on good authority. The afternoon air is laden with miasmic vapors. Unseen to be sure, but there nonetheless, and far beyond any sweet lady's endurance. It is, medically speaking, if I may be so bold, quite injurious to their delicate natures."

Brandon, having been recently convinced that Alexandra's endurance was admirable and her nature even more so, did not flicker a muscle. On the contrary, he sketched a bow and most soberly thanked Mr. Druberry for his instruction.

Begging pardon for his lack of medical knowledge, he wondered aloud if perhaps, since the miasmic vapors of Bath were so hazardous to ladies, they might not also be somewhat deleterious to the gentlemen? Particularly the long-term residents of the town? If so, Brandon inquired in a most amiable fashion, shouldn't Mr. Druberry protect his own health by retiring to his home immediately before the hour grew later and these mysterious vapors even stronger?

"I certainly have no intention of rushing off yet," squawked that worthy. "I've barely greeted Lady Redcliffe."

Turning to her, he reassuringly patted her hand. "Not to worry, dear lady. Medical, ahem, evidence points to the fact that men are more or less immune to this danger. Stronger constitutions and all that, you see."

It occurred to him that Lady Redcliffe's, "How nice — for you," did not sound quite as appreciative as he would have liked. Nor did Mr. Clive's contrite manner seem all that genuine.

Nevertheless, Mr. Druberry was not about to leave the field to his rival. He planted himself staunchly in front of Brandon and declared that, while the gentleman of Bath had become inured to these vapors, it was an entirely different matter with visitors. Male visitors in particular, he emphasized. And quite often with the most unwelcome results.

"If I might suggest," he finished ominously, "for the sake of your own health, Mr. Clive, you might consider leaving Bath to those of us who are accustomed to it!"

"Sage advice," Brandon replied. "I do believe I shall take it in good time."

Neither Alexandra nor Mr. Druberry knew what he meant by that, but the latter could not resist piling on a few more medical statistics. To wit, that many a male visitor had tarried too long in town only to find himself plagued with the most horrible, but of course unmentionable, illnesses.

"The fact is —" began Mr. Druberry.

There were, not surprisingly, a great many more facts to come, and each of them no less fanciful that the first. The sole truth behind Mr. Druberry's mouthings was the source that prompted them.

Jealousy, pure and simple.

Arriving for tea and receiving only the vague information that Miss Winford was out, as was Lady Redcliffe at the

Circulating Library, Mr. Druberry had somewhat naturally inferred that the two young ladies had gone off together.

Leaving the Messs. Cavendish and Sharlett to smile at each other and a distracted Mrs. Cawlwood under the soothing influence of Lord Chambers, Mr. Druberry had positioned himself at the foremost window of the drawing room. Standing at an angle that afforded a rather long view of the street, he had planned what he considered a most gallant touch. At the first glimpse of the two ladies, he would pop out of the house to meet them and offer to carry their books the rest of the way.

Yes, he had thought, idly drumming his fingertips on the windowsill as he had waited, that's just the sort of thing the dear little creatures would appreciate. Carry their books home and they would deem him quite the gallant indeed. Lady Redcliffe, especially, no doubt.

So he had waited by the window. And waited. By the time he had spotted two distant figures climbing the hill, his patience and his gallantry were wearing mighty thin. They snapped completely as the dim figures emerged into clear view. The lady of his dreams was accompanied neither by books nor Miss Winford. Worse, she was smiling up at Mr. Clive as if she actually enjoyed that detestable man's company!

"The blighter!" grunted Mr. Druberry. And stricken with jealousy, he had pounced on the first scathing criticism that had come to mind. How that happened to be "miasmic vapors," no one, Mr. Druberry included, would ever learn. He scarcely knew what the term meant, let alone if the Bath air abounded with them. But, by the end of his diatribe, he had so convinced himself, if no one else, that he actually glanced out the window, half expecting to find the roadway littered with gasping male visitors.

He certainly hoped at least one of them would soon meet that fate.

"Yorkshiremen!" he grunted, so forgetting himself as to utter his thoughts out loud. "Too many of them in town. Cluttering up the streets!"

"Would you mind explaining that?" Brandon said.

Mr. Druberry was not too far gone to recognize the steel behind that quiet voice. He backed down, mumbling that he had meant nothing by the remark. Only that he had chanced to meet another Yorkshireman in town that day. A connection — a relative, or some sort — of Mr. Clive's, he believed.

Brandon stiffened. "A relation of mine?"

Noting this reaction, Alexandra uttered a sharp laugh. "Why so surprised? It's undoubtedly your cousin. I told you he was in town."

She turned to Mr. Druberry. "Where did you meet him? I'd rather like to 'chance' upon the man myself."

Whatever Mr. Druberry might have replied was lost in a despairing wail from Mrs. Cawlwood. "Your cousin — *Brandon*? The poor boy's here? In *Bath*? Oh, dear, and after the frightful way you two girls have gone about muttering over him. Alexandra! Dulcie! Won't someone please tell me what's going on!"

"Now, now there," soothed Lord Chambers, not for the first time that afternoon. Patting her hand, he offered to pour her another cup of tea.

Mrs. Cawlwood flatly refused it. "Heavens, no! I'm fair to drowning in tea! What I should like is a sensible answer of some sort. I simply don't understand. Bath used to be such a quiet, simple little town. Now people seem to keep dashing in and out with never a word of explanation. First your father, Dulcie, and now Brandon. What is he doing here?"

"Now, now —" began Lord Chambers, but Mrs. Cawlwood was far past any such simple assuasions.

"And the luggage?" she cried, brooking no interference not even from his dear lordship. "I come back to hear Chives has been dragging luggage up and down the stairs at all hours. But does anyone tell him why? Does anyone tell *me* why? Whatever is going on? I do wish people would stop dashing about long enough to give me just the slightest explanation!"

She got not even that. All of a sudden, four persons in the room seemed to be in great haste. Dulcie, pleading a headache, declared she could not survive another moment without a restorative of lavender water. As she fled out of the room and up the stairs, Alexandra was right on her heels, claiming loudly enough for all to hear that no doubt such restorative, if they had any, would be in her own room and the poor, ailing dear would never find it without her.

Brandon, with a skeptical look at the remaining habitants of the room, invented a prior engagement and quietly took his leave.

Daniel, whose inventiveness apparently ran along the same lines, promptly followed suit.

Only the Messrs. Sharlett, Cavendish, and Druberry seemed in no hurry to be somewhere else. Two of them smiled politely, and the third looked extremely curious.

Lord Chambers made short shrift of them all. Correctly assuming that, when Mrs. Cawlwood remembered herself, she would be dreadfully embarrassed by her outburst, he politely but firmly sent the three gentlemen packing.

He attempted to suggest the same course for himself, but Mrs. Cawlwood, who found his presence exceedingly comforting, would have none of it. With good-natured acceptance, his lordship resettled himself beside her and began deftly interweaving his hand pats and "now, now, there's" with a number of amusing anecdotes that so pacified the lady she went as far as to say, "I cannot imagine what I should do without you . . . Oliver."

Upstairs in her friend's bedroom, Alexandra was industriously applying lavender water to her own aching head. In the past ten minutes, she had been witness to the most agitated and incoherent argument she had ever heard. The emotional upheaval, she had no trouble sharing. Dabbing at her throbbing temples, she decided agitation was the norm for all females in the Cawlwood household. Had she gone into the kitchen, she thought, she would not have been the least surprised had she found the cook barricaded behind the stove, furiously pitching currant buns at the scullery maid.

It was the gist of this particular upheaval she couldn't quite grasp, mainly because Dulcie seemed to be taking both sides of the argument herself.

Sitting on the edge of the bed, her head feeling like a pendulum in full swing, Alexandra tried in vain to keep track of her madly pacing little friend. The girl switched back and forth, apparently having no difficulty in supplying both accusation and rebuttal for some unseen opponent. "If you truly loved me, we could . . . I do love you, but we can't . . . it simply isn't done!"

Finally, Alexandra could stand no more. She shrilled out a command to halt that even Dulcie could not ignore.

The girl was halfway across the room. She stopped and looked back over her shoulder as she might have at some stranger who had rudely interrupted a private conversation. "For heaven's sake, Lexie, you don't have to screech. Does this mean you have an idea?"

"It means," said Alexandra, sternly pointing a finger at a chair and refusing to continue until Dulcie had somewhat exasperatedly positioned it and herself by the bed, "that I have not understood five words out of any hundred you've just said. Are you actually trying to tell me you wish to elope?"

"I do." Dulcie plopped herself into the chair. "But Daniel doesn't."

Well, thought Alexandra, thank God for that much. Elopements were so . . .

". . . so seedy," she finished, giving voice to her disapproval. "Dulcie, did Lieutenant Symington actually propose to you, or did you ask him?"

The girl thought this over for a moment. "I may have brought up the subject, I suppose. But it doesn't matter. I love him. I do, really and truly, you know. Papa always thinks I flit from one fancy to another and can never make up my mind. But not this time. I love Daniel, and nothing means more to me than to be his wife. Nothing. You do believe me, don't you, Lexie?"

If Alexandra had entertained any doubts, the utter simplicity with which the girl spoke erased those doubts completely. "Yes, I believe you. I'm also rather convinced that Lieutenant Symington loves you."

"Well, of course," Dulcie replied pertly, sounding more like her usual self. "He told me so this afternoon. And he wants to marry me. He told me that too. Only he refuses to elope, which I think is highly shabby of him, considering that he swore on his honor—and his life, mind you—that he'd never let anyone take me away from him. And yet he couldn't seem to think of one simply way to keep Papa and Major Clive from doing just that!"

"So naturally you did. Really, Dulcie, an elopement? If we're speaking of shabby, my dear, that certainly fits the bill. What would you propose he do? Skip off to Gretna Green with you like some crude guttersnipe and his wench?"

The sarcasm brought a heated flush to the Dresden-doll cheeks. Plainly insulted, Dulcie filched an expression from her father to say that she had never heard such a skitter-witted notion. She had, she coolly informed her friend, suggested quite sensibly that they flee to Brighton.

Dear lord, thought Alexandra, not that again. With a sigh, she called Dulcie's attention to the fact that the two of them had already discussed an exodus to Brighton and concluded it was pointless. Mr. Winford would track his daughter down eventually no matter where she fled.

"Eventually, yes," said Dulcie completely unswayed, "But, by then, Daniel and I would already be married. What could Papa do?"

"Have it annulled," Alexandra answered in a weary voice. "You're not yet of age."

"Well, I am very close," snapped Dulcie despite the fact that she was a full three years short of that majority. Having that point brought out to her only brought a pout to her lips, and the opinion that she had never expected her very dearest friend to prove as stubborn as Daniel. "Besides, my age wouldn't matter. Not in Brighton!" she added defiantly. "For heaven's sake, Lexie, use your thinking cap!"

Doing so, Alexandra only further succeeded in irritating

the girl by concluding that she rather thought marital laws were the same throughout the country. Why should Brighton possibly be different?

"Because Aunt Letitia's there!" cried Dulcie. "Oh, Lexie, you're worse than Daniel. He immediately flew up into the boughs. I don't think he heard a thing I was saying. However, it's really quite simple, if you'd only stop interrupting and listen!"

Thus chastised, Alexandra bit back a half-uttered protest and mutely applied her full attention to Dulcie's latest scheme. At least she tried her best to understand. The explanation, punctuated with a great many "There, you see how easy it is" and "I cannot imagine why Daniel considers it such a sad romp when you can plainly see it is nothing of the sort!" interjections, was hardly as simple to follow as Dulcie had predicted.

The gist seemed to be that Aunt Letitia of Brighton—the very same aunt after whom Dulcie Letitia Winford had been named—was not only a godmother to her late sister's child but a part guardian as well. Dulcie, admittedly, wasn't quite certain how that had come about. Most likely her mother had realized on her deathbed that a man raising a baby daughter alone needed help. So she had named Aunt Letitia to aid in the task.

Although, as Dulcie added thoughtfully, she couldn't imagine what difference it had made because Aunt Letitia had not been in London more than once or twice in the past eighteen years. Nonetheless, it was all there very clearly in Mama's will. Aunt Letitia was as much—or perhaps almost as much—her legal guardian as Papa.

And as Dulcie remembered, she and her aunt had gotten along splendidly on the few times they had been together. Furthermore, they would get along splendidly now, if only Daniel would see reason and take her to Brighton. Aunt Letitia could have them married as proper as a churchful of vicars.

"There, you see!" Dulcie ended on an exultant note. "What could be simpler?"

A great deal, thought Alexandra, though she didn't say it. She did question whether Dulcie's aunt would be as amenable as her niece seemed to think.

"Of course she will," said Dulcie. Having leaped up and down several times during her recitation, she now regained her chair and demurely smoothed her skirts. "Aunt Letitia is very sensible. Besides, she's not all that fond of Papa. She think he tries to ride roughshod over too many people — ladies, in particular. She was quite dubious about my marriage to Major Clive." Dulcie giggled. "Your marriage as it turned out."

Alexandra let that ride. "Oh, so you did invite her to the wedding then?"

"Naturally," said Dulcie. "It was only Aunt Tilmatha I forgot. At any rate, Aunt Letitia wrote back, saying she couldn't attend. Have you ever met her, Lexie? No, I daresay you haven't. Well, she's very tall and thin, and of course she's rather old too. She said her brittle bones simply couldn't take the jarring of a trip to London, but that she would send me a very nice present if I married this Major Clive. And was I quite certain I truly did want to marry him? If not, she said she would jounce herself to London, old bones or not, and put Papa in his place."

Despite her woes, Dulcie could not refrain from a second giggle. "She would have too. Aunt Letitia is the only woman in the world Papa's ever tangled with — and always come off the worst of it. But of course I hadn't fallen in love with Daniel then. And there was no one else really. So I wrote her back, saying it was all right, I supposed I had to marry someone sometime, and things had a way of working out in the end."

"Which they did," she added, vaguely staring at the ceiling. "In a way. And I know they'd work out now, too."

Suddenly straightening up, she pounded a small fist on her knee. "They *would* . . . if we could only get to Brighton!"

Alexandra had no such confidence. Neither, apparently, had Lieutenant Symington. Since Dulcie could hardly be married in Brighton, or anywhere else, without the cooperation of a bridegroom, Alexandra advanced no further objections.

Instead, she harked back to what seemed their most sensible plan. Namely, the dissuasion of Major Clive at Friday evening's party.

But this, in lieu of distracting her friend as she had hoped, seemed to have the most crushing effect yet. The Dresden face settled into an expression so glum it would have produced permanent wrinkles in any female over twenty-one.

"He won't come," Dulcie said flatly.

"Nonsense," Alexandra retorted. "He is here in Bath. We learned as much from your father. Peyton will find him, I'm sure, and bring him along tomorrow night."

"No, he won't come."

"Now, really, Dulcie, you can't know that. Peyton—"

"Is merely his cousin," Dulcie interrupted. "He hasn't seen the major for years, but Daniel has. He's his equerry as you might recall. He does know the major, and he is convinced the man will not show his face in this house tomorrow night."

The girl's expression grew even tighter. "And I wouldn't be here either—if only Daniel would take me away. But he won't! Oh, Lexie, why must men be such vexing creatures? He loves me—I know he does—yet all he can say is *this* isn't proper. And in the meanwhile, he's doing absolutely *nothing*!"

If Lieutenant Symington had heard his beloved's complaint, he would have felt much maligned.

The fact was, he had been trying his utmost for the past half-hour. Unfortunately, as Dulcie would have no doubt concurred, he had put his argument very badly.

Now, sitting across from his superior in the common room of the Seven Seas Inn, Daniel felt his collar growing more constrictive by the moment. But he stuck to his guns, just as he had stuck to them when he had dogged the major's footsteps down the hill from Mrs. Cawlwood's house.

Brandon, none too pleased by the dust-up in that lady's

drawing room, had not particularly desired anyone's company on his way back to the inn. At last conceding it was not to be avoided, he had extended an invitation for a joint whiskey and early supper in the common room.

Now, as his expression plainly showed, he was rather regretting that invitation.

The whiskey is doing it perhaps, he thought, watching his equerry down a good part of a second glass. Whatever it was, Brandon was one of the opinion his subordinate had finally overstepped himself.

So did Lieutenant Symington for that matter, but Dulcie, as he reminded himself, was worth fighting for. Whereupon, he kept at it, blundering along in an impossible attempt to be both diplomatic and sternly reproving at the same time. He made such a bungle of it that Brandon finally held up his hand.

"Enough, Lieutenant," he said. Though his tone was quiet, there was no mistaking the authority behind it. "I believe I may infer from all this mishmash, may I not, that you highly disapprove of my association with Lady Redcliffe?"

"Well—" Daniel tugged once more at his collar. Then again reminding himself of his mission, he took another gulp of whiskey and squared his shoulders. "Yes, sir, the fact is, I do, but that's another matter. If I may say—"

"No, let me say," Brandon quietly cut in. "Whatever the friendship between Lady Redcliffe and myself, you might be well advised to remember it is none of your concern."

"Perhaps not, sir! But Miss Winford is! That is, it is my intention that she soon will be my concern."

"And I am to infer, of course, that, along with Lady Redcliffe, I have been trifling with Miss Winford's affections."

"No, sir!" The lieutenant downed the rest of his whiskey and raised his hand to order a third. One look at his superior convinced him this was hardly the appropriate action, and he quickly lowered his hand.

"No, sir, I know you wouldn't trifle with Dulcie. She

wouldn't take to the idea above half."

"I'm sure the lady would appreciate your confidence," Brandon said heavily.

"Oh, you neither, sir!" blurted the lieutenant, trying to thrash his way out of this pitfall. "I mean, I don't exactly understand what you're doing, but I know you wouldn't really—that is, you know, really trifle—with any lady under false pretenses. Including Lady Redcliffe, even though she is your wife, so to speak. But of course she ain't that any more—or won't be as soon as Mr. Winford files those annulment papers in London."

"Which won't be any time soon," muttered Brandon, thinking that, without his own signature, Mr. Winford's copies of those papers would be useless indeed. As before, he vaguely wondered what the old man was up to, but it was only a passing thought.

Mostly he was relieved that, contrary to his earlier suspicions, Daniel seemed to have no idea that his relationship with Lady Redcliffe had gone beyond a mere flirtation. That, he told himself, was definitely no one's business save his and the lady's.

Relenting a little, Brandon leaned back and regarded his subordinate in a somewhat more favorable light. "The lady is still my wife, Daniel. I can assure you of that because the annulment papers—the proper ones, that is—are right here in the innkeeper's safe. Mr. Winford will get nowhere without my cooperation."

"And he's got that right enough, hasn't he?" blurted Daniel. "My God, sir, why'd you do it? You don't love Dulcie. Why'd you tell her father to bring back that special license?"

This time it was Brandon's hand that raised in signal to the barkeep in the otherwise deserted room. And unlike Daniel, he did not change his mind. When the drink arrived, he tipped a bit into his equerry's empty glass, then added a generous dollop of water from a pitcher sitting on the table.

The lieutenant's glum nod of thanks plainly implied he

would have preferred an ampler dollop of whiskey and uncut to boot, but Brandon paid no heed. In his opinion, the lad had already reached his limits. Maj. Brandon Clive's amiability did not extend to nursemaiding besotted equerries. He pushed the watered glass toward the lieutenant, then picked up his own.

"Daniel, if indeed Mr. Winford is planning to return with some sort of license, I can assure you, it was not my idea."

"Well, maybe not," conceded Daniel, retreating a little, yet still refusing to give up the bone. "But you obviously went along with him. He told Dulcie as much, and that's why she wants to—"

The word so dismayed him, it was only with great difficulty that he managed to clear his throat and give it voice. "—to cope. She's frantic that the two of you are mobbing up on her. And the way it sounds, I don't wonder she's right. I must say I think it's most unfair—sir!"

Brandon, looking for all the world as if he were interested in nothing more than the contents of his glass, casually took a sip and returned the barely touched glass to the table. "Miss Winford means to fly off to Gretna Green? With you?"

"Yes, sir! I mean, no—not to Gretna Green. But with me, yes!"

Flushing, Daniel straightened to a painfully rigid position. "Miss Winford and I have plighted a troth, sir. She is in love with me. And I, with her. We wish to be married."

"By eloping?" Brandon said mildly. "If you don't mind my saying so, that's hardly the thing."

Daniel flushed even redder. "I know it's not, sir! I've told Dulcie it was outside of enough. No matter how much she wheedled, I'd have none of it!"

No? thought Brandon. Having some knowledge of Miss Winford's clever wiles, he smiled a bit to himself. If Miss Winford had made up her mind to marry Daniel, the poor lad didn't stand a chance.

Not that Brandon minded, of course. It had already occurred to him that the two would make a very suitable and lively union. But not, by God, by elopement!

He picked up his glass and sipped at it, weighing the consequences. Dulcie Winford was an impetuous little thing. It would no doubt be just like her to attempt some damn-fool elopement. And Daniel was hardly a barrier. Enamored as he was, all Miss Winford had to do was beckon, and his firmest resolves would disappear faster than Berbers in a sandstorm.

Then there was Alexandra. As Brandon thought of her, his attention threatened to wander off into more pleasant memories. With an imperceptible but determined shake of his head, he got himself back on the track. She would be an excellent deterrent, he mused.

Lady Alexandra Redcliffe—Clive, he added unthinkingly—was not only beautiful but practical. She would never allow her friend to go dashing off to Gretna Green . . . or wherever it was the rash little imp had in mind.

The rest, Brandon decided with a grimace, would be up to him. The pair would be married properly and with Papa Winford's blessing. And that, Brandon meant to secure as soon as the old man returned from London.

Now, looking across the table at his flushed young equerry, he decided the best action was to keep his own counsel. With a single question, he began a strategy that was not too different from one of Miss Winford's own. Delaying tactics.

"If not elopement, Daniel, then exactly what do you propose to do?"

The lieutenant, startled by his sudden directness, seemed momentarily at a loss not only for words but for a solitary thought as well. Finally, after much stumbling around and a hefty swig of the watered whiskey, he managed to admit that he had little in mind for himself. Not as yet anyhow. It was his superior's actions he was counting on.

Girding his courage, Daniel drained his glass and set it down with a thump. "I firmly believe, sir, that you must reveal your identity to Miss Winford. And explain your intentions toward her."

Only wish to God I knew myself what they were, Daniel thought. It had suddenly dawned on him that the major had

228

given no sign he still wanted to marry Dulcie. But then he hadn't expressly said he didn't either. And the special license? It might have been Mr. Winford's idea, but the major obviously hadn't objected.

With an inward groan, the lieutenant hitched himself forward in his chair, determined to do the manly thing. "Sir!" I realize Miss Winford is—was your intended. And that now that you've met her—well, she's past price, isn't she? I can see how any man would want to marry her. And if you do, I'll—I'll—oh, blast it all! Sir, I've been straight with you. Dulcie don't love you. Surely you can't still mean to marry her, not on top of that!"

"And if I did?" Brandon said evenly.

"Then I'd—I'd—well, I can promise you I won't give up easily! That's not the proper thing to say, is it? I should say I'd back out gracefully, but I won't. Neither against you nor Mr. Winford!"

"Bold words," muttered Brandon. His voice was without emotion, but in truth he was silently applauding the lieutenant's spunk.

"Yes, sir! I mean them. And for Dulcie's sake, I must insist that you reveal your identity at once. It's only fair, sir. And if you don't tell her, sir . . . I will!"

The former might have been courage, but that last statement was sheer whiskey talking. Even in his muddled state, Daniel had only to take one glance at the hardening features of the face opposite him to to know he had stepped off the edge.

"Lieutenant Symington." The tone, although low, had sent many a man cringing from its presence. "May I remind you I am your superior officer? When I inform Miss Winford or Lady Redcliffe of my identity, it will be at my own doing at my own time. Until then, you are under direct orders to remain silent on any and all accounts concerning me. Is that clear?"

Under this steely barrage, Lieutenant Symington's training brought forth an automatic response. He sprang from his chair and came to ramrod attention. "Yes, sir!"

"Furthermore—and this is another direct order, Lieutenant—you are not to leave Bath for any reason without my permission. Is that clear?"

"Sir!"

"In which case"—Brandon, glancing toward the far end of the room, noticed that the barkeep was no longer at his post—"I believe I should like to order my dinner. You might so inform the proprietor or whoever happens to be about."

"Sir!"

Turning on his heel, Daniel promptly exited the room to seek out the owner of the Seven Seas Inn. When he found the man at the registry desk, he made it quite clear the meal would be for one. Angry, embarrassed, and befuddled as he was, Daniel realized the dinner invitation to himself no longer held.

Wouldn't have accepted it anyway, he grumped to himself. He was turning to leave when the proprietor's "Pardon, Lieutenant?" hailed him back.

The man took a thick envelope from the desk and handed it to him. "Would you mind giving this to the gentleman whilst I fetch his dinner? It came by post rider only a short time ago."

Although much adverse to returning to the common room, Daniel again could not deny his training.

His heels clicking on the highly polished floor, he delivered this burden and stood at rigid attention as Brandon opened it and casually flipped through its contents.

"My decommission papers," Brandon murmured, stuffing them back into the envelope.

"Yes, sir!" Eyes straight ahead, Daniel paid little attention. "Is there anything else—sir?"

"There is," Brandon answered. Although more than a bit ticked off himself, he could not help being amused by the mute indignation in the lieutenant's rigid stance. Nor could he resist a teasing gibe. "With such dignity, Lieutenant, it occurs to me you'd make a splendid best man."

"Sir!"

It was nearly a wail, but Brandon paid no heed. He flicked

a finger toward the envelope. "You might put this in my chambers on your way out. My satchel's in the armoire. Just tuck this in the side pocket if you will."

With the iciest of salutes and the most formal about face this side of Buckingham Palace, Lt. Daniel Symington of His Majesty's Light Horse Guards marched out of the common room, across the reception hall, and up the stairs to his superior's chambers.

Now alone and incredulous as well as frustrated to a peak, he had a mighty urge to kick something, anything, in the blasted room! But, as nothing presented itself to him that might not mar his own spit-and-polish boots in return, he took vengeance on the armoire instead. Giving it a vicious whack with the flat of his hand, he slammed wide its door with a force that nearly tore off the hinges and thrust the envelope into the open satchel without even bothering to look for a side pocket.

He would never have noticed the adjacent object either, had it not fallen across his outstretched hand.

A red parasol?

Now if Lieutenant Symington was no roué, he hadn't precisely cut his wisdoms yesterday either. Ladies seldom visited gentlemen in a public inn and never in their bedrooms. That did not preclude all women of course. Daniel himself had on occasion entertained certain females in such circumstances. Likewise, on mornings after, he had carelessly tucked away such forgotten items as a glove, a hanky — a parasol?

So the major had found himself a bit of muslin in Bath, he thought, and started to push the parasol back into the armoire.

Then a fringe of jet tickled his fingers, and he jerked the parasol out into the bright light of the room.

The intricacies of fashion were often lost on the lieutenant, but it did not take him long to remember he had seen a hat with an identical fringe only a short time earlier. A hat that had lain beside his when he had prepared to leave Mrs. Cawlwood's house.

231

Nor to remember that, when he had arrived, he had met the major with a lady who had been wearing an outfit of the same deep red.

Had she been carrying a parasol? She had not!

Daniel dropped the elegant little sunshade back into the armoire as if he had been burned.

The major—*his* major—had seduced a lady under false pretenses.

And not just any lady.

His major had trifled—really trifled—with Dulcie's dearest friend!

If Daniel had been angry before, he was absolutely livid now. His own superior, the man he trusted, had evinced all the honor of a Spittlefields alley cat!

"And wouldn't I just like to let this cat out of the bag," he snarled. "But I can't, goddamn it! I'm under orders!"

He was halfway out of the room before the thought finally clicked in his head. Diving back into that same cupboard, he grabbed the envelope and rifled through its contents.

"Full and straight-out decommissioned, by God!"

Turning a page, he looked at the date of the signing, then slowly refolded the pages, and put them in the side pocket of the satchel.

Mr. Brandon Clive was no longer anybody's superior officer. In fact, he hadn't been for a week.

232

Chapter 8

By midnight, Lt. Daniel Symington felt as if his body had turned into a one-man battlefield with each part fiercely warring against the other. His head pounded with a surfeit of alcohol and indecision. His stomach not only echoed those symptoms but had further pitted itself into a lively skirmish with its contents. Having wound up at his grandmother's dinner table, he had been coerced by that sweet but determined little lady into a meal that would have fortified a regiment.

The rest of his body tossed and turned in its bed until finally, in desperation, his grandmother had pounded on the connecting wall and demanded he either stop thrashing about, or she would post him off to Turkey in a gunny sack.

Needless to say, it was a tired-eyed and dispirited young officer who presented himself at Mrs. Cawlwood's door on Friday morning. The man he had admired most in the world had suddenly developed into an out-and-out scoundrel.

And the girl he loved most obviously considered him a grave disappointment. She barely acknowledged his presence as he was ushered into the sun-filled morning room.

Carefully seating himself amidst a jumble of white-lacquered wicker furnishings and potted areca palms, the lieutenant felt himself to be a most ill-used young man.

Only Alexandra seemed to be in a cordial mood. Seated across from Dulcie at a table cluttered with breakfast appointments, she glanced from one to the other of her companions. Deciding neither was going to behave with the least semblance of joviality, she proceeded with the best grace possible to make the visitor welcome.

Explaining that Mrs. Cawlwood had not yet risen, she asked if he would care to join them in a cup of chocolate and a scone. No, it seemed she and Dulcie had finished the scones. Perhaps coffee and a poppy seed roll?

"Just coffee, ma'am," Daniel mumbled. His stomach was in no condition to conquer anything heavier.

"Ma'am?" teased Alexandra, pouring a cup and adding a hint of warm milk before she handed it to him. "Don't you suppose by now"—she glanced at Dulcie—"we could dispense with the formalities? Please call me Alexandra. And I shall call you Daniel if that's agreeable?"

The answering "Er, delighted" was polite if not terribly enthusiastic. The truth was, the more Lady Redcliffe tried to put him at ease, the more uncomfortable the lieutenant became. The lady was being most unfairly deceived. And unwilling or not, Daniel felt as if he were almost as much to blame as his superior.

His ex-superior, he sternly reminded himself.

This was small consolation. Dulcie was plainly ignoring him. Alexandra, trying to fill the gulf, chatted pleasantly about this and that as she attempted to draw him into the conversation. Her kindness only made him all the more miserable.

Between his terse "thank you's" and "no thank you's" and Dulcie's pouting silence, Alexandra plowed on bravely for a spell, then acknowledged defeat.

She gave each of them a piercing stare, relieved Daniel of his empty cup, set it on the table, and then primly folded her hands in her lap. "Very well. I have exhausted every polite topic this side of the Antipodes. I suppose I may as well be blunt. Daniel, Dulcie says you are convinced the major will not show himself here tonight. May I ask why? Have you spoken to him?"

The sharpness of the question startled the young officer into an admission. Upon even sharper cross-examination, he admitted he had professed his own love for Dulcie and found all his arguments to no avail. "I'm afraid," he said woefully, "he still means to marry her."

This, quite naturally, ended Dulcie's silence. She began to sputter and spew, throwing herself tragically against the back of her chair, her head sunken onto one outstretched arm, and vowing that all was irrevocably lost. Her life was in shambles. Would no one come to save her?

Meanwhile, there was Daniel protesting he had tried to do just that. And all was not lost. Yet. If Dulcie would only trust him, he pleaded, he would think of something. He was quite sure he could, he insisted. Given a little time and a little quiet, he would come up with some plan.

Dulcie, however, was in no mood to give him either time or quiet. Being overwrought and having a natural bent for theatrics, she was seriously contemplating an outright fit of hysterics.

Daniel, thinking this was pitching it a bit too high, even for his beloved, promptly changed his own tactics.

"Dulcie, stop that caterwauling this instant!"

It worked.

The abrupt silence surprised everyone, not the least of whom was Dulcie. She demurely straightened her skirts and murmured an apology.

"Accepted," said Alexandra, once more stepping into the breach. "I'm sure we're all rather upset. Major Clive seems to bring out the worst in all of us. Even in absentia," she added grimly. "Daniel, you're quite certain he means to go ahead with this marriage?"

With what had to be the glummest expression in the whole of England, Daniel nodded. "He claims I'd make a splendid best man."

"What?" yelped Dulcie. "Why, of all the unmitigated gall! Oh, Daniel, we've simply got to go *now*! I know you said you wouldn't, but, I promise you, it won't be in the least shabby. Not with Aunt Letitia on our side. And now, we've got no choice, don't you see? We've simply got to — and if you really and truly loved me, you would!"

While Dulcie's argument may have been somewhat garbled, its intent was not. Daniel, feeling once more pinned between the irresistible and the immovable, hesitated, looking for the right words.

Alexandra was quicker. "Of course he loves you. I daresay he'd never put up with you if he didn't. But, Aunt Letitia or no, an elopement is simply out of the question, and I feel quite sure that Daniel agrees."

"I did," he muttered so low that Alexandra, fully expecting him to reaffirm her position, was not sure she had heard right.

But Dulcie pounded on it in a wink. *"Did?* Oh, my darling Daniel, I knew it! I knew it! You've seen the light!"

"No, he hasn't!" blurted Alexandra.

Before Dulcie could pounce again, Alexandra told her to stop browbeating the poor man. Couldn't she see she had gotten him so befuddled he didn't know what he was saying?

"You didn't mean any such thing, did you?" she said brightly and then rushed on before the lieutenant could even open his mouth. "No, of course you didn't! Being a sensible person and most unpanicky—as I can well see you are—it's such a relief to know you're not the type to let a little upset send you careening off into the countryside! And you're certainly not that at all, are you?"

"No, I guess not," mumbled the sorely vexed lieutenant. He cast an agonized glance at Dulcie.

"Of course not!" Alexandra took a gulp of air and speeded on before Dulcie would weaken the young officer's resolve even further. He was a perfectly reasonable young man, she insisted. Never the type to lead a girl into such a disastrous romp—which of course an elopement would be. Highly disastrous and most improper as she was sure she needn't tell him. It was simply not the solution!

"Then pray tell me what is?" snapped Dulcie.

Quite aware of what Alexandra was trying to do, Dulcie was not the slightest bit impressed. Arms folded, foot tapping impatiently, she gave her lieutenant an exasperated look, then turned an even more exasperated one on Alexandra.

236

"Well?"

"Well . . ." With two pairs of eyes boring into her, Alexandra did not stop to sort out her thoughts. She simply said the first thing that popped into her mind. "Peyton will take care of it."

"Peyton?" Two bewildered voices cried out in unison.

"None other." Alexandra beamed at them, suddenly feeling the utmost confidence and wondering why she hadn't thought of such a simple solution before. "Blood tells, you see," she added as if that explained everything.

When the expressions of their faces proved it had done nothing of the sort, she sighed and set herself to explaining more fully. Who of all people would the major be most inclined to trust? One of his own kin naturally. And Peyton was his first cousin. Furthermore, Peyton knew Dulcie. He alone was in a position to convince the major that a marriage to her would prove most unsatisfactory to both parties.

"Both?" gasped Dulcie. "You think I'd be unsatisfactory too?"

Alexandra laughed. "Only in one respect, dearest. You're in love with another man. I doubt even the major—indifferent as he seems to be—would relish a bride who's pining away for someone else.

"In fact, I'm rather positive he won't," she added, calmly pouring herself a second cup of chocolate. "The major simply didn't believe it when Daniel told him, but he will after Peyton takes a hand. You may not realize it, but Peyton's grown quite fond of you both. And once he knows you're in love—"

"But he does!" Daniel blurted. The truth, the whole truth, begged to come spilling out. And now was the time, he told himself, but old habits were hard to break. Disobeying an order, even if it wasn't strictly an order because the major had been decommissioned days before he bade Daniel's silence, was still difficult. The lieutenant hesitated an instant too long.

Alexandra, having no idea of the torments raging through the young officer's mind, simply dismissed the outburst with an indulgent wave of her hand. "I daresay he's guessed as much. Seeing you two together, it would be impossible not to suspect. Nevertheless, once he learns your interest is, shall we say, definitely fixed, he'll persuade the major to look elsewhere. And that will be the end of it," she said, climaxing her argument with an afterthought that betrayed more of her feelings than she realized. "Peyton is a very persuasive man."

"Especially in certain ways," muttered Daniel, remembering the red parasol in the armoire.

Dulcie, being privy to no one's thoughts but her own, was quite doubtful of Mr. Clive's powers of persuasion. "I can't see that he'd be all that much help. He hasn't been so far. I'd still rather elope, I think."

Immediately annoyed by the girl's first opinion, Alexandra ignored the second. "Mr. Clive is not the type of gentleman to interfere in others' affairs unless he's asked. Which we haven't, not directly, that is. But we shall today! In fact, I shall go right now to—"

To the Seven Seas Inn, she started to say, then quickly retracted the notion. Peyton might think this was merely another excuse to visit his room.

Even worse was the distinct possibility she might succumb to that temptation and forget her mission. She had done that once, she recalled and flushed anew at the memory. Twice would never do.

"To the Circulating Library," she hastily amended. "I'll send Chives with a message asking Peyton to meet me there. Now if you two will excuse me, I'll go find Chives, then change my dress."

She rose to leave, then seeing the look on Dulcie's face, she impulsively reached across the table to squeeze the girl's hand. "Dearest, don't frown so, you'll wind up wrinkled as a prune. Cheer up, isn't it just as you always say? Things have a way of turning out—with a little help? Well, I'm off to get that help now. And then you'll see, my little doubting Thomas. Peyton won't fail us. Not when he understands how much it means to both of you."

"Not likely he won't," grumbled Daniel but only to himself.

238

Truth was, after watching Alexandra and hearing the undercurrents in her voice and the emotions that played across her face, he simply hadn't the heart to tell her what a rotter she had fallen in love with.

Rotter?

Dismayed by his own thoughts, Lieutenant Symington decided he could have never gotten the word out anyway. For the fact was, he still couldn't believe it himself. Logic said, yes. Ex-Major Brandon DeWitt Clive was all too plainly toying with one lady's affections while ruthlessly forcing marriage on another. Try as he might, Daniel Symington simply couldn't bring feelings and logic into agreement.

Surely, he thought, when the major sees Lady Redcliffe today, he'll make a clean breast of the matter. He'll set everything to rights.

But what if he didn't?

Rising, Daniel waited until Alexandra had left the room. Then he planted himself squarely in front of a very dispirited young lady.

"Dulcie, if Mr. — Clive sets things to rights, fine. However, should he not, I hereby give you my word as an officer and a gentleman. We — we'll elope!"

"Oh, Daniel!" Jumping up, Dulcie threw her arms about his neck. "You've finally come round! I knew you would. I knew it! And it shan't be the least bit shabby, you'll see. Not with Aunt Letitia! Why, we shall have the most romantic — not to mention of course the most circumspect elopement you'd ever wish to—"

"On one condition," said Daniel, ignoring this outburst. Having committed himself thus far, he had determined that, if it was his duty to save one lady, it was equally his duty to save both. With a stern look at his beloved, he removed her arms from around his neck. "Should we be forced to gallop off to Brighton — and I say, 'should,' mind you — Alexandra must go with us."

"Oh." Dulcie sank back into her chair with all the lifelessness of a stone disappearing into a river. "Well, I should certainly like that above all things, truly I should. But,

Daniel, you heard her. She's dead set against it! What if she refused to go?"

"Then neither shall we," said Daniel, his tone brooking no argument. He hoped to hell none of them would have to go. Galloping off went much against his grain. But if they did, Lady Redcliffe was going with them. Daniel was not going to leave her to the mercies of a—of a callous libertine.

Nor would Dulcie, he thought with a dry smile. Whether she knew the real circumstances or not, Dulcie could be counted on to wear down her friend's resistance. Of that Daniel had no doubt.

A few seconds later, having more or less convinced his beloved of the same, he was gratified to see her perk up and more than content to let her prattle on all she liked about hired carriages to Brighton and Aunt Letitia's parlor—which it seemed would make a most excellent locale for a wedding.

A possible locale, he reminded himself, in favor of the idea but still averse to the method.

Nevertheless, he felt he had done everything he could for the moment. Taking the chair Alexandra had vacated, he poured himself a second cup of coffee.

Chives obediently trudged the few blocks to the Seven Seas Inn. He returned with a reply that the gentleman would be delighted to meet Lady Redcliffe within the hour. At the time of encounter, Chives took it upon himself to add, Mr. Clive had just sat down to a rather encompassing breakfast.

An overindulgent repast, his tone implied.

Alexandra grinned. The butler had apparently served too long in a female household. He had forgotten gentlemen normally preferred sturdier nourishment than a cup of chocolate and a bun.

With a polite thank you for his efforts, Alexandra dismissed him, then turned to the hall mirror to tie the ribbons on the small soft-brimmed bonnet with its poke crown. A wide-brimmed leghorn would have suited this dress much better, she decided, and thought of the several she had left behind in London. Unfortunately, they were the very devil to pack; there simply hadn't been room in the Winford coach.

The poke bonnet would do well enough. Its dark-green color did not distract from the paler green of the high-necked ruched silk dress, and the fringed Norwich shawl picked up the colors from both.

You'll do, Alexandra told herself and turned toward the door.

She was several yards down the street when it occurred to her she needn't have hurried. Peyton might be some time at his breakfast, and she would be at the Circulating Library long before him.

She almost turned back, then just as quickly decided otherwise. Hadn't she once promised herself to read up on Yorkshire? What better opportunity to do it?

"Of course," she murmured. "A little education never hurt anybody. One can learn all sorts of interesting things in a reading room."

Draping the shawl more securely about her shoulders, she walked briskly down the hill in the bright morning sunlight.

The Circulating Library was just off lower High Street. Alexandra covered the short distance quite easily, nodding to a few passers-by whose acquaintance she had made during her brief stay and enjoying the rare privilege of a solitary stroll. How unlike London, she mused, and not for the first time.

In fact, it occurred to her that despite the many allures of the city, she was rather glad she had not gone tearing back to London. Bath, too, had its attractions. The uncommonly fine weather was a most definite asset. And while the town might no longer have been considered the tonnish retreat of several years past, it still had its pluses.

Over the tea table, Alexandra had heared mention of concerts, theaters, assemblies, and quite elegant ladies' shops on Milsom Street. Then of course there was Sydney Garden. Someone—Mr. Druberry, no doubt—had described the tree-dappled lanes of the garden, its grottoes and waterfalls, opining that Lady Redcliffe might well fancy a stroll among these wonders.

"And I rather think I should," Alexandra murmured as she pushed open the wrought-iron-trimmed door of the library. It was a pity she had seen so little of Bath's pleasures, she thought, but there simply hadn't been time.

Not as yet, she added to herself, draping her shawl casually over her arm as she entered the reading room.

Unbidden, a vision came to mind of herself and a gentleman strolling through Sydney Garden. And the slight smile that curved her lips made it quite plain that the gentleman in mind was not Mr. Druberry.

Alexandra nodded to the few book-seekers that milled about the room. Noting they seemed as much interested in their own whispered gossip as in the shelves of volumes that lined the walls, she walked directly to the atlas table.

The first thing, it seemed most sensibly to her, was to find out exactly where Yorkshire was. North, hadn't Peyton said? Alexandra ran her finger toward the top of the map, and, after several seconds of squinting this way and that, she figured out she was in Scotland.

Well, it wasn't that far north. With a fleeting wish that her father and his Glaswegian wife were getting along nicely, she traced a zigzag pattern down the map to — Brighton? That, obviously, was too far south. Her finger moved over to the Irish Channel. No, that wasn't it. She zigzagged in the opposite direction and at last found it. On the North Sea, of all places.

My word, she thought as she stood back to look at the squiggly coastline, it must be very rugged up there in the winter. No wonder he had come south to indulge in this lovely weather for a while.

Perhaps they both could enjoy it a while longer. All Peyton had to do was send his cousin packing. It never occurred to Alexandra, he could not or would not, once he understood the whole of their dilemma. She was quite confident a man like Peyton Clive could handle any number of vile-tempered cousins. And once he had? Well, who knew what hidden pleasures Bath might have in store!

The thought of one rather obvious pleasure sent a flush to her cheeks.

No! No more of that, she told herself firmly. She was no naughty widow, carelessly flinging herself from one affair to another. In fact, she couldn't seem to handle one. And the alternative, she told herself just as firmly, did not appeal to her either.

Still, there was the rout party tonight. Alexandra stared at the atlas, trying but unable to ignore the fact that Mrs. Cawlwood's jollification was mere hours away.

Would he propose? Would he. not?

Alexandra shut the map book with a tiny snort of disgust.

Marriage! She had no intention of marrying anyone, not even Peyton Clive, should he ask her. Which at any rate he probably wouldn't.

Yet inside, some niggling little feeling told her she would be sorely disappointed if he didn't.

"—and the news sheets are there to your left, sir," came a loud whisper from somewhere behind her. "The London rags, too—and only a day or so old, I am proud to say. Fast postriders and all that, you see. Nothing backward about our little town. No indeed! If I may profess without bragging, sir, I believe you'll find Bath bang up to the mark. Are you, perhaps, planning a lengthy stay?"

"Hope not," returned a somewhat gruffer voice. "Wife insisted on dragging us down here. Touch of rheumatics, she has. Some meddling pill-poker said the waters here would perk her up in nothing flat. Waste of time if you ask me. We've been here three days, and she's drunk so much water, she gurgles, but she ain't perked up a whit. Got so tired of hearing her, I thought I'd find me a quiet place and read the papers. And frankly I'd not care how old they are as long as they don't gurgle. Now if you'll excuse me, Mr.—uh, Druberry, is it?—I'll get to them."

The stranger was apparently anxious to escape his new-found guide, but no more so than Alexandra. She hadn't needed a name in order to recognize that first voice. As soon

243

as she had heard it, she had carefully kept her back turned and, ostensibly searching for a certain book among the many that lined the walls, she had begun edging toward the door

Blast the man anyway! Once he had attached himself to her, which she was quite sure he would, she would never have a chance to confide in Peyton. If only she could make it to the door, she thought, she would wait outside, hiding behind a tree, if necessary!

That she failed was hardly surprising. The reading room was not all that large, and its present population was far too sparse. Mr. Druberry spotted her at once.

With a piercing "Halloo!" he made his way toward her, proclaiming his delight at this unexpected meeting.

Or was it, perhaps, not so unexpected after all? Lady Redcliffe had been here just the other day, hadn't she? She must be quite a reader. If she didn't take care, he-he, folks would start thinking her a regular bluestocking. Oh, but of course, he was only jesting. No one would ever suppose dear charming Lady Redcliffe to be one of those dreadfully bookish females. And even if she were, she needn't look so terribly abashed. Her secret was safe with him. In fact, exclaimed Mr. Druberry, making a magnanimous bow, Lady Redcliffe might pick out as many books as she liked. He himself would be only too happy to carry them up the hill.

"How kind," muttered Alexandra, who was feeling not the least abashed, only a great deal annoyed. "But I'm afraid there's very little here that catches my interest at the moment. So, as you can see, I have nothing to carry, and I am in bit of a rush. You'll have to excuse me, Mr. Druberry, but I really must run."

"So soon, dear lady? How very disappointing," he exclaimed, accentuating that regret with a most doleful pout. Then instantly he brightened. "But there is! Something to catch your interest, I mean."

A "shush!" from a nearby patron of literature informed him that he might do well to lower his voice. He did somewhat. "That chap at the reading table," he whispered, loudly. "You wanted to meet him."

"I did?" Alexandra barely glanced at the portly gentleman who sprawled back in his chair, holding a newspaper almost at arm's length to accommodate his paunch. She was too busy trying to keep her own arms out of Mr. Druberry's reach.

She didn't succeed. At last grappling a firm hold on her elbow, the man was clearly intent on escorting her across the room whether she wished it or not.

"You did indeed, my dear lady," he whispered, stopping just short of tugging her along with him. "You might recall that you mentioned as much just the other afternoon at tea. I allowed as how I'd happened on a chap from Yorkshire—not that I knew that at first of course. I just chanced to sit myself down beside him at the Pump Room. He brings his wife there for her rheumatism, so he tells me. At any rate, we fell to chatting. Such as it was, I must say the fellow wasn't much forthcoming, but he did admit to being a Yorkshireman. So naturally I asked him about that—that 'other' Yorkshireman in town."

"And he did know Pey—Mr. Clive," Alexandra murmured. "Yes, I recall now. I—I thought you meant someone else. This gentleman, you say, is a relation of Mr. Clive's?"

"Or some such. His name's Muchmore, but not when it comes to chatting, I may assure you of that. I was merely engaging in idle converse, not prying, you understand. But I may tell you it was rather like pulling hen's teeth. The fellow has no conversation except, I'm afraid, when it comes to his wife's afflictions. He seems rather fond of that topic."

Mr. Druberry was no longer tugging. It had finally occurred to him that, in his attempt to keep Lady Redcliffe by his side, he was only reminding her of the one man he very much wished they both could forget.

He started tugging again but this time in the opposite direction. "Pray do forgive me, dear lady. Here I've been rattling on, and you're in such a rush. Please allow me to escort you to your destination, wherever that may be, and we'll speak no more of this fellow. The man seems most contrary at any rate, rather like most Yorkshiremen no doubt. I daresay you shouldn't like to make his acquaintance after all."

"Oh, but I should."

And this time it was Alexandra who propelled the way. Short of committing an outright gaucherie, Altheus Druberry had no choice but to accompany her to the reading table and perform the introductions. Once these niceties were exchanged, Alexandra stole an anxious glance at the door.

"I believe, sir, we have an acquaintance in common. Mr. Peyton Clive? In fact, as I have been informed by Mr. Druberry, you happen to be a kinsman of his, do you not?"

"Only through marriage," said Mr. Muchmore, having heaved himself and his paunch out of his chair to greet this lovely lady. With a gesture, he invited her to take a seat and was a bit disappointed when she declined.

Pity, he thought, it was not every day he was introduced to a real beauty. Then he considered the bright side. If the lady lingered, so doubtless would Mr. Druberry, and Mr. Muchmore was far from enamored with that worthy's presence. He swiftly got back to the subject at hand.

"Peyton's connected with Mrs. Muchmore's side of the family. Brandon, too, a' course. That would be his cousin, did you know? Military man—risen to major's rank, I believe. I ran into him about a year past, in London, as a matter of fact. He was just dashing through on some, oh, diplomatic assignment or another as I recall. But now, Peyton a' course I know much better, being a neighbor of mine so to speak. Though I can't claim I've seen him for a couple of fortnights. He's here in Bath, you say?"

"He is," Mr. Druberry volunteered with an expression that clearly showed he wished at least one Yorkshireman had stayed in his own domain. "Mr. Clive has lodgings at the Seven Seas Inn on Henry Street."

Mr. Muchmore rubbed his chin thoughtfully. "Close by, I take it. Suppose we'll have to look the lad up then. Ah, yes, now that it comes to mind, I'm jolly well sure the missus will insist. She'll want word of his wife."

"Wife?"

The word was no more than a whisper. Without another sound, Alexandra sank into a vacant chair.

"Indeed, yes," said Mr. Muchmore. "Maryanne, her name is."

Pleased to think the beautiful Lady Redcliffe had changed her mind about lingering, he promptly lowered himself into his own chair and hitched it closer.

"Spirited little gal, she is too," he went on jovially. "The last we heard she was nearly due with their seventh babe. Or could it be the eighth?"

Chapter 9

Having overslept, Mrs. Cawlwood trailed downstairs to find her house in rather a commotion. The masses of flowers she had ordered for the evening's festivities had arrived. Much too many flowers, Chives' tone seemed to imply as he greeted his mistress at the foot of the stairs. They were, he explained, now overflowing the hall because the maids had not yet finished dusting the main salons and one could hardly arrange flowers on undusted tables, could one?

Furthermore, it seemed Cook was in rebellion because the scullery girl had not yet arrived but the party provisions had. Too many provisions, the tone again implied. The kitchen was now cluttered with enough supplies to feed an army, not to mention a score of squabs that were not only unplucked, but still alive. Further, several of them had escaped their pen and Cook was now in the process of chasing them around the kitchen with a cleaver. If madam desire breakfast, perhaps she might partake of the remaining chocolate and buns that had been served to the young ladies.

With the additional information that Miss Dulcie was yet in the morning room and Lady Redcliffe had gone to the Circulating Library, Chives quickly took himself off. And his direction, understandably enough, was not toward the kitchen.

Mrs. Cawlwood, thus left deserted at the foot of the stairs, thought her butler's actions rather uncommon, but she was of no mind to dwell on them — a condition which in itself was highly uncommon.

Ordinarily, any one of these minor disasters would have been sufficient to set Tilmatha Cawlwood into a stew. This bright, Friday morning, however, she was quite content with her world despite having overslept. Or, perhaps, because of it. That extra repose had produced several pleasant dreams of a highly intimate nature.

Thus, it was in high good humor that she sailed into the morning room, uncaring that her lace cap was askew and her voluminous dressing gown sported far too many lacy ruffles and beribboned flounces for her little dumpling of a figure.

She certainly was not expecting to find a young officer of His Majesty's Light Horse Guards sprawled in one of her wicker chairs.

"Lieutenant!" she gasped, clutching the errant gown up to her chin and nearly disappearing within a large ruffle. "I hadn't expected—I mean—oh, dear, why didn't Chives tell me? I'm not dressed for company!"

She spun around, determined to exit the room as quickly as she had entered it, but a trailing flounce stopped her. Mrs. Cawlwood found herself inextricably pinned, barely able to see over the top of one ruffle, her heel securely snagged in another.

Dulcie sped to her rescue. "Oh, Auntie," she giggled, sinking to her knees and deftly freeing the slipper from its lacy snare. "You needn't stand on ceremony with Daniel. He's practically family."

"He is?" mumbled Mrs. Cawlwood from somewhere inside the ruffle. Now that her foot was once more unhindered, she turned around very cautiously.

"Of course." Rising, Dulcie took a ribbon from the waist of her own frock and tied it around her aunt's neckline, thereby securing the treacherous gown. "We're going to be married," she added, neatly folding back the encompassing ruffle.

"That's nice, dear," said Mrs. Cawlwood.

Whether her aunt was offering congratulations or merely expressing relief at the ability to see clearly again, Dulcie couldn't tell.

She preferred to assume it was the former. "Thank you,"

she said, gaily taking her aunt's hand and leading her over to the table. "Now do sit down and I shall tell you all about it. Would you care for some chocolate?"

"Yes," declared Mrs. Cawlwood. "I believe I'm fair to starving. Thank you, Lieutenant," she added as Daniel, having politely risen at her entrance, now offered her his own chair, then drew up another for himself.

"Now, you were saying, my dear?" she went on, sipping at her chocolate and paying more attention to the contents of the table than to Dulcie's utterings. Sadly, the table seemed to be better filled with cutlery than food. And the chocolate was decidedly tepid. Mrs. Cawlwood finally got the drift of the conversation just as she lifted the cover from the sole bread basket on the table.

An elopement? Mrs. Cawlwood's contentment with the world crumbled as quickly as a piece of poorly molded clay.

"Impossible!" she wailed. She fixed the lieutenant with a most censorious eye. "I cannot say as I would disapprove of your marrying Dulcie. Your grandmother is a fine woman. Quite first oars as you youngsters would say. Indeed, I misdoubt there is a soul in Bath who would claim less. And as for you, young man! While I might venture to find you a bit too full of dash—"

"Auntie!" Dulcie interrupted with a harsh laugh of disbelief. "Surely you cannot think Daniel's a rake-shame!"

Absently-mindedly, Mrs. Cawlwood had picked up the cup of tepid chocolate. She set it down with a clatter. "Good heavens! Most certainly not! But he did kiss you. Right on the doorsill!"

"Really now, Auntie—" began Dulcie.

Mrs. Cawlwood shushed her with a wave of the hand. "Nevertheless," she went on, looking Daniel square in the face. "If it were up to me, I shouldn't precisely hold that against you, you see. I daresay you had a touch of encouragement."

She paused to give her niece the benefit of that censorious eye, then leveled it once more on Daniel. "On the whole, I'd vow you'd do rather nicely for Dulcie. And if her father disapproves of you, which it seems to me very likely he does, than I'd say that is all the more to your credit. Percy Winford—forgive me, dear, for saying this, but it happens to be true—Percy has never been able to see the forest for the trees when it comes to money. The thing is, of course as we all know, he'd have married Dulcie off to the Bank of England if he could. Which naturally he couldn't although I daresay the notion did occur to him. And barring that, a nabob—which, Daniel dearest, you are not. Still, I happen to have it on good account from your grandmother that you're sufficiently plump in the purse to keep your bride from starving. Far from starving, I might add—if you'll forgive me, dear boy, for being so blunt. And I shouldn't object in the least if it were up to me. Unfortunately, it's not, so I can only give you my blessing, and pray that somehow you can convince Dulcie's father. You must win his permission, you know, it's only fitting. Anything else is not, young man. And we'll hear no more talk of elopement in this house. It's unseemly."

Unused to so much determination, Mrs. Cawlwood collapsed back in her chair with a fluttery "Oh, my, what have I said?"

"Only the truth," Daniel replied with a glaring look at Dulcie. "You're quite correct, ma'am. Anything less than appealing to Mr. Winford is most unseemly, and it was only desperation that drove us to even think of another course. I'm quite hopeful, we shan't ever have to think of it again."

"Hopeful?" Dulcie scoffed. She was getting rather tired of trying to talk Daniel into an elopement, only to have him back away with each new argument. "Daniel, how can you be so foolish? Major Clive won't back away. Absolutely nothing will happen, even if Peyton Clive does agree to talk to him. He won't listen! You said yourself once that the more the major's balked, the more stubborn he gets. He won't listen to a cousin he hasn't seen in years. He won't listen to anyone! The whole thing is an utter goose chase. And I can tell you exactly what will happen. Lexie will come back all moony-eyed from seeing her Mr. Clive. And anything else will come to absolute naught!"

Mrs. Cawlwood who had been trying to follow this

exchange with a total lack of success vowed that an elopement, even the thought of an elopement was horrid enough, without bringing in outsiders. And whatever did the Clive boys have to do with it anyway?

"Dear," she fluttered. "I'm sure you're mistaken somehow. I really can't imagine the Clives caring one way or another whom you marry. Whatever this is about, I do believe you've been misled. Oh, yes, undoubtedly you must have been."

The sound of the front door slamming heralded Lady Redcliffe's return.

And she was definitely not moony-eyed.

Running to greet her, Dulcie took one look at her friend's face and stopped short in her tracks. "Oh, Lexie, it did come to naught, didn't it?"

She didn't wait for an answer. Pushing Alexandra into the morning room, she accosted the love of her life with a spirited reproach. "Daniel Symington, just see what you've done! Sending her off on a fool's errand, and now something terrible's happened. Just look at her, she's crushed beyond words. Oh, Daniel, how could you!"

Daniel, much to his credit, not only ignored this accusation but the couple of rather glaring fallacies behind it. For one, he hadn't sent Lady Redcliffe on her mission. It had been her own idea. Second, to him the lady did not look crushed. She looked absolutely speechless with anger.

With as much dignity as he could muster, Daniel rose and invited her to take his chair. "Alexandra," he said quietly. "What exactly did happen?"

The best he got was a tight-lipped shake of the head, meaning, he inferred, that the lady had no wish to join them at the table.

Still hoping against hope that his former major had done the honorable thing, he persisted. "Didn't he make any attempt to set matters right?"

Again the answer was that same tight-lipped shake of the head. The possibility of any further probing was immediately squelched by Dulcie.

"Can't you see, she doesn't want to talk about it!" Impulsively the girl threw her arms around Alexandra. "Poor darling, you don't have to say a word. It's all perfectly clear. Mr. Clive wasn't the slightest help, was he? No, I can see he wasn't. And I can see how disappointed you are. But you mustn't be—not on our account at any rate. Daniel and I are going to elope now, aren't we, Daniel?"

The lieutenant happened to be standing behind Alexandra at the moment. When there was no response, Dulcie raised herself on tiptoe to throw a glaring look across her friend's shoulder. "Well, aren't we? You promised you would if this ridiculous goose chase failed. And obviously it has!"

Stepping a few paces backward, Daniel glanced from Dulcie to Alexandra and across to Mrs. Cawlwood, who was plainly bereft of words herself.

"Yes," he muttered glumly. "I guess it has."

"Marvelous!" cried Dulcie. Wrapping her arms even tighter around Alexandra, she gave her friend an exuberant hug. "Oh, Lexie, didn't I tell you! Things do have a way of working out. Just imagine! Dashing off through the countryside. How exciting—and so romantic. Daniel, darling, please go hire a coach, won't you? Something roomy would be nice, and well-sprung of course. I shouldn't like to be uncomfortable. It is quite a long trip, you know, and—oh, well, I'm sure you'll manage quite nicely. We'll be off to Brighton in a wink!"

"Only," said Daniel, "if Alexandra goes with us."

"Good heavens, of course!" cried Dulcie. "How could I have forgotten? Oh, Lexie, you will come with us, won't you? You must! If you don't, then Daniel and I should have to go dashing off alone. And I'm afraid, despite all I've said, that would look a bit shabby. You wouldn't like that. And neither would Aunt Letitia when she found out. But with you along, everything would be perfectly proper! So you must go with us. Please, Lexie, say you will!"

Dulcie, clutching her motionless friend even harder, felt as if she were caught between two stubborn mules. Daniel would not elope without Alexandra, and Alexandra had already made her opposition to any such venture quite clear.

Dulcie geared herself for a knotty siege.

She found, to her amazement, not even the hint of a snag.

Alexandra removed herself from Dulcie's embrace. "I'll be delighted to go anywhere," she said coldly, "as long as it is away from Bath."

Thrilled at the outcome and at the same time a shade disappointed that she had had no chance to show off her full powers of persuasion, Dulcie could only stare at her friend in the blankest of fashion.

But she quickly recovered. "Thank goodness, that's settled! Now Daniel can see about the coach."

"Yes, I suppose I may as well," Daniel muttered. He turned to leave, adding rather morosely that he would see himself out since Dulcie no doubt would be in an absolute tear to start packing.

Her reply proved he didn't know his beloved as well as he suspected. "There is plenty of time," she said firmly. "I am going nowhere until I've comforted Lexie."

She waited until the door had closed behind Daniel. Then turning to Alexandra, she murmured gently, "Do sit down, poor darling, and tell me everything."

Chapter 10

By mid-morning, Mrs. Cawlwood's house had reached some semblance of order.

The squab rebellion had been squelched. The plethora of flowers had been arranged in any and all bowls available and now adorned every possible surface from the newel posts of the stairs to the hall table beside the front door.

There, as a matter of fact, Chives had deposited a massive array of asters in a soup tureen that was nearly as large as the table itself. Two full pails of water had been required to fill it.

Alexandra, having formed the habit of tying her bonnet in front of the mirror above this hall table, automatically stopped to do the same this particular morning and was quite put out to discover that asters obscured not only the entire table but the mirror as well.

With the sincere opinion that nothing in this world would ever set itself right again, she fumbled blindly with the bonnet strings and went out the door.

Dulcie, having preceded her by some minutes, was now standing on the lower front step, arms akimbo, directing the placement of the last of the luggage.

"It must go in!" she was exclaiming. "Oh, Daniel, I cannot go to Brighton without my trunk. The coach is so small. Are you certain it was the best you could hire?"

"The very best," grunted the lieutenant, who was obviously doing his utmost to shove a trunk into the closed interior of that conveyance. As that space was already jumbled with a variety of portmanteaus and hatboxes, his efforts were meeting with small success. Three-quarters of the way in, the trunk came to a stop. Farther, despite Lieutenant Symington's most valiant attempts, it would not budge.

With a muttered curse, he heaved it back out and onto the curb. "Blast it all, Dulcie, the only way I can get this thing in is to wedge it between the seats, and then there won't be room for you two. It will have to go on top."

He was soon to learn that Dulcie and her trunk had a great deal in common. The girl moved a bit to one side, allowing Alexandra to join her on the lower step, but, further than that, she would not budge.

"Darling," she said, and the tinge of exasperation in her voice did not go unnoticed. "You know perfectly well it cannot go outside. Good heavens, how would it look if we went driving through town with a trunk in plain view? Everyone would guess our business, and what a scandal broth that would be! We must think of Aunt Tilmatha, you know!"

Daniel, who had turned once more to cast a dubious eye on the jumble inside the coach, suddenly spun around. "Good Lord, she's not going too?"

"Of course not!" Dulcie snapped, now openly annoyed with her beloved's lack of grasp. "But Aunt Tilmatha knows simply everyone in Bath. Some of her friends are apt to see us and recognize us! They're bound to think we're eloping."

"Well, that's what we are doing, aren't we?" grumbled a most frustrated lieutenant.

"We most definitely are not! I mean, we are in a way, I suppose, but certainly not in the shabby manner they'll suspect. After all, we're not going to Gretna Green! But they won't know that, and we can't very well pull up at every street corner to explain, now can we? So you just push that trunk into the coach. And we'll tie down the side curtains nice and tight. Thank goodness, they're black. No one will have the least chance of peeking inside. And"—Dulcie paused to consider the narrow, unprotected driver's seat—"and Lexie and I will ride up front with you. There's plenty of room if we squeeze, which will be loads more fun anyway, don't you think? We'll be a snug as three bugs—"

"In a snuff tin," finished Daniel, who looked as if he would like to leave both the trunk and Dulcie sitting on the curbstone. Nevertheless, he complied with his little taskmaster's wishes.

As they settled themselves on the high front seat, Alexandra, who had had the good sense to keep quiet for the past several minutes, mildly ventured that they had been in luck so far. No one, outside the Cawlwood household, had seemed to witness their departure.

"That's because we were very quick," said Dulcie, quite proud of her strategical maneuvers. With a grin, she rewarded Daniel for his part in those maneuvers. "And we mustn't dawdle through town either. We don't want anyone asking idle questions. If we see anyone we know, we'll simply nod politely and drive on."

"Right," Daniel agreed. "No dawdling." He sprang the horses and off they went at a reassuring brisk clip.

Friday, as any local cit might have told them, was market day in Bath. The lower streets, which on any other day might be filled with pedestrians but only an occasional vehicle, were now cluttered with drays, produce wagons, and pushcarts.

Their brisk clip abruptly slowed to a frustrating clop.

"Oh, dear," sighed Dulcie. Seated between Daniel and Alexandra, she leaned forward, anxiously searching the crowds from one side to the other and praying not one face would prove familiar. "Isn't there another way?"

"Yes," Daniel muttered, "if only I'd thought. Steady, boys, steady," he called out, taking a firmer hold on the reins. The coach he had managed to hire may have had its inadequacies, but the horses that went with it were in fine mettle.

Too fine for this melee, he thought, feeling their straining tension through the reins. He looked ahead, then pointed with his free hand. "There's the Pump Room just yonder. Next to it is an off street I know. We can use that to get to the main high road—if we can ever reach it!"

With expert handling, he began to edge the team through the traffic. Around a cumbersome dray, past a wagon heaped with potatoes. "Hey, be a fine chap and move that pushcart, will you? Much obliged."

Finally, Dulcie drew a ragged breath of relief. "Thank heavens, we're almost there and we haven't passed a soul we recog—"

"Halloo, so we meet again! What a charming coincidence, my dear lady!"

"Yes, isn't it?" Alexandra muttered. She exchanged a glance with Dulcie, then looked down at the man who had just arrived at her side of the coach. "Good morning, once more, Mr. Druberry."

Next to her, she could hear Dulcie frantically whispering, "Move on, Daniel, move on!"

And Daniel did try, but the traffic had closed around them. They were temporarily at an impasse.

It was a very provoking moment for everyone except Altheus Druberry. He beamed up at them as if Providence had showered its blessings on him alone. "My regards, Miss Winford. Lieutenant. And where, may I ask, might you three be off to on this glorious day? A jolly drive through the town perhaps?"

"Yes!" Dulcie blurted, then realized Mr. Druberry was making a bit of a jest. No one in his right mind would believe they had deliberately set off on a pleasure jaunt through this chaos.

"No!" she quickly retracted. "That is, we were planning a short drive. A very short drive to—to the Arthurian ruins! Yes, that's it, to King Arthur's old fort. It's somewhere round about quite close, so we hear. Hardly the slightest drive at all!"

258

For God's sake, thought Alexandra, stop embellishing! She knew what was bound to follow.

It did. Hard upon the wake of Mr. Druberry's delighted laugh.

"Bless you, Miss Winford, I think you'll find it is a bit farther than that, but you are in luck all the same. I know a most convenient route to those ruins, and if you'll pardon my blowing my own yard of tin, he-he, I am probably more conversant with those ruins than any man hereabouts. Fortunately, I am quite at leisure at the moment. I would consider it no less than my duty to accompany you. Indeed, I would consider it a rare pleasure.

"If you've no objection, Lieutenant," he went on, bestowing his most flattering smile on Alexandra and paying not the slightest heed to Daniel, "I'm sure your lovely companions won't object. No lady—or so I've found, he-he—is ever adverse to a second admiring escort."

"Well, this lady is!" Dulcie snapped. Feeling Alexandra's warning touch on her sleeve, she amended her tone, but only slightly. "Very kind of you to offer, sir, but as you can see, there's hardly space on this seat for the three of us. Good day, Mr. Druberry."

Any other man would have taken this less-then-veiled hint and hied himself off, but not Altheus Druberry. So eager was he to supplant himself in the place of the deceitful Mr. Peyton Clive (married? And a father several times over? No wonder Lady Redcliffe had stormed out of the library without a word) that it would have taken a broadsword to deter that worthy.

Favoring Dulcie with a forgiving smile, he glanced toward the tightly curtained interior of the coach. "My dear Miss Winford, I'm sure you and your young officer have a great many *on dits* to share. I would not think to intrude for a moment. Your lovely chaperone and I will be quite content to ride inside the coach. We might even, he-he, find our own little *on dits* to share, mightn't we, my dear Lady Redcliffe?"

He reached out a hand to open the coach door.

259

Three "no's!" rang out at the same time, and a startled Mr Druberry jumped back a good foot.

"My stars! Is there something in there I shouldn't see?"

"Yes!" It was Alexandra's turn to blurt out the first thing that came to mind. "I mean, no, of course not. There' nothing inside save our parasols. And a few other things. It' just that—"

In desperation, she glanced around. A familiar building just ahead caught her eye.

"—that I myself wasn't going to the ruins!" she finished overjoyed at the sudden inspiration. "It's been a dreadfully nervy morning. I thought I'd go to the Pump Room for glass of restorative water. Daniel and Dulcie were simply dropping me off on their way."

This respite, temporary as it was, brought four sighs o relief. Three from the coach's occupants and one, for an entirely different reason, from Mr. Altheus Druberry. Despite his offer to guide them, he hadn't the vaguest notion where any Arthurian fort might be or even if it existed.

"Wonderful!" he exclaimed. "Naturally, my dear lady, I' be most honored to escort you there instead."

"Naturally," muttered Alexandra. After a whispered aside to Dulcie, "Drive around to the side of the Pump Room and wait for me, I'll get rid of him somehow," she bestowed glittering smile on Mr. Druberry and gave him her hand

As he assisted her down, she heard a muffled giggle behind her, followed by a most insincere expression o sympathy for her poor beleaguered nerves.

"Thank you, Dulcie," Alexandra responded dryly. "You concern is most touching."

She took Mr. Druberry's arm, and they walked off toward the Pump Room.

At the door, Alexandra cast a glance backward and wa happy to note that Daniel was at last making progres through the crowd. She hustled her new escort inside with the insistence that she simply couldn't wait another instan for a sip of those wondrous, healing waters.

"But of course," burbled Mr. Druberry. "Pray allow me to etch you a glass immediately." With that, he went trotting off toward the pump in the center of the room, leaving Alexandra just inside the entrance.

Idly surveying the assembly room with its usual complement of gossiping and sipping dowagers, she edged sideways a step and came bump up against a slender table. Atop it was a bowl of flowers equal to the mass in Mrs. Cawlwood's hallway and filled with just as much water.

Asters again, she thought, and vaguely wondered if they were the only flowers in season. Even more she wondered why she didn't simply duck out now while Mr. Druberry was at the pump. It would be so easy, she thought, to just disappear while no one was looking.

Unhappily, Alexandra's luck had been running uphill for some time. It was not about to change course now.

Someone was looking.

Even as she turned, Alexandra heard her name called. A portly gentleman rose from his chair and hurried to her side.

"Lady Redcliffe, good to see you out and about. Frankly— well, you must forgive an old man's curiosity, my dear, but I was a bit concerned. When you rushed out of the library this morning, you seemed so pale. I'm afraid I couldn't help wondering if you were suddenly taken ill. You're back in fettle now, I do hope."

"Why, yes, thank you, Mr. — Mr. Muchmore, isn't it?"

Alexandra judged the distance to the door. Barely four or five steps and she would be gone . . .

But she couldn't bring herself to do it.

She had run out on this kindly man once. Twice would be impossibly rude. It wasn't his fault Peyton Clive was such a rotter. With a resigned shrug, Alexandra abandoned her first, and quickest, prospect of escape.

"I do appreciate your asking, sir. But it was merely a passing indisposition. I am quite recovered now, I assure you."

And to herself, she added, And myself as well. I no longer

care a fig for a certain Mr. Clive. No matter what, that man will never get a rise out of me again.

"Tell me, Mr. Muchmore," she said, taking his arm and moving several paces farther into the room, "have you tried the waters yet? Some people find them quite refreshing."

"Not I," replied Mr. Muchmore. "Wouldn't touch the stuff. I'm only waiting for the missus. She's back rumbling around in one of those infernal pools, so they tell me. And so, I fancy, is her stomach," he added with a droll smile. "Be delighted to introduce you if you've time to wait until they bring her out."

"Well, I haven't really," said Alexandra, looking around to see that Mr. Druberry had been waylaid by a garrulous dowager. She glanced toward the entrance. "I must run actually. I—"

Without knowing it, she stepped behind Mr. Muchmore, putting his portly figure between her and the doorway.

Remember, she told herself firmly. You don't care. Not a fig. You shall simply utter a politeness and then leave in a most dignified manner.

"Why, there's Mr. Clive," she said brightly. "Perhaps you'd like to ask him about his wife. Maryanne, I believe you called her."

"So I should." Turning toward the newcomer, who appeared to be scanning the room for a particular face, Mr. Muchmore strode a pace forward. Then he stopped, looked again, and chuckled. "I'll ask, but I doubt he'll know any more than I do. That's not Peyton, you know."

At Alexandra's incredulous expression, Mr. Muchmore chuckled again. "I can hardly be mistaken, my dear. Maryanne not only takes to motherhood, she sets a fine table. Peyton is nearly as paunchy as I am these days."

"Then—then—" Alexandra could barely get the words out. "Then who's *that*?"

"Why, his cousin Brandon, of course."

As if in slow motion, Alexandra walked toward the door.

"Ah, there you are," said Brandon, a teasing smile curving

his lips as he spied her. "Alexandra, my sweet, you are a hard woman to find. From your message, I inferred that you wanted my help in some way, but, when I got to the library, you weren't there. I've been looking all over. What is it, darling? What can I do for you?"

"Why, absolutely nothing," Alexandra said with icy politeness.

In a most dignified manner, she picked up the bowl of asters from the nearby table and dumped it over his head.

Chapter 11

To passers-by, the sight of a thoroughly soaked gentleman stalking along Abbey Square was enough to provoke many a stare and a smile.

That the gentleman also seemed oblivious to a stray aster that protruded from the back of his collar, not to mention a couple more that had managed to slip themselves halfway into the front of his waistcoat was downright laughable.

The only person who seemed to find absolutely nothing comical about this predicament was the former Maj. Brandon Clive. In a seething rage, he strode toward the Seven Seas Inn, thinking this damned town had been all too aptly named. He had never been drenched so many times in his life!

Once in his room, effecting a complete change of raiment did not make him feel a whit better. The inn's valet, summoned to revive the wet clothing, offered a polite murmur of sympathy for its sad state. He nearly had his nose bitten off for his efforts.

The man departed for the lower regions of the inn, convinced that Mr. Clive was either prone to some strange fetish or else in love.

"Likely both," he muttered to himself, remembering the parasol he had tucked into the gentleman's armoire and its apparent owner, the lady he had glimpsed descending the rear stairs.

In the meantime, Brandon had stalked the length of his chambers a good dozen times and had shown no sign of relenting. He had no idea whether he was more furious with himself for being a bloody fool or with Lady Alexandra Redcliffe for being the damnedest jade this side of the Bosporus.

Which, he told himself savagely, he should never have left!

But, oh, no, he had had to do the honorable thing. He had agreed to that ridiculous betrothal with Dulcie Winford, and what had he gotten for his pains?

Hoodwinked at every turn!

Finding himself married to the wrong woman should have been hoax enough for a lifetime. But not for *his*, Brandon fumed, kicking a chair out of the way. *That* particular mishap had been only the beginning.

And a mere snap compared to the bride herself!

Giving the carpet a brief respite, Brandon ceased pacing from north to south and started a new track from east to west. He was, he concluded, the most accursed bridegroom who had ever drawn breath.

An unsolicited bride, twice widowed and thrice wed? What else could he have expected except a well-traveled piece of baggage. What else would any man have expected! Certainly not a beauty, whose husbands had left her so virtually untouched that one might as well say she had never been married at all.

This reflection enraged him still further. He had, he told himself, every justification for his own small hoax. It was the blasted jade's fault anyway. If she had been fair enough not to condemn him sight unseen, he would never have considered switching names on her. Furthermore, if she had been the old raddled-cheek she should have been, the thought would never have occurred to him!

"Serves her right," he muttered, pausing only to plant his boot against the back of another chair and send it skittering. She hadn't even given him time to explain, which he had been ready to, had he been given the chance!

In fact, while searching for her, he had been of a mind not only to confess his true name but to ask the lady if she would care to share it with him permanently.

"Lady!" he sneered aloud.

Ladies did not leave a gentleman drenched and sputting amid a roomful of gape-jawed dowagers.

The renewed remembrance of that humiliation brought irreparable damage to the carpet.

His heels digging into the fibers as he continued to pace, Brandon found himself torn between the desire to render some like humiliation to his tormentor and the memory of how entrancing she had been on the first day they had met. Unbidden came the thought that, in complete privacy and sans clothing, any sort of dunking with Lady Redcliffe might well prove enjoyable.

He came to an abrupt halt.

"You damned fool! She's a headlong, ill-mannered addle-pate, and you're well rid of her!"

He flung himself into a chair, then immediately jumped up again. "Or you soon will be," he muttered, striding toward the door. "That's one trick they didn't get away with!"

The notion had just occurred to him that the annulment papers were still in the safe downstairs. Percy Winford had obviously tried some sort of boggle, claiming he was off to London to file for the annulment. At least that ruse had failed, Brandon assured himself as he went stalking down the stairs.

The only documents that would count officially were those with his own signature on them. And those, he was confident, were yet in the Seven Seas safe.

Rousting the innkeeper from the common room, Brandon demanded his property. The moment it was in his possession, he told himself firmly, he was going to march up the hill to the Cawlwood house and demand Alexandra's signature. This farce of a marriage would be ended right then and there!

It took some time for him to realize he had been deluded once more. The baffled innkeeper, in turn, finally rousted the valet who confessed he had not only penned the gentleman's name on the outside of the packet but had left it in plain view on the desk.

Whereupon, the innkeeper, amid much head scratching, at last recalled that a Mr. Wisford — or was it Winford? — had been present during the great egg spill. It had been a dreadful mess, Mr. Clive must understand. Anything could have happened.

Well, Brandon mused as he went out the door, so Percival Winford very likely did have the right papers. And if he had actually filed them in London, that was just fine with former Maj. Brandon Clive.

But he wanted to make sure, and if anyone would know, it would be Lady Alexandra Redcliffe!

There was only one drawback. He could hardly confront her when she wasn't there.

Once having arrived at the Cawlwood house, he found the only persons available were the owner of said house and a strangely mischievous-looking Lord Chambers.

The former couldn't—or woudn't—tell him where her guests had gone. His lordship, with an even more mischievous wink, merely offered to escort him back to the Seven Seas for a late-morning libation.

Considering it was the only courteous offer he had had that day, Brandon took him up on it.

"Excellent. The treat shall be mine," returned Lord Chambers. "I expect we both could use a bit of calming down."

After pressing Mrs. Cawlwood's hand and whispering a few words that seemed to heighten her complexion a great deal, he took Brandon's arm and the two men walked down the hill in mutual silence.

By the demise of his second tankard of ale, Brandon had discovered what Mrs. Cawlwood had known for some time. His lordship was a very soothing and perspicacious listener.

Also more than a bit wily, Brandon noticed as, at a discreet signal from his host, a third tankard suddenly appeared before him. Lord Chambers, on the other hand, seemed quite content with a single glass of sherry.

Brandon raised the tankard in a mock salute. "You wouldn't by any chance be trying to tipple me, would you, sir?"

"By no means," his lordship replied in a grave voice, but

his eyes twinkled. "I daresay it would take more than a couple of ales to loosen your tongue — Major Clive."

"Ex-Major," Brandon automatically corrected, then realization broke over him. He looked up, taking the joke on himself with a harsh laugh.

"Touché! I've been running on like a bloody fool, haven't I? Please accept my apologies, sir. And my gratitude that you weren't some Turkish inquisitioner. I'd have doubtless spilled every military secret from the Bosporus to the Crimea!"

Disgusted, he shook his head in disbelief at his own garrulousness. "I should never have resigned my commission. A few days of civilian life, and I've turned into a regular gabble-grinder. Is there nothing I didn't blurt out?"

"Quite a bit, I imagine," his lordship replied graciously. He refrained from saying that, what little had been omitted, he had surmised rather easily. "No need to belabor yourself, my boy. I'm confident there's never been a military problem you've not handled with admirable stoicism. But then, I would also fancy you have never encountered an adversary quite like Lady Redcliffe."

"Damned right, I haven't!" Brandon retorted. "Still, that's no excuse for —"

Lord Chambers quickly threw up a forestalling hand. "Please, no more apologies. On the contrary, I'm gratified that you chose to confide in me. I, ahem, have almost come to consider myself a member of the family, so to speak. And I assure you, I am most interested. Now, from what you've told me, it would seem nearly certain that you and Lady Redcliffe are no longer wed. What do you intend to do next?"

"Leave!"

Angrily, Brandon took a swig of ale, then set the tankard down hard. "I've had my fill of Bath. And its denizens — present company excepted, that is. I am returning to London, and, I may promise you, sir, my very first stop will be the registry office. I intend to make damned sure that annulment has been filed. After that, decommissioned or not, I've a good mind to head straight back to Turkey!"

Unperturbed by this outburst, Lord Chambers merely sipped at his sherry and agreed that the Continent no doubt would provide a convenient escape. "If indeed," he added dryly, "one is quite certain he wishes to escape. But then, in our case of course, I daresay it's the only solution. As you've so graphically stated, there's nothing—and no one—to hold you in England. No obligations of any sort."

"Not a one!" Brandon muttered and told himself he had not a thing to feel guilty about. Alexandra had come to him willingly. He hadn't coerced her. He had made her no false promises. And, by damn, despite all her trickery, he had been prepared to make a clean breast of it—even do the right thing by her—if she had only been reasonable.

With a snort, Brandon Clive absolved himself of all guilt. *Reasonable?* Any hornet who would crown a man with a bowl of asters didn't know the meaning of the word!

"No obligations," he repeated coldly as much, or so it sounded, to convince himself as Lord Chambers. "Not to anyone—including Miss Winford. In fact, I suspect she'll view my departure as a definite boon."

His lordship, having watched with interest the play of emotions across his companion's face, merely smiled and drained the last of his sherry. "Oh, I daresay she might have once. But not now. You won't be marrying her, you know."

Brandon smiled with genuine amusement for the first time since they had sat down. "So I gathered," he replied, turning the tables on his lordship and signaling for a second sherry without asking if the older gentleman preferred one or not.

"Although," he went on, "her father's still set on the match as I understand, but I'll set that straight when I get to London. I believe, once I've made it unmistakably clear that his daughter's affections are otherwise engaged and that I've no intention of forcing the girl into marriage, he'll come around. He will, that is, if he's got the slightest grain of sense. Daniel Symington's a good man—and there's no ignoring his feelings toward her. I think, within a few weeks, Mr. Percival Winford will find himself with an excellent son-in-law."

"Sooner than that," came the murmured response, or at least so it sounded to Brandon. He gave Lord Chambers a sharp look.

"Sir?"

But Lord Chambers seemed in no hurry to repeat himself. He turned away, ostensibly sipping his sherry and studying its clarity against the light.

It was some seconds later before he set the glass down. "Forgive me, my boy, I was wrestling with my conscience. Been a while," he added, chuckling. "Suppose I'm a bit rusty at the task. But it would seem in the interest of—well, of all concerned. I'd best tell you what my dear, agitated Mrs. Cawlwood swore me not to tell."

"You mean you know where Alexandra's gone?" Brandon sat forward abruptly, then just as quickly sat back again. With a great show of nonchalance, he stretched out his long legs and crossed his ankles, looking for all the world as if he were more intrigued by the shine on his boots than in any confidences.

"Don't trouble yourself, sir. Or your conscience either. Lady Redcliffe's direction is not of the least consequence to me."

Lord Chambers, ignoring the words and correctly assessing the actions, just smiled and congratulated himself on making the right choice. "They're on their way to Brighton."

"They?" drawled Brandon, still looking extremely bored. "Alexandra and Dulcie Winford with her, I suppose."

"And Lieutenant Symington as well. He and Miss Winford are eloping." Two could play at this, thought Lord Chambers. Without bothering to glance at the man across the table, he casually pulled out his watch and made note of the hour. "Almost noontime," he said, affecting a good facsimile of his companion's bored drawl. "And well on their way by now, I'd say. Of course, I know you're not the least interested. Particularly since Lady Redcliffe is with them—and has no intention of returning to Bath, I might add."

Brandon yawned. "Really? Well, I'm afraid it's none of my concern."

"No, of course not, my boy. Still—just thinking out loud, you see—a hired coach, even with a decent team, which I understand they have, shouldn't get all that far in one day's time. No match for a man on horseback, I daresay. And I am familiar with the route to Brighton. Only one good post road. One can connect with it just a few blocks off Abbey Square. Then they'll have to stop for the night. The Three Bells would be my guess. Choicest inn halfway to Brighton . . ."

Lord Chambers consulted his watch again. "Ah, well, no interest to you, as you say. You must forgive an old man's ramblings. And rumblings," he added, patting his stomach. "If you will excuse me, I think I'll be getting home to my nuncheon."

Brandon rose to his feet. "Of course, sir. I didn't mean to keep you so long."

"Nonsense, my boy. The pleasure was all mine."

Lord Chambers collected his hat. Then, leaving a generous payment for the barkeep, he went off to a most satisfying meal.

Chapter 12

It was not to be supposed the remainder of the exodus to Brighton would be an especially cheery jaunt.

And indeed it was not.

Daniel, having taken Alexandra up just outside the Pump Room, had done his best to obey the lady's sole utterance, "Spring 'em!" But the side streets of Bath had turned out to be as congested as the main thoroughfares. The coach and horses, which had apparently decided to prove themselves thoroughbreds by spooking at every wagon and cart in their path, demanded all Daniel's attention.

Dulcie, in the meanwhile, had let the delays work her into a desperate fret. Visions of her father and some faceless but demonic suitor with swords abristling had inflamed her imagination.

Long before reaching the high road, she had convinced herself they were in hot pursuit. Try as she might, she could not resist peering frantically over her shoulder from one instant to the next, while delivering a constant barrage of urgings in between.

"Daniel, darling, there's an opening, go this way! There's another, go that way! Oh, Daniel dearest, let's do hurry!"

When Alexandra had remounted the coach, her face had been partially obscured by her bonnet. Dulcie, in her haste to get them moving, had not bothered to look beneath that charming concoction of velvet and ruching. If she had thought about her friend at all, it was only to assume she had rid them of Mr. Druberry as promised and to wish she had done it even faster. They could chat about it later.

Which was just as well. Lady Alexandra Redcliffe was in no mood to chat with anyone.

For the second time that day, a certain man named Clive had rendered her speechless. The first time, although she would have been hard-pressed to admit it, her little Dresden-faced friend had been right. She had been as crushed as she was furious. Now, she told herself in very strong terms, she was simply furious!

Stealing a hard look at her driver, she clamped her mouth shut and concentrated on the road ahead.

Daniel was doing likewise.

"Thank God, we've reached the high road," he at last muttered, then promptly followed that utterance with a distinct, "Blast!"

The first splat of rain had hit his face.

With magnificent restraint, Lieutenant Symington swallowed a good deal of appropriate blasphemy and pulled his team off to the side. "I've traveled this road before, ladies. It shortly is going to become exceedingly wet and exceedingly sloggy. I suggest you get inside."

"We can't, there's no room!" protested Dulcie. She cast a glance skyward, then stubbornly folded her arms across her small bosom. "Furthermore, if you think for one moment that I'd sit in there all dry and cozy while you're out here freezing—and likely catching your death besides—you're very sadly mistaken! We'll . . ."

She took a fearful look backward, then staunchly called upon the sum of her reserves. "Dump the luggage out. We'll *all* sit inside the coach until the rain stops."

Daniel, whose mood had been scarcely more cheerful than Alexandra's, suddenly burst into laughter. Knowing how much Dulcie wanted to forge ahead and just how valiant had been her offer of yet another delay, he pulled her to him and gave her a resounding kiss.

"Thank you, my sweet, but I've been soaked, and none the

273

worse for it, before. Wait here, I'll manage something. I promise you, it won't including dumping your paraphernalia into the mud. Blasted chore stuffing it in the first time! I don't relish repeating the job in a downpour."

Which is definitely what we're in for, he opined to himself as he jumped down from the seat and wrenched open the door. The drops were coming heavier now, and he wanted to make as much time as possible before the road mired. Maybe, he thought, they could even outrun the rain.

That notion inspired him to juggle the assorted boxes and portmanteaus with considerable speed. Then a second thought inspired him further.

Once his dear, frantic little Dulcie was inside the coach, he would no longer be able to see or hear her. She would have to stop second-guessing his driving.

With a chuckle, Daniel proceeded to work even faster. Soon hatboxes and portmanteaus were stacked high on the forward seat. The uncooperative trunk was upended, half of it resting on the floor, half of it taking up the center of the rear seat, with Dulcie and Alexandra neatly squeezed in on either side.

"Good heavens, we're packed tighter than herrings!" was all Dulcie managed to say before Daniel slammed the door and leaped back onto the driver's perch.

He sprang the team and, for a while at least, it did seem they might outrun the weather. But the pelting drops, teasing for a mile here and another there, seemed as intent upon reaching Brighton as soon as the elopers. Eventually the road mired and the coach wheels began to clot with mud. It was tough slogging at best.

His driving coat buttoned tightly around him, his hat brim nearly covering his eyes, Lt. Daniel Symington settled down for a long, chilly ride.

Once or twice, he glanced backward a tad enviously and wondered how the ladies were faring. They might be cramped, he thought, but, by God, they must be a damned sight warmer.

274

With a bulky obstacle between them and their individual thoughts flying, Alexandra and Dulcie evinced no more than an occasional "Ouch!" as the lurch of the vehicle brought an unwary elbow or knee into painful contact with the trunk.

Finally, after several attempts to peer out the window at the road behind them and getting little more for her efforts than a blinding slap of rain, Dulcie settled as best she could into her tiny corner and proceeded to distract herself with all sorts of cheering comments. Wouldn't it be wonderful when they arrived in Brighton? Wouldn't Aunt Letitia Bereston be surprised?

Her companion's monosyllabic replies did not deter her.

"My, aren't we the grumpy one," Dulcie went on, determined to be rosy at all costs. "Likely you're just hungry. I know I am. And poor Daniel out there all alone, he must be famished! I do wish we'd thought to bring a picnic basket. A pity, but—then again, I suppose it's just as well we didn't. If I ate even one tea sandwich, I'd doubtless be too plump to fit into this corner."

"That," muttered Alexandra, "is certainly looking on the bright side."

"Oh, come on now, Lexie, it isn't all that sad. Daniel said we'd stop at some inn called the Three Bells. He says it is the finest one on the road. Near Salisbury, I believe. And surely, even at this ridiculous pace, it cannot be very far now. The three of us will have a lovely dinner beside a roaring fire—"

"How would you know?" Alexandra interrupted. "You've never been there."

Dulcie dismissed this quibbling with a wave of her hand. At least, she appeared to. All Alexandra saw was a brief fluttering of fingers. The rest of Dulcie was hidden behind the trunk.

But, above the sound of the rain and the rumblings of the coach, Dulcie's nonchalant, "Country inns always have roaring fireplaces," came through clear enough. "Lexie, for heaven's sake, do cheer up. We'll have an absolutely engulfing dinner. Then you and I will share a room. We can tuck into bed and chat across our pillows just like schoolgirls. And I vow I shan't bore you very much talking about my wedding. Or Daniel either. Although—" Dulcie giggled—"I expect his name might come up accidentally. Oh, Lexie, hasn't he been simply the grandest! All the time not wanting an elopement—which it isn't, not in a shabby way, I mean—and still, here he is. Out there in the pouring rain, rescuing me just when I needed it. My poor, wonderful darling! How could I have ever railed at him? Just imagine! I was so put out, thinking he was dragging his heels. Why, I very nearly called him a pudding heart!"

She uttered a loud sigh. "That was terrible of me, wasn't it? I should have trusted him. And from now on, I shall! He is simply the dearest, sweetest, most honorable man in the whole world. No matter what, I shall never, ever be angry with him again!"

Looking up at the roof of the coach, she blew her unseen knight a kiss. "He is, isn't he, Lexie?" she added dreamily. "Rather wonderful, I mean?"

Hearing no sound from the far side of the trunk, Dulcie suddenly pushed herself forward and peered around it. "Really, Lexie! If nothing else will take your mind off your empty stomach, then let's talk about—about the Pump Room! You still haven't told me how you stole away from Mr. Druberry. It must have been hilarious. Now do tell me."

Alexandra, too, glanced toward the front of the coach and the unseen lieutenant who steered them through the rain. Then she looked back at her friend's eager face.

"Yes, I suppose you'll have to know sometime."

A bit puzzled by the obvious reluctance in this statement, Dulcie leaned farther around the trunk. "Well, I certainly cannot see why it should matter very much one way or the other. Just tell me what happened."

And so Alexandra did.

Given Dulcie's love for the dramatic, it was to be expected her outrage would easily match Lady Redcliffe's own. Between consoling "her poor Lexie" and calling the deceitful Brandon Clive every name she could think of (including a few Alexandra reminded herself to add to her own vocabulary), Dulcie's rantings lasted some distance.

At last, apparently having fallen short of words and breath, she lapsed into silence and set herself to musing over the treacheries of the common male. Particularly, of course, the treachery of one Major Clive as compared to her own stalwart lieutenant. Thank the saints, dearest Daniel would never be so deceitful, so dishonest, so . . .

Miss Dulcie Letitia Winford let out a shriek that might have broken any number of crystal goblets.

"Lexie! He knew! Daniel knew all the time!"

Her first tirade had been remarkable. Her second was nothing less than awesome. In her efforts to tell her "former" beloved exactly what she thought of his perfidy, she almost pitched herself out the window.

Alexandra pulled her back with the weary comment that she might as well save that indignation. With all the wind and the rain, the lieutenant couldn't possibly hear her.

At last the coach drove into the courtyard of, not the Three Bells as Daniel had intended, but the Sign of the Merry Wayfarer. He helped Dulcie, then Alexandra, down, explaining that the road had become quite impossible and the Wayfarer, if not as elegant as the Three Bells, had the reputation of being clean and comfortable. They would tarry the night there. Daniel, of course, had no idea how near a tongue-lashing he was nor that the hovering presence of two ostlers and a helpful innkeeper was the sole deterrent.

They were shown into a fairly commodious public room while their chambers were being prepared. Dulcie lingered just inside the door, scrutinizing the area with a glittering eye. She looked from one side of the room to the other, from the nearby sofas upon which Alexandra and Daniel had immediately sunk in total exhaustion to the rather insignificant fire at the far end of the room and the oversized, high-backed chair that faced it.

Coming to the decision that, apart from the three of them, the room was devoid of another human presence, she grimly closed the door.

Lt. Daniel Symington was treated to a tongue-lashing the likes of which he had ever before experienced. And, most thankfully, never would again.

It must be said that, to an outsider, none of it would have made the least sense. Dulcie, having worked herself up to a complete sputter, at last burst into tears.

This, in a perverse way, played to one advantage. It made her outpourings intelligible, mainly because the need for an occasional, sobbing breath made her space out her words instead of running them into one, senseless jumble.

It also gave an astounded, and also very guilty-feeling, young lieutenant time to put some space between himself and this furious little tiger.

But hardly an appreciable space, he noticed woefully. With every step he backed, Dulcie was hard on his toes.

"How *could* you?" she wailed, driving him toward the fireplace as ruthlessly as any enemy legion. "I trusted you—I thought we'd be happily married. *You said we would be!* But you deceived me, Daniel—*you lied to me!* Oh, how could you let us make such fools of ourselves!"

Daniel, still steadily retreating, tried to justify himself. "Now sweetheart, I know you've a right to be—a little angry. I was going to tell you—"

"*When?*" exploded Dulcie, pinning him against the high back of the chair by the fireplace. "Oh, why did I ever come with you? I thought it would be so lovely, so romantic to elope. I thought you were a man of your word. But you've been toying with me all along. You—you *rake-screw!*"

"Now, Dulcie, don't excite yourself," began Daniel.

That was as far as he got.

At the same moment, an unerringly wielded, silver-topped cane came up over the top of the chair and landed him a resounding whack on the head.

The next moment left only Alexandra sitting still in open-mouthed astonishment. As Daniel staggered forward, a tall, thin old woman rose from the chair. And Dulcie, feeling it her prerogative to attack the lieutenant as much as she liked but woe betide anyone else who tried to harm him, leaped at his assailant in blind fury.

"Don't you dare touch him, you horrid old . . . Aunt Letitia!"

Chapter 13

Entering upon the climax of this hoo-rah, an appalled innkeeper had rolled his eyes heavenward and had sincerely wished these strange travelers had indeed gone to the Three Bells.

An hour or so later, he was somewhat mollified. Having supplied bandages as well as a nourishing dinner and having been profusely thanked for both, he had begun to think his inn had not turned into a madhouse after all. In fact, his establishment seemed to be living up to its name.

For amid a great deal of discussion, his unruly guests had grown not only civil but outright jovial.

"Gentry!" he muttered to himself as he trotted in with a slab of Stilton and apples to round off the meal. "Change temperaments as oft as they change their togs, I reckon."

Depositing the fruit and cheese on the table, he announced that three bedchambers were ready any time his guests were. Then he bowed himself out.

Miss Dulcie Winford, having most satisfactorily indulged herself to the limits of outrage and betrayal, had taken one glimpse of her battered knight and promptly forgiven him all his sins.

In her new role as nurse—a role that she had always fancied that, given the opportunity, she would be quite valiant at—she had proceeded to wrap Daniel in such a swath of linen as to completely blind him.

Alexandra, wryly pointing out that it was a rather slight

wound and hardly worth such aggressive mummification, had reduced the mass to a small patch on the crown of Daniel's head.

Neither of the younger couple had seemed to mind. In fact, it could be said they had hardly even noticed. Dulcie had moved on to yet another new role, having discovered it was much more romantic to solace a convalescent than to stick plaster on a bloody scalp.

Daniel had appeared to think so, too. He had been rejuvenated in no time amid Dulcie's reassurances that his worst fault had been an overly tender heart. He simply hadn't wanted to hurt her dear friend's feelings, had he? How well she understood that — now.

Leaving Alexandra and Aunt Letitia at the dinner table, she suggested perhaps she and Daniel should move to the sofa. Only to make him more comfortable of course.

As they resettled themselves, Dulcie demurely lowered her eyes and murmured that perhaps she had been the teensiest bit impetuous earlier. But — well, she would forgive him if he would forgive her.

Judging from the kiss that followed, the lieutenant seemed to think that a very sage compromise.

Fortunately, Dulcie's aunt had been apprised of the details during dinner. Else poor Daniel's scalp might have received another drubbing. As it was, the elderly lady merely shrugged and commented that she had anticipated much worse.

Alexandra, who had been nibbling at a slice of apple, promptly returned it to her plate. "Anticipated? But surely this was a chance encounter. You can't mean you *expected* to find Dulcie?"

"Naturally," said the older woman. "You don't suppose I'd be racketing my bones over this godforsaken road for mere pleasure, do you? I was most definitely expecting to encounter my niece."

She cast a glance at the two lovers busily discussing their future. "Only not here. And certainly not under the circumstances as I—ahem—perceived them. It would seem," she added dryly, picking up the cane that rested by her chair and testing the hefty weight of its silver knob, "I may have acted a bit impetuously myself."

Alexandra could not help but grin. Recalling Dulcie's hysterical diatribe, it was easy to see why her aunt had sprung to the wrong conclusions. "I imagine Lieutenant Symington has forgiven you."

"Of course he has," came the brisk reply. "I am going to help him marry my only niece now that I know the whole of the matter. Although I must say I am a shade provoked with that nattering grandson of Hannah Cavendish. If he'd kept his business to himself for a few days longer, I'd have never set out for Bath. I could have settled this farradiddle just as quickly in my own home. And in a great deal more comfort, I might add!"

Unable to make heads or tails of this speech, Alexandra murmured some polite sympathy about the rigors of travel and was immediately treated to a brief but harsh discourse on the skimpiness of modern fashions.

Not that Dulcie's aunt subscribed to any such nonsense as dampened muslins of course. She was sensibly dressed in black bombazine with any number of petticoats beneath. Yet even that, it seemed, did not supply adequate padding for a lady of plentiful years but a sparsity of flesh.

"Always was the skinny one," she said, dismissing her own complaints with a flick of her long fingers. "You never saw three sisters so unalike. Me, the bag of bones. Tilmatha, ever the little dumpling. And Dulcie's mother—God rest her sweet soul—right in between. She'd approve of her prospective son-in-law, I daresay. And so will Percy Winford when I've done with him. He's soon to return to Bath, you told me?"

Alexandra nodded. "Those were his intentions, Mrs. Bereston."

"Miss," she was promptly corrected. "Only one of the three of us who never found a man. Too picky, I suppose. Ah,

282

well, water under the bridge and all that. We'll all have ourselves a good night's rest, and tomorrow morning we'll sally forth to Bath. I'm sure Dulcie and her young man won't object to returning now that I've joined forces with them."

"No, I'm quite sure they won't," Alexandra murmured while thinking, But I object. I object very much!

Not realizing an anguished look had played across her face or the fact that the older woman had observed it all too well, Alexandra retreated to less painful ground.

"I'm afraid I still don't understand," she said. "Exactly what, if I may ask, brought you here?"

"Here? The rain, of course. I rather thought I explained as much, my dear."

"Yes, ma'am," Alexandra said meekly. That part she understood in full detail. How Miss Bereston, quite intending to reach Bath that day, had finally grown so irate over "this bone-cracking mud pit of a road" she had commanded her driver to pull her coach into the first decent inn he could find.

And how once there, she had been quietly awaiting her dinner when Dulcie's disjointed accusations had leaped out at her. Naturally, she had had no choice but to assume Daniel was some cad who had lured her niece away under empty promises of marriage and was therefore quite deserving of a clout on the head.

It hadn't seemed to do him much harm, Alexandra observed. Daniel, sitting with his arm around Dulcie's waist, looked at the moment as if he would hardly notice a complete battery of thumbscrews.

She turned back to her hostess (Miss Bereston had insisted on sporting them all to dinner) and amended her question. "Pardon me, I don't believe I made myself clear. Seeing as you appear to hate traveling so awfully, I was wondering what prompted you to set off for Bath."

The old lady gave a distinct "Humph! Thought I just explained that as well. It was Henry Cavendish's letter, of course. You and Dulcie know the boy. At least he claims as much."

Oh? thought Alexandra. Then a picture of the mute, tea-imbibing Messrs. Sharlett and Cavendish sprang to mind. She smiled. "I believe he's right. We are acquainted. However, I would scarcely describe him as 'nattering.'"

Miss Bereston shrugged her thin shoulders. "Must save it for his letters then, that boy could outscribble Mr. Boswell. His grandmother lives next door to me, you ken. She's forever bringing over his letters, reading every interminable word, and pleased as a poppet that he never fails to write each single week. Too bad he couldn't have forgotten just once," she grumbled, gingerly rubbing a sore spot where an elbow had collided with the door handle of a jouncing coach. "No matter. I'll have my own back once I get home. I intend to bore the old dear with every creak and groan I've endured on this trip. That should show her, don't you think?"

"No doubt," agreed Alexandra. She was beginning to like this elderly woman and her dry sense of humor very much. "I daresay you're entitled after listening through such faithful correspondence."

Miss Bereston nodded gravely. "Fit the revenge to the punishment is my motto. This is all her doing anyhow. Apparently she's forever badgering the boy to find himself a wife. So he wrote that he'd met a certain Miss Dulcie Winford, who seemed quite charming. But unfortunately her attentions seemed to have already been set on a young lieutenant. Up to this point I'd been fair to dozing off, mind you, Alexandra. I may call you Alexandra, mayn't I?"

"Please do."

"Yes, well, at any rate. I may tell you I came awake in a nonce. From the last I'd heard, my niece should have already been married. To your Major Clive, as a matter of fact."

"He is not 'my' Major Clive!" Alexandra blurted.

Miss Bereston paid no heed to this interruption. "So naturally that set me a-puzzling. I decided there was nothing to do but haul myself to Bath and discover what in tarnation had gone awry."

She paused to select an apple, then continued in that same dry voice. "Which apparently has turned out to be not a thing—judging from the pair of them yonder. At least, nothing I cannot set right in a few days."

She held up a piece of fruit, critically inspecting it on every side, as she added, "Now, my dear, let's see if I can do as much for you."

"*Me?* I—I appreciate your interest, Miss Bereston. But I'm afraid I haven't the least idea what you mean. There's nothing to do for me. There's nothing I want done!"

"Isn't there?" Unperturbed, Dulcie's aunt pared her fruit and began to slice it into precise sections. "It seems to me you're in a bit of a stew, aren't you?"

Alexandra started to lie, but she faltered under the piercing scrutiny of the other woman's gaze. In the past hour or so, precious little of her history had been left unexposed. Dulcie had seen to that. There was no point in dissembling.

"Oh, very well—yes, I am upset. Of course, I am! Who wouldn't be? I made an absolute fool of myself. Impossible dunce that I was, I believed him. I even went so far as to think I was falling in—"

She uttered a harsh sound. "Never mind, that hardly signifies now. I have learned my lesson. No more the complete fool, I! Trusting a man who lied to me, deceived me at every turn! And all the while, doubtless laughing at me behind my—"

"I think not," Miss Bereston calmly interrupted. She laid down her paring knife. "I am not acquainted with your Major Clive, my dear, but it appears to me that no one has bothered to view his side of this farradiddle. Do you mind if I try?"

Alexandra did mind. The expression on her face left no doubt. Miss Bereston simply ignored it.

"It would seem—and of course you may correct me should I err, my dear—but it would seem your major has been dealt an unfair hand."

"Unfair!" Alexandra yelped. "I never once lied to that—

that man. He lied to me! And please stop calling him *my* major!"

Miss Bereston ignored this furor as well. Selecting a section of apple, she serenely munched on it as she marshaled the information she had so recently acquired.

"Yes, definitely an unsporting hand if you'll forgive the vulgar comparison, my dear. I have, I'm afraid, a most unremitting affinity for the pasteboards. Quite a whist sharpster, in fact. Nonetheless, as I see it, Major Clive has every right to feel cheated. No, don't interrupt, girl. I firmly believe he did. First Percy's shenanigans of foisting that ridiculous prior betrothal on him — absolute nonsense having to honor the humbuggery of two meddling old men — assuming, that is, his own father was anything like Percy Winford. Which was no doubt the case, I daresay. Then more double dealing at the altar. For all the major knew, he'd married a pig in a sack."

Miss Bereston cut a bit of cheese, laid it on a slice of apple, and slowly devoured the result.

She dabbed a napkin to her mouth. "And finally," she continued, returning the linen to her lap, "you, my dear, dealt him the trickiest hand of all."

At the expected protest, Miss Bereston emitted a dry chuckle. "Tricked him twice over. Had you been a skinny old tough like me, he'd never have fallen in love with you. On top of that, you condemned him sight unseen. Most unfair of you, my dear. You never gave the poor fellow a chance."

Alexandra needed several attempts to get her mouth working. "Miss Bereston, you gave me leave to correct you. And I shall! You are totally in error! Brandon Clive is no more in love with me than — than a . . ."

While she groped for a fitting term, Miss Bereston quietly folded her napkin and rose from the table. "Than a befuddled Romeo perhaps?" she suggested. "Sounds to me that's quite likely the sum of it."

With a pleasant "Good evening, my dear," she walked over to Dulcie.

"That's enough love-birding for one night. Up the stairs with you, girl. Else you'll be coo-ed out before the wedding."

As Dulcie reluctantly obeyed orders, Miss Bereston cast a glance out of one of the unshuttered windows. "Hmm, rain appears to have stopped. And high time, I must say. This damp's cursed hard on my bones. But then so's traveling," she added, taking Dulcie's arm. "If not for the rain, I'd have missed you altogether. Seems to have turned out a blessing in disguise after all, wouldn't you say?"

Chapter 14

A damned impossible disguise, Brandon would have called it.

Having waited through the dusk, through the nightfall, and finally through a much unappreciated dinner, ex-Major Brandon Clive was glaring at a glass of the finest brandy the Three Bells had to offer and wondering how in the hell he had managed to pass a coach on that near-deserted road without noticing it.

His host, reentering the public room, saw the continuing glower on his guest's face and sighed. He had done his best. The gentleman's horse had been efficiently rubbed down and stabled. The mud-caked saddle as well as the gentleman's boots had been cleaned and polished. The many-collared riding cape and the wide-brimmed hat had been refurbished with all possible care. One of the finest rooms upstairs was ready and waiting.

And having had the same question put to him innumerable times, he had answered with the patience of several saints. No, sir, no officer and two young ladies had arrived for the evening. No, sir, they could not have gone farther in a coach, not in this weather. Yes, sir, it would appear they had stopped somewhere earlier, perhaps hoping to outwait the rain. No, sir, he had no idea where.

It was only in the past few minutes that a helpful notion had sifted to mind. He approached the gentleman's chair with some trepidation. "It comes to me, sir. They might have stopped by the Merry Wayfarer."

"What's that?"

"An inn — of sorts," added the innkeeper, unable to resist a glance around at the superiority of his own establishment. Far from lavish, of course, but adequate. And being as they are gentry, as you say, I imagine there's no place else they could have found, ahem, acceptable for the night."

"Where is it?"

"I believe —" the innkeeper stopped to do some mental arithmetic. "I'd judge it to be some seven leagues, sir. About midpoint between here and Bath, I would hazard. It is a small inn, a bit off the main road. But I do believe there's a sign of sorts directing one to it. A wooden sign, sir. Somewhat faded, as I recall, and rather pock-riddled as well —"

He stopped, marveling at the glower on his guest's face. Impossible to credit, but it was even more pronounced than before. He hardly heard the muttered oath, but the "Seven leagues? Blast it all, you mean I overjumped them *that* far?" was quite audible.

The innkeeper's spine stiffened abruptly. "I wouldn't know, sir. It was merely a suggestion. Will there be anything else?"

Brandon grabbed his glass and drained the contents in a single gulp.

To hell with it, he thought. To hell with them all! He had tried to stop Daniel from eloping; he had ordered the lad not leave town. And what had been his reward? A miserable day's ride and a missing equerry who hadn't had the grace to be where he should have been for a proper dressing-down!

As for Lady Alexandra Redcliffe — now there was a fine one. He had chased that exasperating wench from London to Bath and halfway to Brighton. He would be damned if he was going to chase her halfway back again.

To hell with the lot of them!

As he rose, the innkeeper stiffly repeated his question. "Will there be anything else, sir?"

"Yes," Brandon snarled. "Show me to my room. I am going to bed!"

After reflecting on this newest attitude and grimly deciding he should have come to it long ago, Brandon had promised his saddle-weary body three indulgences. A lengthy, undisturbed night's sleep, a leisurely breakfast, and an even more leisurely ride back to Bath.

If he was unable to sleep, it was merely the bed which was damnably uncomfortable. If he wasn't able to partake of much breakfast, it was due to its inferior quality. And if the leisurely ride had somehow turned into a pounding gallop, it was only because his horse was fresh and in need of a healthy run. All the better anyway in Brandon's opinion. The sooner back to the Seven Seas, the sooner he could grab his belongings and hie himself far from anything that smacked of Bath. Or Brighton.

Nor was he interested in some faded, pock-riddled sign. Should he happen to spot it, he would merely tip his hat — and pass it right by.

Having passed a sleepless night, Alexandra had arrived at the same conclusion. The sooner she was gone from Bath, the better!

At breakfast, she nibbled at a crust of toast and told herself her sleeplessness had been due to only one culprit. A lumpy mattress.

Certainly it had nothing to do with Miss Bereston's conjectures!

Pah! thought Alexandra. Fanciful old woman with her ridiculous notions. The facts were perfectly obvious. Brandon Clive was an out-and-out rotter. If he loved anyone, it was himself! Furthermore, she should be thanking her lucky stars she was well rid of him. On the off chance they should ever meet again, she would merely nod — and pass right on by.

Congratulating herself on this most sensible attitude, Alexandra pushed back her chair and went out the door of he Merry Wayfarer into the bright morning sunlight.

Miss Bereston had insisted on overseeing the readiness of he two coaches. When Alexandra came upon her in the arriage yard, the old lady was flourishing her cane like a ield commander's baton. Two ostlers were smartly stepping o her directions.

"Ah, there you are, my girl," sang out Miss Bereston. She ame over, looking exceedingly spry for a woman with so nany self-confessed creaks and groans. "Are we ready to get his caravan under way?"

"I am," said Alexandra. "But Dulcie and Daniel seem to be paying more attention to each other, I'm afraid, than to inishing their tea and eggs. They didn't even notice my eaving."

Miss Bereston, still keeping a sharp eye on her troops, chuckled dryly. "Likely holding hands instead of their forks, daresay. Makes for too much dawdling. And even messier ating. I'd best roust them out or we'll never get away. I say! You there, ostler! The luggage in my coach, I told you, not he other!"

"My word," gasped Alexandra, for the first time taking a good look at the two conveyances. Miss Bereston's coach eemed to be bristling with boxes and portmanteaus. The poot was already filled. The remainder was now being lashed atop the roof.

"Miss Bereston, do you usually travel with so much uggage?"

"I fully expect any nosy pokes in Bath to think so," eturned the older lady. "Tilmatha's such a fidget, I fancied a pit of precautionary deception might please her. So I had the ot of it — yours and Dulcie's trappings and Daniel's mite — piled on my coach.

"You were lucky yesterday apparently. Hardly anyone noticed your leaving and nobody, thank goodness, got a look inside your coach. But you mightn't be so lucky today. Therefore — with no telltale trappings to show — who's to say you didn't merely drive out this morning to escort Dulcie's poor old, 'overladen' auntie back to Bath?"

"Who indeed?" quipped Alexandra. "Miss Bereston, I am beginning to see where Dulcie gets some of her slyness."

"Well, you certainly wouldn't suppose she got it from Tilmatha, would—who on earth is that?"

"My God!"

Miss Bereston rather doubted the accuracy of such identification. The man who had just thrown himself from his horse and was now bearing down on them, looked quite human.

Miss Bereston turned to the obvious objective of his advance. "My dear, could this fellow possibly be—"

But Alexandra had already fled.

And the gentleman, striding purposefully, was hard on her trail.

"Not 'possibly,' " Miss Bereston corrected herself. "I would say he most definitely is!"

Surmising this new turn of events would require some delay, she signaled the ostlers to take away the teams. Then, just as quickly, she countermanded that order.

"Leave 'em hitched!" she called out as she marched into the Merry Wayfarer's dining room. Dulcie and Daniel were still holding hands over their breakfast. Miss Bereston thumped her cane to get their attention. "Come along, we're leaving now. You two will ride with me. We'll leave the hired coach for Lady Redcliffe."

Dulcie scrambled to her feet in surprise. "Lexie's staying. She can't do that!"

Daniel rose in swift agreement. "Of course not! Who's drive the coach for her?"

Ushering them both out the door, Miss Bereston serenely murmured, "Oh, I expect she'll find someone."

The little path that meandered away from the inn was quite charming. The sun glinted through the overhanging trees. Birds darted here and there, chirping their contentment with the morning.

Alexandra, of course, noticed none of this as she scurried

292

ong. She was too engrossed with looking over her shoulder. "Go away! I have nothing to say to you!"

Her pursuer was by now only a few steps behind her. "Fair nough," he called. "If you intend to keep up this pace, you on't have the breath for it at any rate."

"And neither will you, I hope!" Alexandra flung back over er shoulder.

Of all the impossible situations she had ever found herself , this had to be the worst. Dignity—or what was left of it, e thought—would not let her run, but she was walking for l she was worth.

He was right behind her, making no attempt to stop her, mply staying at her heels. Dear God, how humiliating!

"Don't you dare touch me!" she fumed. There was no need yell. He was practically walking beside her.

"Very well," he replied amiably. "You know, this is quite a leasant idea. Nothing like a little stroll after breakfast, I ways say. Glad you thought of it. And I must compliment u on your choice of routes. So quiet and peaceful—leafy adows playing across the path—reminds me of a poem. Or e bit of it I can remember, anyway. Would you care to hear ?"

"I would not! I don't know what kind of game you think u're playing, but you may as well stop hounding me. I am ot turning back until you leave!"

As this seemed to elicit no comment or change of course om her tormenter, Alexandra barged ahead. The trail visted and turned—back toward the inn, she hoped. She ad been lost with Brandon Clive once—and wound up in a ayloft! Alexandra nearly tripped over a wayward root. ood lord, was that why he had suddenly shown up? For ore of the same?

As she stumbled a little, she felt a steadying hand on her rm. She whirled around. "You—you rake screw! Touch me gain, and I'll claw your eyes out!"

"My, my, such language," he teased. Then he glanced cross her shoulder for a second and stepped to one side. Perhaps we should return to the inn."

"Not we, Mr. Clive! You! I intend to continue on solitary stroll."

With a toss of her head, Alexandra spun around and wa almost immediately confronted with the fact that the pa had become a bridge.

"Looks a bit rickety," observed Brandon. "Sure yo wouldn't rather start back?"

"Quite sure! But you're much heavier than I, of course. certainly shouldn't risk crossing to the other side if I wer you!"

"Oh, I don't intend to."

Fine! thought Alexandra. Now he would have to retrac his steps, and she could continue on her way in blissfu solitude.

"Good-bye, Mr. Clive," she snapped.

Without a second glance, she sallied forth.

A step or two on the bridge convinced her Brandon Cliv was not only a rogue, but a timothy mouse as well. Th boards under foot seemed perfectly sturdy. Besides, it was very low bridge. Even the stumpy little side railings were n more than a couple of feet above the water.

And the stream itself?

Alexandra peered down, judging the depth as she walke Good heavens, the stream might be fairly wide, but it cou scarcely be more than three feet deep, even at midpoint. Sh couldn't drown if she tried!

"What a lot of fuss and feathers over nothing," sh muttered as she suddenly found herself on solid ground onc more. "Now I'll just continue along the path. It must lea somewh—"

It did. Right into what must have been a very nast rockslide at one time. There was no more path. There wa no more anything except a monstrous pile of rocks and o each side an overgrown and most uninviting terrain.

Well! she thought. There was nothing to do but retrac her steps. And if Mr. Timothy Mouse was still lurkin about, she would sail right past him without a word.

She turned around.

Mr. Clive was far from lurking. He was in plain view. He was positioned in the exact center of the bridge, his arms folded as he sat on the low railing. His long legs were stretched across the bridge with his booted feet firmly propped against the opposite railing.

It occurred to Alexandra that she would have to speak to him — at least once.

She marched to the center of the bridge. "I should like to pass, sir!"

Brandon grinned up at her. "Not until I've had my say."

Since there was little she could do save further embarrass herself by leaping across him, she folded her own arms and turned her back to him. "I shan't listen!"

"No? Well, perhaps you'll change your mind. Judging from those faint but nonetheless endearing shadows under your eyes, I'd say your slumber was no more peaceful than mine. Come to think of it, as a matter of fact, I can't remember a more damnedable night!"

Alexandra did not turn around. "Your memory, Mr. Clive, or your discomfort is of no interest to me."

"Well, it is to me. Tossing and turning aren't precisely my favorite pastimes. Moreover, it occurred to me about ten miles down the road that, unless we come to terms, neither of us is ever likely to see a restful night."

"Speak for yourself!"

"Thank you, Lady Redcliffe. Since you've so kindly given me permission, I'll do just that. I think we should get married."

"*What?*" Alexandra spun around like a minor whirlwind. "Just so you can have a good night's *sleep*?"

Brandon shrugged, his expression completely noncommittal. "That's an important factor, of course. But I suppose, if pressed, I might think of a few others. For example, we've already been married once, however briefly. And the second attempt at anything's usually easier, so they say. Besides," he added, casually drawing a small bit of straw from his pocket and holding it up to the light, "there were a few hours in that first marriage I found quite pleasant."

"Why, you—"

Her eyes glittering furiously, Alexandra took a step forward.

Brandon shot a glance at the water behind him, then he looked back at her and grinned. "You wouldn't, my sweet. You couldn't, not to a man who's about to make the most serious admission of his life. The truth is—"

"The *truth*! You wouldn't know the truth if you drowned in it! Let me pass. And if you dare use that word once more, *I will push you in*!"

"Alexandra, will you please stop making idle threats and listen to me. This time I'm serious. It is the—hey!"

He came up dripping and sputtering. "You damned double-dealing wench! *I love you*!"

Alexandra was already at the end of the bridge. She came to a dead halt.

She stood there for a long moment. Then she slowly turned around and came back. "You know," she said thoughtfully, "Miss Bereston told me you did."

Brandon, standing barely two feet below her, dashed the water from his eyes. "Well, whoever she is, she's got twice the sense you have! Every time I come near you, I nearly get myself drowned! Yet I seem to keep coming back for more. *Doesn't that prove I love you?*"

Alexandra pondered this for a minute. "Yes, I expect it does."

"And you love me?"

Another pause. "So it would seem."

"Prove it!"

Alexandra took a deep breath and jumped into the water.

The coach rolled at a very leisurely pace toward Bath.

Alexandra, snuggled in Brandon's arms, looked down at the blankets covering them and then at the welter of wet garments tossed upon the opposite seat.

She gave a sleepy little chuckle. "Let's hope they're dry enough to put on before we reach upper High Street.

Somehow, I rather doubt Miss Bereston is expecting us to arrive in the nude."

Brandon, who by now was most anxious to meet that estimable lady, returned the chuckle with an outright laugh. "Probably not, but I'm sure she'd manage quite admirably if we did. Which, by the way, I assure you, we won't. I'll think of some excuse for our bedraggled appearance."

If need be, he added to himself. The members of the Cawlwood household likely had become so accustomed to dousings, they wouldn't even notice.

He shifted a little, nestling Alexandra's slim, soft body even closer. "Comfortable?" he murmured, his lips soft against her ear.

"Um, wonderfully so," came the drowsy response. "We really must thank Miss Bereston for providing a driver."

"We certainly must," agreed Brandon, once again admiring that lady's foresight. Not only had she seen to it that Brandon's horse was securely tied behind the hired coach, but she had tipped one of the ostlers so generously, he had been more than happy to wait for the tardy couple and drive them to Bath.

They were almost there when Brandon roused Alexandra with a kiss. "Wake up, my gorgeous little sleepyhead. It's time to get dressed."

Reluctantly, Alexandra came out of the warmth of his arms and reached for her clothes. She made a face as she picked up a still-damp chemise.

Brandon helped her struggle into it. "Regret now you jumped in after me? You really didn't have to, you know."

"Yes, I did," said Alexandra, calmly pulling on her stockings. "Because you wouldn't come after me. I nearly died standing there on the end of that bridge, I was so sure you'd come thrashing and flailing after me, but you didn't. Why not?"

"Couldn't," muttered Brandon, struggling into his trousers. "Not if I wanted to follow Ben Jonson's advice." He picked up his shirt. "The bit of poem, remember? You didn't want to listen."

"Oh." Alexandra squirmed into a ruffled petticoat. "Well, I believe I should like to hear it now."

"My pleasure, milady."

Brandon stomped his foot into a boot, then cleared his throat with portentious solemnity:

Follow a shadow, it still flies you;
   Seem to fly it, it will pursue:
So court a mistress, she denies you;
   Let her alone, she will court you.

Chapter 15

For no less than the thirtieth time, Dulcie declared she had never been so happy in her life.

"Just look at us," she said, beaming across the tea table. "We're all exactly like Noah's ark. There's you and I—"

Grabbing Daniel's hand, which indeed seldom strayed more than an inch from hers, she proceeded to draft his forefinger as a convenient pointer. "—and Lexie and her dear Brandon by the window. Aunt Tilmatha and Lord Chambers together on the settee. And Papa and Aunt Letitia on the other—"

Miss Bereston cut her niece's burbling short. "Dulcie, some of us may happen to be sitting together. But that hardly qualifies us for a category of 'two by two.'"

"No, I suppose not," Dulcie giggled. It certainly didn't apply to Papa and Aunt Letitia. After the sermon that redoubtable lady had preached to him not ten minutes following his arrival, Papa Winford had scarcely opened his mouth, but he was beginning to look as if he considered Daniel Symington a godsend compared to his late wife's barb-tongued sister.

Dulcie leaned over and gave him an exuberant buss on the cheek. "Oh, Papa, I am so happy. Daniel and I do have your most heartfelt consent, don't we?"

Percy Winford glanced at his future son-in-law, then at the quelling visage of Letitia Bereston. He grumbled something that, if not quite heartfelt, was at least a capitulation.

"Oh, thank you, Papa! You, too, Aunt Letitia—and of

course, you, Aunt Tilmatha!" Relinquishing herself momentarily from her betrothed, Dulcie threw her arms around Mrs. Cawlwood and gave her a mighty hug.

"My dear, please!" that lady protested good-naturedly. "You've almost pushed Lord Chambers onto the floor."

"No, no, far from it," replied his lordship. With a great deal of amused tolerance, he edged himself back from the brink of disaster. "Your aunt tells me you're going to have the wedding here."

"Yes! Isn't it lovely! And now that Lexie is—Lexie, dearest, I've just had an absolutely brilliant idea! Let's make it a double wedding!"

Alexandra laughed and looked up at Brandon. "Shall we?"

He took both her hands in his, and the look in his eyes said much more than his nonchalant answer. "Why not."

Hardly able to contain her excitement, Dulcie was immediately full of plans. The ceremony had to be absolutely, no, exquisitely splendid! Two bridal gowns, two wedding cakes . . .

Lord Chambers discreetly cleared his throat. "I wonder, Miss Dulcie, if it might not be even a bit more splendid with three?"

"Three wedding cakes? What on earth for?"

Lord Chambers rose and bowed. Then with a smile at Mrs. Cawlwood, he looked back to her astonished niece. "Only if you young people shouldn't mind of course. Perhaps your aunt should explain it."

This naturally sent Mrs. Cawlwood into a flurry of agitation, but, with a calming pat on her wrist from his lordship, she managed to rise to her feet and to the occasion quite nicely. "Well, to begin with. There was my little jollification last night."

Dulcie gasped. "My goodness, the rout party! Oh, Auntie, I'm so sorry we couldn't be there!"

"It didn't matter in the slightest, my dear," her aunt returned graciously. "But of course I had no way of realizing that beforehand. Oh, no, not at all!" she added, coloring prettily.

"So there I was. Or so I thought at the time, you see. I'd

nvited all those people for a special occasion — and there was nothing special to offer. My guests of honor were on their way to Brighton."

It was Alexandra's turn to apologize. "Mrs. Cawlwood, how dreadful of us to leave you in such a lurch."

"Nonsense. Nothing lurchy about it, my dear. It was a great success. His lordship—"

Here Mrs. Cawlwood turned as rosy as a young girl. "His lordship provided a most gratifying solution. Didn't you— Oliver?"

"I definitely found it to be such," said Lord Chambers. He slipped an arm around Mrs. Cawlwood's plump waist. "Ladies and gentlemen, I have asked Tilmatha to be my wife. We celebrated our engagement at the rout party."

If Dulcie had been exuberant before, she was now past rapture.

"A *triple wedding*! I've never been so happy in my life! We'll invite simply everyone! Your friends, Auntie — his lordship's friends — Daniel's grandmother and her friends. Why—"

Dulcie suddenly spun around in a complete circle. "Why, I'm so happy, I'll even invite . . . *Mr. Druberry!*"

HISTORICAL ROMANCES BY VICTORIA THOMPSON

BOLD TEXAS EMBRACE   (2835, $4.50)
Art teacher Catherine Eaton could hardly believe how stubbor
Sam Connors was! Even though the rancher's young stepbrothe
was an exceptionally talented painter, Sam forbade Catherine t
instruct him, fearing that art would make a sissy out of him
Spunky and determined, the blond schoolmarm confronted th
muleheaded cowboy . . . only to find that he was as handsome a
he was hard-headed and as desirable as he was dictatorial. Befor
long she had nearly forgotten what she'd come for, as Sam'
brash, breathless embrace drove from her mind all thought o
anything save wanting him . . .

TEXAS BLONDE   (2183, $3.95)
When dashing Josh Logan resuced her from death by exposure
petite Felicity Morrow realized she'd never survive rugged frontie
life without a man by her side. And when she gazed at the Texa
rancher's lean hard frame and strong rippling muscles, the deter
mined beauty decided he was the one for her. To reach her goal
feisty Felicity pretended to be meek and mild: the only kind of ga
Josh proclaimed he'd wed. But after she'd won his hand, the blue
eyed temptress swore she'd quit playing his game—and still wi
his heart!

ANGEL HEART   (2426, $3.95)
Ever since Angelica's father died, Harlan Snyder had been an
gling to get his hands on her ranch, the Diamond R. And now
just when she had an important government contract to fulfil
she couldn't find a single cowhand to hire on—all because of Sny
der's threats. It was only a matter of time before she lost th
ranch. . . . That is, until the legendary gunfighter Kid Collin
turned up on her doorstep, badly wounded. Angelica assessed hi
firmly muscled physique and stared into his startling blue eyes
Beneath all that blood and dirt he was the handsomest man sh
had ever seen, and the one person who could help her beat Snyde
at his own game—if the price were not too high. . . .

*Available wherever paperbacks are sold, or order direct from th
Publisher. Send cover price plus 50¢ per copy for mailing an
handling to Zebra Books, Dept. 2880, 475 Park Avenue South
New York, N.Y. 10016. Residents of New York, New Jersey an
Pennsylvania must include sales tax. DO NOT SEND CASH.*